THE
GODS OF
LAKI

THE
GODS OF
LAKI

A THRILLER

CHRIS ANGUS

YUCCA

Yucca Publishing books may be purchased in bulk at special discounts for sales promotion, corporate gifts, fund-raising, or educational purposes. Special editions can also be created to specifications. For details, contact the Special Sales Department, Yucca Publishing, 307 West 36th Street, 11th Floor, New York, NY 10018 or yucca@skyhorsepublishing.com.

Yucca Publishing® is an imprint of Skyhorse Publishing, Inc.®, a Delaware corporation.

Visit our website at www.yuccapub.com.

10 9 8 7 6 5 4 3 2 1

Library of Congress Cataloging-in-Publication Data is available on file.

Cover design by Yucca Publishing

Print ISBN: 978-1-63158-046-8
Ebook ISBN: 978-1-63158-056-7

Printed in the United States of America

THE
GODS OF
LAKI

Chapter One

Runa was cold. She was cold and wet and hungry. She had been all of these for nearly three weeks, which was exactly how long they had been at sea.

She turned her back on the angry spray that stung her eyes every time their Viking longboat cratered into another deep North Atlantic trough.

"Fish!" Skari yelled at her, pointing to his mouth in case she hadn't heard over the crashing of the waves and the constant, blowing wind.

She paused in her endless attempts to bail water from the bottom of the boat, took a piece of dried fish from a wooden box, and tossed it to him. He caught it expertly and began to chew, never taking his hand off the tiller that was guiding them relentlessly westward.

Runa stared at the others in the boat. Ragni and Asa had been husband and wife for only three months, yet Runa suspected Asa was already pregnant. She huddled in her husband's arms, shivering. Anyone could read the concern in Ragni's eyes, the fear that the journey would be too much for a woman with child.

Agnarr, whose boat this was, sat in the bow. He was mostly responsible for their being here, though they had all, in their ways, needed to leave the homeland. Agnarr was twice Runa's age of sixteen, but even so, he was unmarried. He wasn't bad looking, she decided, but he had a reputation for being wild. He had fought in the raids in Scotland and been wounded three times. He still walked with a slight limp and had a scar that ran down the length of his right arm. But despite this, he was good-natured and smiled often.

He smiled now at Runa from his place near the bow. She gave a small grimace in return, but it was hard. She was so cold.

Last was Amma, Runa's grandmother. No one knew how old Amma was, least of all Amma herself. Few Vikings lived much past sixty. Theirs was a brutal life, one in which the slightest mishap or illness could spell the end. But the elderly woman was resilient and a bit mysterious to all of them. She deferred to the men in the group, but everyone relied on her vast reservoir of knowledge. Amma was their link to the gods. She knew the rituals and prayers that would guide their success.

Just six souls altogether. A desperately small contingent to begin a new life in the land of fire and ice, some nine hundred miles from their homeland, across the vast, storm-tossed and icy waters of the North Atlantic. They would need every ounce of their combined efforts if they were to have any hope of survival.

Runa stared at Skari again, chewing on his fish. She'd met him only the day they were to leave and had not liked him from the first. He was a brooding, stolid fellow, who spoke infrequently and then in an ordering tone that Runa found distasteful. She didn't like the way he looked at her. She was a woman and understood such looks.

She stared past Agnarr and blinked, brought both hands to her face, rubbed her eyes and looked again.

Land!

"Look," she said, then had to repeat herself to be heard over the waves. "Look!"

Everyone in the boat followed her pointing finger. For a moment, they saw nothing. The headland had disappeared behind the ever-present fog. But then they all saw it, a dark and fearsome landscape rising from the sea through wisps of fog that gave the appearance of something straight out of the Norse Hel.

"The land of fire and ice!" Skari cried aloud. "We made it!"

The boat crashed in over a sharp reef, and Runa heard the terrible sound of the hull being torn. A moment later they were all in the water. It felt like ice even though it was August. Cold fingers gripped Runa's arm, as Agnarr pulled her toward shore. Then they were on the pebbled beach, Ragni and Asa helping old Amma.

The men pulled the damaged boat above the high tide line and examined it briefly. It could be repaired, but there was no rush. They had made it to the land of fire and ice. No one had followed them, Runa was certain. There was bad blood behind them, a rent in the community that would never heal. This was how Vikings lived. Families split and moved apart, always searching for new lands. Now this small group would begin again, a new community. Three adult men, two young women, and Amma. Enough to start over.

The first days in the cold land were hard. Food was scarce. Runa searched for shellfish along the coast, but fish or seal was what they needed. Until the boat was fixed, that would not be possible.

They hauled the longboat ashore and turned it over to make a rudimentary shelter. Agnarr made several forages inland but found no wood suitable for repairing the boat. Their landfall had come in a place heavily covered with lava flows from an eruption just a decade earlier. As a result, only a few small bushes and shrubs covered the barren landscape.

Amma sat in the shelter, preparing what little food they had, some pitiful bits of dried fish left from their journey along with limpets, a few clams and seaweed, mixed to make a kind of soup.

The land was forbidding. Steep volcanoes rose from the ocean, smoking ominously. Heavy fogs ran in from the sea, blanketing the slopes, so that they were never quite afforded an open view. There was something hostile, almost brooding to the landscape. They felt closed in and longed for the sweeping fiords of their homeland.

Runa worked with Amma, shelling limpets for their meager pot. It was overcast and dark, the mountains only dimly visible through periodic waves of pelting rain. When they could see it, the ocean foamed with whitecaps.

Amma was covered in furs, for her old body could not produce enough warmth, even in summer. She said, "Skari told me he wants you for his wife."

Runa's heart went cold. "I do not like him," she said. "I like Agnarr."

"Has he asked you?" Amma threw a handful of seaweed into their cooking pot.

Runa could only shake her head.

"There are only two breeding women here for three adult men," Amma said. "Asa is spoken for. That leaves you. You cannot make both men content. You need to choose."

"I don't want to be married . . . at least not right away," Runa said. "I don't want to have a baby."

"Now is baby-making time," said Amma. "So it will be born in the spring." She stood up with effort and moved out from beneath the boat. The conversation was over.

Skari returned with an armload of firewood. He dropped it in front of the boat and stared at Runa. "I will make good babies," he said, his eyes heavy with desire. He reached one hand down and fondled her breast. "And so will you," he said.

Runa retreated farther beneath the boat but then looked up as a shadow crossed her face. Agnarr.

He shoved Skari aside roughly and said, "Runa will be my wife."

The two men stood facing each other for long moments, their fists clenched. But Skari knew Agnarr was experienced in battle and very strong. He dared not confront him outright. With a snarl, he turned and walked away.

The weather turned even colder. Snow spotted the slopes, reminding them all that the frigid northern winter would soon be upon them and they had no shelter or dried fish put away for the long, dark months.

Runa and Asa spent their days trying to catch fish with a bit of line and their few iron hooks. The fish were plentiful enough but nearly impossible to catch.

"We would do better with a net," said Asa, but there was nothing with which to make one.

Agnarr went away overnight on a long forage. He eventually found a place with sizeable trees and brought back wood to repair the longboat. The patch would be temporary and not something they'd want to put to sea with. But for fishing along the coast, it would do.

Agnarr and Skari worked together out of necessity. But their dislike for each other simmered beneath the surface. Fortunately, the need to prepare for winter took everyone's complete effort. If they were unprepared for the cold when it came, then whoever got Runa would not matter. They would all die.

Firewood collection was another urgent task. Every free moment went into gathering dead wood and driftwood along the shore. The pile grew slowly next to the longboat. They would need a great deal of wood to keep warm through the winter, and finding it once the snows came would be next to impossible. Amma, unable to fish, took this task upon herself and gathered more than anyone, moving at her slow, arthritic pace across the low hills.

Then the first hard storm hit with gale-force winds and a blizzard that dropped a blanket of snow. The sky hung low and forbidding for many days, temperatures falling into the single digits. They watched as their pitiful pile of firewood slowly diminished. In addition, the fish they had gathered began to rot, for there had not been enough warmth from the sun to dry it properly.

But then there came a reprieve in the weather. The snow melted away and they redoubled their efforts to increase their supplies. Runa, Asa, and Amma roamed the highlands gathering fuel, while

Skari, Ragni, and Agnarr, with the longboat repaired, went fishing every day. Slowly, their provisions increased, but still the inability to dry fish was a problem. If winter came fast and stayed cold, they could freeze the fish. But drying was preferable.

One day, Runa went foraging high on the side of the volcano. What wood there was came from stunted trees and brush that grew ever smaller as she moved higher. Still, it was a clear day and she enjoyed a rare view of their new land.

As she neared the rim of the volcano, she saw steam coming from an opening in the ground. This was very curious, and she approached the opening. Suddenly, something seemed to push her forward, propelling her toward the strange mist rising from the hole. Try as she might, she couldn't resist the force. She was not in control of her own movements. Her heart pounded. Had she somehow angered the gods? Were they about to punish her? She wished Amma were here to tell her what to do.

The opening was like a small cave and as she slumped beside it, the unseen hand went away. She knew she should be terrified, but instead, a sense of peace settled over her. Tentatively, she reached one hand into the steam. How warm it was! She uncovered her legs and let the warmth soak into her body. Suddenly, despite the warmth, goose bumps rose on her legs and a shiver coursed across her shoulders and down her back, as if something had passed through her entire body.

Then, out of nowhere, a thought came into her head. She inched her body down into the hole, the warmth enveloping her. She found breathing the steam to be strangely invigorating. The hole descended about ten feet, then widened, and Runa found herself in a space the size of a small room. Enough light came in from the entrance to allow her to see her surroundings.

Another tunnel led lower at the far end of the space, and she could feel even more heat coming from there. She hadn't been so warm since they left the Norseland. Why couldn't this be their home for the winter? If the heat continued, they would need firewood for cooking only.

It took every bit of her willpower to climb back out of the hole. Not because it was difficult but because she felt an overwhelming desire to stay there, in the bosom of the earth. It was the strangest sensation, as though someone else's thoughts had invaded her own.

She rushed back to tell the others. Everyone climbed to the small opening in the ground and marveled at the warmth. For people who had been cold for months, it was intoxicating. Amma, especially, sighed with pleasure as the heat penetrated her withered flesh. They quickly moved their few belongings into the cave, and the men went to work lining the space with stones that would further reflect the heat back into the living area.

Laboriously, they moved their pile of firewood to the entrance to their new home and settled in. Runa felt serenity come over her. She felt utterly at peace here, enveloped in the warm earth. She couldn't explain why she felt this way, only that it was so.

Though there was still much work to do, no one wanted to leave the warm confines of their new home. They had to force themselves to go forth and look for food, and all the time they were gone, they yearned to be back again in the strangely exhilarating heart of the volcano.

There was more than enough room for six people. Ragni formed a partition by weaving branches together that allowed Asa a small bit of privacy. She was nearly six months pregnant now, but Ragni still insisted on the right of the marriage bed. The sound of their love-making just a few feet away made Agnarr, Skari, and Runa painfully aware of their own situation.

Finally, one day while it snowed heavily and they were all lounging in their heated home, Runa announced her decision.

"We need to make babies to increase the size of our community," she said firmly. "It would not be fair to either Skari or Agnarr for the only woman to be denied to them. I will take both for my husbands. I will sleep one night with Agnarr and the next with Skari. But this I will only do if both of you agree, so that there will be harmony among all of us."

Neither man was happy and there was much grumbling, but Runa realized, with some surprise, that she was in control. She owned the most valuable commodity in their world: her fertile, young body. Though Skari and Agnarr disliked one another, there was no question of them fighting, or killing each other. If they were to survive, they needed the collective talents of every member of their tiny group, even old Amma. This they understood intuitively.

So Runa took two husbands and very quickly, peace settled on the group as each man's needs were met. Indeed, everyone seemed to get along much better than before. Runa wondered at the harmony that had settled over their little clan. She had known nothing like it back home. Vikings were always a contentious, battle-ready group. She had been glad to leave that world behind. Here, everything felt different.

Though harmony reigned, the winter was wretched, cold and bleak, worse even than back in the old country. The frigid winds howled out of the Arctic, and during blizzards they had to push snow away from the entrance to their home. Food was scarce, except when the men occasionally managed to kill a seal in their boat. Without the unending source of heat, they would never have survived the terrible cold. But even on the most frigid nights when Runa snuggled close to Agnarr, they were toasty warm.

Amma seemed to thrive with the constant warmth applied to her aged bones. She took to sitting in the back of the cave where she could breathe in the warm, moist steam that emanated from below. Runa had never seen the old woman more content. Her strength returned. Her breathing cleared and she slept peacefully.

Indeed, with the arrival of spring, they all felt stronger. Asa delivered her baby at the end of February, a boy. They named him Haraldr. He was healthy and grew quickly.

Runa was happy that she hadn't yet become pregnant, though it was not for lack of trying by both her husbands. She felt she was becoming a strong young woman, and she explored their island by herself, going far afield, discovering many more underground caves that were warm from the earth's heat.

Once, she heard a strange rumbling sound. It was something she'd never experienced before. The land moved beneath her feet, and she fell to the ground, terrified. Then she had a vision. She saw a strange, heavily cloaked figure floating above the volcano's rim, beckoning to her. The figure had long tentacles where there should have been fingers. The tentacles snaked down the slope toward her. Runa closed her eyes tightly until the frightening image went away.

On one of her outings, she found clusters of mushrooms that stood out from the green mosses prevailing on the open slopes. The mushrooms seemed to thrive around the entrances to the underground caves.

She gathered some and brought them to Amma. "Do you think we could eat them?" she asked her grandmother.

The old woman was well acquainted with the flora of their former homeland, but she had never seen mushrooms like these.

"We will eat a little and see if it makes us sick," said Amma. She heated them in water over the fire. They gave off a strange odor that Runa didn't care for, but when they ate them, they found that they were quite tasty and didn't make them sick. Over time, they discovered that the mushrooms made a good addition to the thin soups, stews, and fish chowders that made up most of their diet, adding flavor to the largely plain fare.

They made one collective trip in their repaired longboat, traveling many miles along the coast, searching for others who might have come to this part of the land of fire and ice. They knew that others now made the trip from the old land, but they encountered no one. All of them felt a fierce longing to be back at their home in the earth, and there was much discontent within the group until they returned.

By the beginning of their second winter, many changes had taken place. Agnarr and Skari built an enclosure around the entrance to their underground home so they didn't have to fight to keep the winter snows out. The men went far offshore in their longboat and dried hundreds of pounds of fish for the winter. Working together and sharing a wife, Agnarr and Skari managed to coexist. Yet Skari remained unhappy and distant. He spent much of his time in a deep venthole, carving religious offerings to the gods.

Haraldr was a happy, bubbly boy and they all loved him and watched over him. After the second long winter, Runa felt herself bursting with new life. In April, she gave birth to twins, a boy and a girl. There were now three new members of the clan. It was exciting to see life take hold in this hard land.

They were all very healthy. In their small community with no outside contact, they were not exposed to disease. It was unusual for Vikings to enjoy such a long period of strength and vitality. Amma seemed to be growing more vital and stronger with each passing month. It was as if she were growing younger as the children grew older. Everyone marveled at it, and they made offerings to the gods for their good fortune.

Chapter Two

Present Day

The security guard looked up from Ryan's ID. "Been a long time for you," he said. "Miss the action?"

"Not even a little," he replied.

The guard returned the papers. He had that glazed, done-it-all-a-thousand-times-before look that Ryan remembered so well. "Know where you're going?" the man asked.

He shook his head. "I have a meeting with Senator Shelby Graham."

"Straight down the hall till you reach the elevators. Go to the third floor, turn right and you'll find the senator's suite in front of you."

"Since when did they start calling them suites?"

"Don't know," the guard replied, already looking away. "Probably has something to do with the sweet deals these SOBs give themselves with our hard-earned tax dollars. Hope you're here to cash in like everybody else."

That would be the day. It was ten years since he'd left government employ. The entire decade of his thirties had been spent with the Secret Service, protecting the President. It had been one of the most boring jobs of his life. Advance work checking sniper lines of sight, emergency escape routes, and donor credentials. Then came endless hours staring at throngs of adoring fans, checking their hands, trying to determine if that camera or cell phone or peanut butter sandwich was a threat.

The money was good, but he still looked upon the day he quit as emancipation day. After all, what would be the result of failure? Another politician would slip automatically into place. No shortage there. After ten years on the job, he had come to believe that it would make no difference whatsoever. History would go on in its usual peripatetic fashion. It wasn't an attitude that went over well in the Service.

He'd grimaced upon learning recently of the thirteen-billion-dollar program to upgrade the President's helicopters, making them terrorist- and nuclear-proof. What utter nonsense. Thirteen billion dollars to secure the safety of one man who could be replaced in a nanosecond. Indeed, every one of the self-serving pols in line for the Presidency secretly longed for that day.

Senator Graham's suite was sweet indeed. The hallway expanded suddenly and a set of glass doors gave entrance to a large reception area, decorated in what Ryan could only call Washington Regal. Muted, gold striped wallpaper, sitting areas with color-coordinated couches perfectly aligned, three secretaries busy on the phones. Graham was the majority leader and had one of the most coveted offices in the capital.

"Oh yes, Mr. Baldwin," said the voluptuous and preternaturally put-together blonde-haired woman at the primary desk. "The senator said to keep an eye out for you. You may go straight through to the inner waiting room." She gestured to a door. "He'll be with you directly."

Avoiding the eyes of half a dozen other supplicants who stared at him with instant dislike for his immediate access, he passed into the inner sanctum.

The old feelings of privilege and power washed over him. It had been heady stuff, working for the President. Doors opened without hesitation, and as security for the great man, Baldwin had often been the first through those doors. He'd acquired the Secret Service stare. Everyone was suspicious, and he quickly came to realize that most people viewed the men sporting the mysterious earpieces with a degree of fear.

He was alone for only a minute, looking at the pictures of the senator on the wall with various heads of state. In one corner was a workout center with an elliptical trainer, weight machine, and rubber mat. The senator was known to be a health nut. A door opened behind him.

At first glance, Shelby Graham from the great state of Tennessee presented the central casting image of what a senator should look like. He was in his early seventies, over six feet in height, with hair graying at the temples. That was all standard. But in direct contrast to his obvious fitness and intensity, he dressed in famously rumpled attire. The creased jacket, scuffed brown loafers and decidedly chaotic haircut allowed him to cultivate the image of one so busy and important that he couldn't be bothered with the amenities. Perhaps incongruously, that relaxed image had gone a long way toward cementing his popularity in his home state, as had a penchant for dropping his final g's on the campaign trail.

The voice had become more graveled in the years since Ryan had last seen him.

"I appreciate your coming on such short notice," the senator said, moving forward with his hand out.

Ryan took the hand and said, "My coming on short notice was in response to what I took as a summons. Delivered by patrol car."

"Not my intention, I assure you. You're not an easy man to get hold of, either in your U.S. or Icelandic offices. We've never really met, but of course I saw you often in the company of two of our former presidents."

Ryan shrugged. "I remember you as well, Senator." Then, because he couldn't think of anything complimentary to say, added, "Congratulations on being chosen majority leader."

"Thanks . . . uh . . . shall we sit by the window?"

When they were settled, Graham stared out at the Mall and was quiet for a moment.

"Though I am, as you say, the newly appointed majority leader, the reason I've asked you here has nothing to do with my office . . . directly. This is a personal matter."

Ryan raised an eyebrow. After leaving the Service, he'd gone back to school and earned his PhD from Georgetown, then worked for British Petroleum before going into business for himself as a consultant to energy companies. Not on security matters. He'd long since given that up. He now helped companies develop alternative energy sources, primarily geothermal. He couldn't imagine what personal matter the senator wished to consult him on.

"You have any children, Mr. Baldwin?"

"No sir. Never been married."

"Well then . . ." Graham was quiet, staring outside again. Then he began.

"My daughter's name is Samantha. Sam for short." He turned slightly and picked up a photo from the table next to him. It wasn't very clear, but showed a windblown young woman with short, dark hair, standing on a rocky ledge next to an array of strange-looking instruments. She held a clipboard and appeared oblivious to the photo taker.

"This was taken several years ago in Papua New Guinea. She was only a few years out of graduate school. My daughter is a volcanologist." He replaced the picture on the table. "I don't see her very often. Sam's life has taken a very different direction from mine."

"Interesting field," Ryan said. "I considered it for a time. And of course, it's related to my own interest in geothermal energy."

"Which is why I thought I might be able to engage you in this . . . project," said the senator.

"Project?"

"Simply put, I believe Sam needs protection. She's always been fearless in her travels to remote places around the globe. In addition to her professional duties as a research volcanologist, she's also a science journalist. You may have seen some of her articles in *Science News* and occasionally the *New York Times*. She's currently working in Iceland, one of the most volcanic places on earth, as you know."

"Yes, my office there is studying what they're doing with new geothermal and fuel cell technologies. Some extraordinary things, really."

"Precisely why I want you for this. You have a unique set of abilities and are familiar with Iceland. I thought you might not be averse to taking on a slightly enlarged set of duties."

Ryan crossed his legs, noting that his own shoes were more scuffed than the senator's. "From what you say, your daughter—Samantha?—has spent years working in her field. I wouldn't think she'd need much protection from dangerous locations or potential volcanic eruptions. She must have much more experience with all of that than I do."

"She doesn't need protection from the elements, Mr. Baldwin." He hesitated. "What I'm going to tell you is not generally known, and I probably shouldn't reveal it, but . . . we're talking about my daughter's safety." He sighed. "Sam has upset certain interests in Iceland, as a result of her research. A great deal of foreign investment has come into the country since the financial meltdown a few years ago. The failure of the nation's banks provided an opening for foreign investors. From one nation in particular, as I suspect you know."

"Iran," said Ryan.

The senator let the word hang in the air for a moment. "I'm also Chairman of the Foreign Relations Committee, which makes this whole business even more touchy. I've tried to talk to Sam about it, but she refuses to believe there's any danger. I can tell you, however, that these Iranians are ruthless characters. I don't know exactly what they're up to, whether it's manipulation of the financial markets or oil prices or simply laundering money, but they have moved into

Iceland in a big way. My daughter's work may put her directly in their path.

"Sam speaks her mind, not unlike her mother, and she's written two pieces for the *Times* in which she argues that Iceland's economy will suffer even more than it already has from the cheap energy the Iranians have flooded the local market with. She believes it will stifle the alternative energy programs that are the way ahead for the country, indeed, that have already made Iceland a world leader in that area. Frankly, she's stirred up a hornet's nest.

"I don't want her to have an accident. I want you to go there and watch her back, is that clear enough?"

Ryan shifted uncomfortably. "I'm not in that business anymore, Senator. I have my own clientele and frankly, I have a lot on my plate at the moment. I can't just drop everything and go . . . if you will excuse the expression . . . baby-sit. That sort of assignment is precisely why I gave up working for the Service."

Graham was nodding. "I anticipated your response, which is why I have something else to offer. One of your major clients, I believe, is British Petroleum, is it not? I have a degree of influence over certain of their projects that have come before the committee. A word from me and they'll have no problem with your taking a slight detour from your normal obligations. Hell, they'd probably provide you with an expense account if they thought it might put them in my good graces. But I think it's better not to go there. I'll be paying your expenses myself, out of my own pocket, along with your fee. I assure you it will be more than enough to recoup any losses from pending business you may have. And I will personally put in a good word for you with BP."

Ryan took a breath and looked away. He didn't like being manipulated. It was another reason he'd left government service. Manipulation was the coin of the realm. Graham had obviously studied his business situation, and he knew that Ryan's firm had just suffered the cancellation of one of its biggest accounts. For a moment, he wondered if the senator might have had something to do with that. Graham was known for his political ambiguity and freewheeling use of power when it suited his purposes. Ryan knew he was more than capable of such a devious move.

Still, a proven relationship with the senator would cement his BP connection. Permanently. He suddenly remembered the one thing he had liked about working on the public dime: the bottomless money spigot.

Graham leaned forward. "You had an interesting reputation at the Service. The Director himself told me he regretted your departure, said you were one of his most skilled agents. But he also said you had an attitude problem, that you tended to philosophize about the job too openly."

Ryan tilted his head. "The Service tends to think highly of itself. Thinks the free world will come to a screeching halt if a President is ever assassinated. I haven't seen any evidence for that yet. They train us to take the assassin's bullet. I maybe put too much value on my own life to be certain I would do that for another dumb-ass politician. Anyway, it's why I got out."

"Still," Graham said, "Your skills were the best, and I only hire the best. I might actually agree with you about interchangeable politicians. My daughter is *not* replaceable. You have some knowledge of her field and you have contacts in Iceland. Those facts alone will serve as cover for your presence. Try not to let Sam know the real reason for your being there. At least as long as you can. She would never agree to a babysitter. I want you for this, Baldwin. No one else will do. I won't take no for an answer."

Ryan spread his hands in resignation. He'd spent enough time in Washington to know that powerful men usually got what they wanted. Graham obviously knew he couldn't afford to pass up the money or the connections that were being laid before him. He wondered if the senator wanted him as much for his business connections as his Secret Service credentials.

The majority leader's penetrating gaze seemed to be trying to see into Ryan's head, evaluating and calculating every nuance. "There's something else. I don't know that I should mention it, but you just never know where these things will take you."

Ryan waited.

"I divorced Sam's mother when Sam was a college freshman. Sam's never really forgiven me. Her mother's dead now and we're the only family each of us has. But she refuses to have any serious relationship with me." He sighed heavily. "I haven't even seen her in two years. I've never met any of her friends. What I know about her I glean from her writings and from quiet inquiries with local officials. She won't be happy if she learns why you're there."

Ryan stared at him. "So I'm supposed to protect her without her knowing about it? That certainly won't make it easier."

"I don't know any other way to go about it. Perhaps you can befriend her somehow. Your shared interests in Iceland, volcanology and geothermals should give you an opening. I leave that to you.

"I'm counting on you, Baldwin."

It took two whirlwind days for Ryan to wind up his affairs and inform his D.C. business partner that he'd be returning to Iceland for a while.

"What the hell's going on?" Will had said. "When I told that bloke at BP, the one who's always giving us all manner of hell about being behind in our work, that you were taking a leave of absence, he was all sweetness and light."

That was Senator Graham's doing. The man had a long reach.

Now, he stared out the window of his plane as it prepared to land on an uncharacteristically sunny Reykjavik morning. He could see volcanic steam venting in the distance, a promising landscape if one happened to be in the thermal energy business.

Eva Berenson, who managed his business office in Reykjavik, met him at the airport. She was a tall, striking Danish woman, at forty-three still attractive enough to turn heads. Eva had been invaluable in courting business owners, but she came with an edge, most of which had to do with Jon Gudnasson, who was Ryan's chief staff geologist. He'd clashed with Eva, who didn't suffer fools lightly, from the start.

"How's my number one employee?" Ryan smiled broadly as he got in her car and kissed her on the cheek.

"I won't be number one until you fire Gudnasson. He undermines everyone in the office and has us all looking over our shoulders, waiting for the knife in the back."

He sighed. "Look, there will be no knives in the back as long as I'm in charge. You know that, Eva. And you also know it's been next to impossible for us to find a good geologist willing to take the job at the kind of wages we can afford right now."

"*Good* being the operative word in that sentence. No secret why Jon was available. Who the hell else would hire him?"

He said, "How's David?"

"You're changing the subject."

"But it's a good subject."

David was her seventeen-year-old son from a marriage when she was fresh out of college that had lasted only until David was eight. Ryan knew little about her former husband, except that he'd been a cop.

"He's smart as a whip, handsome—like his dad—and beginning to have trouble keeping the girls at bay."

"Yeah, that was always my problem too."

She gave him a look. "That might actually be true, but you've had an attitude as long as I've known you. As a teenager, it probably made you unapproachable."

"Whoa, way too early in the day for psychoanalysis, okay?"

She shrugged. "Anyway, David said he hopes to see you. And what I want to know is why you're not staying with Helga and me?"

He often stayed with Eva and her sister, Helga, who shared a house together. Helga was younger and even more beautiful than her sister. She was also divorced and neither woman seemed to have any interest in getting back in the market. That fact alone had been enough to drive Jon crazy. "What a waste of good feminine pulchritude," he'd told Ryan when he first learned of the arrangement, as though there was anything there that might ever be available to him.

"Out of my hands, I'm afraid," Ryan said. "My new employer arranged the lodgings for me." In fact, the place was the same one the senator's daughter was staying in. He'd present himself as a researcher, which, hopefully, would allow him to fall into Miss Graham's orbit. He consulted his reservation papers. "Evidently a small home. Only three rooms to let and I got the last one."

Eva glanced over his shoulder. "Hildisdottir's place. Well, you could have done worse. I actually know another of her guests, Samantha Graham."

His surprise showed—until he remembered how insular a city Reykjavik really was.

"Only met her a couple of times," she went on. "Quite a brilliant scientist. Doing some sort of volcanic research up on Laki. I don't know how often you'll run into her at your boarding house, though. I've heard that lately, she prefers to camp out on site."

This wasn't good news. It would be hard to justify setting up his own tent right next to Sam's in a half million acres of wilderness. She'd be suspicious immediately.

Eva looked at him. "What's going on, Ryan? Who's this mysterious new client? Are we going to see any of you? There are some problems you could deal with right now, you know."

"I know, and I'm sorry. You're just going to have to handle them yourself for the time being. This new deal will bring in some badly needed financing. I couldn't afford to pass it up. Anyway, I have full confidence in you."

Before she could speak, he added, "Look, why don't you send Jon out into the field. Get him away from the office for a while. God knows there must be plenty for him to do."

"I've tried, believe me. But he resists it. Says he's behind in his own office work and geological studies, blah, blah, blah. Truth is, he likes the nightlife. I'm telling you, boss, he's not worth what you're paying him."

"Probably not. But we have to have a full PhD geologist on staff or our clients won't take us seriously. I'll see if I can come up with something for him to do, okay?"

Reykjavik had perhaps the most spectacular setting for a city anywhere, with a backdrop of magnificent mountains set against the sharply contrasting blues of sky and ocean, at least when the weather allowed them to be seen. Located between the Arctic Circle and the warm Gulf Stream current, its climate constantly shifted back and forth, from balmy one day to wet and frigid the next. As if to compensate, the city rocked with a vibrant nightlife, crowded green parks, and a brisk salmon river that flowed through the center of town.

Much of this had been tempered, of course, since the collapse of the banking and financial industry in the fall of 2008. However, the hardship had declined over the succeeding years, and Icelanders refused to let it dampen their spirits.

He got to visit his Reykjavik office only once or twice a year. Under Eva's management, they'd begun to acquire a number of new, high-level accounts. Geothermal technology was poised to take off on an international scale, and Ryan hoped they'd be in on the ground floor when that happened.

"Is that wonderful little seafood restaurant still down by the waterfront?" he asked.

She glanced at him. "It's still there, all right, but under new management. They serve Middle Eastern food now. Owned by an Iranian chain. Truth is, you'll see a lot of that. Sometimes it seems like the Iranians have bought up half of Reykjavik, apartment buildings, high rises, malls, restaurants."

He raised an eyebrow. "I knew they were one of the foreign interests that had been capitalizing on the economic weakness," he said. "But I didn't realize it had gone that far."

"After the collapse, things were available at fire sale prices, as you know," said Eva. "There's long been resistance to foreign investment in Iceland. The government has tried to keep it under strict control, but there's been pressure to open things more and more. A lot of it has been surreptitious, locals partnering with foreign nationals to make it more palatable. The truth is, the Iranians like Iceland. Seem to find it exotic. They love the wildness of it."

"I wouldn't think they'd care for the cold weather and overcast skies."

"Well, if they don't, they're doing an awfully good job of concealing their discomfort." She pulled the car up to a small clapboard building with a bright red roof. "Here we are—Hildisdottir's place."

He got out and looked around. They were in the center of town. Ingolfsstraeti was a quiet street with a small park across the way. The National Theater and the waterfront were nearby. He took his bags out and gave her a hug.

"You have to at least come for dinner," she said. "Saturday night?"

"Will David be able to fight the girls off long enough to stop by?"

"I promise."

"Okay. Tell him I'll give him a lesson in attitude adjustment that will help keep the young things at bay."

She smiled. "You'll want to rent a car. There's a place just round the corner. See you, then." She roared off, leaving him on the curb with his bags.

He went up the stoop and rang the bell.

An efficient, ruddy-faced woman greeted him. She wore a white apron and shook his hand with her own, lightly floured one.

"Sorry," she said. "There is a pie, you see." She took one of his bags and bustled him inside. "Expecting you. My name is Bjorg. Nice it will be to have a full house again."

"How many others are there?"

"Only two. An Iranian business owner. Here to look for investments, he is, though Lord knows what is left to buy. He is gone most of the day. And a scientist, a woman. But she is out there somewhere." She waved a hand, leaving Ryan uncertain if she meant to indicate the distant mountains or that the woman was a bit crazy.

"Gone for days at a time, almost a week this time. I do not know why she keeps a room at all. Perhaps it is subletting I should be doing." She looked him up and down. "I do hope you will spend more time with us. It is a full English breakfast I am providing every morning at seven thirty."

"That's marvelous!" he said and meant it. He was addicted to the English idea of breakfast.

The house gave off a Victorian flavor with busy wallpaper, over-stuffed furniture, and bric-a-brac everywhere. Upstairs, a hallway had three doors off it. She opened one and he stepped into a large, bright room with a queen-size bed, a sitting area, and a small balcony that looked out on the park.

"Beautiful," he said. "I'll be very comfortable here."

"Oh, I am glad. The door at the end of the hall is the bathroom. With Miss Graham, you will share, when she is here. The Iranian gentleman has the downstairs toilet off his own bedroom."

"Uh . . . what did you say his name was?"

"Hassan . . . something. I am not remembering. They are all named Hassan or Mohammad. Confusing, it is."

He wondered if her remark revealed prejudice or simply discomfort with the new order in Iceland and decided to probe a little further. "I haven't been back in some time. My friend said there's been a lot more foreign investment."

"Ya! That is putting it . . . how do you Americans say? Softly? Mildly? Bought up half the country, they have. Did you see all the new fuel tanks down by the docks? Iranian oil. Makes it hard for folks to complain, it does. Cheap fuel . . . they undercut the price of local gas . . . and hotels and businesses filled with Hassans spreading money around like water."

"What's in it for them?"

"I could not be saying. It is more money they have than good sense. Seem to enjoy the stark beauty of this place. Must be quite a change from the desert, I am thinking. But Hassan—he never takes off his down coat. Not adapted to the cold." She gave him a smile and spun out one of her Americanisms. "It all beats me."

Bjorg disappeared to continue with her pie. Ryan stepped out onto the balcony and stared at the distant mountains. In spite of his unusual mission, he felt the tension in his shoulders slip away. He loved this country and even thought he might make it his home

someday. He started to turn away when he noticed a gray Land
Rover parked across the street in front of the park. The two men
sitting inside stared straight ahead. They weren't conversing or consulting a map. There was just something a little . . . odd . . . about it.
His security training kicked in. The men looked for all the world like
they were on some sort of stakeout.

Looking for Sam?

The thought made him nervous. He kept an eye on them into
the early afternoon as he unpacked and settled in. Bjorg brought a
lunch to his room.

He decided to ask her directly. "Um . . . have you noticed those
two men sitting in that car across the way? They've been there
all day."

She looked out the window. "I am forgetting about them," she
said. "Showed up three days ago, now, and been there ever since.
A bit strange, I am thinking."

He felt alarm bells go off. They had to be looking for someone
and it made sense it would be Sam.

"Is there another way out of the house, Bjorg?"

She looked at him with a questioning tilt of her head. "Ya. The
back door goes into the garden. There is a gate you will be taking to
a path and then to Lindargata street. The way I go to market."

"I think I'll wander out that way if you don't mind. I want to
rent a car."

"There is a shop right on that street. Turn left when you get to
the end of the path." She started to leave the room. "If you leave a
light on," she said. "They will be thinking you are still here."

"Who will?"

"Why . . . anyone would," she said, turning away with a smile.

The rental was a reasonably fuel-efficient 4WD vehicle. He
threw in a pack with some warm clothes and a few bits of food he'd
picked up at a local grocery. He wasn't at all sure what he was doing,
but the fact that someone seemed already on the lookout for Sam
made him nervous.

Bjorg said she'd been gone almost a week, so Sam might walk right into something unexpected when she returned. Or potentially, she'd run into trouble already. That was something he didn't want to think about.

He'd been to Laki once during a tour Eva had given him when he first came to Iceland to open his office. It was located in the barren south-central highlands near the Vatnajökull glacier in an area of volcanic fissures. Barren . . . but also incredibly beautiful.

He knew what he was doing was foolish. What were the odds he could find a single person in all that vast wilderness? Yet he recalled that Laki was at the end of a spur connecting with the Ring Road that encircled the entire country. Perhaps Sam's car would be there, and he could figure out which direction she'd gone. You could see a long way in that open landscape. A colorful tent would stick out like a beacon.

It was after five when he reached the small parking lot at the end of Rt. 206, connecting the Laki Craters to the Ring Road. There had been several difficult river crossings he'd never have been able to negotiate without 4WD. Once or twice he feared he'd gotten mired in the water but he'd managed finally to get through, gears grinding. Sure enough, a blue 4WD pickup was pulled off to one side of the lot, its bed modified with fitted metal storage bins.

He got out, walked over to the truck, and peered in the window. Aside from a sweater and a few magazines or journals, there was nothing else inside that might identify the owner. But it had to be hers. Who else would be in such a place with night coming on?

He walked about the brown earth, a mixture of volcanic detritus and hardened lava flows, though a layer of gray moss covered much of the landscape. He knew the moss turned a vibrant green following a rainfall. After making two circuits, he found faint footprints in the moss leading up the side of the crater. It was hard to know if they were recent, but they seemed too small for a man's.

He put his pack on. He had moved perhaps a hundred meters up the side when he heard another vehicle coming. He crouched behind a large boulder and waited.

In a moment, the same Land Rover that had been parked outside his boarding house chugged noisily to a halt beside the other
two vehicles. Four men got out and scanned the surrounding slopes.
One man with a stoop and a large nose seemed to be in charge.

There ensued a lengthy conversation, much peering into the cars
and pointing in various directions. He wished he could hear what
they were saying. But then it wasn't necessary, as Big Nose pulled
out a blade and carefully punctured the tires, all of them, on Ryan's
car and the pickup.

He stared in disbelief. The action left no doubt as to why the
men were here. They intended that whoever owned those vehicles
would not be able to leave. Not be able to escape.

If further evidence was needed, it was forthcoming. From the
trunk of the Land Rover, one man issued rifles to each of the others.
Ryan's hand went down and felt the familiar weight of his SIG P229
pistol, the weapon of choice for the Secret Service. Without the help
of the majority leader and his own record with the Service, he would
never have been able to bring the firearm into the country. It gave
him some reassurance, though a pistol against four men with rifles
was small comfort.

He watched long enough to see the men study the ground
and find the same tracks he was following. Then he scurried away,
keeping behind the rocks. Cover was limited and darkness of any
kind was still many hours away.

The tracks petered out, as the moss gave way to loose shale.
He continued upward, finally out of sight, taking the path of least
resistance, which he felt anyone would follow in the rough terrain.
God, what a bleak place! Eva had barely allowed him out of the car
when he'd visited before, simply pointing out the volcanic mountain as a tourist site. But from what he understood, tourism on Laki
had taken a big hit following Graham's published suggestions that
an eruption might be imminent. That had not made her a popular
figure in the tourism industry.

Laki was part of a volcanic system that centered on the
Grímsvötn volcano and included the Eldgjá canyon and Katla

volcano. It lay between the glaciers of Mýrdalsjökull and Vatnajökull, in an area of fissures that ran in a southwest-northeast direction. He knew that the volcanoes in this region had a long history of eruptions, so Samantha's cautions undoubtedly had some basis in fact.

As the side of the crater grew steeper, he entered a region rent with fissures, rocky overhangs, treacherous drop-offs, and dangerous, slippery footing. He was now just two hundred feet below the rim. He peered over a boulder and could see the men far below, working their way slowly upward. They were clearly not mountaineering types. Their city shoes slipped on the uneven ground, and he heard Big Nose curse as he lost his balance and fell on the hard rock.

As he circled to the backside of the volcano, he saw a bright orange tent a hundred yards away, situated in a cluster of boulders near the rim. The sides of the tent were held down with rocks, the ground being too hard for stakes.

He picked up his pace, stumbling and cursing like the men behind. As he neared the tent, he saw sudden movement to one side. A woman carrying a heavily weighted pack was carefully making her way down from the rim. She looked up and saw him.

"Who are you?" she asked. She held her walking stick in both hands like a weapon. Ryan was struck by the intensity in her gaze. Her black hair had grown longer since the picture he'd seen. It was tied back in a ponytail, a pair of sunglasses resting on top of her head. From what little he could see beneath the pack and coat, she appeared very slight. She was completely and utterly alone in this wilderness and had just been confronted by a strange man. Yet he had no sense that she was afraid. Indeed, she seemed ready to interrogate him.

Before he could respond, the crack of a rifle split the air and a bullet ricocheted off a rock next to them. The sound reverberated in the vastness of their surroundings and seemed to echo away into the distance.

He looked back and saw that the four men had spread out and were making better time than he'd originally anticipated. When he turned back to the woman, he caught just a glimpse of her as she disappeared over the rim.

"Wait!" he cried, then cursed as another bullet smacked near his feet. He dropped his pack and took off up the crater after her. He considered firing a return shot, just to make them think twice, but rejected the idea. Better to let them think he was unarmed.

He struggled up the steep final feet to the rim, realizing that the quickness with which the girl had climbed while carrying a heavy pack was impressive. She was in good shape.

At the top, he was silhouetted against the sky for a moment and two shots nicked close to him before he ducked over the edge.

The inside of Laki crater descended steeply. He found himself in a maze of rock ledges, fissures and, lower down, smoking ventholes. At the bottom, a small crater lake nestled in the rock. It was a desolate place. But what stopped him in his tracks was the realization that the woman was nowhere to be seen.

He whirled around, looking in every direction. There wasn't a sign of her. She had vanished as completely as if she'd fallen down a rabbit hole. It was impossible.

"Damn!" He swore out loud. He had no option but to call out. "Samantha! Where are you? Sam?"

He stumbled lower. He needed to find a place to make a stand. Once the men topped the crater rim, they'd make quick work of him. He found a fissure that wound along the side of the crater. It offered some protection. But then the men were on top and they saw him before he could get out of sight. They opened fire in an almost continuous fusillade. Bullets rang and ricocheted off the rocks.

He worked his way along the fissure until he reached a small ledge that blocked further progress. He'd got himself trapped in a dead end.

The men were talking among themselves. They could see his predicament and began to spread out along the rim searching for a spot where they'd be able to fire down on him.

He looked about desperately for some way out. Then a voice whispered sharply from above.

"Up here!"

He looked up and saw a hand wave to him from the top of the ledge. It would be a tough scramble, and he'd have to hurry before the men got into position to fire on him.

He maneuvered until he was out of sight of the men, then began to pull himself up using a series of shale-like steps. Just before he reached the top, he heard the voice again.

"That's far enough . . . now slip through here."

A small depression existed near the top of the ledge, no bigger than a man's waist. It looked like nothing more than a bit of rock of a slightly different color. He lowered himself into it, realizing that it was the opening of a venthole. He squeezed through a small entryway and found himself completely enclosed in a larger fissure that wound away, disappearing into darkness.

"Come lower," the voice said. "And try not to make any noise."

He eased farther into the fissure, sliding on his rear where it became steeper, finally stopping beside the woman.

"Thanks," he said. "They would have had me in another minute."

Her face was turned away as she removed her pack and lowered it to the ground. Then she sat down, leaning against it.

"Maybe we should keep going," he said.

"No. They'll never find the entrance. I've been doing research here for two years, walking past that ledge and opening nearly every day and I never saw it until I slipped one time and fell into the depression. They'll look for a while and then give up. We're too far from the entrance now for them to hear us."

He examined her face for the first time. She had prominent cheekbones and smooth, dark skin that had obviously spent time in tropical climates. Her features were small and sharp, with penetrating black eyes that were studying him hard.

"Now maybe you can explain," she said, "why you brought these people here. And how you happen to know my name."

He sighed. "I'm sorry. I feel like a damn fool. I'm here—I come to Iceland I mean—on business, to do research in geothermal energy. I have a small consulting business that works with energy firms.

Believe it or not, I'm actually staying at Bjorg's place, just down the hall from you. She mentioned . . . or maybe it was my friend Eva, that you were out here. I only just arrived and decided to come out for something to do. I was here once years ago. I . . . I think those men followed me." He hesitated, then added, "Why would they do that? And why are they trying to kill me?"

Her intense eyes stared at him. She seemed to be trying to decide whether or not to believe him. Finally, she said, "They aren't trying to kill you. They're trying to kill me, and it's not the first time."

She held up a hand as he started to speak. "You called me Sam," she said. "Why?"

"What do you mean? It's your name, isn't it?"

"My name is Samantha. There's only one person in the world who calls me Sam. That's my father." She glared at him. "He sent you here didn't he?"

He swore. So much for being undercover. He wondered just how badly her father had underestimated his daughter's ability to take care of herself. There was nothing he could do but nod.

She lowered her head. In a resigned voice, she said, "Mr. Majority Leader always has to be the one who makes the decisions. It's why I don't spend any more time in the States than I have to." She put both hands to her face and pressed them against her eyes. "I never cared for that nickname, you know. Sam Graham. Sounds like some sort of wire service, though I guess I've gotten used to it."

She looked him up and down. "I suppose if he hired you, you must be good. I rather doubt you are any sort of . . . what did you call it? Geothermal researcher."

"Funny thing is, I am. It's what I do now. But I was in the Secret Service for many years. That's how your dad knew about me."

"It figures."

"So now that you know all about me, can I ask a couple of questions, since I'm supposed to be protecting you—at least until you tell me to take a hike."

"I just may do that," she said, but he detected the hint of a smile around her eyes. "I suppose it's stupid, really, given what's just happened, not to be grateful that someone wants to help me."

"Some help. I led them straight to you and damn near got us both killed. We still may be. So . . . the obvious question is, why are they trying to kill you? You would appear to be a fairly undangerous-looking volcanologist going about her business. What gives?"

***

Eva was washing dishes in her kitchen. The window looked out on a sidewalk and a small garden. About twenty feet away, she could see into the windows of the home next door. A new family had moved in. She hadn't met them yet but thought it would only be a matter of time. Neighbors were cordial in Iceland.

They appeared to be Iranian. Nothing unusual about that these days, though they certainly lived modestly. They weren't the rich oil barons of late. More likely labor or help for the upper classes. There was a cute little boy of about eight and a daughter who looked like she was maybe sixteen. Eva had taken to waving at the girl whenever she came home from school. She was slim and pretty and had a dazzling smile.

As she finished up the dishes, a school bus stopped at the corner and several kids got off. One was the Iranian girl. She hunched over her books and walked quickly down the sidewalk.

Eva opened her window and called hello. The girl didn't look at her or acknowledge her in any way. She disappeared inside. A moment later, Eva saw her through the open window of her bedroom.

She started to turn away, when she heard a low wail. Looking back, she saw the girl hunched over, holding her stomach, and crying as she lay curled up on her bed.

Eva stood in indecision. She didn't know these people. But her heart went out to the girl. She was probably having a hard time in her new school. She watched until the crying stopped and the child seemed to go to sleep.

Helga came over and stood beside her. "What's wrong?" she asked.

Eva nodded out the window. "Our new neighbor's daughter isn't happy."

Helga looked out at the still form across the way.

"Life's hard in a new home," she said.

"In a new country."

"In a new school."

Helga looked at her. She knew Eva. "You going to do something?"

Eva shook her head. "Try not to be a busybody. That's probably the last thing she needs."

Chapter Three

August 5, 1940

Reykjavik

Fritz Kraus was the only German graduate student at the University of Iceland. He was also the only one studying the island's geology. In just a week, he had to defend his PhD thesis on the geology and volcanology of the Laki chain.

His interest in Iceland had come about as the result of a climbing trip several years earlier. He and a friend had gone ice climbing on one of the glaciers. The awe-inspiring beauty of the place hooked him, as had the geology. He was particularly intrigued by subglacial volcanoes. It was a new wonder, a terrain of earth-shaping powers, and Germany had nothing like it.

He looked at his watch for the tenth time in annoyance. His Icelandic girlfriend, Greta, was late as usual. Then he saw her slip into the library and toss her blonde hair as she looked for him.

His heart took the little leap it always did whenever he saw her. She was so damn beautiful. If he didn't watch out, he might never

return to Germany. That wouldn't be good for his employment pos-
sibilities. Since the rise of the Nazis, Germans had not been looked
upon favorably in Iceland. It had taken an extraordinary effort, along
with letters of reference from several teachers back in Germany, to
get him into the country to study in the first place.

Greta saw him and worked her way down the long study tables.
The eyes of every young male student followed her progress, and
Fritz felt that incredible sense of pride when they all saw her stop in
front of him, lean over and give him a quick kiss.

She sat beside him and snuggled close, whispering, "How's the
most handsome geology PhD candidate in Reykjavik?"

"I'm the *only* PhD geology candidate," he reminded her.

"And the most handsome one too. Imagine that?" she said, gig-
gling. "You promised we'd go ice climbing this weekend."

"Yes. Everything's ready, though I really should be studying, you
know, or I may soon be the only ex-PhD candidate in geology."

"Nonsense. You're too brilliant. Be a feather in the cap of this
place to issue you a degree. They wouldn't dare deny you."

He wished he shared her feelings. "Germans aren't all that popular around here, you know. Not since Germany invaded Denmark
last April. Yours may be the only friendly face I see on a regular basis."

"Yes, well, we Icelanders are sick to death of Der Führer and his
nasty Storm Troopers. He's a disgusting, little man. And that ridiculous moustache . . ."

"You better not talk that way if you ever come visit me at home,"
he said.

"I'm not going to visit your home as long as that monster is in
charge. You're going to have to stay here and be my sex slave and
make love to me whenever I order you to."

He looked around self-consciously. Greta was deliciously sexual,
but she seemed to have little idea of the effect she had on men. Even
now, he could see several students unable to take their eyes off her. It
was time to get out of here.

He gathered up his books and papers and they made their
way outside to his car. It was already loaded down with the gear

they would need for the weekend. In a few minutes they were outside the city, motoring down the Ring Road toward the southern Laki chain.

"Where are you taking me?" asked Greta. She perched her feet on the dashboard, bare legs soaking in the sunshine. "And how long till we set up our tent and you ravish me in the wastelands?"

He glanced at her. "I can pull over right here and have the tent up in five minutes," he said.

She laughed. "No, no. It has to be the wastelands. Otherwise, the effect is not the same."

"It's the same for me no matter where we do it," he said.

"Tell me what you're studying," she said. "It'll take your mind off my legs . . . and be good practice for the defense of your thesis when the time comes."

He reached out a hand and stroked her bare thigh. Maybe it would be a good idea to think of something else. "Well . . . I've been studying the effects of subglacial eruptions in the Grimsvotn volcano beneath the Vatnajökull icecap. There have been a number of glacial outburst floods, called jökulhlaup, in recorded history. I've been studying two documented jökulhlaups probably caused by Grimsvotn eruptions beneath the glacier in 1933 and 1934."

"So . . . what?" she interrupted. "The volcano erupts and it causes ice to melt, right? Forming a lake?"

"Exactly. The eruptions can melt huge volumes of water. Some of it may become trapped beneath or within the glacier and build up pressure until it breaks through. The damage when that happens can be unbelievable, though it rarely happens in inhabited areas. I've estimated runoffs equal to a week's outflow of the Amazon."

"Wow! I guess that could cause a bit of damage, huh?"

"There've been lots of Grimsvotn eruptions through history. The word jökulhlaup is actually an Icelandic term that's been adapted by the rest of the world to describe the phenomenon. One scientist friend of mine believes the English Channel may have been created two hundred thousand years ago by a glacial lake outburst flood, probably caused by an earthquake. The flood would have lasted for many months, releasing perhaps a million cubic meters of water per second."

Greta stared at him. "Per second?"

He nodded. "I've been expanding on my friend's theory. I think such an outflow might have destroyed the isthmus that connected Britain to continental Europe. It's one small part of my PhD thesis, along with the idea that it would have carved a deep valley down the length of the English Channel."

She stared at him. "How on Earth could you ever prove that?"

He laughed. "We'll have to leave that to the science of the future, I'm afraid. That's the great thing about far-out theories. No one can really refute them." He stared at the horizon where the slopes of the volcano, Laki, loomed barren and bleak. "I love this place. Ever since I first visited the southern coast and especially Laki, I've felt a strange attraction to it. Overwhelming, really."

He glanced at her. "I can't explain it. This place simply makes me feel alive." He added quickly, "Almost the same way you do."

"I hope my charms are a little more enticing than those of a volcano," she said. "But I think I understand. You have a poetic soul, you know. It's one of the things I like about you." She looked out at the rising hills. "It does look a bit like a woman. Laki, I mean. Those lean, lanky slopes, like a woman's curves, leading to something more, something promised in a dark, warm center."

He grinned, light-hearted again. "That's a metaphor I'd like to get to the bottom of," he said, reaching over a hand and squeezing her bottom.

Laki retreated behind them and the road began to get marginal as they approached Vatnajökull glacier. He'd done this before and knew how to get as close to the glacier as possible by vehicle. Then they'd hike for an hour to a spot where they could easily access the glacier via a short ice climb.

It was early evening by the time they reached the glacial wall. Greta stared up at it in awe. "It's beautiful. Just like you said."

"Come on. We'll pitch our tent over there. It's too late to climb tonight, and as I recall you said you needed the attentions of your sex slave."

By midnight, Fritz was tapped out completely. He couldn't remember a time when he'd had such sexual stamina. Greta put him through his paces for close to two hours, until they fell asleep in each other's arms. They didn't wake until the bright sunshine broke through their tent window.

An hour later, they had crampons on and a rope tied between them, as they made their way slowly up the glacial wall. The going was not difficult, even though Greta was largely inexperienced. Fritz had taken that into account in choosing a fairly easy path to the top.

Once they were seated in the snow on top of the glacier, Greta's eyes sparkled.

"It's absolutely everything you said it would be, Fritz! I'm in love with this place—and with you." She leaned over and kissed him deeply.

"Let's hike a ways," he said. "This looks pretty stable up here. I'd like to see what's over that next rise."

They reached the top of the rise and Fritz stopped abruptly.

"What is it?" Greta asked.

"It's a subsidence bowl. My God, it's unbelievable! I've never actually seen one."

They stared down at what looked for all the world like a crater crafted out of snow. It was immense, stretching at least half a mile in circumference. The sides were filled with striations and small crevices. And at the bottom was a small black hole, almost like a cave entrance.

"There's your warm, dark center," Fritz said with a grin. "Like the one I explored last night. Come on! I want to see what's down there."

They circumnavigated the rim of the bowl until they were directly above the black, cave-like entrance.

"I don't know, Fritz," Greta said. "It looks dangerous, and the snow seems loose, like it could give way."

"Actually, it's probably a quite stable formation, but we'll be careful anyway."

He knelt down at the rim and pounded two pitons into an ice-covered rock, then ran his line through them and over the lip into the crater. It reached all the way to the opening.

Greta sat in the snow, eyeing the bowl. "Look at those crevices. It doesn't look safe at all to me."

"Look, you can just sit here on the rim while I climb down. It'll be a piece of cake." He leaned over and planted a kiss on her mouth. "I just want to see what's down there."

He began to back down into the bowl. His feet punched small holes in the snow, causing miniature avalanches that trickled down into the black hole below. Greta sat on the rim and watched him uneasily.

Fritz stopped just above the opening and tried to peer inside, but the angle was wrong. He was almost out of rope, too. He tied himself off firmly and studied an overhang of snow that was blocking his view.

"I think I can knock this bit of snow loose," he called up to her. "And then I'll be able to see what's down there."

"Be careful!" came her cry from above.

He maneuvered himself onto the overhang and gave a little jump with both feet. The overhang seemed to loosen. "One more should do it," he called up.

He jumped in the air and came down hard with both feet. The overhang broke away and disappeared into the opening. Fritz stared after the crumbling snow, then noticed that the snow around the sides of the crater had started to trickle downward into the hole as well.

"Fritz! Be careful!" Greta called. She was standing on the rim watching the loose snow collapse inward. Then, all of a sudden, the entire inside of the crater simply crumbled from rim to rim.

Fritz looked up in time to see Greta being washed downward in the collapsing snow.

Avalanche!

Greta's white face looked over at him. She was no more than a dozen feet from him, but it might as well have been the dark side of the moon.

"Greta!" he cried. "Grab onto something."

But the snow collapsed in ever-widening circles, drawing Greta downward in a vortex of motion.

There was nothing he could do.

The snow disappeared into the black hole, then the hole itself collapsed and Fritz had one last glimpse of Greta, her blonde hair whipped upward by a whirlpool of wind.

"Fritz! Help me!" she cried, and then she disappeared along with the rush of snow. Fritz felt something give and the entire interior of the bowl collapsed inward, leaving him hanging from his rope above a massive opening. He stared into it in horror. A river of icy meltwater flowed away beneath the glacier, carrying the snow and Greta into oblivion.

Chapter Four

Present Day

They heard a distant shout. It seemed very far away from their enclosed hideaway.

Sam looked at her watch. "They'll give up soon," she said confidently. "It gets cold up here in the evening, and they didn't look to be terribly well dressed."

She took her heavy jacket off. Inside the venthole, out of the wind, it was comfortable. More than comfortable. Ryan wondered if there might be some thermal heat being generated by Laki that reached up from the earth beneath them. Despite the presence of gunmen outside, he felt strangely relaxed and content.

"You said you'd been here before," she went on. "How much do you actually know about Laki?"

He shrugged. "Precious little. It's not been the focus of my interest directly. I've pretty much kept to examining the research being done on thermal and fuel cell technology in Reykjavik."

She nodded thoughtfully. "This is a very interesting volcano, not only for its interior design, so to speak, but also for its history. There have been two major eruptions in recorded history and of course many more before that. This is a very active region geologically. Iceland has over two hundred active volcanoes, you know. I've recorded a surprising amount of seismic activity here in the last two years."

He raised an eyebrow. "Which could mean a new eruption is imminent?"

"Perhaps. The correlation is not always exact, but yes, it's a possibility. I've written about that possibility, which hasn't made me the most popular person in Iceland."

"I imagine it could frighten people."

"More than that, it pisses them off, especially those in the tourist industry. Guides, tour buses, hotels, restaurants, car rentals. It all ties together. Since I started writing about it, tourism has fallen off a cliff. No one wants to be around if this thing goes off."

"What happens if you're here when it erupts?"

She shrugged. "I'm a volcanologist. I have to be here to study. It goes with the territory. Anyway, I'm happier here than any other place I've ever been. It just seems right, somehow, to be here."

They listened silently for a moment. There was no sound from their pursuers.

"Laki's last major eruption was huge," She went on. "It happened in 1783 and extended over a period of months into 1784. Thirty billion tons of lava poured out of a twenty-mile-long fissure. It was the largest recorded lava flow in history."

He whistled softly. "This entire region must be undermined by vents and lava tunnels."

"You have no idea. Some of the fissure is now actually beneath the Myrdalsjokull glacier. There are several lifetimes of study and research to be done here." She leaned forward suddenly and stared at him with hungry eyes. "I intend to do my share."

"I believe you will," he said.

She relaxed a little, settled back again. "Anyway, ninety million tons of sulfuric acid was released. Nine thousand people died, twenty percent of Iceland's population at the time. The eruption set off one of the coldest winters on record in Europe, North America, and Central Asia, as far away as Siberia. An estimated twenty-three thousand people in Britain alone died from inhaling sulfurous gases that descended in the form of deadly fogs in August and September."

"I had no clue," Ryan said.

"The effects on human history were significant. It's even thought it may have been one cause of the French Revolution, because the destruction of crops and livestock brought famine and poverty leading to unrest in France before the revolution in 1789.

"In North America, the winter of 1783-84 was one of the longest and coldest in history—the longest period of below-zero temperatures in New England, the largest accumulation of snow in New Jersey, the longest freezing over of Chesapeake Bay. A huge snowstorm hit the South and the Mississippi river at New Orleans froze over. There were ice flows in the Gulf of Mexico."

"And you think an eruption of similar magnitude may be building now?"

She stretched out her legs and leaned back against her pack. The effect was to make her seem taller. It also made him uncomfortably aware of her physical presence. There was something vital, almost intimidating about her. She exuded independence and self-confidence. Given the fact that men had just tried to kill her, she looked remarkably composed.

"Many volcanoes erupt on a regular basis, though that regularity may only amount to every few hundred or even thousand years. There was another major eruption of Laki in AD 934, called the Eldgjá eruption. We know much less about this one, of course, since it occurred before recorded history in Iceland, even before the Norse Sagas, which were written from the twelfth to the fourteenth centuries, though they recorded stories that went back to the Saga Age, about 900–1050."

THE GODS OF LAKI

Ryan shook his head in wonder. "You must have been researching this place for a long time."

She went on as if he hadn't spoken. "The Eldgjá eruption, like the one in 1783, produced a cloud of sulfuric acid aerosols that traversed northern Europe, dimming and reddening the sun. King Henry of Saxony observed one of these heavy, dry fogs in AD 934. It was the same phenomenon that Ben Franklin described after the 1783 catastrophe."

"I know a little something about what the release of aerosol gas and dust into the atmosphere can do," Ryan said. "Sulfuric gas changes rapidly into sulfuric acid aerosol in the atmosphere. It alters the radiative budget and leads to cooling of the earth's surface as the aerosol reflects solar radiation back to space. It can be a major factor in climate change."

Samantha looked at him with grudging respect. "You're right and furthermore . . ."

A loud voice suddenly shouted from the top of the vent. In a moment, more voices could be heard all talking rapidly. They had found the entrance to their hiding place.

"Son of a bitch!" said Ryan.

Samantha grabbed her pack and jacket. "Follow me," she said.

As they moved, rifle fire resounded in the vent, deafening them. Ryan heard bullets whiz past, ricocheting off the walls.

As they moved lower, Samantha took out a small flashlight to help guide them. They could hear the men entering the tunnel, grunting and sliding somewhere behind them.

Ryan could definitely feel heat coming through the floor of the vent now.

"There must be volcanic activity not far below us," he said.

"More than you know," she replied. "It gets steeper from here."

"You mean you've been down here before?"

"It's very interesting structure, volcanically speaking." She slowed as the ground beneath them began to slope steeply. "Be careful. It's easy to lose your footing now. Put your hand on the floor."

He wasn't sure what she meant, but he leaned over and put one palm on the vent floor. It was warm to the touch. Before he could say anything, Samantha sat down and began to slide.

"Try not to get going too fast," she said. "There's a fork in the tunnel below us. We'll slide to the left, entering the smaller tunnel. Those following will more likely choose the larger opening. It'll be the last decision they ever make."

He wanted to ask what she meant, but there was no time. He sat and began to slide, barely able to control his increasing speed with his hands and feet. The branch in the tunnels came upon them suddenly, and he followed Samantha's lead into the left opening by dragging one hand as if it were a rudder. The rock was much warmer now.

Their sliding gradually slowed as the angle of the vent decreased until they stopped altogether. Samantha turned off her flashlight.

"Keep quiet," she whispered.

They could hear the men, who had decided to come after them. Ryan saw the flicker of a flashlight. Then one of the men cried out and they saw a rifle go sliding past into the other tunnel. A moment later the men followed it, their speed completely unarrested now.

One. Two. Three. Four. Like mountain climbers tied together being pulled off a sheer face one after the other, the men disappeared down the venthole. There was no further sound.

Sam turned the light on and played it on Ryan's face.

"They're gone," she said.

"Gone? Gone where?" Ryan asked.

"I haven't seen it, but that other vent passage must empty into a caldera of lava. They would have all died instantly." She stood up and considered their path back upward. The death of four men did not appear to have upset her in the least.

"I hope they left their car keys behind," he said.

She gave him a puzzled look.

"They destroyed all the tires on our cars. That made it pretty clear what their intentions were. You said it wasn't the first time."

"I've been followed for weeks now. There have been two near accidents, one in which the brakes on my car failed without warning.

Then the gas heater in Bjorg's house malfunctioned and everyone inside was nearly asphyxiated from the fumes. I was afraid I'd get someone killed, so I started spending most of my time up here, living in my tent."

He stared at her in dismay. "People were trying to kill you, so you decided to go out into total wilderness where no one else was around? Were you trying to make it easy for them? You have a death wish?"

She smiled grudgingly. He noted the crinkle around her nose. She looked almost pixyish, except for the steel in her eyes.

"Probably wasn't the smartest thing I've ever done," she said. "But now that you're here to protect me, everything should be okay."

While they talked they'd been moving higher. At the confluence with the other vent opening, Samantha stopped and turned off the light. Ryan could see an orange glow shimmering far in the distance. A wave of heat emanated from the tunnel that he hadn't had time to note as they hurtled into the adjacent opening. His stomach did a turn, as he thought how close they'd come to the same fate as the men following them.

"They might have arrested themselves if they'd had any idea what lay ahead," Sam said. "By the time they realized, if they did, it was too late."

She smiled secretly. "Come on. I want to show you something very special."

He followed her back to the entrance to the venthole. Then she led the way over the rim and down the outside another hundred yards to where yet another opening beckoned.

"This place is a bloody honeycomb."

"Ten thousand years of lava and gas vents. At least. Fact is, I never took much notice of this one before, but when I returned at the beginning of the season this year, it appeared to have been widened. I thought that was curious, so I took a look inside. Come on." She slipped the pack off and left it, then wriggled through the opening.

Ryan found it a bit tighter for his frame but made it through to a low space, where Sam waited for him, flashlight pointing to the floor.

"I should prepare you," she said. "Because when I saw it the first time, it nearly gave me a heart attack."

"What?"

She played the light on the floor and he saw several clay vessels and some reed mats, very primitive looking.

"What on earth . . .?" He stared at the items incomprehensibly.

She slowly played the light higher until he could see human bones lying against the walls. They were obviously many hundreds of years old.

"Who are they?" he whispered.

"Vikings," she said without hesitation.

"What? I can't believe that. I thought they buried their dead at sea or something."

"When it was convenient, they did. Or sometimes in or under a boat. But if they were in a hurry, they probably would have found these ready-made ventholes a real time-saver. Look."

She played the light around them and he realized that the venthole had been widened into a room. Stones had been stood on end to form a nearly rectangular living space. There was even a slab-like hearth at one end. Beside it were a number of implements. He moved closer and identified several primitive blades and what looked for all the world like a battleaxe. Resting on a hearthstone were several carvings or pieces of jewelry that appeared to be heavily soot-covered.

She nodded at his look. "That's jet, a locally mined black coal mineral from northern England that was used to make jewelry. The Vikings traded for it from York in England. It was often left with the dead along with other belongings, sometimes including horses or dogs."

"So this is a burial?"

"That was my first thought. But I've begun to wonder. See the way the stones are situated, and the hearth. I think this was actually someone's home."

"They lived inside a volcano?" He whistled softly. "I guess they trusted those Norse gods a whole lot."

"Well, think about it. It's pretty comfortable in here right now. I bet they relied on the heat of the Earth to keep them warm. It must have been an incredible find for them. Central heating. An endless source of warmth for the cold months." She stared about at the contents of the room. "What's surprising is that this survived the eruption of 1783. It's located on the downside of the rim, away from the direction the lava flows took. But it's still incredible that it survived at all."

He shook his head. "There's the makings of a pretty good marketing campaign here for geothermal energy. I can see the ads now: Keep warm the Viking way!"

"Assuming people don't take that to mean by raging around looting, raping and pillaging in order to keep warm—a sort of exercise program for the socially misfit." She smiled that crinkly-nosed smile. "Anyway, it'll have to be exhaustively excavated and studied." She gave him a hard look. "I wouldn't want it part of any ad campaign, drawing all sorts of yahoos up here, disturbing the site."

"Point taken." He stared at one of the skulls. It had a blackened jet necklace lying on what remained of the neck. He reached out a hand and touched it. Then he placed his hand on the skull. Instantly, a woman's face appeared in his mind. He could see her as clearly as he saw Samantha. It was so real he lurched backward, his heart beating like a sledgehammer. The image went away as soon as his hand left the skull.

Sam was staring at him.

"I . . . I saw something. Someone."

"Good," she said. "At least I'm not totally crazy."

"It happened to you too?"

"Only once. The first time I touched it. Like you."

"What did you see?"

"I don't know, a sort of vision. There's something down here that plays tricks on the mind. It's probably the volcanic gas." She shook herself, as though dismissing the idea.

"You don't suppose this could have anything to do with those men? That they could have wanted the discovery to themselves?"

She stared at him. "You're suggesting they were rogue archaeologists willing to kill for the site? I think that's a stretch. But maybe . . ."

"What?"

"Maybe it's the opposite. They don't want this to get out because it would mean lots of people up here."

"What earthly difference could it make to anyone whether or not there are lots of people on Laki?"

"Well, it matters to the authorities for one. My articles have completely stifled tourism. Virtually no one has visited the area in the past year. I'm not terribly popular in government circles."

"I imagine that's putting it lightly."

"The point is, all of a sudden, someone seems to be very interested in this place."

"Or in you," he said. He started to put his hand back on the skull, then thought better of it. The image of the woman was still vivid in his head. It had seemed so real.

***

The distinguished-looking man wore a sharply cut dark suit, black tie, and even darker demeanor. He spoke precise English as he handed Ryan's passport back to him. His name was Johann Dagursson, and he was national police commissioner. Ryan and Samantha had been shunted to the man's office in Reykjavik after reporting what they believed had happened to the men who attacked them. That was two days ago. Now, they'd been called back on the carpet.

The commissioner sat behind his desk, tapping his pen thoughtfully. He had striking Nordic features, thick silver-blonde hair, and eyes that bore into his two guests. His hands were huge, the knuckles misshapen. Despite his fastidious taste in clothes, Ryan suspected the man might at one time have been a professional fighter. It was impossible to guess his age.

"We've investigated your story," he said, looking at them. "And not the first one we've heard from you, Miss Graham."

"You know each other?" Ryan asked.

"I told you I was being followed," said Sam. "I'm not a complete idiot. I reported it."

"We've identified the owner of the vehicle you drove back from Laki after your own cars were disabled," Dagursson said. "It's registered with IranOil, an energy firm that has offices on the waterfront. One of the larger foreign interests in our country at the moment, actually."

"And did you ask them why their people were trying to kill us?" said Ryan.

"They avow no knowledge of the men," said the commissioner. "Claim the car was stolen."

"When?"

"Last week."

"Convenient."

Dagursson stared at Ryan beneath block-shaped eyebrows. "It is also convenient that there are no bodies. My men are searching the area in question but so far have found nothing."

"I already told you what you would find," said Sam. "The temperature of lava runs to two thousand degrees Fahrenheit. They would have been incinerated instantly."

"Yes. Unfortunate for their next of kin," said Dagursson.

"Look. Put them down as lost at sea, for all I care," said Ryan. "A sea of lava. I have no qualms about what happened to them. They were trying to kill us. We'd like to know why."

Dagursson looked at some papers in front of him. "You're the owner of a business here in Reykjavik, Mr. Baldwin. You are also a former member of the United States Secret Service. As such, you've been issued a permit to carry a gun while in my country, an extraordinary privilege. It would seem that both of you are well connected." He looked at Sam. "I spoke with your father this morning."

She sighed. There was no getting away from her powerful family.

"He was quite worried about you. Even suggested I revoke your visa and send you home."

She leaned forward. "You can't do that. I'm involved in very important research. My seismic readings strongly suggest another Laki eruption could be building. Lives may be at stake. Your countrymen's lives."

"Yes, the government is well aware of that. The publicity you've garnered surrounding your reports that an eruption might be imminent has effectively shut down tourism at Laki and much of the southern coastline, I might add. Given our current economic difficulties, you couldn't have picked a worse time."

"I suppose you'd rather a few hundred tourists got incinerated?" said Sam. "That should do wonders for tourism."

"Nevertheless, your work could be handed over to the university. I actually appreciate what you are doing, Dr. Graham, but evidently it has already cost four lives, if we are to take your word. I don't need any more disappearing people. Half a dozen tourists have gone missing in the last few months."

"Yes. I read about that," said Sam. "Any progress on what happened to them?"

"It's been an absolute dead end, as though they simply vanished. We continue to work with the families, tracking down every lead. As you know, inexperienced visitors have a habit of heading off into the hinterlands, completely unprepared for the harshness of this climate."

Dagursson stood abruptly. "I told your father I won't revoke your visa without due cause. Being the subject of an attack hardly seems a fair reason. For now, you may continue. And we will continue our own investigations." He gave Ryan a look. "Your training may come in handy Mr. Baldwin. I'd advise that you not let Dr. Graham out of your sight. The senator has made it abundantly clear that he would take a dim view if anything happens to her."

Ryan nodded. The same thought had occurred to him.

Outside, he said, "There's something to that bit about not letting you out of my sight. But I want to do some investigating of my own. Where are you going now?"

"Home," she said. "I want one of Bjorg's breakfasts. Then I'm going to take a very long bath."

"I guess you'll be okay for a while, then. Whoever's been after you will have to regroup and find some new men if they're serious about this. Or maybe they'll want to lay low for a while, until the police investigation dies down. But that's no excuse to let our guard down. Will you let me know if you go out?"

"I seem to recall that it was you who led those men straight to me. I might be safer on my own. But . . ." Her eyes sparkled as she considered him. "I suppose as long as my dad is paying you what is no doubt an outrageous sum, I ought to make use of you. Just try not to get into any more trouble. It will be awkward if I have to tell my father that his bodyguard turned up missing—or dead."

***

Ryan decided to touch base with Eva at his business address on Oldugata Street, a few blocks from the waterfront. He had complete trust in her ability to manage the office and in her knowledge of the business climate in her hometown.

Her father had once been mayor of the city. He'd been pushed out of the job in nasty political infighting when Eva was just a teenager. She spoke sometimes to Ryan about that time and how difficult it had been for the family. There was no question it had affected her deeply, for she'd been working in her father's office as an intern during the upheaval. But her experience had proved invaluable to Ryan. There was no one of importance in Reykjavik that Eva didn't know.

The office currently held six employees. They worked on establishing contacts with various businesses, exploring, and keeping up with new technological developments and laying the groundwork for joint ventures in the field of geothermal energy between U.S. and Icelandic concerns. Under Eva's capable management, Ryan knew his own currently divergent interests would not harm the business.

His main worry was Jon Gudnasson. He was concerned that his chief geologist could so poison the atmosphere that Eva might be tempted to jump ship. She'd had offers in the past.

Eva listened to his story of the past two days with growing concern. "Well . . . it doesn't usually take people long to figure out what an asshole you are," she said facetiously. "But shooting at you takes it to a new level." She stared at him. "I don't suppose you might get Gudnasson to join you the next time you go careening down a lava tube."

"That bad, huh?"

"The man doesn't know the meaning of the word work. Spends most of his time, as near as I can determine, reading in his office, going out to lunch and carousing in nightclubs. He'd like to have my job, along with both salaries, thank you very much. Everyone in the office thinks he's a self-important fool."

There was no better moment for the fool to make an appearance. Gudnasson opened Eva's office door with a bit of a flourish. "Ah, the boss has arrived," he said, coming forward with his hand out.

He was about forty, with a fading boyish look and a receding hairline, carefully combed over. He was thin but had begun to put on extra pounds through lack of exercise and too much nightlife. He affected the tweedy look, wearing suits from a well-known London haberdasher.

"Hello Jon," Ryan said. "Keeping busy?"

The geologist sat down, unasked. He'd long since given up waiting to be invited to sit by Eva. Shaking his head, he said, "An awful lot of work needs doing here. Darn good thing you managed to hire me, really. There's a shortage of good geologists in the market, you know."

"There's a shortage of geologists, anyway," Eva said.

The remark seemed to escape Gudnasson.

"Like to talk to you sometime, boss. I have a number of ideas for ways to improve our bottom line. We need more outreach to local companies and that includes, by the way, the new Iranian firms that have moved in."

Ryan nodded slowly. "I understand the Iranians are supplying cheap foreign oil. Obviously that means competition for renewables."

"Most people in Reykjavik rely on geothermal already for energy," said Eva. "Where the Iranians have really had an impact is in the dirt-cheap price they're selling gasoline for."

"It all relates to the market, doesn't it?" Gudnasson said with a wink. "When one sector goes up, the other goes down. We need to cover all our bases, the same way big industry gives contributions to both Republicans and Democrats in America."

"You're saying we should give money to the Iranians? I'm afraid I don't see how that helps us."

"It's not money they want. It's attention. Outreach is the key. Grease the wheels of commerce. They're spreading a lot of money around. Maybe we can get them to give some to us—for renewable research."

"Why would they want to do that? It cuts their own throats."

"Good will?" he answered vacuously.

Gudnasson's ideas were never fully thought out. They flowed from his mouth like spittle after a shot of Novocain. It was time to redirect.

"I don't have time on this trip to become involved. But I want you to get out into the field more, Jon. Call it outreach if you want. We have a number of projects that need your input. Leave the office politics to Eva."

Gudnasson made a face. "Not trying to undermine anyone, but we really could use a tighter ship. I have some ideas, as I said . . ."

The man was unstoppable. Ryan looked at Eva, who was seething so close to the boiling point that he feared there might soon be a puddle beneath her chair.

"As I said, no time for it now. I've given Eva several field projects for you to look into. I'd like full reports on them next time I'm in town. Now, if you'll excuse us Jon, I have a few other things to discuss with Eva." He stood and took Gudnasson's hand like it was a pump that he could use to suction the irritating prig from the room.

"Well . . . uh . . . sure. Just say the word. But I do have a lot on my plate right now . . . ."

And he was gone, back to his cubicle, where he did Lord knew what through the long Icelandic days.

"Thanks," Eva said.

"It probably won't keep him entirely off your back. Just remember that I think you are the most important person in this firm. If it ever comes down to a direct confrontation, I will support you, no questions asked, okay? But please keep in mind that we need that PhD on staff. If you want to keep an eye out for a replacement, you can do so."

That mollified her enough to produce a smile.

"Now tell me what you know about IranOil."

"Well . . . much as I hate to admit it, Jon said one thing that makes a certain amount of sense—though I don't think he had a clue about what he was suggesting. A number of countries in the Middle East are beginning to see the handwriting on the wall. Their oil isn't going to last forever. They've begun to invest in new technologies."

"That include IranOil?"

"I'm not aware of any such efforts, but that doesn't mean they aren't happening. Mind you, with a very long time horizon in mind. The truth is, no one really knows why they're here. But there's no question they're spreading money around liberally, and it's had an impact. The lousy economy since the financial collapse has made it easier for them to polish local politicians."

"Like the police commissioner?"

She hesitated. "Actually, no. I think he's one of the more honest ones around. Got a reputation for being ethical, if hard-nosed."

He stared at the floor. "I simply can't buy it. Why would the Iranians want to come here and give their oil away? It doesn't make any sense. Hasn't anyone wondered about that?"

"Sure, everyone talks about it, but most people don't really care. Cheap energy is cheap energy, even if it does undermine local industry. And the new refinery they built over the last couple of years provides all the gasoline Iceland can possibly use. As you well know, the financial catastrophe hurt us badly. So there's an opening for them to exploit. To what end is anyone's guess. The price of oil on the international market has plummeted to less than thirty-eight dollars a barrel. That's down from a high of almost one hundred seventy dollars. They might just as well give it away." Her face tightened.

"I'm more concerned about the connection between IranOil and the people who tried to kill you."

"The thought had occurred to me. According to Commissioner Dagursson, the firm says they had nothing to do with those men, that the car was stolen. End of story."

She laughed out loud. "Do you know how many cars are stolen in Iceland in any given year?"

He shook his head.

"Few to none. It's a no-win crime on an island this size with so few roads. There's nowhere to hide."

"So it's a lie?"

"Just watch your back, boss. Something stinks about this." She smiled. "Besides, I need you around to fire Gudnasson when the time comes."

***

Eva looked on as her son played soccer at a school event. He wasn't the best player, but he played hard and with great intensity. He'd always been like that. Focused. She wondered how much of his personality grew out of not having a father at home.

A siren blew and the game ended. David's team had won and he came running over with two friends, sweaty, dirty and beaming with their triumph. After a moment, the friends disappeared and David sat beside her.

"Thanks for coming," he said.

"What? I have another son I could be spending time with?" She tousled his hair. "You played well."

"Thanks, mom."

"I wanted to ask you something," she said. "Do you know our new neighbor's daughter?"

"Sure. Her name's Sahar."

"What is she, a sophomore?"

"No. She's just a freshman. I think she's fifteen. She's very pretty, though. A lot of the guys talk about her. I guess they think she's exotic."

"Is she having any trouble in school?"

David looked at her. "What do you mean?"

"Well, I've been waving at her when I see her out the window and she always gives me this wonderful smile. Lately, though, she's completely ignored me. And I saw her crying once. I wondered— you know, it's hard being at a new school."

He shrugged. "I really don't know her personally. I'm a hotshot senior, you know. We don't pay attention to freshmen."

She smiled, remembering how it was. "Could you, maybe, keep an eye on her?"

He grinned. "You doing social work again? Does Ryan know you're moonlighting?"

"I'm serious. Sahar's been very unhappy lately. I'm worried no one is looking out for her. Her parents both work and she's alone at home after school. Just keep an eye on her, okay? See if anyone is bothering her or if she's being ostracized, but keep it quiet. Don't tell anyone what you're doing."

He looked at her with the same intensity he'd shown in the game. Then he leaned over and hugged her. "I guess everyone can't get as lucky in the mom department as I did."

She squeezed him back. "That's a nice thing to say, especially since I know what the divorce put you through."

"No sweat, mom. I love living with you and Helga. You know that. She's like a second mom, and I love dad too. So I got two families instead of one. You don't need to worry about me. I'm happy, all right?"

Eva couldn't speak. She just nodded and squeezed some more.

Chapter Five

AD 970

Iceland

Runa watched as her son, now twenty-eight years old, rowed the boat he'd so laboriously built over the last two years. He was proud of his creation and it showed in every ripple of his muscles. He paused, craft bobbing in the choppy bay, and waved to her. She waved back happily.

Now forty-six years old, Runa was still a beautiful woman. Her skin remained smooth, though darkened by long hours gathering food and firewood in the relentless Icelandic sun. She'd had six children, but Afastr was the only boy. He looked just like his father, Agnarr. There could be no doubt, even though Skari had believed otherwise right up until he had disappeared mysteriously years ago.

Skari had taken to working beneath the basalt rock of Laki in a deep vent, where he set up a workshop. He'd become an accomplished stone carver, designing amulets and offerings to the gods. He spent many hours a day at this task, sometimes so engrossed in the work that he failed to show up for meals. When no one had seen him for two days, they went looking for him and found his venthole had collapsed. The entire clan frantically dug out the hole only to find that he wasn't there. His body was never found.

Runa had tried to be sad over his disappearance, but it wasn't easy. Despite treating him as one of her two husbands, she'd never grown fond of him. He was too cold and full of himself. She often wondered what she would have done if it had been Agnarr who had died that long-ago day.

She shuddered at the unpleasant thought.

Their small community had grown. Each of her daughters now had children of her own. They'd made contact with other settlers in the land of fire and ice, and Runa's beautiful daughters had been in great demand. She now had seventeen grandchildren and the shoreline sprouted many small summer homes, built from wood and native stone. Still, the homes were of a semi-permanent, seasonal nature. During the cold winters, everyone resided in vent tunnel homes heated by the gods of the earth.

Amma climbed the rise and stood beside her granddaughter. "He is a good son," she said, staring out at Afastr. "Too bad you could only have one."

"I would have liked more," Runa admitted. "But instead I have five sons-in-law. They are all good men and our community grows."

Amma nodded. Runa marveled at her grandmother. No one knew her exact age. Her parents had been killed in one of the end-less raids when she was a child, and she'd been raised by outlanders. Viking women often began to have children by the age of fourteen. Runa herself had begun at sixteen, as had her mother before her. Amma told of having Runa's mother when she was still a very young girl, from a marriage she'd been forced into. That meant Amma had to be nearing eighty by now, an almost unheard-of age.

Yet she remained young in spirit. This new land seemed to agree with her. Her long-ago breathing problems had disappeared, and she still walked many miles over the headlands gathering firewood, col-lecting shellfish and harvesting the mushrooms they used in virtually all of their cooking. The arthritis that had once bothered her was all but gone. Her flesh was firm and unwrinkled, her face unmarred by age spots.

Maybe, Runa thought, she would live as long as Amma. She wouldn't mind . . . so long as Agnarr lived just as long.

The two women began to climb toward the rim of the volcano. Today, they would make an offering to the gods of this place. It was a ritual begun long ago, shortly after Runa had had her frightening vision of the cloaked figure floating above her.

There had been other visions. Many members of the clan experienced them. Though it was commonplace and expected now, Runa still found the strange sightings, often accompanied by the ever-present rumblings, disconcerting, even frightening, as though Laki was trying to communicate with them.

They reached the rim and Amma knelt, holding the fish in front of her. Runa knelt by her side.

"We offer this fish to the gods of Laki," said Amma. "You have given us life and warmth . . ." she paused, "but you have also taken Skari from us."

Runa looked at her grandmother. This was not a normal prayer.

"I believe you have taken Skari to your heart," the old woman continued. "He has been absorbed into the underworld. Perhaps it is because of the work he did, which was in your honor. Perhaps you wanted him to be with you. We ask that you not take any more members of the clan in this way. For this we make our offering."

Amma lifted the fish above her head for a moment, then threw it into the volcano.

As they walked back down the mountain, Runa said, "Why do you think Laki took my husband?"

"I don't know. Skari was a strange man. Quiet. Difficult. Angry. He never seemed happy his whole life. Even when you were first married, along with Agnarr, he didn't seem happy. We've all been content here, except Skari." She shrugged. "He was different. Maybe he was closer to the gods, which is why they took him away."

Runa thought about Amma's words. She didn't miss Skari and if the mountain wanted him, she was glad to let it have him. But she remained a little frightened of the volcano. Amma's words made her think of Laki as a living thing. A spirit that sometimes wanted things from them. Runa hoped Laki would never want her that way, or Agnarr, or any of her children.

Chapter Six

Present Day

Much as Ryan hated to admit it, Gudnasson had said one thing that just might prove useful, although for a very different reason.

Because a big part of his business, one that had helped get the concern off the ground, was a contract with British Petroleum, he'd done a great deal of research on the behemoth international company. As a result, he was aware that BP had begun as the Anglo-Persian Oil Company, or APOC, which became BP in 1954.

This might give him an opening. If he approached IranOil as an independent business owner, as Jon had suggested, but with a connection to BP, it would give him an excuse to talk to people on the inside. There was a risk, of course, that they already knew about him. But he was willing to bet against it. He'd been on the job less than a week. The men who were looking for Samantha may have followed him simply because he was staying at the same lodging and they were running out of ideas.

A few calls put him in contact with IranOil's Reykjavik Director of Community Relations. He made an appointment without any difficulty. It appeared that requests from local business owners asking for handouts were pouring through the doors these days.

IranOil had an enormous fuel depot, along with a small refinery, a few miles outside of the city, but their corporate headquarters was located along the waterfront off Grandagardur Street, an eight-story glass and steel monolith with the company logo on a block of granite out front. Ryan felt a twinge of jealousy. Perhaps someday, renewable concerns like his would be able to go similarly upscale.

Renewables were the future. Everyone acknowledged the fact. But it was still oil that ruled the international roost.

He'd thrown together a briefcase full of papers about his company's ongoing projects. Now he parked his rental car, complete with new tires courtesy of the agency, along the busy portside street and entered the building.

He was met cordially but firmly at a security station. A beefy guard asked his business, confirmed his appointment, and directed him to pass through a metal detector that was operated by two more men. It seemed like an undue amount of security for a firm in laid-back Reykjavik. Fortunately, he'd left his firearm in the car.

Rather than telling him where to go, one of the men on the metal detector escorted him to the third floor in an elevator and stayed by his side until they reached their destination.

Mohammad Reza was precisely what Ryan would have expected, a lower functionary whose job was to advance good relations with the host country. He was young, perhaps thirty, a small, neat man with a tightly cropped beard and an expensive suit. He had a smile on his face from the moment they shook hands. There was no evidence he knew anything at all about his guest.

Reza poured him a coffee and said, 'How may I help you, Mr. Baldwin?"

"I run a small concern that facilitates joint ventures in renewable energy, particularly geothermal, between firms here in Iceland and in the United States. I thought you might be interested in

investing in the future." He looked around at the opulent surroundings. "Clearly, you are doing well in the present," he smiled. "But
renewables are the wave of the new century, and you must admit,
your oil won't last forever."

Reza smiled self-deprecatingly. "We want to be good neighbors.
What sort of joint ventures are you working on?"

"There's a great deal of new research being done at the moment,
new techniques for deep drilling and energy generation at the surface. The basics are simple enough. Water is injected deep into the
earth, where it absorbs heat from the surrounding rock. As the fluid
returns to the surface, the transferred heat is used to generate elec-
tricity. Then the water is re-injected. The system forms a closed
loop, creates virtually no emissions, and is entirely renewable. As
you know, this is what fuels most of Reykjavik, but my firm is also
looking into new fuel cell technology. If you'd like I can give you the
details." He reached for his briefcase.

Reza said benignly, "How much would you like?"

Ryan almost choked. The man hadn't asked to see any plans,
hadn't inquired as to his credentials or even the main thrust of his
business. Just, how much do you want? It was breathtaking. And it
caught him off guard. The last thing he had in mind was any kind
of a figure.

Well, nothing ventured. "We thought something on the order of
one hundred thousand dollars would give a start." He smiled weakly
at his own brazenness.

"We do have a policy," Reza said with a slight sadness in his
eyes that such a matter had even to be discussed, "Of providing
no more than eighty percent of any request. Will eighty thousand
dollars be acceptable? Of course, you can apply for additional funds
later on."

Much as the money would have been welcome for his business,
Ryan couldn't really accept such a payment. Not under the current
circumstances. Indeed, he found the meeting almost surreal. He
was no stranger to approaching potential investors. But he'd never
been handed a check on his first meeting, without ever discussing

specifics. He decided to see what might happen if he mentioned something else.

Reza was standing, offering his hand. "If you'll sign a few papers with our legal department, I'll have my secretary cut the check. You can pick it up on your way out. I wish you luck in your endeavors."

Ryan took a deep breath. "You've been most generous," he said. "This will give a big boost to our new geothermal research program on Laki."

It was as though a light went out in Reza's face. His eyes grew sad; his very hand seemed to grow heavy in Ryan's grasp.

"Ah . . . there may actually be a problem," he said. There followed the most expert bit of waffling that Ryan had ever experienced. Too many research programs in the same area, a requirement that specific research be vetted first, government restrictions, perhaps another program might be more beneficial—money was suddenly tighter than it had been thirty seconds earlier.

Ryan was swept out the door with the same efficiency one might use to get rid of a septic tank salesperson. He found himself standing on the pavement staring at the door, hand empty of the briefly proffered check.

He felt goose bumps crawl on his skin. The reaction left little doubt. Something was happening on Laki that IranOil considered entirely proprietary. He was also worried that he might have left his employees vulnerable. IranOil now believed that his business was planning major research on Laki. What their reaction to that news would be was anyone's guess.

He'd have to tell Eva what he'd done and why. He didn't want to bring her in on this. But something was going on and he couldn't leave her hanging out there completely unaware.

***

David had a pass to leave study hall early so he could make his way across the school to shop class, which was held in a converted portion of the attached bus garage.

He liked shop and was a pretty good carpenter. He'd been making a medicine cabinet out of cherry for his mother's bathroom.

This part of the school was usually deserted between classes, and he walked at a good clip down a long hall that had the swimming pool on one side and a currently empty gymnasium on the other. Boys' and girls' locker rooms were on either side of the gym. He decided to duck into the boys' locker and use the facilities.

Inside, the place smelled of sweat, wet towels and the usual closeness of probably every locker room since the first caveman bounced the first basketball.

The bathroom was at the back and as he neared it, he heard voices. This wasn't unusual. It was late in the school day and some of the players sometimes skipped out of class early to begin to get ready for practice.

But then he heard a female voice, which *was* unusual, to say the least, in the boys' locker room. It was clearly a girl's voice, not a teacher, and it was obviously in distress. He followed the voices down rows of lockers and peered around the end.

At the far end of the row were two seniors he knew. One was Sven Svensson, the tall, muscular, crew cut captain of the soccer team. The other was a buddy of Sven's named Nils Nilsson. He wore gray workout shorts and had no shirt on.

The two seniors had Sahar pinned back against one of the lockers, their hands all over her. She had her eyes closed and tears stained her cheeks. Sven took something from a folder on the bench beside him and showed it to the girl.

She let out a little moan and slumped down.

Before David could decide what to do, the alarm sounded, announcing the end of the school day. They could all hear the doors to the locker room slam open as students came in to change for after-school athletic programs.

Sven whispered something into Sahar's ear, ran his hand quickly under her skirt, and then pulled her to a rear exit that led out to the athletic fields and pushed her through the door. Then

he and Nils laughed some more and settled down to wait for the
locker room to fill up.

David went out another door and looked for Sahar. He found
her behind a tree near one of the soccer goals. She was sitting on the
ground, her legs pulled up to her chest, her whole body shivering.

She jumped when David appeared, stood up, and stared at him
for a moment. Her face was wet with tears and her eyes were blank
and glassy, like those of a deer staring at a wolf. Before David could
open his mouth, she fled back into the school.

Chapter Seven

Dubai

Ali Akbari sighed contentedly. The prostitute lying next to him had been perfect. Long blonde hair, slim, tan legs, a perfect ass. He would have to ask his host where he got her, or even make arrangements to take her with him.

That might be difficult, given his highly visible position as Iranian minister of oil. Certain sacrifices had to be made when one was on the world stage. Still, he stared at the perfection beside him and began to stroke her long, smooth flank. The thought of going back to his plain, overweight wife made him physically nauseous.

He slipped out of the bed and crossed over to an expansive window that looked out on Dubai. The sky was brilliant blue and the sun shone on the water and gleamed along the metallic struts and supports of more high-rises than he could count. Too many of the buildings were now in limbo, construction halted after the world economic downturn that had hit Dubai hard.

He was here for the meeting of OPEC. Despite the economic malaise, the desert kingdom was the perfect place for such a get-together. Reporters from around the globe, waiting to hear whether another production cut would be ordered, had been denied access to the hotel where the ministers were staying. This allowed for the hard-working members to enjoy the secret amenities provided to them.

Akbari picked up a phone and listened as his assistant, Mahmud Farshidi, gave him the day's schedule.

"The meeting of ministers will begin at noon," Mahmud said, "with the final vote on the production cut to be held at two sharp. Then there will be a news conference. Senate Majority Leader Graham has asked you to call him immediately upon knowing the outcome. Also," Ali heard the rustle of papers, then, "the Laki Working Group has set up a conference call for four PM."

A frown crossed Akbari's face. The Laki Working Group was the most secret of his endeavors. It consisted of the head of IranOil, the minister of the interior and the foreign minister. There had been problems. Four Iranian operatives on the ground in Iceland had disappeared. Local officials had little to go on other than that the car belonging to the men had been found. IranOil had denied any knowledge of the incident, of course. That might have been a mistake. Dead men were not always that easy to disavow.

Then there was Senator Graham, a politician of the first order. And one who knew about the Laki Working Group. More than knew about it.

Graham was engaged in a high-wire balancing act. That an American majority leader, indeed the chairman of the Foreign Relations Committee, would possess secret knowledge of an Iranian group led one to consider all sorts of implications. The senator was walking a tightrope. His entire career would be on the line if news ever leaked that he knew what he knew without telling anyone.

The senator was concerned, too, about his troublesome daughter. Indeed, she was becoming a thorn in everyone's side. But even that was not enough to sway the majority leader's own, private interests in this matter. Not when so very much was at stake.

Ali knew all about private interests. He too was taking a risk having this exquisite woman in his bed. He glanced back at her. She was sitting up now, naked, wiping sleep from her eyes.

He would worry about these things later. The girl watched him approach and smiled. She turned over onto her stomach and lifted her exquisite behind into the air. She knew just what he liked, and it had taken her only one time to learn it.

Chapter Eight

Ryan returned to Bjorg's just before lunchtime. He went up to his room without seeing the housekeeper and started to knock on Sam's door, then heard water begin to run in the bathroom. She was in the shower.

He went to his room and straight out onto the balcony. No new bad guys in evidence. He kicked his shoes off and lay down on the bed. It had been a long day. In a moment he was asleep.

When he woke, he was disoriented. He rarely slept soundly during the daytime. Since there was a lot of daytime in Iceland, he tended to run a sizeable sleep deficit whenever he visited.

He got up, splashed water on his face from the room's sink and went to find Sam.

When she didn't answer her door, he tried the knob and found it locked. At least she was taking his warning seriously.

Downstairs, he found Bjorg cleaning in the kitchen, a habitual activity. The small hotel was as spotless as any place he'd ever stayed.

"Do you know where Miss Graham is? I just heard her in the shower a while ago and now I can't find her."

Bjorg shook her head. "After lunch she went out. I have not been seeing her since."

He swallowed hard. It was now mid-afternoon, and Sam had been out there alone for hours.

"I believe . . ." Bjorg said, "she mentioned something about going to see a Professor Hauptmann at the university."

"Hauptmann," he repeated. "Do you know what department? Is he German . . . languages, perhaps?"

"No. History, I am thinking."

She bustled out on some inscrutable cleaning errand.

Uneasy at having Sam out of his protection, such as it was, he made straight for the university's Main Building, also called the Aðalbygging, in the heart of Reykjavik.

He was familiar with the university, having taken several courses there over the years, mostly on the renewable energy sources of Iceland. The Main Building was an enormous Art Deco construction dating from the Second World War. It reminded him of the huge mausoleums created by the Third Reich.

Inside, he checked the roster and found a Professor Hauptmann listed on the third floor. At the door he heard voices and rapped lightly. There was an immediate silence. In Icelandic, a deep, German-accented voice said to come in.

He opened the door to find a professorial type of perhaps sixty sitting behind a desk covered in papers. He had a baldpate, a fringe of wild, brown hair and coke-bottle-thick glasses. His magnified eyes looked at Ryan questioningly.

"Professor, I'm looking for a friend of mine . . ." He moved into the room and stopped as he saw Samantha sitting in a chair across from the professor.

"Sam! I've been looking everywhere for you. I thought we had a deal?"

"Yes, well, I can't really sit around all day waiting for you to show up, can I?" she said. "I have a few responsibilities of my own, you know." She waved a hand. "Professor, this is the man I told you about. Ryan Baldwin . . . Professor Ernst Hauptmann."

Ryan nodded, hardly mollified at Sam having ditched him, but he was too relieved to carry on any sort of high dudgeon. He shook the professor's hand.

Samantha leaned back in her chair. Ryan could smell lotion from her morning shower, and her hair was pulled back, still looking damp. She wore tight jeans along with a black Liz Claiborne jacket over a cream-colored blouse and matching scarf. Very chic. Quite a change from the outfit she'd worn on Laki. She seemed to enjoy his once-over and it made him feel awkward. She motioned him to an empty chair beside her.

"Close the door first," she said. Then, "Professor Hauptmann was an advisor of mine years ago when I was at school in Germany. He's a historian and also a linguist who has studied the Icelandic sagas in great detail. Ernst has been working the last couple of years on a book about something quite interesting. Why don't you tell him, Ernst?"

"I'm all ears," Ryan said.

"You are, aren't you?" said Sam with an amused grin.

But Hauptmann needed no further prodding.

"I've uncovered information regarding a very interesting plan concocted by Hitler's scientists during the war," he began.

Ryan found it disconcerting to look at the man's enormously magnified eyes topped by a pair of very bushy and expressive eyebrows that went up and down almost as though powered by some sort of battery.

Now the eyebrows were at their full height. "How much do you know about the historical eruptions at Laki?" he asked.

Ryan looked at Sam. "Only what she's told me, that there were two large ones in recorded history, one in the seventeen hundreds and another much earlier."

"The 1783 eruption is the one we are most concerned with," said Hauptmann. "It was studied extensively by the Nazis, by Hitler's geologists specifically. Before the war, in 1938, the Reich began to see the strategic importance of Iceland next to the North Atlantic sea-lanes. U-boats visited Reykjavik and the Lufthansa attempted, unsuccessfully, to establish an air service. For a time, the Reich even offered free instruction in gliding by German experts. Perfect cover, in the British view, for compiling maps and discovering suitable landing grounds."

Ryan looked at Sam. "I don't mean to interrupt the history lesson, but I fail to see what this has to do with . . . anything."

"Just listen and you'll figure it out," said Sam. She nodded at Hauptmann to continue.

"Denmark was occupied by Nazi Germany on April 9, 1940," the owl-eyed professor went on. "Communications between Denmark and Iceland were severed, and the latter declared its neutrality, creating the Alpingi, Iceland's parliament. A month later, British military forces invaded with twenty-five thousand troops. A year after that, some forty thousand American troops, commanded by Major General Charles Bonesteel, replaced the British. In 1943, as the tide of the war turned against Germany and it was felt there was no longer any fear of a German invasion, U.S. troops were withdrawn." Hauptmann stared at Ryan balefully. "Prematurely, as it turns out."

Ryan looked nonplussed. "You're saying the Nazis came back?"

"In a manner of speaking . . . yes. Though no one knew about it until I uncovered it," he said proudly. "All American ground troops were withdrawn, except for some coastal artillery, anti-aircraft, and a small naval presence."

Now, Ryan was completely bewildered. He couldn't fathom what the professor was getting at.

"I've been studying the log books of several German U-boats that made repeated trips to Iceland during the American occupation. After most of the Americans withdrew in 1943, there was a sudden uptick in submarine visits . . . and here is where it really gets interesting. The U-boats were taking German geologists, volcanologists, and explosives experts to Iceland, dropping them off secretly in remote bays and then picking them up later on. It appears that quite an enormous amount of material was transported to the island, as well."

Ryan began to get interested in the tale now. He leaned forward. "What on earth were they up to?" he asked.

"The precise details have taken a great deal of time to unravel," said Hauptmann. "And it requires a certain amount of interpretation. It was a scheme so fantastic as to be difficult to believe. All formulated in the mind of the German Reich Minister, Hermann Goering, and under the direction of a young Nazi geologist named Kraus. He had studied in Iceland before the war. Indeed, he wrote a monograph on the explosions at Laki. Kraus knew everything there was to know about the volcano."

"Specifically," Sam suddenly chimed in, "the devastating effects the 1783 eruption had on England and Europe."

Suddenly, Ryan had a glimmer of what they were talking about.

"In 1783, twenty-three thousand British people died from inhaling the sulfurous gases released by Laki in just August and September. Many thousands more were killed by the severe winter of 1784, which affected Britain, France and . . . yes, Germany. A lingering fog hung over the Channel and much of North America as well." The professor halted theatrically. "Are you beginning to see, my friend?"

It was almost too bizarre to take seriously. But Ryan did see. "You're saying the Nazis wanted to try to make Laki erupt again in order to affect the outcome of the war."

"Yes!" Hauptmann struck his desk with a loud bang. "Very good. That is precisely what they wanted to do. They believed the eruption would completely disrupt allied shipping over the North Atlantic, that it would demoralize and kill many of the British people, and would even make any Allied attempt at an invasion across the Channel impossible. It was the most audacious of plans!"

Ryan slumped in his chair. He looked from the professor to Sam and back again. "How . . . how in the world could they cause an eruption?"

Hauptmann nodded patiently. "Indeed, their understanding of volcanic structure was not good. We've learned a great deal since then. Basically, they intended to place huge amounts of explosives in the crater and set them off. Simple . . . but highly unlikely to be effective. Certainly not with the sort of explosives they had access to at the time."

"In fact, it was an utterly crazy idea," said Sam. "To set off massive explosions in such an unstable area could cause any number of unforeseen chain reactions, earthquakes, minor eruptions, gas emissions, lava flows, subglacial eruptions. The list goes on and probably one of the least likely outcomes would be a precise repeat of what occurred in 1783."

"So what happened? Did they actually carry the plan out?"

Hauptmann shrugged for the first time. "This I have not been able to determine. Obviously, there's no record of an eruption during the war, so if they set off their explosions, they didn't have the desired effect. My former student here," he smiled at Sam, "has been keeping an eye out for any signs of damage from explosives or residue from that period."

"But I've found nothing," she injected.

"Viking burials excepted," Ryan said. "It's utterly fantastical."

"Not at all," said Hauptmann. "The Nazis tried all sorts of things during the war. They were extraordinarily inventive. A vortex gun that used a combination of coal dust and a virtual tornado of air to bring down planes, tanks that ran underwater using snorkels, the largest glider ever conceived that could carry hundreds of troops and even tanks, a one-man rocket that launched vertically, traveled at six hundred miles an hour to an altitude of thirty thousand feet, then glided back to earth, firing rockets at enemy aircraft. Hitler loved these schemes, the crazier the better."

Ryan thought for a moment. "Could this . . . eruption scheme . . . have anything to do with the men who've been interested in Sam's work on Laki?"

"I'm convinced there must be a connection," said Sam, "though what it could be escapes me." She turned to the professor. "Tell him about the saga."

Hauptmann looked off into space. "What do you know about the sagas?"

Again, Ryan looked baffled. "They were stories about early Viking history, weren't they? Written in Old Norse. No one knows how accurate they are."

"Yes, you are partly correct. Actually, they are epic tales in prose of heroic deeds from the distant past, about ancient Scandinavian and German history, as well as the Vikings. They relate the early Viking voyages to Iceland and tell of feuds between Icelandic families, tales of kings, commoners, and larger-than-life figures. Most sagas of Icelanders record events that occurred between AD 930 and 1030 known as the Age of the Sagas. They were passed on as oral history for more than two hundred years before being written down, which accounts for the questions about their accuracy."

"I understand," said Ryan. "But what does this have to do with anything?"

"I have found a previously unknown saga," he said with obvious relish.

Ryan raised an eyebrow and glanced at Sam. She was focused intently on the professor.

"It relates the story of a woman, a sort of holy woman, who lived in a small clan on the southern coast of Iceland in the tenth century. Her name was Amma. She tells of living beneath the spirit god Laki."

Ryan looked quickly at Sam. "*Your* Vikings?" he asked.

"Certainly a possibility. How many clans could have lived in the ventholes of Laki?"

But Hauptmann was rolling. "Amma relates the history of her many family members, in particular a man named Skari who became a craftsman of religious ornaments and who disappeared. Another man, whose name we don't know, became a mystical figure and was struck dumb one day while beneath the volcano. There are others. Amma believed the volcano was a living spirit. They made sacrifices to it and lived in fear of it, even while enjoying its warmth.

"Theirs was a very long-lived clan, and they seemed to enjoy extreme good health. Amma spoke of it and she couldn't explain it other than to say she believed the spirit of Laki was strong."

"Tell him about the end," Sam prodded.

"Amma relates how the clan broke apart suddenly. There was bad blood that rose quickly. This wasn't all that unusual for Vikings, but it was most unusual on Laki. The clan had enjoyed many years of harmony. This is where the tale begins to deteriorate. She speaks of turmoil in the earth, of unexplained deaths and disappearances and of some sort of final stand made by the clan beneath the earth."

"You see?" Sam said, excitedly. "Something killed them all at once, and that's why we found those bodies together underground. Were they hiding from something? How were they killed? We need to study those remains and find out what happened to them."

"Hold on," Ryan said. "I think you're jumping to conclusions. In the first place, we don't know if they all died together. Those bodies could have been placed in there one at a time, over a period of years, hell, maybe even hundreds of years. Like a family burial plot."

Sam shook her head. "I *know* there's something strange about Laki. Amma talks about the spirituality of the place. I've felt it . . . and so have you. It's real."

He stared at her, at a loss for how to respond. The vision he'd had of a woman . . . could it have been this Amma? The idea was crazy. More than crazy. Lunatic.

Hauptmann looked down at his desk. "It won't be easy to determine how these people died. I'm continuing to search for more sagas about Amma. It's all a great puzzle, not unlike the story of the Nazis' own involvement on Laki."

They left the professor staring balefully at a pile of student papers. It was clear he would have spent all his time working on his research and his book, if not for the unfortunate necessity of providing for one's upkeep.

Outside, the day had turned quite suddenly gray. They could hear the moan of the marker buoy at the harbor entrance. It was early Friday evening and the workaday city was beginning to bustle as residents prepared to help Reykjavik live up to its bawdy nightlife reputation.

"It's Freaky Friday," said Sam. "You've heard of it?"

He shook his head.

"The first Friday of every month, all day long and into the evening, our trendy youngsters line up to have their hair turned into a variety of whimsical cuts by the stylists of Galleri Gel on

Hverfisgata Street. It turns into something of a party as onlookers socialize and drink beer and wine."

She considered him. "No, on second thought . . . probably not your thing. Being a straitlaced Secret Service agent and all. Your hair looks like it was chopped by a lawnmower. Anyway, I know a little place where we can get a decent meal . . . if you're interested."

She looked to Ryan like something out of Vogue magazine. Quite extraordinarily beautiful, he realized with a start. Had she dressed up in anticipation of their going out to eat?

"Um . . . yes, that would be nice," he said awkwardly.

"My treat," she said, avoiding his eyes. "We need to get to know each other if I'm going to have you following me around like . . . a . . . a . . . Secret Service agent."

She led the way down the street to a waterfront bistro that stuck out over the water on pilings. They went inside and Sam said something to a waiter who led them out to a terrace over the water.

They ordered frigidly cold martinis made with Icelandic vodka, clinked glasses and stared contentedly at Reykjavik's magnificent harbor. There were only two other couples on the terrace.

"Beautiful," he said.

"You don't have to go far for a good sea view in Iceland. I've come to think of this place as home," she said. "It's far enough from Washington that I don't have to look behind my back every other minute . . . at least until recently."

"Sounds like you and your father have quite a bit of history."

"I suppose some of it's my fault. I'm not what he wanted in a child. Frankly, he wanted a boy. In some ways, he got one . . . a tomboy, anyway."

"He seems pretty worried about you. I understand you've been stirring the pot with some articles in the *New York Times*. Your father seems to think that may be the reason you might be a target."

She stared out at the ocean. A brisk, warm breeze curled back the edges of her hair. "I hate what IranOil is doing here. By spreading their money around, they're hurting local industry—yours included. People are so easily bought out. They just want to save money and the hell with what's best for Iceland, for controlling global warming, for the whole bloody world. A little cheap gasoline is all it takes." She looked completely exasperated. "It doesn't make any sense that IranOil would be doing this. It's driving me crazy. So, yes, I wrote about it, and it got some people angry."

"You know who?"

"No, but obviously the Iranians are a good bet." She sighed. "Sometimes I wish I'd lived a thousand years ago, like those Vikings. Life was a lot simpler back then. All you had to do was find food and manage to keep warm. That was it."

He looked dubious. "I suspect they had other things on their minds, just like we do today. How to placate the gods, for instance. Amma said something about turmoil in the clan and disappearances, didn't she?" He hesitated. "I've been wanting to ask you. You said you felt something spiritual about Laki. Were you serious? You don't just think it was the effects of the rising gases?"

They were interrupted by the waiter. Ryan ordered grilled whale meat, which had the texture of beef but a faintly saline taste. Sam selected Arctic char. The prices were steep, which made him uncomfortable until he remembered that she came from a very well-to-do family.

When the man disappeared with their order, Sam played with her napkin, avoiding his eyes.

"It's hard to explain," she said finally. "The moment I first went underground on Laki, I felt something."

"What?"

"I don't know . . . a presence."

"A spirit?"

"Maybe . . . something like that."

He could tell she was afraid of sounding foolish. "You know," he said, "when they opened the tombs of the Pharaohs, people felt things. There were strange disappearances, people became sick and even died. There was talk of spirits. Scientists speculated there might have been deadly microbes inside that were released when they opened the tombs."

"Yes, I know about that. I suppose there could be some effects of the gas. But I've been overcome by volcanic gas before. This feels different. Like . . . don't laugh at me . . . being possessed."

"Whoa! I can see Amma, some kind of shaman, believing something like that. But you're a scientist. You know there has to be a rational explanation."

She let the subject drop, as though she just didn't want to think about it anymore. "So what's your story?" she asked as they contemplated desert.

"Me?"

"Yes, you. You've let me do most of the talking. Time to give. You married? Got a family?"

He shook his head. "No. I lived with someone for a number of years, but the hours a Secret Service agent works are not conducive to conjugal bliss. She left five years ago."

"And since then?"

"Since then, I've pretty much put all my eggs into one basket—my business. It's taken almost total commitment." He hesitated. "Probably not unlike your commitment to volcanology. A fascinating field by the way. One I considered for a while."

"What stopped you?"

"No money in it," he said honestly.

She laughed, and he saw her face light up fully for the first time. "Precisely why I chose it! To make my father angry. He sees everything in terms of dollars and cents, so I deliberately chose a field where I'd make a pittance."

He glanced at the menu. "Maybe we should go Dutch."

"Don't worry," she smiled, her nose crinkling. "I can afford it. There's a little matter of a trust fund." She took a sip of martini and leaned back in her chair. "Why did you give up being in the Secret Service?"

"Boredom, partly. Disgust with the way Washington works. Everyone in town sees themselves as crucially important and significant. I thought they were all completely self-involved and totally deluded, right up to and including the President himself." He shrugged. "It wasn't an attitude that sat well with the Service."

"I know exactly what you mean. I grew up with it and felt pretty much the same way. People were always coming to my father seeking favors. Most of it was petty and all of it self-serving. You ask me, you're well out of it."

Outside, they walked along the waterfront, enjoying one of those sudden Reykjavik weather surprises, a balmy breeze blowing in from the south. The smell of the sea was strong. Ryan started to say something and then stopped as a large, black sedan pulled up beside them. A huge man got out, glanced at them briefly, then opened a rear door and they both gaped in astonishment as Senator Graham emerged.

"Good to see you, Sam," he said, giving her a quick hug. He nodded at Ryan. "Glad to see you're on the job, Baldwin, but your services will no longer be required. Sam is leaving Iceland."

Samantha's face turned white. "The hell I am!" she said.

Graham turned to her with a look that Ryan could only describe as something between fatherly affection and total exasperation.

"I've just been visiting with the police commissioner. He told me what happened to you up on Laki." He glanced at Ryan. "And how those men managed to find you, I might add. I know you think your work is important, Sam. But this is no laughing matter. Someone is trying to kill you. I won't have you taking such a risk."

"It's none of your damn business what risks I take," she said. "It's my goddamn life!"

"Baldwin, can you talk sense to her? You're a professional. You know how easy it is to kill someone. Even the most protected person on Earth."

This was one argument Ryan didn't want to be caught in the middle of, between Sam and her father, who just also happened to be his employer. He held his hands out helplessly.

"I barely know your daughter, sir, but from what I do know, she's not likely to take my advice any more than she apparently will take yours."

"You don't need to speak for me," Sam said, still seething. "I'm an adult and no one tells me what to do."

"I can't argue with you," Graham said in exasperation. "I never could. Your things are in the trunk. We collected them from your boarding house, along with your passport." He turned to the man looming over them all. "Put my daughter in the car," he said, turning away.

"What the hell . . ." said Sam. "You're going to kidnap me? I don't believe it."

"Senator," Ryan said, moving to intercept the man. "You can't do this. I won't be party to an attempted abduction."

"You work for me, Baldwin. Don't interfere if you want to be paid."

Sam began to back away as the muscle-bound man approached her. He glanced easily at Baldwin, whose slim build gave him no reason to hesitate. It was a miscalculation.

He might have been a little rusty, but Ryan had had some of the best training in the world. He put one hand on the man's chest and shook his head.

Graham's bodyguard looked at the senator, who seemed mired in indecision. Then he simply nodded. The man smiled like a pet Doberman let off its leash. He made a move for Ryan.

Though obviously strong, the big man was a step too slow. He seemed inclined to want to grab his opponent and squeeze him like a rag doll. But Ryan avoided him easily. Each time the man tried to get close, he received a series of lightning-quick punches to his kidneys. Before long he was huffing and puffing and even slower than he had been. Ryan finished him off with a roundhouse that knocked him to the ground, where he sat looking dazed. It was all over in little more than a minute.

"What the hell do you think you're doing, Baldwin?" Graham cried.

Ryan didn't answer. He opened the car door, reached inside, and popped the trunk release. He pulled Sam's bags out and slammed the lid down. He stared at the senator. "I'll have her passport too," he said.

"What you're going to have from me," said Graham, "is a legal nightmare. This will cost you your business, Ryan."

"Oh, daddy, shut up!" Samantha moved forward and lifted her father's suit jacket, deftly removing the passport from its inner pocket. Then she planted a kiss on his cheek.

"And you're not going to do anything to harm Mr. Baldwin. Are we clear on that?"

There was a steel in her voice that Ryan hadn't heard since she'd first confronted him with her walking stick on top of Laki. It was almost comical to watch this tiny woman stand down the great majority leader of the U.S. Senate.

Graham looked defeated. "Sam, I just don't want to see you hurt. I love you more than anything. You know that."

"I do know it. And I love you too. But you do the stupidest things sometimes. I wonder how you manage to run a country. I really do. Now please go home. I'm not completely helpless, you know. And I'm willing to accept Mr. Baldwin's protection, which . . ." she looked down at the man still recovering on the ground, "is not, evidently, inconsiderable."

Her father shook his head. "You don't know what these people are capable of," he muttered. He looked from Sam to Ryan and sighed helplessly. "I'm counting on you, Baldwin," he said. Then he helped the bodyguard into the car and they drove away.

Samantha seemed none the worse for their experience. If anything, she appeared even more relaxed than the martinis had made her.

"Pretty impressive handiwork, Baldwin," she said.

"What do you mean?" he asked, knowing exactly what she meant.

"Ha! You put that goon down faster than I finished my first martini. And trust me, if he worked for my father, he was no slouch."

"He underestimated me. My size is helpful sometimes in that regard. Next time won't be so easy."

"Right." She was holding onto his arm now, for she really was tipsy. "How about we go bake this alcohol out of our systems?" she asked.

"How do you suggest we do that?"

"There's a pretty good geothermal pool not far from here," she replied.

He knew the one she had in mind. Reykjavik was full of thermal pools and tubs scattered about the city. When the winter air was biting cold, it was exquisite luxury to envelope yourself in warm water while your head remained exposed to the night chill. The pools sported thick mist over the water, and there could be currents so hot they would curl your toes.

But he was pretty sure he didn't want to do it. Patrons entered the water in the skimpiest of attire and more than a few then took off the rest. Sam was inebriated enough that she might be so tempted. Though he found her petite body undeniably sensual, he'd had more than enough frustration the past couple of days.

"I don't think so," he said. "Let's call it a night."

She released his arm and looked at him oddly. "Must be losing my touch," she murmured. Then she waved a hand at him. "I can find my own way home, Mr. Bodyguard."

He watched her go, puzzled at her reaction, but staying close at hand in case any trouble should arise. When she entered Bjorg's, he walked on for a few blocks, not wanting to have to confront her in the hallway or bathroom. By the time he got back to his room, her door was firmly shut.

***

He slept soundly, certain that his internal clock would wake him at three AM. Being able to rouse himself whenever he wanted was a skill he'd learned in the Service. It was something actually taught by the behaviorists. Through concentration prior to sleep, he could program his brain to wake at a certain time. It was a useful skill and saved money on alarm clocks to boot.

He got up, dressed quietly in dark pants, jacket, and black sneakers. He pulled a knit hat over his head, checked his pistol, and slipped out of Bjorg's into the rear garden. He passed through the gate to Lindargata Street and walked briskly toward the waterfront.

THE GODS OF LAKI

It took twenty minutes to reach IranOil's headquarters. The front of the building was well lit. He walked all the way around it, checking for surveillance cameras and security movements. For all the careful vetting he'd received as a visitor, the off-hours security appeared to be considerably more lax. There were no cameras that he could detect, though that didn't mean there weren't hidden ones. Nothing he could do about that.

He walked onto a pier that thrust into the harbor opposite the building and sat on a bench. During daytime hours, it was a popular tourist spot with food stands, a band platform, and several historic old crafts from another age that were now exhibits. He was alone, except for a man who appeared to be sleeping off a bender from the night before.

He watched the building for an hour. A single police car drove past a little after four, on routine patrol. It paid no special attention to IranOil headquarters.

He saw no security details moving about the building, no changing of the guards, no lights going on or off inside. Either IranOil had complete confidence in its alarm systems or it had nothing whatsoever to hide.

Fine. That was what he was here to determine.

At a quarter to five, he got up and walked around to the rear of the building. He pulled out a small, hooded flashlight and studied the back entrance. The door was flanked by large trash bins that cast a shadow nicely across the area where he stood.

Lock picking was a carefully studied art in the Service. One never knew when an agent might want quick access to a suspect's apartment or need to find an alternate escape route, should a carefully planned attack on the President lead his protectors to take an unexpected path through a hotel or convention center. Ryan had been one of the best.

He removed a small device from a zippered inner pocket of his pullover and held it up to the lock. He slowly ran it around the entire surface of the door. The LED light on the device stayed green. There was no alarm system.

A moment later, he was inside. He stood silently, listening to the building. He could hear the muffled sound of a heating system but his instincts told him he was alone. He avoided the elevators and took the stairs to the top floor, where he expected to find the executive offices.

Except there were no executive offices.

Room after room contained nothing at all. No desks, no copy machines, no file cabinets, no chairs, no Mr. Coffee. Nothing. Not so much as a paper clip.

Maybe IranOil didn't need the extra space, or maybe they planned to rent it out to some other concern. But it was pretty strange given the massive infusion of capital the business was putting into Iceland. They'd constructed holding tanks on the waterfront and a refinery outside of the city. They'd invested in shopping malls, housing developments and numerous small local industries. Certainly, they would need executives to run an operation of such size.

He descended several floors and found the office of Mohammad Reza, the Community Relations man who'd nearly coughed up eighty grand to Ryan's firm. The floor contained a reception area with two secretary stations, a small conference room, a smaller kitchenette, and a spacious lounge. Reza's was the only private office.

He went through the man's files, checking the drawers of his desk and generally making a snoop of himself, careful not to leave any evidence of his intrusion. The files contained mostly records of the various donations and investments IranOil had made over the last year. There were a lot of them but even so, it was a remarkably small record trail. No follow-up information about any of the investments that Ryan could find. No secret plans to exploit some gigantic new natural gas discovery, no business models for future expansion of the oil giant itself. Just file after file of ordinary, run-of-the-mill, charitable and business donations.

After half an hour, he slumped on a sofa in Reza's office. He was utterly stumped. Why was IranOil here at all? It made no sense. He stared out the window at Reykjavik's waterfront. It was almost five-thirty and the sun was coming up. He needed to leave.

As he went down the stairs, he stopped on each floor long enough to assure himself of what he now knew for certain. The lower floors were as empty as the top ones had been. The great IranOil headquarters building was making use of just a single floor. Reza's office was perfectly situated on a middle level. Visitors would assume that lower floors held busy offices full of employees and that upper offices held the top executives who made the big decisions.

It was all a sham. Even the security procedures he'd undergone during his visit were for show, since there was no other security whatsoever. It was all a pretense for visitors seeking IranOil money. He remembered how he'd been escorted directly to Reza's office. So he wouldn't stray onto empty floors by accident?

He left the building, locking the door behind him, and walked slowly back to Bjorg's. Whatever IranOil was doing in Iceland, it was clearly a front for something else entirely.

***

Eva listened to David's description of what he'd seen in the boys' locker room with a growing sense of fury. She'd known something was wrong. The poor girl must be scared out of her mind. A new kid in a strange environment being molested by some of the biggest, strongest, and most popular seniors in the school.

"I couldn't get her to sit still long enough to talk to her," said David. "Not that I think I could have been much help . . . maybe let her know someone else knew what was going on."

"That may have scared her more than anything," said Eva. "She might be scared of her parents finding out. Some cultures blame the girl when she's molested by men."

"Are you serious?" David asked.

"Yes. The argument is that she brought it on by her own come-hither actions, by the way she dressed, by being somewhere she shouldn't, like in or near the boys' athletic locker room."

"Jeez . . . she wasn't there voluntarily, mom. It would have been easy for Sven and Nils to wait till she was alone somewhere and force her to go with them." David stared at the floor. "If she's too scared to do anything about this, it could go on all year. We *have* to tell someone. Maybe we should tell dad."

Eva put a hand on his arm. "Yes, but we've got to be careful. I don't think we should tell her parents . . . at least not right away. It's hard to know what their reaction would be. They might blame Sahar. Let me talk to your father, see if he can do anything."

"Well do it quick, mom. She looked scared as a rabbit."

Eva nodded tightly. She knew her son was right. Something like this could drive a young girl into a serious depression or psychosis. Even suicide. The girls' parents probably sensed that something was wrong. Sahar was certainly not her usual, cheerful self. Even a neighbor who'd done nothing more than wave at the girl could tell that.

David left and Eva got into her car and drove straight to the police commissioner's office. Dagursson was her ex-husband. She'd only been dissembling a little when she told Ryan that the commissioner was ethical but hard-nosed. It was the hard-nosed part that led to the divorce. She'd never had any reason to tell her boss who her ex was. She wanted to put that part of her life behind her. Dagursson had taken the divorce reasonably well and he was a good father to David. They remained on friendly terms.

Dagursson looked up as Eva walked into his office. She'd never come to the station before.

"Eva. Is anything wrong? David . . ."

"David's fine. I need to talk to you about something though." She closed his office door and sat across from him.

Before she could start, Dagursson said, "I met your boss the other day."

"Does he know who you are?"

"He knows I'm police commissioner. It was pretty clear he didn't connect me with you."

"Someone's been trying to kill him," said Eva. "It would be nice if you didn't let that happen."

"I'll do my best . . . though I get the distinct impression that Mr. Baldwin is not so easy to kill. What's on your mind?"

She told him what David had seen.

His face grew dark as he listened. "That girl needs help. You were right to come to me."

"You have to help her without telling her parents," said Eva.

"I'm not sure that's the best thing, Eva."

"You know what can happen," she said. "She could be blamed for it. The family is not well to do. Both parents work. They probably wouldn't want to make waves in the community. And it would almost certainly make things even worse for Sahar."

"They could take her out of the school."

"You know it's the only public school there is. I'm sure her parents can't afford private. What are they going to do? Home-school her?"

Her husband stared at her silently for almost a minute. Then he pressed a button on his intercom and said, "Would you ask Officer Berenson to come in please."

A moment later a young woman entered. She was short, dark-haired, and pretty.

"This is Officer Margret Berenson. Margret, my ex-wife, Eva. Tell her what you told me, Eva."

When Eva was through, Margret's face wore a black cloud. "I went to that school," she said. "We need to do something for that girl."

"Here's what I want you to do," said Dagursson. "I'm going to call the school and tell them that we're putting an undercover agent into the school because we believe there are drugs being marketed to the kids. You will pose as a substitute teacher, Margret, and you'll keep an eye on Sahar."

"Just keep an eye on her?"

"If you happen to learn anything about our two playful youths, Sven and Nils, that wouldn't hurt."

Margret smiled a hard smile. "Always hated jocks," she said.

Chapter Nine

May 1943

Carinhall, outside Berlin

Fritz Kraus fidgeted. The drive from Berlin to Carinhall, Hermann Goering's ostentatious hunting lodge on a lake fifty miles from Berlin, was just long enough for those summoned into the great man's presence to imagine all manner of horrors.

He had no idea why he'd been called, and by the time the Reich Supreme Commander's private car arrived to pick him up from his apartment in Berlin, his thoughts were awash with possible infractions he might have committed.

It had been a long journey that had taken him from that awful glacier to a post in the Third Reich. Greta's disappearance had placed him at the center of an investigation, for his girlfriend's family was well known in Iceland. However, with the lack of either a body or witnesses, there was little that could be charged, much less proven. Still, he had suffered. As a German citizen, he was persona non grata and the government deported him. He would never defend his PhD thesis or be able to prove that he was as brilliant as Greta had always maintained.

Back in Germany, he was quickly absorbed into Hitler's Third Reich, becoming a low-level science advisor to the great industrial war machine. Greta became a bittersweet memory that he fought to repress, only partly successfully.

The car left the main highway and passed through heavy forest, winding along the shores of a lake until the first view of the lodge appeared. It was the picture of ostentatious luxury and poor taste. The building sprouted wing after wing, additions to provide gallery space for Goering's stolen art collection. After the war, this looted art, taken mostly from Jews, would be valued at more than sixty million pounds.

The building, Fritz knew, had been named after Goering's first wife, Carin, who died of tuberculosis in 1931. Here, Goering organized great bacchanals and state hunts where he affected an archaic Germanic style of hunting dress centering on green leather jackets, boar spears, and medieval peasant hats. He flaunted his medals, styling himself as "the last Renaissance man."

The car pulled to a halt before the three-story mansion's pillared front entrance and Kraus got out. He was met by an aide who nodded and indicated that he should follow. They passed inside, through a large hall, and out to a central courtyard surrounded by hunting statues. Here, Goering stood holding a rifle, dressed in his ridiculous garb that Fritz thought made him look even fatter than he had heard.

"Ah, Kraus. Good. I'm about to leave on a hunt. But we'll have a few minutes to talk."

He indicated a table where glasses of heavy, dark German beer had been put out, along with Goering's favorite Bavarian meal, thick black bread with gänseschmaltz or goose fat drippings. The two men sat and Fritz watched as the Reich Commander downed a tumbler almost in a single draught, burped heavily, and leaned back in his chair.

"What do you think of my hunting lodge?" he asked.

Fritz offered a weak smile, still completely in the dark as to why he was here. "Quite extraordinary, Reich Commander. It's even more magnificent than I'd heard."

His host beamed.

Time had not been kind to the man. Like all Germans, Fritz had followed newsreels of Goering's career. Instrumental in Hitler's rise to power, he'd been rewarded with numerous titles and positions, including Commander-in-Chief of the Luftwaffe. He was considered the number two man in the Third Reich. But that began to change following the Battle of Britain, when Goering made the great tactical error of switching from attacking British fighter defenses to the massive nighttime bombings of London in September of 1940. The move gave British defenses time to recover and resulted in the cancellation of Operation Sea Lion, the planned invasion of England. Hitler never forgave his Reich Commander and the subsequent failures of the Luftwaffe on the Russian front and in protecting the Homeland from bombing, exposed Goering's incompetence as Supreme Commander.

By 1943, Goering was being eclipsed by Himmler, Goebbels, and Speer. Martin Bormann's intrigues had further undermined him and even Hitler had come to despise the man who had orchestrated the Führer's rise to power. Goering had grown fat, discredited, and isolated. In short, he was reduced to grasping at any straw that might increase his influence at the same time that his mental stability was disintegrating.

Fritz was aware of only bits of this history. It was widely known that Goering valued personal heroism and denigrated scientific know-how. He had actually promoted the idea of ramming enemy aircraft as an aerial technique. As a scientist, albeit one without an advanced degree, Fritz had little respect for the pseudo-science that permeated Hitler's Germany. The deportation and murder of the Jews had largely stripped the country of its best minds.

"You are familiar with Iceland, I understand," Goering said.

Fritz almost choked. What the blazes was the man going on about?

"Yes, Reich Commander. I studied at the university in Reykjavik for several years."

"A fine institution, I have heard. One of my advisors recently informed me about the history of volcanic eruptions on the island, especially of a volcano called Laki."

Greta's face, frozen in fear and slipping past him down into that terrible maelstrom of ice water, flashed before his eyes. He shook his head. It was an image that would never leave him.

He managed a weak, "Yes, Reich Commander."

"I want you to lead a group of our finest scientists, experts in geology, volcanology, and earthquake tectonics," Goering said. "You will be taken to Iceland by U-boat, along with whatever supplies you may need. We will also supply troops and explosives experts who will operate under your command."

Fritz's face showed bewilderment. "What will be the purpose of the mission, Reich Commander?"

"The purpose is to cause an eruption of Laki similar to the one that occurred in 1783."

Fritz's heart nearly stopped. He tried to cover his astonishment. "Reich Commander, I know the history of the Laki eruption you mention, but nothing at all about explosives. And isn't Iceland occupied by the Americans?"

Goering waved a hand. "The Americans have only a token force on the island. As for explosives, you will have the best experts the Homeland can provide. Your expertise will inform them where best to place the charges and how to maximize the effects. With luck, we will alter the course of the war. You . . . and I . . . will be heroes of the Reich." His gaze wandered off to the distant woods. "The Führer will learn to appreciate my abilities once more."

The idea of returning to Iceland did not immediately dismay Fritz. He had missed the stark beauty of the place, but memories of Greta and of his deportation still left a bad taste in his mouth, even after three years. The idea of causing an eruption he believed to be a complete fantasy, something to be expected from the mind of a pseudo-scientist like Goering. But perhaps he could use the situation to remove himself from Berlin. Anyone with half a brain could see that the war was going badly. Berlin would not be a happy place during the next year. He would play this to his own best advantage, which was what everyone in Germany was doing at this point in the war.

"How soon do I leave?" he asked.

Chapter Ten

Present Day

Mahmoud Farshidi was crisply efficient. The oil minister was his sole concern. He'd been taking care of Ali Akbari for more than ten years, through some very interesting times. An assassination attempt his first year with the minister had cemented their mutual trust, as Farshidi had seen the bomb carrier at the last moment and pushed Akbari behind a concrete barrier just before the assassin set himself off. Neither of them had been hurt.

Nevertheless, he always addressed the man he now considered his friend as Mr. Minister.

"There have been inquiries from the families of the four men who disappeared on Laki, Mr. Minister," he said.

They were alone in a sauna in downtown Tehran, a luxurious spa that Akbari rented in its entirety whenever he wanted to use it. The men sat, like two wrestlers preparing for a match, sweat pouring from their glistening bodies.

"Rashid was an idiot to send them," Akbari said. "He tries to prevent anyone from going to Laki and ends up instead with police swarming over the place." He sighed. "Pay the families off. And make sure they understand that they had better be quiet once they get the money."

Mahmoud nodded. "It will not be hard. Or expensive. The families are not well-to-do, and they have no idea what happened in any event." He hesitated.

"What is it, my friend? Something else is bothering you."

"The meeting of the Laki Working Group."

"Yes?"

"It's to be held in Iceland. At our facility outside Reykjavik."

"I know."

"It may be hard to keep secret. The arrival of half a dozen high-level officials is sure to attract attention. The press will want to know what's going on."

Akbari shrugged. "Perfectly normal for the minister of oil and a few of his employees to periodically visit IranOil headquarters around the globe. What is so unreasonable about that?"

"Senator Graham will be there."

"What the American majority leader does is up to him. I understand he plans to mix business with a family vacation to visit his daughter. No one could question his having a meeting with the minister of oil when they both happen to be in the same place. These are difficult times. All sorts of American leaders have asked me to discuss the price of oil."

"Perhaps," Mahmoud said. "But Rashid has indicated he wants to be at the meeting."

For the first time, Akbari raised an eyebrow.

"How did he find out about it?"

"I don't know. His resources are considerable. I told him it was a closed group, by invitation only."

Akbari stared at the floor. "Do you think he knows?"

"He knows something is going on. He doesn't know what. My sense is he's only interested if it might interfere with his own agenda."

"Play along with him, then. Tell him just what you must. Nothing more."

"I wish I had your confidence, Mr. Minister. His knowing about the meeting means there's a leak somewhere. That's not good. And Rashid, as you know, is single-minded. He goes forward with his plan. He's convinced his lunatic scheme will work. And he sees opposition everywhere. I suspect it's why he thinks the Laki Group may be a threat to him and why he wants to attend the meeting."

"Perhaps we should simply invite him, so he can see we have no interest in what he's doing."

Mahmoud looked shocked. "Do not joke, Mr. Minister. You should not trust him with such information. Besides, as you know, if he were to be successful, it could mean the end of our own endeavors."

The minister patted his hand. "Of course you are right, Mahmoud. I did not mean it seriously. He is still a long way from carrying out his plans, is he not?"

Mahmoud's brow furrowed. "I think that is true," he said slowly, "though we really don't know. Frankly, our sources are not as good as Rashid's. I believe he is already on the ground in Iceland."

"So far along? Truly?"

"Yes. That's why he wanted to get rid of the Graham woman. Her presence was slowing down his ability to execute his plan."

Akbari's face clouded. "If that is so, we do not have a leak. We have a broken water main. Tell me again, Mahmoud. Do you think what Rashid intends could be possible?"

'No," Mahmoud answered without hesitation.

"Good. Then let him play his games. It will keep him occupied and out of our business." The minister flicked the sweat off his forehead. "Let's keep our eyes on the real prize, my friend. We will change human history . . . and get even richer than we already are."

***

Ryan sat on his tiny balcony and stared at the small park across the way without really seeing it. He had a lot to think about. IranOil's empty corporate headquarters for one. For another, Professor

Hauptman's story about Nazi plans to make Laki erupt. It was a fantastic scheme and a bizarrely improbable one.

He'd long since come to the conclusion that Mother Nature was not so easy to control. Plumbing the depths of thermal power for his business had helped him realize how puny humans truly were. It was the ultimate in hubris for those Nazi geologists to have thought they could cause an eruption that would affect the course of world history.

He watched as three cars pulled up in front of Bjorg's little hostel. Two of them were obviously police vehicles, their lights flashing. He stood up as a man got out of the third vehicle and quickly made his way into the hotel.

He knew this man. In a moment there was a sharp rap on the door. He opened it to find an agitated Johann Dagursson facing him. The national police commissioner walked past him into the room without being invited.

"Come in, by all means," Ryan said, a bit ruffled at the abrupt nature of the visit.

"We have a situation, Mr. Baldwin," Dagursson said without preamble. "The prime minister has asked me to show you and Miss Graham a recent discovery made near the volcano of Laki."

Ryan's surprise was evident. Could the bodies of the Vikings have already been discovered? So much for keeping that particular find under wraps.

The door to the room opened again and a young police officer entered with Sam, who looked as surprised as Ryan.

"What's going on?" she asked.

"Good. I'm glad you're here too," Dagursson said. "I'll give you the details on the way."

With that, the commissioner turned abruptly, and they could only follow him to the cars out front, leaving an astonished Bjorg gaping at the door.

Ryan and Sam got into the back seat of the cramped police vehicle while Dagursson got in the passenger seat and motioned for the driver to head out.

The commissioner was quiet for the first few minutes, leaving Sam and Ryan exchanging looks of puzzlement. Finally, as they passed out of the city and began to pick up speed, he put one gnarled hand over the seat and looked back at them.

"The prime minister is in an awkward situation," he said. "Our small country is in continuing financial crisis, more serious than most of our people realize. As a result, we're hard pressed to ignore the contributions the Iranians have made to our bottom line."

"You mean cheap energy," said Ryan.

"Partly. Also, they've contributed to many local and national charities and have made substantial loans to numerous businesses. No one really has any idea why IranOil has decided to invest to such an extent in Iceland. However, my men have discovered something very unsettling on Laki that perhaps you . . . Miss Graham especially . . . may be able to shed some light on."

Before Sam could respond, the cars whipped into a military installation and pulled up to a waiting helicopter. A few moments later, they were airborne. The noise of the aircraft made conversation difficult, and Dagursson lapsed once more into silence. An hour later they hovered over Laki, staring down at a volcano now crawling with tiny figures.

"Oh my God!" Sam said. "What's going on down there?"

Dagursson simply raised a hand for them to wait as the helicopter slowly settled to earth near the parking lot where Ryan and Sam's cars had had their tires mutilated the previous week. The barren lot now sported more than a dozen official-looking vehicles.

They followed the commissioner as he walked quickly along the side of the volcano to a place where neither Ryan nor Sam had been before. It was an area below the rim where the volcano connected via a ridge to the next volcanic cone in the Laki chain. He proceeded past a small clutch of men, who parted like the Red Sea to let them through, and then stopped.

Dagursson waved a hand, indicating a stretch of the landscape that encompassed an unusual-looking rift, a sort of overhang of volcanic rock. Ryan could see at once that the overhang would not have been readily seen by someone climbing or working around the rim of Laki itself. It cast a shadow along a crevice hiding something that now struck Sam like a thunderbolt.

"My God!" she said. "What in the world?"

"Yes," Dagursson said. "My men have been crisscrossing Laki looking for any signs of the four men you say were killed . . . and for the other tourists who have disappeared in the past few months. Instead, they found these."

What they were staring at seemed inconsequential enough. A line of pipes, like oversized car exhaust tailpipes, emerged from the earth. Each had a grillwork of metal around it. They were perhaps six inches in diameter and rose out of the earth to a height of several feet. At least seven or eight could be seen running along the overhang. They gave the appearance of being very old and looked to have been freshly uncovered by the workers who stood nearby, watching the commissioner.

"One of my officers literally tripped over the first of these," said Dagursson. "All of these protrusions you see were carefully concealed by piles of rock and ash. My men have since cleared around them. You can see that the line of pipes runs for nearly a quarter mile."

"But what are they?" asked Sam.

"Manmade ventilation openings," the commissioner replied.

"Ventilation?" Sam seemed completely mystified, and Ryan had to admit he was baffled as well.

"Come this way." Dagursson led them around an outcrop to where there was an opening in the earth. It was about five feet in diameter and Ryan could see light coming from within. Two dirt-covered police officers emerged from the hole and nodded to the commissioner.

"You can go in now sir," said one of the men. "The place was booby trapped, all right. Pretty outdated stuff, but you can never tell with ancient ordnance. It could still be effective. And whoever did this clearly didn't want their handiwork discovered. But we've cleared it. It's safe now."

A mystified Ryan and Sam followed Dagursson as he picked his way down into the shaft.

Ryan heard the dull thrum of a generator and saw that a string of lights had been strung along one side of the tunnel. But the lights were the least of the improbable sights before them.

As they made their way along the shaft, a number of small openings appeared, carved out of the soft lava rock. There were a few bits of trash here and there, but for the most part, it seemed that what or whoever had once been here was long gone and had taken whatever contents there might once have been with them.

Sam paused at the entrance to one of the spaces, leaned over and poked at a pile of earth, dislodging a filthy bit of cloth. She held it up, revealing that it was some sort of military garb. Then she caught her breath, as they all stared at the clear insignia of an SS officer.

"This is a Nazi installation," Ryan said softly, hardly believing the words coming out of his mouth.

Dagursson too stared at the bit of cloth in wonder. "That's the first indication we've had of who might be behind all of this," he said. "Do you have any explanation for what we're looking at?"

Sam dropped the cloth on the ground and poked farther into the room. "Hauptmann was right," she almost whispered.

"Who?" asked Dagursson.

"Professor Hauptmann at the university," Ryan answered. "He has a theory that the Nazis intended to try to cause an eruption on Laki during the war."

"An eruption?" Dagursson looked blankly at him. "What on earth for?"

"The plan," Ryan said, "was to cause an enormous eruption on the scale of the last one in 1783. That blast caused tens of thousands of deaths in Britain and Europe from sulfuric acids in the air. The Nazis thought it might also disrupt Allied shipping and maybe even the D-Day landing."

"You can't be serious." Dagursson seemed unable to get his head around the incredible idea. "Could such a thing have been possible?"

"I doubt it," said Sam. "But clearly the Nazis must have thought it was. Look at the way they constructed these openings, all along one side of Laki and connecting with the next volcano in the chain. If they placed charges in each of these recesses, they must have thought they could focus the blasts and cause some sort of split or rent in the sides of both volcanoes, perhaps setting off a cataclysmic release of hot gases and lava."

"But we've found no evidence of explosives or much of anything else at all down here," said Dagursson.

"Maybe they gave up on the idea," Ryan said. "Maybe someone finally came to his senses and realized that Germany could be affected just as easily as Britain. Or maybe the war simply ended before they had a chance to finish."

"As long as we're doing maybes," said Sam. "Here's another one. Maybe the men working down here got scared that they might get themselves killed in the process. Some of them must have known that what they were doing was incredibly risky. We should tell Hauptmann and get him down here. He might be able to piece together more of the plan."

"No," Dagursson said firmly. "The fewer people know about this the better. At least until we figure out who's behind the new opening."

Sam and Ryan stared at him. "What new opening?" they said in unison.

"Follow me," Dagursson said and continued down the tunnel.

Near the end of the sloping trench, he stopped and brought his flashlight to bear on what indeed appeared to be a new opening. Ryan and Sam stared at it in incomprehension.

"This is newly constructed," Dagursson said simply. "You see the blast marks and drill holes? And this is freshly moved debris. Someone has cut through here, opening up a whole new connection of ventholes and channels. That's what I brought you here to see. You've been working up here for two years, Miss Graham. Frankly, I find it hard to believe you could be unaware that someone else has been blasting and working here on Laki."

The utter mystification on Sam's face was so evident that even Dagursson had to accept it. He grunted.

"Who . . . who would be doing such a thing?" She asked quietly. "It's as if they were continuing the Nazis' work. But that makes no sense at all. What would be the point?"

"What indeed?" said the commissioner.

"Wait a minute," said Ryan. "When we were driving out here, you seemed to suggest the Iranians might be up to something. You think they're behind this, don't you?"

"The thought crossed my mind," he said evenly.

Ryan held up a hand. "Listen . . . something strange happened at the meeting I had the other day with the information officer at IranOil. He was all ready to give my business a sizeable donation . . . until I said we were planning some research on Laki. Then he shut me down like a leaky valve. He didn't want me or my business anywhere near Laki."

Dagursson stared at him. "Maybe now we know why."

Sam said, "Do you think they could have found oil here? That that's why they've moved into Iceland in such a big way? To tap into an oil deposit?"

"Anything's possible, I suppose," said Dagursson. "Oil . . . or natural gas perhaps."

Ryan shook his head. "I can't buy it. Offshore oil . . . maybe. But here in a volcanic region? I don't know everything about it, but the geology seems unlikely. And besides, no one invests in huge new oil fields when the price of oil worldwide is falling. They go in the opposite direction, shutting down production. The way IranOil has been pouring money into Iceland makes no sense if that were the reason. Explorations push into new areas when the price of oil skyrockets, not when it tanks."

"Perhaps they're looking ahead," said Dagursson, "to when markets revive. Or maybe it's such a big find that they know it will be profitable no matter the market price of oil."

"No." Ryan was adamant. "It simply doesn't work that way. You can't raise billions from investors when no one is making money at current market rates. And a sudden, massive new oil source would only depress prices even further. Besides, there's no drilling equipment, just some carved-out passageways of rock. Something else is going on down here. And it's pretty clear that whatever it is, someone intends to keep it secret—no matter the cost."

Ryan hesitated. "I think you should show the commissioner your other discovery," he said to Sam.

She looked at him for a long moment, then shrugged. "Why not? With this many people up here, they'll find it eventually anyway."

She led the way to the entrance to the Viking burial and stood to one side as Dagursson and Ryan entered the hidden room. Then she heard Ryan mutter a curse. She ducked inside and stood with her mouth open, staring at the space she'd grown so familiar with.

"What's the big deal?" Dagursson asked, surveying the enclosure.

Ryan met Sam's bewildered eyes. "They're gone," he said flatly.

Dagursson looked from one to the other. "Who's gone?" he asked.

Sam moved forward, her eyes sweeping every corner of the vent hole.

"This was the site of a Viking burial . . . or some sort of living space," Ryan said. "When we were here last, there were skeletons of at least half a dozen souls, pottery, ancient blades, battleaxes, and the like. Maybe a thousand years old."

"Well . . ." Dagursson said, skepticism lining his voice "they're not here now."

"Obviously, someone has removed them," Sam said. "If we figure out why, we may have an answer for your question about what those ventilation holes were for." She stared sadly at the empty room. "Whoever did this had no interest in archaeology. By removing the contents of this room, they've destroyed any hope of identifying those bodies or putting them in the context of their surroundings. Whatever else is going on here, we're standing on the site of a major cultural crime."

Ryan couldn't put into words what he was feeling. Something more was missing here than a few old bones and knives. The space seemed oddly empty . . . barren. The missing bodies had filled this hole in the ground not just physically but in another way.

Spiritually? He met Sam's eyes and could tell she was thinking the same thing.

"How long have your men been working up here?" he asked.

"Just since you reported the deaths of those men."

"And have you seen anyone else up here in that time?"

"No." Dagursson said. "What are you getting at, Baldwin?"

"I think you should close up shop here right away. Tell your men to recover the vent openings and remove any sign that they've been here."

"What for?"

"Because whoever's been doing this will be back—if you don't scare them away. I intend to stay here and catch them at whatever they're up to. They've gotten used to Sam's presence, and my guess is they work around it, doing most of their work at night or when they're sure she's not on the mountain. Though the recent attempts to kill her suggest they were becoming tired of her.

"We'll close up her tent and make it look like no one's around. That's the way she leaves it when she goes back to Bjorg's, and of course, there won't be any cars down below. It'll be an open invitation to them."

Dagursson looked skeptical. "It gets cold up here at night," he said. "They might not come around right away . . . or ever, for that matter."

"I'll stay in one of the vent openings or even here in the Viking home. No one's likely to come back now that it's been emptied." He thought for a moment. "Maybe you could put something in the paper about detaining Samantha Graham for questioning. Make them believe they have free rein to get on with their work."

"What you're suggesting will be dangerous," said Dagursson. "But I have to admit, it's not a bad plan. I could leave a couple of men with you for protection . . ."

"Why don't you leave me a radio instead? Your men can monitor it. I'll call for help if anything happens."

He could see Dagursson's mind working. The commissioner didn't like the idea of leaving Ryan alone, but the truth was he was shorthanded. The financial difficulties had cut deeply into his force. Leaving men doing nothing for days or even weeks was not an option.

"All right," he said slowly. "We'll try it your way, but I expect regular reports. If you need us, we can be here by chopper in an hour at the outside."

Sam smiled. "A real stakeout," she said. "It's a good idea. I have just one thing to add. I'll be staying with you."

Ryan's eyes went wide. "No way. Like the commissioner said, this could be dangerous. These people are playing for keeps, Sam. If your dad ever found out I allowed you to do this, he'd have my hide."

The moment the words were out of his mouth, he realized he'd made a mistake in mentioning her father.

"I told you before," she said darkly. "I make my own decisions. Anyway, I'm pissed off at the idea that someone's been up here on Laki the whole time and I was never aware of it. I want to know what the hell's going on. Besides, you just might find me useful. I've already saved your ass once on this mountain, buster."

He shook his head resignedly. "Sometimes you make me sympathetic to your father's point of view." He held up a hand to stop her from speaking. "All right, God help me, we'll do it together."

***

Officer Berenson wore a gray, pleated skirt, white blouse, and black loafers. Though she'd been out of high school for almost a decade, she felt that same strange queasiness in her stomach that she'd had almost every day she'd been there. Like she was on display and being tested every minute. And she'd actually had a reasonably good time in high school. She couldn't imagine what Sahar must be going through.

She was assigned to help out in the art class and had been sent by the teacher to get supplies from the storeroom. But Margret didn't care a hoot if the kids ran out of brushes and paints. She had a copy of Sahar's class schedule and knew where the girl was supposed to be every minute of the day. Margret shadowed her from the moment she entered the school.

What she saw was painful to observe. Sahar seemed to have no real friends. Though she was pretty and smart, according to her teachers, she simply didn't fit in easily.

Partly it was, as David had said, her exotic looks. She was beautiful and that made the other girls wary of her. As for the boys, they watched her like a fox watches a chicken. They jostled her in the halls, joked about her behind her back, and made lewd gestures. It brought back all the stuff Margret had hated the most about high school.

At lunchtime, Sahar took her tray and went to an empty table as far away from everyone as possible. Margret decided to make contact.

With her own tray filled with macaroni and cheese, rock hard green peas, and something that looked like gray Jell-O, she approached the girl.

"Hi there," she said. "Mind if I join you?"

Sahar looked at her, startled, but nodded and moved her tray to make room.

"I'm Margret Berenson. I'm the new art assistant and I don't know anyone."

In a soft voice, Sahar said, "I'm Sahar. It's hard not knowing anyone."

"Well, you got that right," said Margret. "I could use a friend. Someone who can tell me where things are. Like I don't even really know where the art supply room is, can you believe that?"

"I know," said Sahar. "I'll show you after lunch if you like."

"Really? Thanks. That's very nice of you." Margret made a show of eating the nauseating food on her plate. God. It hadn't changed a bit in ten years.

"Where are you from?" she asked.

"Tehran," Sahar said.

"Wow. You've come a long way. You know, I used to go here myself. What do you think of our school?"

Her eyes darted away. "Okay, I guess."

"Probably takes a while to make friends," Margret said. "I know. It took me a long time and I only came from the other side of Iceland."

The bell sounded, ending the lunch hour. Sahar began to gather up her things. Margret knew she had history class next.

"You got time to show me where the art stuff is?" she asked.

"Sure."

Sahar moved slowly, obviously wanting the other kids to leave first, so she didn't have to interact with them. Margret saw several boys looking at the girl and snickering. She gave them her best Mother Superior stare and they turned away.

Down the hall, Sahar pointed out the art supply closet and then said she had to get to class.

"Thanks for being my friend, Sahar," Margret said. "Will you let me know if I can do anything for you?"

The girl smiled shyly. "Will you have lunch with me again tomorrow?"

"You bet. Every day, if you like. We're buddies, right?"

Sahar beamed at her and went into her class.

Margret sighed. Poor girl was starved for attention—from anyone. She pulled a slip of paper out of her pocket. It contained the class schedules of Sven and Nils. They were currently in chemistry class, if they hadn't skipped it. She also had their locker combinations, courtesy of the administration.

Once the halls emptied out, she found Sven's locker in a cul-de-sac with no classrooms and opened it. Junk fell out. The thing was a mess, filled with clothes, uniforms, a lacrosse stick. On the top shelf she pulled out a box of condoms and a small whisky bottle. Contraband. In a folder on the shelf, she found a picture of Sahar. The girl's hands were being held above her head by a boy whose face was hidden, while another boy had lifted up her skirt and pulled down Sahar's panties. He crouched in front of her, his tongue on her stomach and his hands behind, grabbing her buttocks. It was clearly Sven.

"What the hell you doing?"

She looked up to see Sven standing next to her. He towered over her and had a disbelieving look on his face.

"I said what the hell you doing in my locker?"

"Searching for contraband," she said. "Found some too." She waved the picture, then put it in her pocket.

"Give me that." Sven reached for her jacket, pressing his body against her and pushing her up against the wall.

Margret smiled at him sweetly and brought her leg up into his groin with all the force she could muster. He howled in pain and collapsed on the floor, legs pulled up tight to his chest.

"I'm glad we had this little discussion," she said. "I hope you enjoyed it as much as I did." She slammed the locker shut and moved on down the hall, a decided bounce in her step.

Chapter Eleven

Stanley Budelmann pulled the collar of his down jacket up around his neck and slapped his hands together. Iceland was too damn cold, and he hated the cold. He hated this assignment as well, writing about the ongoing repercussions of the country's disastrous economic downfall for his paper, the *Wall Street Journal*.

Why couldn't he get assigned to some place warm . . . say, Costa Rica, writing about fancy restaurants, eco-tourism, and posh hotels for the rich? He knew the paper's culture editor had an enormous expense account for such things. He distracted himself from the cold for a few minutes by thinking about finagling a ticket for his girlfriend, Shawntel, to join him on such an assignment. They'd lie on the beach drinking piña coladas, eating fabulous meals by the bay and enjoying long nights wrapped in each other's arms. Damn! He was in the wrong end of this business.

But maybe things were looking up. He'd received a tip that some important bigwigs were coming into Keflavik Airport. Evidently, their arrival had been kept largely secret. But a bunch of IranOil executives flying in shortly after the recent OPEC meeting in Dubai had to have significance. Or at least his editor thought so when he told him about it.

"Find out what those bloody rich Arabs are up to," was how his chief had so indelicately put it.

And he had to admit, he was intrigued. He'd already poked about enough to learn that IranOil was spreading money around Iceland like cow manure. And no one had any idea why.

He'd been camped out at the airport for three days now, checking every flight in from the Middle East, tramping about the freezing parking lots checking for rentals charged out to IranOil.

He reentered the reservation hall and sighed with contentment at the warmth. He checked the list of incoming flights. Two from the Mideast had landed only moments ago. He went to the arrivals section and had to first watch as a stream of tourists disembarked from a New York flight. The struggling Icelandic economy had spurred a boom in vacation bargain-seekers.

His eyes roamed the line and kept coming back to a distinguished-looking man who seemed vaguely familiar. He moved in for a closer look. Damned if the fellow didn't bear a striking resemblance to the American Senate Majority Leader, Shelby Graham.

He followed the man through the airport uncertainly. After clearing customs, his target went and collected his luggage. This wasn't how senators traveled, alone, without any entourage whatsoever. Such a well-known political figure probably wouldn't even have to clear customs in the normal manner. Maybe he was mistaken. Finally, he decided to confront the man.

The moment they were face to face, he knew he was right. He'd covered enough stories on the Hill to have seen Graham before. There was no doubt.

"Evening, Senator Graham," he said. "I hadn't heard you were coming to Iceland."

The majority leader looked like a deer caught in the headlights. "I beg your pardon?"

Budelmann smiled self-deprecatingly. "Knew it was you straight off. Stan Budelmann, *Wall Street Journal*."

Graham looked like he was going to have a coronary. He obviously didn't recognize the reporter. "You must have me mistaken for someone else," he said, moving away.

Budelmann stayed with him. There was nothing unusual about famous people denying who they were to reporters.

"Just a vacation, Senator? Or a business trip?"

"I'm not a senator. Now please leave me alone or I'll have to call security."

Budelmann couldn't have been more pleased if someone had told him he'd won the lottery. Graham was clearly here for something of a clandestine nature. No way was he going to call security and have to identify himself. But there was no upside in pushing the matter. He allowed the senator to slip away, making sure he could keep an eye on him in the crowd.

The proof of the pudding came when Graham hooked up with the Iranian minister of oil, Ali Akbari. There wasn't a financial writer in the western world who didn't know Akbari on sight. The two men left the airport together by private sedan.

Budelmann hailed a taxi and followed them for an hour as they drove out of the city and turned into a gated drive that led to a remote headland. He dismissed his driver and hiked overland to a point where he could see a large, rambling, modern building of glass and steel. Built entirely on one level, the building sprawled over a rocky headland that jutted into the ocean. There must have been spectacular views from every room.

Something big was happening. He could feel it in his reporter's bones. He needed to get closer, to get inside if possible, and hear what was being talked about.

He began to circle the building. The rocky landscape provided good cover in the form of outcrops that allowed him to get close to several of the big windows.

The place was certainly suitable for the wealthy guests who now inhabited it. He saw bedrooms with original artwork on the walls and sliding glass doors to decks constructed of imported teak. One large room completely enclosed by glass contained an indoor pool and sauna. Another held a small theater or lecture hall. There also appeared to be two wings that contained what looked like laboratory equipment.

The place must be some sort of high-level research center. With the poshest accommodations imaginable. He eased himself out of the rocks and crossed an open section of lawn to reach a room where he could see men sitting around a conference table.

He felt very cold. And exposed. Even though it was now late evening, visibility was still good. The men inside could probably see out the windows, though reflections on the glass from the lights would somewhat retard their vision.

But as he crouched beside the building, it was evident the men were not concerned with the view. Indeed, there appeared to be a heated discussion going on, and Senator Graham was at the center of it. Whatever they were arguing about, the debate went on for some time. Finally, the dispute died down. Akbari stood up and motioned to Senator Graham to follow him.

Budelmann watched them leave the room and pass down a long glass corridor that led to one of the research laboratories. He frog-walked along the foundation, lowered himself over a cement slab, and climbed back up to a lawn where there was a window that looked into one of the labs. There was less glass here, and he felt less exposed.

He watched Graham and Akbari enter the room and proceed to a series of tables that seemed to hold what looked like . . . what the hell was that? He peered uncertainly at the objects that were partially obscured by the two men's bodies.

Then Akbari reached down and lifted some sort of tool. Budelmann squinted at it. It appeared to be an axe. Primitive looking, though, almost like a . . . a battleaxe. He stared in incomprehension. For half a moment, he thought the oil minister was going to split the senator's skull. But the Iranian only laughed and handed the thing to Graham, who studied it briefly, then placed it back on the table.

Akbari picked up a bone. Yes! That's what was on the tables. Bodies. No. Not bodies. Bones. A collection of bones and skulls. The two men spent some time talking about the bone in Akbari's hand.

Then another man, dressed in a white frock, came in, and all three of them talked about the bone. The man who looked like a doctor was quite animated, gesticulating with his arms and waving one of the bones around. Then he directed them across the room to a series of large, rectangular vats. They all stared into the vats while the man in the white frock talked some more.

Finally, Graham nodded and he and Akbari left the room. The man doing all the talking also left, leaving Budelmann crouched by the window, trying to make sense of what he'd seen.

If only he could get into that lab for a few minutes. He tried all of the windows, but they were locked. Indeed, it looked like they were constructed not to open, period. He considered breaking the glass, but was afraid someone would hear the noise, and of course, there was probably an alarm system.

What the hell was going on here? He'd imagined the meeting must have something to do with the international price of oil, maybe with some new discovery that would influence world markets. Instead, Graham and Akbari seemed to be arguing over a pile of old bones and a battleaxe.

It made no sense.

Suddenly, a shaft of light flashed across the lawn next to him. He shrank back against the wall. Someone had opened a door from the lab. He watched the doctor emerge, take out a long, slim cigar, light it, inhale with pleasure, and stroll toward the end of the headland a hundred yards away. A smoke break. Some doctor, if that's what he was. *Well, if the guy wants to kill himself,* Budelmann thought, *I'm not going to argue with him.*

As soon as the man was a good distance away, the reporter slipped down the slope and entered the lab through the open door. From the size of that cigar, he figured he had at least twenty minutes.

He whistled softly at the display of sophisticated equipment that lined the work areas. He had no idea what any of it was for, though there were plenty of computers and electronics. He'd seen oil company research labs before. Computers were de rigueur for any business nowadays, but something about the entire work area struck him as having little to do with any sort of geological research.

He reached the tables and examined the bones. They were clearly very old. Several had been neatly sawed in half, and the dismembered pieces were missing.

He heard something and went to the door. The doctor was still fifty or sixty yards away, but he was coming back.

Quickly, he grabbed one of the smaller, cut bones and a piece of jawbone with several teeth still attached. He glanced at the vats the men had been staring into. They were filled with some sort of bubbling, whitish liquid. It smelled pretty bad, and he had no idea what it could be. He found a small container and quickly scooped up some of the liquid. Then he slipped outside and into the dark shadows cast by the building. The man in the lab coat stopped by the door, took one final puff of his cigar, and dropped the stub. He ground it out with his foot and went inside, closing the door behind him.

There was nothing left to do but begin the long walk home. Maybe he could hitch a ride if he was lucky. He pulled his collar up, shivering. Damn, but Iceland was appropriately named.

Chapter Twelve

Rashid stared at the men sitting around the conference table. They were a scruffy lot. Mercenaries and would-be terrorists he'd hired on the open market. It wasn't easy finding men willing to go out on a limb for something of this nature, even if they were being well paid.

It didn't hurt, of course, that he was one of Iran's wealthiest business owners. Or had been until the recent tumble in the price of oil. Petroleum was now flirting with thirty-five dollars a barrel, an unheard-of figure that was swiftly draining his resources.

It was hard to believe it had only been a year since he'd uncovered Goering's audacious plan to turn the war around in its final days by causing the volcano of Laki to erupt in Iceland. It had sounded like the ridiculous fantasy of a deranged lunatic, which Goering surely was by 1943, and he had dismissed it. But that was before he met Abdullah Ali al-Shihri, a Saudi who had also latched onto the information. Far from being dismissive, Abdullah recognized at once the possibility of affecting the worldwide price of oil.

Rashid stared at Abdullah with a mixture of envy and distaste. Physically, the man was a disgrace. Hugely overweight with a girth only barely concealed by his robes, he had small black eyes and even smaller stubby fingers. His slothful demeanor belied a fierce passion for wealth and this was where the envy came in. Abdullah's own capital was not directly tied to oil and thus subject to the vagaries of the market, as was Rashid's.

Abdullah was connected to the royal family. All the Saudi money had come initially from oil, but many decades of control of the world's primary energy supply had given the family broad investments around the globe. Despite Abdullah's independent means, Rashid had never come across anyone more money-hungry.

It hadn't taken long for Abdullah to infect Rashid's own greed. In just a single meeting, he laid out his scheme in great detail, along with the history of Goering's plot. By the end of the presentation, Rashid had to admit the plan might have merit. He knew nothing at all of the science of volcanology. No matter. Results were what counted, and Abdullah had already fielded a team of his own and begun to expand the Nazi tunnel system.

What the fat Arab needed from the man at the head of the table was access to explosives and experts to use them. Both were tightly controlled in Iceland. Rashid's connections through IranOil would make it possible for him to smuggle in the necessary expertise.

Such an expert now sat across the table from both men. His name was Abu Qarawi, a Yemeni who'd been released from Guantanamo after being held in detention for more than a year. It hadn't taken him long to find an employer. A frightening-looking figure with the coldest eyes Rashid had ever seen, Qarawi had an ugly scar across one cheek and spoke in a raspy, low tone that sent chills down Rashid's spine every time he heard it. Fortunately, the man rarely had much to say.

From beneath the layers of fat that took the place of his chin, Abdullah said, "We've made considerable progress, but it was necessary to shut down operations while the police investigated the disappearance of your men." It was a sore point.

"We needed to keep to our timetable," said Rashid, irritated. "OPEC is under tremendous pressure from the West to maintain production levels. If it does, the price of oil will fall even further, pushing Iran's and my own resources toward bankruptcy. The Graham woman had taken to living on the volcano. We had no choice. We didn't know who her father was. She was simply a scientist who was in the way."

Rashid's remark was irrelevant as far as Abdullah was concerned. The point was that no one had bothered to consult him about the plan to go after Samantha Graham. Even without knowing about the woman's father, such a move was bound to bring the scrutiny of the police. It had made him question the wisdom of working with Rashid in the first place.

Even Rashid had to admit it had been a major screw-up. Four men dead, or at least missing, and the police investigating. Irrationally, he blamed Akbari. The oil minister clearly had his own agenda, one Rashid would dearly love to uncover. He resented being cut out of the meetings of something called the Laki Working Group. His spies had uncovered the existence of the group but had been unable to determine its purpose. One thing they had learned was that Senator Graham, the American majority leader, was involved. And that meant the Laki Working Group must have global significance.

By the time he learned of the connection between the senator and the scientist, it was too late. And the fact that the senator's daughter had very nearly been killed could have thrown a real monkey wrench into whatever Akbari was up to. Serve the minister right, Rashid thought, for freezing him out. And there was no question the blasted woman had been a pain in the neck. Aside from her presence on Laki, which made everything difficult, she continued to draw attention to IranOil's inexplicable actions in Iceland through her articles in the *New York Times*.

"When will you begin operations again?" Rashid asked.

Abdullah shrugged. "We've been monitoring official activity in Reykjavik. Police vans and men have been leaving the city headed toward Laki all week. When they're on site at the volcano, we can't get close enough to see what's going on. However, one of my men told me this morning he believes the police action is winding down. He made a trip to the volcano yesterday, pretending to be a lost tourist, and saw no evidence of anyone around. What is more, there was a notice in the morning papers saying the police had detained Samantha Graham for questioning regarding the disappearance of four men on Laki."

Rashid leaned forward. "That's perfect!" he said. "You must make good use of the time."

Abdullah nodded at Abu Qarawi. "Your explosives man will accompany our people tomorrow to examine the preparations. It's à tricky business. The principle of focusing the blasts will be critical."

Rashid leaned back. "Tell me again what will happen."

The fat Arab smiled, for there was nothing he enjoyed contemplating more. "If we succeed in setting off the sort of cataclysmic eruption we intend, much of the world . . . at least all of Europe, a good deal of Asia, and perhaps even North America . . . will become mired in below-normal temperatures. You've heard of the Little Ice Age that began in the thirteen hundreds and lasted for several hundred years? Well, we hope to achieve something similar.

"Perhaps . . ." his eyes took on a faraway look, "the cold will even cause a deviation of the Gulf Stream and other ocean currents, resulting in a permanent lowering of the earth's temperatures."

"Making oil the most sought-after commodity in the world to deal with the extreme cold," said Rashid.

"I conservatively estimate," Abdullah replied, "that oil will quickly spike to three hundred dollars a barrel. And that will only be the beginning."

Concern washed over Rashid's face. "No one must ever learn who was behind such a catastrophe. I don't fancy another Nuremberg Trial. We all recognize there will be a certain number of deaths as a result of the toxic gases that will be released. Do you have any estimates on how many?"

The detail was of little interest to Abdullah. "There's no way to tell. Some tens of thousands, perhaps. Maybe more. It all depends on whether we manage to cause a reaction throughout the entire Laki volcanic chain. That's our goal, and it's essential to the success of the mission. The bigger the eruption, the more sulfuric gases released, the greater the effects upon world climate."

"What are the chances that the cause of the eruption will be detected?"

"Virtually none. If we trigger the massive release of lava that we expect, all signs of our work will be buried beneath solid rock."

Rashid smiled. It all seemed so simple.

***

Ryan's back started to ache as soon as he saw Sam's enormous pack. "I thought you said we needed to travel light?"

"This *is* light . . . for a woman." She leaned over and picked up his small daypack. "I'll carry yours if you carry mine," she said brightly and headed out the door that Bjorg was holding for them.

They'd told the housekeeper they were going to visit friends outside the city and would be gone for a few days.

"A warming of my heart it is, to see my boarders getting along so well," Bjorg said, smiling sweetly. She clearly thought they were more than getting along. But in Iceland, sexual freedom was rampant and not a big deal.

Ryan had arranged for them to be picked up a few blocks away by one of Dagursson's men. They couldn't leave a car at Laki, signaling their presence, and he thought it was probably wise not to be picked up at Bjorg's. The fewer people who knew anything at all about their plans, the better.

Sam's pack was filled with food and water, enough for a week at least. They would requisition sleeping bags and some other gear from her tent before closing it up in permanent fashion.

Then it would be a matter of not being bored to death, sitting in a hole in the ground waiting for something to happen.

A few hours later, they were dropped off by their driver, who gave Ryan a radiophone to be used to stay in touch with the police.

"The range can be iffy," the man said. "You need to get elevation for the best reception, and of course it won't work at all if you're underground."

"Might as well use smoke signals," Ryan grunted, but he took the thing and stuffed it in his bag.

There were no cars in the small parking lot and no signs of anyone at all on the volcano. They hiked quickly to Sam's tent, where she removed sleeping bags, a lantern, and a few other odds and ends. Then she closed the tent up, placing heavy rocks along the zippered fly, plain evidence to anyone interested that no one was home.

They observed the care with which Dagursson's men had replaced the rocks around the exposed ventholes. There was almost no sign that they'd been tampered with.

The Viking home would serve as their headquarters. After setting out their belongings, Ryan suggested they reconnoiter the area.

"Probably best to look around now," he said. "Get our bearings. If my hunch is correct, we won't be alone for long."

It was already nine in the evening, but Iceland's pale skies showed barely a hint of darkness. They trekked down the far side of the mountain until they reached the entrance to the Nazi tunnel system. Sam took out her flashlight, and they moved into the opening.

"It's bloody amazing," Ryan said, as they moved through the passageways. "This place is extensive. It must have taken extraordinary effort and resources to create, but Hitler didn't have a lot of resources at his disposal toward the end of the war."

"He wasn't all that sane at the end, either," said Sam, shining her light into a darkened recess. "If this was some sort of pet project, I bet he redirected whatever resources he had. Still, it's not like they dug out all these passageways. These tunnels are natural volcanic vents, which they must have simply connected."

They reached the area of the current excavation that Dagursson had pointed out. The evidence of recent blasting was obvious. Someone had cut through rock in order to connect with still more natural passages. One of the newly connected tunnels took a steep downward tilt, as Sam slipped and slid along it.

He eyed what she was doing uneasily. "You don't suppose this could end in a caldera, do you? I'm not anxious to become a crispy critter like our Arab friends."

"Not likely. We'd be able to feel the heat if there were any danger."

She played the light along the floor. The passage had grown damp, probably from a recent rainfall. "I don't see any evidence that Dagursson or his men went down this far," she said. "Look, you can see our footprints in all this wetness."

The passage began to widen. They could see many newly carved recesses in the walls here. *Places to put explosives to focus the blast?* Ryan wondered.

Suddenly, they heard voices. Sam immediately turned off her light, and they stood, shoulder to shoulder, listening tensely in the darkness.

The voices echoed through the passageways in a manner that made it difficult to gauge precisely where they were coming from.

"Who do you think it is?" she whispered.

"Doesn't sound like English to me, though the way the sound echoes and carries down here, it's hard to be sure. I think we should keep moving ahead of them. Can you feel your way without the light?"

She squeezed his arm and held on as they began to move slowly away. It was tough going without the light, as black as walking down a sewer.

"Maybe it's Dagursson or his men," Sam said, still keeping her voice low.

"No reason he'd be down here without telling us. Certainly not this soon."

Suddenly, Sam slipped and fell hard on her butt, crying out for a moment. They froze. The voices stopped instantly. Then they heard them rise again, this time excited and wary.

"That sounds like Farsi if I had to guess," Ryan said tightly. "Come on!"

He grabbed her hand and took the light from her, turning it on.

"They'll see it!" Sam said.

"Can't worry about that now. They know we're here. If we don't use the light to see where we're going, they'll catch up to us in a moment."

In fact, they could hear men running, sloshing through the wet tunnel.

"Faster!" he said, his heart beating a mile a minute. What had he gotten them into? Bringing Sam down here had been madness. A Secret Service agent's folly. Like taking the President alone to the Bronx for a cheeseburger. Senator Graham was going to kill him . . . if someone else didn't beat him to it.

"There must be other tunnels down here," Sam said. "Ventholes or something. We need some way to throw them off."

But the sole passageway continued on by itself, still steeply downward, with no branches or recesses. There was absolutely no place to hide.

They both jumped a foot as a rifle shot rang out and reverberated over and over against the rock. It was impossible to tell how far away it was, but whoever had fired the weapon had to be shooting at something. Who that might be was immediately evident as more shots rang out and bullets ricocheted off the walls.

All they could do was try to run even faster. Finally, they came to a place where the walls began to close in, tightening on them. Despite their surging adrenalin, they were both getting tired. Ryan looked for some place to make a stand. He still had his pistol. At least he could make them pay a price for killing them.

They came to a dogleg in the tunnel, and he squeezed Sam's hand. "Stop," he said. "Rest here."

"Are you crazy? They'll be on us in a second." But she slid to the ground breathing heavily.

He peered around the dogleg and could see several figures, blackened behind their flashlights. They were no more than twenty feet behind them. Time to make them think twice. He raised the pistol and fired. One of the men slumped to the ground.

There was immediate darkness as the others extinguished their lights, followed by a flurry of unintelligible language, as the men dove to the ground and took whatever small cover they could find. Guns began to blast indiscriminately. Ryan drew back as bullets whined and ricocheted all around them.

Then there was silence. For several minutes there was no sound at all. With his light off, Ryan poked his head around the dogleg. Whoever was out there wasn't about to provide any light. They'd learned their lesson. It was dark as night.

"What do you think they're doing?" Sam asked.

He shook his head, then realized she couldn't see him. "Trying to decide what to do about us."

Then a voice floated across the intervening space, eerily disembodied in the blackness. There was a strange sort of singsong quality to the heavily accented English.

"Yes, please. Whoever is there, we are sorry for shooting. You frightened us. No one is supposed to be down here. You may come out. We no shoot anymore. Yes? Okay?"

Ryan said nothing.

"Really," the voice said. "There is no problem. This is restricted area, that is all. You must to explain your presence here, but no longer any danger, I assure you."

"In a pig's eye," Sam said softly.

After a couple of minutes, the voices renewed, this time in Farsi again. They were arguing over what to do. Ryan estimated there had to be at least five or six men. The talk went on for some time. Then they heard movement.

"I'm going to take a look," he said. Lowering himself until he was on his belly, he slid out around the dogleg. Then he turned the flashlight on and pointed it down the tunnel. What he saw made his insides go cold. Two men were running fuse up the tunnel walls while another was preparing to place a charge of what looked like plastic explosive of some kind. Immediately, two men began to fire at Ryan's light. He turned it off and backed away.

"Son of a bitch!"

"What are they doing?"

"They're setting charges."

"Charges?"

"To collapse the tunnel and seal us in down here."

He flicked his light back on. Even in the yellow of the flashlight, he could see her face go white. The voices began to move farther away. They were ready.

"Come on," he said. "We've got to move." He pulled her and they stumbled down the shaft. A moment later, there was a horrific blast that stung their ears and nearly threw them to the ground. A cloud of rock dust floated down the tunnel, making them choke. They moved farther away from it and sat down. After a few minutes, the fine particles began to settle out.

"Might as well go see the damage," he said in a resigned voice.

They stood and made their way back to the dogleg. As soon as they passed it, Sam took her breath in suddenly. "Oh my God!" she exclaimed.

The shaft was completely blocked by tons of rock. They were effectively entombed.

***

"Exactly where did you find these?"

Dr. Leif Haarde was referring to the bone and small jaw fragment supporting three teeth that Stanley Budelmann had presented to him for analysis several days earlier.

Haarde was a forensic scientist who did contract work for the Reykjavik police. He and Stanley had struck up a friendship after meeting in a nightclub. Like every good reporter, Budelmann was quick to cultivate a source, and he had immediately sized up the doctor as a potentially rich one, though not necessarily one to be fully trusted, given who he worked for.

"I found them while hiking along the southwest coast," the reporter said vaguely.

Haarde looked at him skeptically.

"Why, is there something significant about the bones? You're not suggesting it could be a murder victim?"

"A possibility, I suppose, but I think the statute of limitations will have run out on this poor fellow."

Budelmann looked at him blankly.

"There are two . . . well . . . three interesting things about these bones. To begin with, they are very old. I date the specimens to between one thousand and eleven hundred years of age."

"What?" Budelmann's mouth fell open. "Are you sure?"

"The dating technique is quite precise. The second thing of interest is this end that has been cut off on the rib bone. You see the cleanness of the cut? It looks very much like a fine-toothed, high-tech spiral cutting tool was used, the sort I have right here in my lab. There is no way . . . I repeat, no way . . . this cut could have occurred naturally. Nor could it have been done by any human back in the tenth century."

"So who did it?"

Haarde carried the bone over and sat down at a desk, examining the piece under a bright light. "A very good question. You say you found this, right?"

Budelmann hesitated. He didn't want anyone to know he'd broken into some secret research center. At the same time, he wanted the doctor to give him the best information he could. "Yes, I found it, just on the beach, but . . . there was a large building nearby, industrial maybe or some other type of facility."

Haarde grunted. "That's the first thing that makes any sense." He held the bone in one hand and tapped it lightly in his palm. "Someone else has obviously worked on this specimen."

"You said there were three things about the bones that intrigued you," said Budelmann. "So far you've only told me two."

"The third thing is quite inexplicable. I'd go so far as to say it is an impossibility. For the person this came from was old. Very old. I'd hazard that this person may well have been the oldest person in the world at the time."

"What?"

"The sternal ends of the fourth rib, which this is, change as people get older. If you look at the depth of the pitting on this bone, you can pinpoint age fairly accurately plus or minus two years. Also, the teeth are a useful age indicator. The development of ridges in enamel growth can give an approximate idea of age at the time of death. My best determination is that these remains came from an individual who was at least one hundred years old. Possibly . . . older than that."

Budelmann looked at him in complete disbelief. "You're telling me that someone from the tenth century lived to be over one hundred years old?"

"At least."

"What's the likelihood of that?"

"Before working on this bone, I would have said none. The average lifespan at the time was probably somewhere around thirty or thirty-five years. A very rare and very lucky individual, who avoided the diseases of childhood, might make it to fifty-five. And there's one more thing." He looked Budelmann straight in the eye. "I believe this represents some kind of hoax."

"What do you mean?"

"There's no question about the age of the person this came from . . ." He raised the bone and stared at it as if for the first time. "But the paleopathology is unusual to say the least . . . ."

"The what?"

"Paleopathology. It has to do with ancient diseases. After age thirty, you begin to see signs of deterioration in everyone. You get lower back problems, bones becoming less dense and more porous, increases in little arthritic projections, work-related injuries, and so forth.

"This very old person had very young bones. Some infectious diseases like tuberculosis and syphilis can be found in bones. Anthropathies—that's joint diseases—like osteoarthritis and gout can also be seen. Bone spurs and other deformities in the knees, toes, and backs also show up, indicating, for example, a woman who might have spent her days squatting, grinding maize into flour. There's no sign of arthritis in these samples, no age-related deterioration of any kind. It's as if someone lived to be over a hundred but their body composition never changed after reaching maturity. Never changed at all, despite living in what must have been a very harsh environment."

He handed the bone to Budelmann. "This is some kind of trick or hoax, as I said. Something along the lines of Piltdown Man . . . only more so. If you can find out who's actually perpetrating this hoax and why, I'd guess you'll have one of the biggest stories of your career."

Budelmann's face registered complete befuddlement. Instead of the answers he'd hoped for, he had only more questions. With a sigh, he asked, "What about the liquid? Did you examine that?"

"I did. All I can tell you is that it's some sort of fungus . . . in solution, as though someone were trying to make a concentrate."

"Fungus? What sort of fungus?"

"Impossible to tell without a lot more study. There are at least a hundred thousand known species, probably a million more yet to be discovered." He gave the reporter a hard look. "I suppose you found this also, lying on the beach?"

Budelmann ignored the question. "I don't understand this. What would they be doing with a fungus? Do you use anything like it in your lab?"

The scientist shook his head. "Fungi are major decomposers, more effective than bacteria, worms, or maggots. I suppose someone could be trying to use it to remove flesh from bone, but I've never heard of it being used for such a purpose."

Budelmann stared at him in utter frustration. What in bloody hell were they up to in that laboratory?

***

Eva stared at the pages of recent mineral rights acquisitions in the hall of records with a growing sense of unease. Studying these listings was a regular part of her job. In addition to learning which companies were doing what with regard to thermal acquisitions, something that told her a whole lot about which areas were on the fast track, what their competition was up to and so forth, it sometimes gave a heads-up to places that Ryan's firm might want to focus its own resources.

Normally, Laki was not an area that caught her attention, for much of the land surrounding the volcanic ring, including the Laki Craters, was protected as part of the Skaftafell National Park. Occasionally, the authorities had been known to sell the rights to exploration and development if it was felt to be in the national interest, though this was a rare occurrence.

But what she was seeing piqued her curiosity. Private interests had been buying rights just outside the protected crater area. Exactly who these purchasers were was not entirely clear. There seemed to be an array of holding companies involved, with names that meant little to her. However, what was clear was that foreign interests were involved. That fact had to be delineated by law, and a number of the purchasing companies were German.

Why was there suddenly so much interest in the areas surrounding Laki? She made copies of the public records of the purchases. It might all be meaningless, but it deserved some attention, especially in light of what had happened to her boss.

She was concerned Ryan might be in over his head and more than glad that Dagursson was involved. She had faith in his abilities. Whatever personal failings he may have had as a husband, he was a damn good police commissioner. And he was certainly capable of handling more than one serious case at a time. His quick action to send an officer undercover to protect Sahar was commendable.

She took the copies and returned to her office. Everyone was busy of course, except Jon. She sighed. At least it would keep him out of her hair for a day or two. She called him in.

Gudnasson looked completely burnt out after the weekend. He usually was barely able to function on a Monday. Or a Tuesday through Friday, she thought bitterly. He took a chair without being asked and gave her a baleful look.

"Hard weekend," he said, sheepishly. Then, as the look she gave him registered, "I took a lot of work home."

What a sorry excuse for a man. Or a geologist. But she wouldn't bite. Instead, she shoved the pile of papers across the desk at him. "I want you to look into these recent acquisitions, Jon."

He stared at the pile like a high school freshman being handed an extra assignment on a Friday afternoon.

"What are they?" he asked.

Eva noted his bloodshot eyes and general disheveled appearance. She had serious doubts he had the capacity to sign his own name, much less take on something like this. But he was all she had . . . for now. She already had feelers out with two possible replacements.

"Mineral rights sold recently to a number of holding companies. I want to know if we're missing something here. There seems to be an awful lot of interest in the Laki area and I don't know why. I want you to go down there and poke around. See what you can find out."

He picked up one of the pages, scanning it warily. "That's pretty unusual." His brow furrowed as he paged through the material. "Maybe they're trying to expand government holdings for the Preserve. It's no secret they want to turn the whole area into a huge tourist attraction. Increase foreign tourism and get more dollars and Euros flowing into the ol' coffers."

"Maybe," Eva said slowly. "But it seems a strange time. Tourism has all but shut down from the fear of volcanic activity that's been touted in the papers over the last couple of years. Why would they choose now to expand their interests? Anyway, if you dig down into that pile, you'll find that the registered holding companies are based in Germany."

Jon perked up at this. He leaned forward and shuffled through the papers more intently. "That *is* strange. Do you think someone could have found something? A major discovery? Maybe a big oil or natural gas . . . or even precious metals . . . strike." He gathered the papers together and stood up. "Good thing you have me on payroll. This is my area, for sure. I'll look into it."

Almost in spite of herself, Eva felt the need to give a warning. "Be careful, Jon. Ryan's already had trouble, you know. If this does have something to do with a new find . . . you know as well as I do that companies can get pretty proprietary about this stuff."

"Not to worry. I'll find out what's going on. This is my specialty, you'll see." The challenge seemed to have sparked something in Gudnasson that Eva hadn't seen before. His hangover was gone.

"Just go easy, that's all. And be careful. Let me know what you find out."

She watched him leave, a sense of foreboding coming over her. Something strange was going on. What if someone *had* made some stupendous discovery? Maybe Ryan had gotten too close for the comfort of whoever was behind this.

***

Eva had a plan for the evening. She was constitutionally incapable of sitting around doing nothing while Dagursson and Berenson went to work. This was as much her problem as it was theirs. Sahar's father always worked late, so it was time, she decided, to meet her new neighbors.

The evening before she'd baked a casserole and some cookies. She stopped at her house long enough to grab them and headed across the garden. She could see Sahar's mother doing something inside but didn't know if the kids were home. Of course, where else was Sahar going to go with no friends?

She knocked at the door, and in a moment a woman dressed in a colorful robe answered. Suddenly Eva panicked. What if she didn't speak Icelandic, for god's sake? Few foreigners did.

But the woman smiled at her and said in what was obviously her only Icelandic phrase, "Do you speak English?"

Eva gave a sigh of relief and said, "Yes. Thank goodness. I wasn't sure if we'd be able to communicate. I've been feeling bad that I haven't come over sooner. I brought some dinner and cookies."

"Oh that is so nice of you," said the woman. "My name is Paree. Please come in and meet my children. My husband is still at work."

Eva entered a small foyer decorated with Mideastern copper pots and a colorful mosaic of a peacock. It felt a little like the entrance to an Iranian restaurant. The house smelled of curry.

Paree took Eva's offerings and put them on a small table. "May I give you some tea? Or perhaps you would stay and eat with us?"

"That's very kind of you, but I don't want to barge in uninvited."

"No, no, you are most welcome. I love to be able to practice my English."

"You speak very well," Eva said. "Much better than I speak Farsi."

"My husband and I lived in New York when we were younger."

"What does he do?"

Paree hesitated, as though looking for the right words. "He was—is—a personal assistant for a well-to-do executive. It does not pay so well, but we have traveled all over the world. That has been very good for my children. They have much better education and more freedom than they would back in Iran."

The little boy came in, shyly, and held his mother's skirt.

"This is Amir. He is seven."

Eva knelt down and put out her hand. The boy looked at his mother, who nodded, and then shook hands.

"You are a big boy for your age," said Eva.

Amir smiled shyly.

"I am teaching both my children how to speak English," Paree said. "It is the language of the world, no?"

Eva said, "Is your daughter here?"

"No. She is late from school. I was just beginning to worry a little. But she will be fine."

It was an opening Eva couldn't pass up. "It can be difficult being in a strange country and a strange school both," she said. "How has she been doing?"

"She is very good student," Paree said proudly.

"She used to wave and smile at me when I saw her come home," Eva said. "But lately, she seems . . . preoccupied."

Something passed over Paree's face. "Yes. I think school is difficult—not the work—but the . . . social part? She has not made any friends. Though she told me the other day that one of the teacher's aides had eaten lunch with her and asked to be her friend."

That had to be Margret, Eva thought. How awful for Sahar's first friend to be a police officer.

There was a sound from the front door and Sahar came in, carrying her book bag.

"You are late," her mother said.

"I decided to walk home," said Sahar, looking at Eva. "I walked part way with my new friend, Margret."

Paree said, "This is our neighbor. She said you have waved to each other."

Sahar came forward and put one delicate hand out. "I am sorry not to be friendly lately. School has been . . . hard."

"Nice to meet you, Sahar. Was it hard today?"

The girl smiled. "It was better. Some of the . . . less friendly . . . kids were not there today."

"Why are they unfriendly?" asked Paree. "You must be nice to them."

Eva saw the haunted look cross Sahar's face. If only her mother knew how "friendly" she had been forced to be. But it was clear the girl felt she couldn't confide in her parents. They expected certain things of her and one of those things was to fit in and be a good student.

Sahar excused herself and went upstairs. Eva accepted tea and sat on the couch.

Paree looked tired. "I know it is difficult for her. I had similar problems adapting to school when I was in New York. But she is a good girl. Her father and I work long days and have little time to help with schoolwork. Still, she gets good grades."

Eva wondered what astonishing effort it must have taken Sahar to keep her grades up while dealing with all the terrible things going on in her life.

"You know, they have counselors at the school. Maybe they could help her."

"Hassan . . . my husband . . . would not permit it. He feels it is an invasion of privacy. It is already difficult for him to accept how much learning Sahar is getting. It is much different from back in Tehran. Hassan is old school. A woman has certain duties—you understand—and is not allowed certain things. He is a man and so does not understand what this means to a woman. His employer is also very strict."

So that's how it is, Eva thought. There would be little help from the parents. It would be up to Margret and Dagursson to do something about Sahar's terrible problem.

Chapter Thirteen

Adrenaline still firing, they stared at the blocked tunnel. Ryan berated himself for bringing Sam along, but his companion seemed unconcerned, already assessing their predicament.

"There's got to be another way out," she said confidently. "You said so yourself, remember? This place is like a gigantic Swiss cheese. All right. We just have to find another hole in the cheese. One that rises to the surface."

"I bow to your superior knowledge of the Laki chain. Let's just hope our flashlight holds out."

"It will. Come on." She led off down the tunnel.

The passage still trended at a downward angle, and it was hard to imagine reaching the surface as long as they were descending. But it wasn't as if they had a lot of choices.

They walked a long way. It was impossible to know how far. When the tunnel ran straight, Sam turned the light off to conserve batteries, but they soon realized this might make them miss a possible branch. A venthole might even come in above them, which they would certainly miss if they had no light.

After a while, Ryan noticed what looked like a discoloration on the rock walls.

"Let me see that light," he said.

He turned the beam on the discoloration.

"What is that?" asked Sam.

There appeared to be lines along the rock, very thin, very fine. Almost like veins, Ryan thought. As they continued, the lines grew thicker and wandered over the entire rock face. Sam rubbed one with her finger and a fine dust rose in a cloud.

"Don't breathe it," he said. "We don't know what the hell it is."

He shivered. He wasn't as warmly dressed as Sam. "Wherever we're headed," he said, "It doesn't appear to be toward any thermal activity, that's for damn sure. It's bloody cold down here."

Sam unzipped her down coat and pulled him close. He sighed with the warmth but also not a little from the full body contact with her.

"That better?" She said, rubbing her hands against his back.

"Um, it feels great," he said stiffly. "Maybe a little too good." He pulled back. "I'm okay now. Thanks. We better keep moving."

"We've gone quite a way," Sam said as they continued. "Hard to know what direction we're heading, but if we're approaching Vatnajökull Glacier, that would account for the cooling temperature . . . and the lack of thermal activity."

The passage continued on. At least it showed no signs of petering out, which would have meant their death warrant. The strange, wavering lines on the walls continued as well. Finally, however, the passage came to an abrupt end against a wall of ice.

"Son of a bitch!" Ryan exclaimed. He put one hand on the ice. It was cold, hard, and dry, almost like dry ice.

"We must be at the glacial wall," Sam said in a subdued voice. She stared at the frigid ice that blocked their passage. "I guess this is the end of the line."

"I don't get it," Ryan said. "How can a lava tube or venthole come straight out of a glacier?"

"A number of volcanoes lie beneath the glacier. During the last Ice Age, there were numerous subglacial eruptions."

"An eruption beneath a glacier? Is that possible?"

"Oh yes. When volcanic activity occurs under a glacier, all sorts of nasty things can happen. The heat causes enormous amounts of meltwater to form, which then percolates through cracks and fissures. That can lead to a sudden glacial lake outburst flood. It's happened even in modern times."

She moved a dozen feet away from the ice and sat down, turning off the light. "Not a very heartwarming place to end one's life."

He wanted to say something positive, but there really wasn't anything to say. They couldn't go forward and they couldn't go back. They were going to die here, no question about it. He felt his way over and sat down beside her.

"I'm sorry I got you into this, Sam. Your father was right. I should have let him kidnap you and take you out of here."

"It was my decision. You had nothing to say about it, just as my father had nothing to say about it."

"If this is the end of the line for us, you should try not to think bad things about your father. Everything he's done comes out of his love for you."

"Don't you think I know that? I was a wild kid, big trouble for him from the time I was twelve. As a teenager, I was completely captivated by adventure stories. Casablanca, Lost Horizon. I envied those people enduring the Blitz in wartime London or exploring the African savanna. *Mogambo* with Clark Gable and Grace Kelly was one of my favorites. I wanted to live in exciting times. Instead, I was completely stifled. My father did everything to see that I was protected from any danger whatsoever. And so, of course, I craved it. I was desperate for some sort of meaning in my life beyond tutors and private schools in Switzerland.

"Even after I went away to college, my father had people watching me, protecting me. The Royal Family had nothing on me. I would have done anything to get away from that. Finally, I just blew up, told him to get the hell out of my life. I went to Europe to graduate school in volcanology and didn't see him for three years."

"How did he take it?"

"It hurt him badly. He had this thing, you know? This sort of politician thing about always being in control, in charge of any situation. He's always had a sort of weird fixation on his health, but it got a lot worse around that time. I think it came out of his predicament with me. He couldn't control me so he concentrated on controlling his own body. He worked out all the time, took endless vitamins, and tried every wacky health scheme that came along."

"Well, he's what? In his mid-seventies? He looks to be in great shape, so maybe it's not a bad thing." He began to shiver again.

"Come here." He heard her unzip and take off her jacket. They lay down on the ground, pulling the warm down over them. Sam snuggled close to him, pressing one slim thigh between his legs.

The warmth and closeness was intoxicating in their dark and joyless surroundings. He could feel her sweet breath against his neck. She kept snuggling, and he wished she'd keep still. He was tired and warm and . . . suddenly . . . horny. She pressed her leg against him, feeling him grow hard.

"I guess it's true what they say," she said softly.

"What?" he managed to croak hoarsely.

"Men can get horny in any situation."

He tried to move. "Listen, I'm sorry, Sam. It's not something I can control."

"Well, it's not as if I've been trying to get you to control it." She pressed her thigh firmly against him and he shuddered. Their lips found each other in the dark.

Then they spread the coat beneath them and despite the cold air and the hopelessness of their predicament, spent half an hour transported to another place. When they were finished, they wrapped the coat around them as far as it would go and slept in each other's arms.

When he woke, Ryan lay for several minutes, enjoying the firm warmth of her skin against his. She really was tiny. Her entire body lay on top of him and felt almost weightless. He found himself wanting to see her. They'd been as intimate as two people could be, but in the blackness of the tunnel, had been unable to see each other.

Slowly he became aware that there was some definition to their surroundings. His eyes were suddenly able to focus on something. He could see the slope of Sam's smooth shoulders. How was that possible? He stirred and she woke, murmuring against him, then clutching him tightly.

"Let's just stay like this," she said.

But he was already sitting up, cradling her in his arms. "I . . . I can see something, Sam."

She opened her eyes for the first time. 'How can you see anything? There's no light . . ." she hesitated, then sat up. "I can see too."

Quickly, they put their clothes on and stood up, staring at the wall of ice in front of them. It gave off a faintly greenish glow. So dim, they hadn't been able to see it when their light was on. But now, with their eyes totally adjusted to the dark, there was no mistaking it. They could even make out the contours of the tunnel.

Ryan went up to the ice and stared into it. "What *is* that?" he said.

"There must be light on the other side," Sam said, hardly believing what she was saying. She put one hand on the cold, hard surface. "This can't be very thick or the light source, whatever it is, wouldn't come through."

Ryan backed away, searching the floor of the tunnel until he found a loose rock.

"Look out," he said. He struck the rock against the ice and they felt the greenish blue wall shake. He retreated several feet and threw the rock with all his strength at the ice.

There was a hollow splitting sound as the ice filled with fractures. He moved in closer and thrust his shoulder against the surface. Instantly, the ice shattered into pieces and they were bathed in a soft, green glow.

They stared at what lay on the other side. Light poured down from what must have been a crevasse far above them. But the new opening in the tunnel that had imprisoned them revealed something almost impossible to comprehend. A large space, almost cavernous in size, loomed in front of them.

"My God," Sam said in a hushed tone. "People have been down here."

That was an understatement. As they moved slowly into the space, it was like entering some sort of crystal palace. Everything dripped with stalactites and stalagmites. Several huge cones ran from the ceiling to the floor, almost like pillars. The strange veins that had appeared on the walls of the passage had grown larger and were now everywhere. They snaked across the floor and walls, crept up the sides of the ice cones, and seemed to actually penetrate objects that were in its path.

A fine rime of ice covered everything, giving an otherworldly look to what were all too worldly things. Some of the dripping ice cones were black.

"*Lavasicles,*" said Sam.

"What?"

"Like icicles, only they're formed by dripping volcanic ash that freezes."

They passed long lines of worktables, chairs, even sinks and what looked like storage bins or filing cabinets. Walls filled with them. Everything was covered with frost. Ryan tried to open one of the file cabinets, but it was frozen shut, the vein-like tentacles swarming up and over it.

As they moved forward, they found additional rooms carved out of the ice-covered rock. There were sleeping quarters, like a dormitory, a kitchen, even what appeared to be some sort of shower facility. A catchment system of pipes ran along the sides of the cavern, collecting meltwater from the glacier and directing it into storage tanks.

"It's some sort of research facility," said Sam, incredulity lacing her voice. "People actually lived and worked down here."

She went over to one of the storage tanks, stood on tiptoe and peered in. Ryan heard her exclaim softly.

"What is it?"

"Look at this," she said.

He went over and stood beside her. The inside of the tank was filled with the crawling, snaking tentacles. Whatever they were, they had coalesced into a throbbing mass of gelatinous-looking . . . something.

"What in hell . . ."?

Suddenly, Sam shivered violently. Ryan looked at her, surprised. In her years working in frigid Iceland, she'd become inured to cold and he'd never seen her react in such a manner.

"What's wrong, Sam? Are you cold?" He put his arm around her.

Slowly the shaking went away. "Th-that was the strangest thing I've ever felt. It—it was like something just went right through my body. I wasn't cold . . . but I *felt* something cold."

He looked at her blankly. "What do you mean?"

"I don't know how to explain it." She started to look around anxiously. "We shouldn't be here."

"Well, I don't particularly want to be here either. But we'll find a way out."

"No. I mean, *something* doesn't want us here."

She was having a full-blown paranoia attack.

"Come on," he said. "You'll be all right. Let's keep moving. We'll get out of here."

They moved through the space, mouths agape in wonder. The scale of whatever had gone on down here was huge. Room followed room. One contained lines of large open vats, several feet deep and connected to the primitive plumbing system. All of them contained the strange, gelatinous substance.

"Looks like a giant brewery," he said. "Laki Lager." But it was here that they got their first inkling of who might be behind the vast construction.

They'd been following the lines of plumbing and seen a system of valves. On closer inspection, they found words on one of the controls.

"Do you know what this says?"

Sam leaned forward and read *Not-Aus-Schalter*. "It's like . . . um . . . close or shut off, maybe emergency shut off."

She grabbed his arm, and their eyes met. "It's a German installation," they said in unison.

"And from the age, dating from WW II would be a fair guess," Ryan said. "But how could they have carved this out seventy years ago and it's still here? Wouldn't the movement of the ice have crushed everything?"

"Not necessarily, if it happened to be a very stable section of rock, perhaps locked off from the main glacier somehow. I suspect the glacier may have begun to overrun the area, which is why we see melt ice covering everything now. We need Professor Hauptmann to see this."

"Well what the hell were they doing down here? This can't have anything to do with setting off a blast to cause an eruption. They wouldn't need all of this stuff to do that. This place must have cost Hitler a pretty penny. What was he getting for his money?"

***

Jon Gudnasson pulled his jeep into the small parking lot at the base of the Laki volcanic chain, got out, and considered the bleak area. There were two other 4WD vehicles in the lot.

He walked about, trying to decide what to do. This assignment from Eva was one he actually took seriously. He knew what the others in the firm thought about him. He'd spent his whole life being put down by others. No one recognized his real talents. He was a damn good geologist. Sure, he liked to enjoy life too. The nightlife of Reykjavik had been an unexpected bonus. His family had been from Iceland and he'd heard stories about the place all his life growing up in the American Midwest. When he finally got the job offer, he leaped at it.

He felt his talents were being underutilized by Ryan's firm, and so he spent even more time living the high life. But this revelation that German companies were buying up land around Laki struck him as very odd.

There had to be a reason the Germans were coming in. They were pretty savvy business people. He was convinced it had to do with a new find of some kind. He stared out at the barren landscape. Why in hell else would anyone buy land here? If he could determine what was going on, it might cement his place in his new firm, but more than that, he might find a way to wedge himself into the action. Secrets could be a valuable commodity in their own right—if marketed correctly.

He started up the steep, slippery slope toward Laki's rim. Every now and then he stopped to dig his hammer into the rock and examine the geology. It certainly wasn't the type of terrain, largely basalt lava flows, where one would expect to find oil or natural gas. Thermal, yes, though developing that was not the sort of proposition he might expect from the Germans.

He reached the top and stopped to rest. Too many vodka martinis had taken their toll in the months since he'd arrived here. His eyes swept the length of the Laki chain, then down into the crater itself, where they stopped abruptly.

Staring up at him were two figures sitting calmly by an opening in the earth. They were obviously talking about the new arrival. Jon made his way down to them.

"Afternoon," he said. The men were warmly dressed. One looked to be about thirty. The other was older, middle aged. Probably tourists, he thought.

The older man nodded. "Interesting place, is it not?" he asked.

Jon looked around, as though noticing this fact for the first time. "Long as we don't get caught in the middle of an eruption," he said.

"Do you think that's a possibility?" asked the younger man, looking suddenly concerned.

Before Jon could answer, the older man said something to his friend in German. That made Gudnasson prick up his ears. "Actually," he said, "I'm a geologist and I don't think there's anything to worry about. There's been some seismic activity here over the last year or so. That could be a sign of something building, but these things take a long time to work themselves into a serious eruption. We're talking many years and there will be telltale, small eruptions or steam releases before anything serious happens. A Mount St. Helens blast, out of the blue, is a pretty rare event."

The older man considered him with new interest. "You must know this area pretty well, being a geologist and all."

Jon could never resist any reference to his expertise, which he considered vastly underappreciated.

"Of course," he said.

"We were just observing these mushrooms around the cave here. Any idea what they are?"

Jon looked at the strangely shaped fungi. He'd been on Laki a couple of times but hadn't seen them before. He hated to show his ignorance, though.

"Oh yes, they're quite common . . . this time of year." He suddenly remembered what someone had told him about the ground cover. "The moss is called Woolly Fringe Moss," he said authoritatively. "It covers most of the Laki chain."

"I see," the man said.

Jon had a question of his own. He nodded at the cave entrance. "Where does that go?" he asked.

"We wondered that too." The man hesitated, then came forward and stuck out his hand. "My name is Kraus. Hans Kraus. This is Ernst." He didn't bother with the other man's surname.

"Glad to meet you." Jon shook hands. "I'm Gudnasson. Jon Gudnasson."

"We might be interested in hiring a geologist," Kraus said.

"Are you serious?" Jon moved closer to the man. Conspiratorially, he said, "I have a job you know, but they don't pay very well. Always keep one ear to the ground. Serve my boss right if something better came along. Almost hate to do it to them, though. They need me to run the office."

"What kind of business do you work for?"

"We investigate geothermal energy sources and new technologies and develop joint ventures between firms here and in America."

"Perhaps you could take a walk down this particular tube with us," the man said. "We'd appreciate your expertise. We have . . . uh . . . bought the rights to some land across the way there, outside the preserve."

"Why?" Jon asked, his curiosity rising.

"Well, that information is proprietary at the moment. If you came on board with us, we could tell you, but not before."

They're either completely bonkers, Gudnasson thought, or they really do have designs on this place. Dollar signs flew before his eyes. He just might make one hell of a lot more money than he did currently.

He followed them into the earth, where he was astonished to see the connecting tunnels leading away. One of the men turned on a powerful flashlight.

Kraus said, "My father did some work here during the war. He wrote a monograph on the Laki Craters."

"Really?" Jon said. "Which side was he on?"

Kraus cleared his throat. "He did research here before the war, then he worked for the German regime as a young geologist. Not that he had a choice in the matter."

"Why would the Nazis be interested in an Icelandic volcano?"

Kraus considered him. He waved an arm at the passage they were walking through. "I believe a significant number of these sub-terranean lava tubes were connected or expanded under the direction of my father," he said, somewhat proudly.

"Whatever for?"

"Initially, as part of a fantastical plan to cause an eruption that might affect the outcome of the war . . ."

The younger man said something sharply to Kraus. They exchanged words for several moments. Then Kraus turned back to Jon.

"My young friend thinks I talk too much. Perhaps he's right. In any event, the scheme was never carried out. The plans were waylaid by the Führer after another discovery was made."

Aha! Jon thought. Here it comes. The Nazis must have dis-covered something valuable. Gold perhaps? Hitler was mad about gold, had stolen it all over Europe to help finance his vision of world domination. Causing an eruption would have buried all that mineral wealth under fresh layers of lava.

"What discovery?" he asked.

But this time, the younger German took Kraus's arm and almost shouted, "*Nein!*"

Kraus shrugged his shoulders and smiled benignly at Jon. "You'll have to come work for us and sign a confidentiality agreement, I'm afraid, before I can tell you that."

This was big all right. Jon began to fantasize about his immediate future. He'd buy out Ryan Baldwin. That was the first thing he'd do. Then he'd fire Eva. "What sort of salary are we talking about?" he asked, as they moved deeper.

***

Abu Qarawi set the final charge and stood back to examine his efforts. Would it work? He really had no idea. He knew explosives. That wasn't the problem. What he knew nothing about was volcano tectonics. Frankly, he had his doubts. But it didn't matter. Either way, he'd already been paid. Get the money up front was the first tenet of his profession.

His coworkers finished running lines connecting all the charges to one timer. "Everything's ready," said one of the men. "All sixteen charges are linked. They'll go off simultaneously. Gonna cause some damned big fireworks."

"Wasted," said the other man. "No one to see it. All underground."

"Well, I for one don't want to be around to see it," the first man said. "Who the hell knows what's going to happen? Biggest crap shoot I've ever been a part of."

Charges had been set along the line agreed upon. A quarter mile of massive explosions would take place, all focused along the weakest part of the Laki fault. Qarawi had no doubt something cataclysmic would happen. Perhaps a massive landslide or lava outflow. Anything was possible, the Arab thought. Maybe *even* the gaseous release that Rashid hoped would alter the world's climate.

Rashid had ordered them to work much faster than originally planned, having no idea how long the window of opportunity around Samantha Graham's detention might last. The woman had been an incredible nuisance. Too bad her dispatch had been fouled up.

Qarawi didn't know whom the people were that they'd entombed in the tunnel and didn't much care. They'd been in the wrong place at the wrong time. Soon, they would be encased in lava if they weren't already dead of asphyxiation. It was possibly the best body disposal he'd ever effected in his work. No body, no crime. Of course, if anything like what Rashid intended came to pass, there were going to be a whole lot of bodies, possibly all over the world.

Qarawi had listened to Rashid fret endlessly about Ali Akbari. The oil minister was up to something, working in concert with the American majority leader. Whatever it was, Rashid knew Akbari thought little of the scheme to blow up Laki. More fool him.

Qarawi understood that Rashid would allow nothing to stand in the way of his plan. The man was a fanatic, a type he was quite familiar with in his line of work, and a type he had little use for, other than to take their money. Rashid envisioned enormous wealth flowing into his private accounts from a worldwide spike in oil prices. Well, maybe. What Qarawi was sure of was that the money deposited in his own account was considerable.

He ordered his men out of the passage. Then he set the timer to give them a full hour to get away before the blasts occurred. No way he wanted to be anywhere near when it happened. Whatever "it" was, lava, landslide, gas release. It made no difference to him. He had his money. Let the fanatics figure out the rest.

***

Margret sat with Eva and David in Dagursson's office. She'd explained what had happened at the school and what she'd found in Sven's locker.

"I suppose you're not going to let me see the picture," said David.

"Need to know," said Margret. "There's no need for you to see it."

"Other than the fact I'm a normal, healthy, seventeen-year-old boy."

"David," said Eva.

"I'm only kidding, mom. I feel really awful for Sahar. That picture must have been what I saw Sven and Nils show her in the locker room. They must have threatened to show it to the whole school if she told anyone what they did."

Margret nodded. "They have a sure thing over Sahar with that picture. She'd never want her parents to see it, let alone everyone at school. Sven and Nils must realize they have complete control over her. They can take advantage of her whenever they want."

"And they have," said Eva, her voice barely controlled. "The question is what do we do about it now?"

"The picture is proof that Sahar is being molested," said Dagursson. "She's being held by one boy while the other takes advantage. It's obvious enough from her face that she's not a willing participant. And we can clearly identify Sven. That's enough for me to bring charges. But Sahar would have to be willing to testify."

"Which would humiliate her in front of the whole school," said Margret, "and probably gain her no sympathy from her parents either. Be nice if we could figure some way to deal with this without making Sahar even more of a victim than she already is."

Dagursson stood up and went over to his window and stared out. The others watched him.

"I could get in real trouble by not informing the girl's parents," he said. "She's a minor. They have a right to know about this regardless of what their reaction might be."

"Parents need to be talked to all right," said Eva. "But not Sahar's. You need to bring Sven's and Nils's parents in. Tell them what their sweethearts are up to, show them the picture and ask them what they think should be done."

Dagursson grunted. This thing threatened to blow up into the biggest hairball the Reykjavik school district had ever seen.

"There's something else," he said. "Sven Svensson's father is a leading member of the Althing."

"He's a member of Parliament?" Margret looked stricken. This was going to get very bad.

"Makes no difference," said Eva. "You both know that. Unless you give special dispensation to break the law to members of the Althing. If this blows up into a big public scandal, though, it will be devastating to Sahar. She can't expect help from her parents. The pressure could literally destroy her. Is that what you want?"

Dagursson stared at his ex-wife. "There's another element," he said. "An Iranian girl being molested by locals. We've already got plenty of bad blood here over the high-handed way the Iranians have come into Iceland. This could ignite a cultural powder keg. So I guess I agree with you. We need to try to deal with this quietly. I'll talk to the boys' parents. And if it doesn't go well, I may be looking for a new job."

***

Sven's parents came in late in the afternoon. His father, Stephan, was dressed meticulously, as though he'd come straight from some high meeting. The unspoken message was clear—see how important I am? Why are you wasting my time? He was tall and well built, like his son, but he also had the same cold eyes that Margret had seen on Sven's face.

The mother was attractive, with bottle blonde hair and makeup so thick it would probably stop a bullet. She was barely seated before she started.

"I want to know what this is all about," she said. "The officer who called said it had to do with something about Sven at school. Our son is a model student, captain of the soccer team. He has lots of friends and is very popular."

"Popularity is a strange thing," said Margret. "You can intimidate people into saying they like you."

Mrs. Svensson stared at Margret like she was a bug. "I don't care for insinuations," she said. "If you have something to say, say it."

"All right," said Margret. "Your son is a self-centered lout. He drinks, beats people up, probably does drugs, and molests, if not rapes, young girls. His school record is hardly exemplary, though I gather the worst stuff has been suppressed. I suspect you've had something to do with that."

The boy's father held up a hand. "Commissioner, if you have something to say to us about our son, I wish you would do so."

Dagursson nodded. "We seem to have gotten off to a rough start. Let me just say that this is not pleasant for anyone." He took a deep breath. "We have clear evidence that your son and at least one other student have been sexually molesting a fifteen-year-old girl."

Both parents' faces went white. Eva could see Mr. Svensson calculating whether or not this might cost him his seat. Mrs. Svensson looked ready to vomit.

"Whatever this underage girl has told you," she said, "it's a lie. She's probably jealous of Sven. Lots of girls like him. He doesn't need to molest a girl to get what he wants."

Dagursson opened a file on his desk, took out the picture of Sahar, and slid it across, so both parents could see it.

They stared at it, shock building in their faces as they recognized what the picture showed and that Sven was obviously at the center of the action.

"Oh my God!" said Mrs. Svensson.

Mr. Svensson seemed to be fighting to control himself. "Do you intend to bring charges, Commissioner?"

"Well, we are in a bit of a situation here," said Dagursson. "If charges are brought, the girl will suffer even more. The boys have no records, and they would probably get off with suspended sentences and community service. The victim is likely to suffer more than the perpetrators."

"She must have asked for it," said Mrs. Svensson. "Little slut's probably a tease."

Everyone in the room looked shocked, even Mrs. Svensson's husband. He stared at her like he was seeing her for the first time. "Shut up, Ingrid," he said. "You're only making things worse for Sven."

Her mouth opened, and then she saw the look in her husband's eyes and shut it again.

Svensson looked at Dagursson. "I take it you have some deal you want to make."

The commissioner spread his hands. "The deal is this. The boys will do community service. I will determine what and when. There will be a restraining order to keep them away from Sahar."

"That's it?" asked Svensson.

"One more thing. Sahar will continue at school. She'll be under our protection and the guidance of school counselors who will help her. Sven and Nils will leave the school and finish their educations elsewhere. Where is up to you."

"No!" said Mrs. Svensson. "This is their senior year. You want to take the best year of their lives away from them. Sven is captain of the soccer team. He's going to university."

Mr. Svensson looked sober. "You know there are no other schools in Reykjavik," he said. "They'll have to be tutored and pass a public exam to get their degrees. Colleges will understand why they had to take this route, even if there is no record. This could affect the rest of their lives."

"You can be damn sure it will affect the rest of Sahar's life," said Margret. "If it were up to me, I'd put your lout of a son in jail and throw away the key. He's reached this stage as a result of your parenting . . . or lack thereof. My opinion is he'll never amount to anything anyway."

Mr. Svensson stared at the photograph. He stood abruptly and offered his hand to Dagursson. "I think you've done the best for the boys that you could under the circumstances, Commissioner. If there is ever an appropriate time, I wish you would offer my apologies to the girl."

He took his wife's arm and guided her out the door before she could say anything more.

The entire episode was then repeated with Nils's parents. They held no prestigious positions in the community and quickly agreed to Dagursson's deal once they learned that Sven would accept it.

When they left, the air in the room seemed to go flat. Dagursson took a phone call from one of his men. He hung up the phone and put on his jacket. "I have to go," he said. "Margret, will you tell Sahar what's happened here and make sure she understands she has nothing to worry about anymore."

"I can't wait," she said. "And for what it's worth, I think you are a damned good commissioner."

Chapter Fourteen

June, 1944

Laki Craters

Fritz stood on Laki's rim and stared out at the view. It never failed to enthrall him. Beyond Laki's splattered, scabby landscape, carpeted after several days of rain in bright green mosses, lay the distant, white mass of Vatnajökull Glacier. To the south was the bleak glacial flood plain known as Skeiðarársandur, The Sandur, surrounded by a panoramic theater of piercing mountains and glistening ice. The sight of Vatnajökull inevitably sent him into a reverie of Greta's flowing blond hair and slim white thighs. She'd been his first great love, and he would never forget her. That would be his lifelong tribute to her.

Turning his attentions back to Laki Crater, he watched as more than a hundred men labored below. They removed piles of debris, a steady stream of blasted lava rock, which was then deposited in other, unused lava tubes. Every effort was made to hide their activities from any random overflight by a commercial or military plane. The men dressed in civilian clothes in the unlikely event someone might stumble upon them. To date only two unfortunate hikers had intruded. Their bodies were deposited in a bottomless crevasse miles away.

This portion of the southern coast was remote and inhospitable. Roads were nearly impassable. The war had dried up any sort of commerce or tourism. Virtually no one else came here, which was perfect for their purposes. Only a few remote fishing villages had to be carefully avoided by the U-boats that had been bringing in a steady stream of equipment and men for the last few months. Twice, freighters made late-night stops, unloading, among other necessities, a pair of bulldozers that were used to cut a primitive road to Laki.

Fritz dismissed the planned eruption of Laki as utter folly. He was a skilled enough geologist to realize that the possibility of causing the precise sort of eruption that would be required was a pipe dream. Another one of Goering's many fantasies. In the meantime, however, something far more interesting had come to light.

After just a few weeks on site, Fritz began to realize that something unusual was happening to his men. Working inside the thermal tubes, surrounded by the warm, volcanic gases slowly being released into the air, the men had begun to display renewed vigor. Their productivity increased dramatically, as did their overall health. It was astonishing and completely impossible to ignore. Something was affecting them in a most inexplicable way.

Fritz reported the strange findings to his superiors. Soon, word came down that Hitler himself had taken an interest. Almost overnight, teams of researchers and medical doctors began to arrive to examine the men, to take air samples and to gather specimens of the limited flora of the area, mostly the gray moss and strangely shaped mushrooms.

Shortly thereafter, Hitler abruptly canceled Goering's eruption scheme. One more failure for the Reich minister, who retreated even further into his narcotics addiction. Instead, the focus would now be on exploring the tunnel systems and developing a research facility to examine the men's reactions and to track down the cause of the unusual physical effects.

Fritz was glad to end what he'd always considered a ridiculous attempt to affect the outcome of the war. But at the same time, he was astonished that the Führer, weighed down with all the problems of a war gone bad, had nevertheless become fascinated by what was happening in Iceland. The German leader was known to be something of a paranoid health fanatic. Though he took no pains to exercise beyond walking, he believed in the cleansing powers of the Austrian Alpine air and was open to any new astrological signs or findings. He feared diseases or contamination and tried to avoid direct contact with most people.

Fritz believed that the Führer had decided there was something on Laki that might improve the health of his men . . . and of himself. The idea complemented Hitler's delusionary belief in the "master race." Here was a way to make it happen.

The young Nazi geologist was ordered to begin constructing a secret laboratory beneath the earth. The men and materiel brought in by submarine hemorrhaged into a vast flow of supplies and equipment. Fritz had no idea where the Führer was getting the resources that were being pumped into Iceland. He feared, too, that the massive infusion must soon come to the attention of the local authorities.

But that was a problem for the elite SS forces in charge of security. Fritz's orders were to concentrate on the construction of the research laboratory, and he soon became completely fascinated by the entire operation. A tunnel connection was discovered that led directly to the face of Vatnajökull glacier. Here, in the very shadow of the great ice mass, they created their research facility. Throughout the process, Fritz's main sounding board came from an unexpected source.

Karl Müller was a bishop, a member of the German Conference of Bishops. Formerly a medical doctor before being called to the cloth, he was a tall, lean man who spoke softly, but had eyes that commanded attention. Also commanding attention was the fact he'd been sent by Hitler himself to oversee the Führer's new pet project in Iceland. The intersection between the Nazis and the Catholic Church had been a difficult one. But Müller was clearly willing to try to breach the gap.

The bishop came up to stand beside Fritz on Laki's rim. "We've nearly completed the vats," he said. "And I have men gathering the mushrooms and samples of the moss to form concentrates from which we hope to be able to determine if the effects can be increased."

Fritz stared at him. "My men showed health improvements simply from working in the tubes and breathing the gases from the Earth. I still believe that hydrogen sulfide is the effective agent. We've detected its rotten egg smell since we first came here. I don't see how your mushrooms could be part of the answer to what has been happening."

"A simple equation, my friend," said Müller. "The mushrooms show up only around the entries to the lava tubes. They are nowhere else. It stands to reason that they would soak in the gas and concentrate whatever is the causative factor. This is what I believe, in any event, and the direction that our investigations will take." He stared across the forbidding landscape. "Fortunate for all of us that this region is so remote. A bit of a joke on our Icelandic friends, that we come here under their very noses to conduct such important studies."

"I still consider the entire matter to be an unlikely premise," said Fritz, stubbornly. "True, there appear to be modest health benefits from the gas, but to think we may have discovered some sort of Holy Grail is absurd. This massive expenditure is a waste, a fantasy that will drain the Third Reich."

Müller considered him. "I would keep such thoughts to myself, my young friend. The war is grinding to its inevitable end. Better you should believe that you are undertaking research that will benefit all of humankind long after the war is over. If we succeed in this, you and I and perhaps Germany itself may yet find a way to survive the catastrophe that will soon engulf our homeland."

And that was the vision that Fritz took to heart. Whatever the outcome of their studies here, the results would redound to the betterment of the world, not just Nazi Germany. If the Führer wished to spend his last resources in such a manner, who was he, Fritz Kraus, to object? And the more distracted Hitler became, the quicker this awful war might come to an end.

But then things began to go wrong. Several accidents underground seriously injured a dozen men who had to be evacuated to Germany by U-boat. Even more mysterious, two men simply disappeared. They were at work in the tunnels beneath the volcano, only a short distance from other workers. Even so, no one had any idea what happened to them. There was no other way out of the passage except past the other workers, all of whom swore the men never came out.

The mystery utterly baffled Kraus and seriously undermined the men's morale. Fritz was inclined to believe the men had decided to desert and had help from the soldiers who claimed they never left the tunnel. Still, there was no proof of anything. Combined with the accidents, the soldiers became increasingly agitated about the gloomy underground maze of passageways. Rumors swirled that Laki and the research laboratory beneath Vatnajökull were somehow haunted.

It was nonsense, of course, but most of the men were very young . . . the last dregs of Hitler's youth . . . poorly educated, and subject to superstition. Fritz countered the feelings by working them hard, to the point of exhaustion, so they had little time or energy to think about their fears.

Then one day, shortly after the vats began to be used in the laboratory, Fritz was near the tunnel entrance to the lab, when men suddenly began to pour out of the research area. They came running from every corner, nearly trampling Fritz in their frenzy to get out. The men made little noise, simply evacuating the lab in rapid fashion, the older scientists and medical people acting just as strangely as the young soldiers. The quiet, focused faces of the panicked men were eerie to contemplate.

Fritz was beside himself with bewilderment. He entered the deserted lab, moving slowly through the warren of rooms, searching for anything out of the ordinary. He worked his way past the vats and poked into the smallest rock crevices. There was a strange discoloration on the walls of the passageways. Like veins, the unusual coloration wove back and forth, permeating the smallest cracks. He had no idea what it was.

Finally, alone, frustrated, angry, he came upon something that nearly caused him to run out of the lab like the other men. He'd been feeling a chill . . . something was making him paranoid. Obviously, a hundred men running silently away from this place would be enough to make anyone a bit paranoid.

But standing in a rock crevice that ran deep beneath the vats, where visibility was marginal at best, he came upon the strangest thing he'd ever encountered. It was like a cocoon, pale yellow in color, and it hung from the rock face . . . almost like a sort of chrysalis . . . except it was the size of a man.

Fritz stared at the object for a long time, shivers running straight into the core of his being. Fighting back a sense of foreboding and the impulse to run away, he reached out one hand and touched the strange object. It was spongy, soft, with a sort of papery consistency.

Cautiously, he brought his hand up to the top of the cocoon, took a breath, and then quickly grabbed the spongy material and pulled away a large piece.

His heart nearly stopped beating. Staring at him was a human face, or what was left of one. It had turned spongy and pale, but there was no mistaking what it was. It was one of the two missing men.

He backed away, petrified. Moving like an automaton, he made his way out of the laboratory. He had no intention of telling anyone what he'd seen. Something about this place was not natural. He no longer had any doubts on that score.

Afterward, under questioning, the men gave almost as many explanations for their actions as there were soldiers. It was as if some sort of mass hysteria had overcome them, and no one could agree on what triggered the event.

The series of strange incidents spooked everyone. It took every ounce of Fritz's leadership to get even a handful of the older men to return to work. When these men disappeared like the earlier ones had, without a trace, the dye was cast. He ordered the research lab closed and the entrance sealed. There was no argument about the decision from those who'd come under the influence of events. Even Müller acquiesced.

By the time word floated back to the Führer that his pet project had been halted, the war was in its final throes, and no one cared any longer about strangely shaped mushrooms in the remote wastelands of Iceland.

Chapter Fifteen

Present Day

Ryan clambered up the side of one of the strange vats that seemed to be central to whatever the creators of this vast underground laboratory had been doing. Using the piping system to scramble higher and trying to avoid any contact with the strange substance in the vat, he reached the lip of a small, rocky crevasse.

"Seems stable," he called to Sam. "Come on up." He took a turn of rope around his shoulder. They'd found the line below. Though old and fraying, it was all they had.

Sam climbed quickly to his side. She was an accomplished mountaineer, a virtual requirement in her line of work.

"How are you doing?" he asked.

"Better," she replied. "Strange. As soon as we started to climb higher, my sense of . . . I don't know . . . like I was being watched or something, diminished." She shivered. "I still really, really want to get out of here though."

He pointed to the slippery route upward. "You can see where the light's coming from, about a hundred feet up. We're at the bottom of a great crevasse."

She stared up at their proposed route. "The glacier must have overrun the abandoned lab. Then crevices formed that allowed the meltwater to drip down, causing all the formations we've seen. This place would make one hell of a tourist attraction . . . 'See the secret World War II Laboratory' . . . Might even put me back in good graces with the government."

"I'm going to make for that next platform of ice." Ryan pointed to a flat projection some twenty feet higher. "Wish to hell we had crampons. Climbing this ice is going to be difficult enough."

She watched him go higher, playing out the fraying rope. The crevasse sloped at about a thirty-degree angle, which was fortunate. It could just as easily have been a straight ninety-degree cliff that would have been impossible for them to scale without proper gear.

When she climbed to Ryan's side, she could see he was cold.

"I'll take the lead this time," she said. "My jacket keeps me a lot warmer against the ice."

He played the rope out, calling encouragement when she reached a particularly difficult section. Once past it, she wedged herself into a slit in the icy ramp they were following.

"I'm going to take a breather," she called down.

He watched as she disappeared into the space. He heard her moving about, trying to get comfortable, when suddenly she let out an almost indecipherable cry.

"What is it?" he yelled. "Are you all right? What's the matter?"

For a very long moment, there was no answer. He couldn't see her from where he was and feared something had happened to her. Maybe an ice slide or collapse of the structure had trapped her.

"Sam!" he called as loud as he could.

"I'm . . . okay . . ." her voice came shakily. "Come on up. You're not going to believe what's up here."

He worked his way slowly upward until he was level with the slit where Sam waited. Her face was white . . . with cold, he thought. "You gave me a hell of a scare," he said. "Why did you cry out?"

She just nodded her head at the icy wall in front of her. He turned to look in the direction she indicated.

"Jesus, Holy Mother of God!" He lost his grip and slipped backward several feet before he could arrest himself. Then he slowly pulled back to Sam's level and stared at the most horrible thing he'd ever seen.

In the translucent ice, but only just covered, was a body. Exposed for the full frontal length, it was clothed in leather climbing pants, a faded wool shirt, and hobnailed boots of a sort that had been out of fashion for half a century.

The face was fully visible and completely preserved in the ice, so that it might easily have seemed a living person when Sam first saw it. Surrounding the face and frozen in a shoulder-length spray was the woman's clearly blonde hair. It was still possible to see that this poor woman had once been beautiful.

"Who do you suppose she was?" Ryan asked in a near whisper.

"Anyone's guess," Sam replied. "Climbers often disappear down crevasses, never to be seen again. I suppose with enough research, it might be possible to figure out who she was, checking old papers and announcements of climbers who were lost. From her outfit, I'd say she's been here a while, maybe even predating the war."

"When we get out of here, we should tell the authorities," he said. "They can come retrieve her body. There might still be family members who'd want to know what happened to her."

She shuddered. "Not sure I'd want to know, or . . . God forbid . . . see her, if she was someone close to me. But I suppose you're right. We have to report it to Dagursson."

She stood up in the icy slit. "Let's get the hell out of here. I don't want to look at her anymore. If we hadn't found a way out of the tunnel back there, someone might have found us someday just like her."

"Frozen lovers," he said speculatively. "That would give the tour guide something to talk about."

"Don't even joke about it, okay?" She looked one last time at the ghostly figure in the ice. "She *was* beautiful. Someone must have loved her once."

They didn't speak about the woman in the ice again. The remainder of the climb was tortuous and exhausting, but they emerged finally into the bright sunshine.

They lay on their backs, soaking the warm rays into their bodies. After so many hours in what was essentially an enormous meat locker, the warmth was intoxicating.

Finally, Ryan rolled over and rested on one elbow. He looked at Sam and couldn't resist planting a kiss on her lips.

"Welcome back to the real world," he said.

She kissed him hungrily. "I really thought we were done for when we came up against that wall of ice down in the tunnel."

"I suppose that was the only reason you made love to me," he said. "Just to pass the time. A brief fling in the dark."

"There won't be anything brief about it, mister, and if you think . . ."

She stopped and they both looked at each other strangely.

"You feel that?" Ryan asked.

She nodded. They stood up. There was a distant rumble, almost like thunder but very low on the sound scale. The sky was crystal clear. There were no storms on the horizon.

"What is that?"

They felt the snow beneath their feet tremble.

"Earthquake!" Sam said.

But Ryan shook his head. "I don't think so. I think our friends down below have set off more of their charges."

"My God! You think they're actually trying to cause an eruption, like the Nazis wanted to do? Why would anyone do that?"

"I don't know, Sam. But you said yourself you thought it would be impossible. So there's nothing to worry about, right?"

"Nothing to worry about? If some crazy SOB's actually attempting something like that, anything could be the result. It doesn't have to be a massive eruption. There are all sorts of other scenarios. And whatever happens might not happen right away. It could cause subtle changes in the fissures and subterranean levels that might take time to work their way through. The entire area could be de-stabilized." She looked around uneasily. "We need to get out of here. That much I do know."

"All right. I can't disagree with you there. It's going to be a grunt getting down off this ice field, but it can't happen too soon for my comfort."

***

In fact, it took hours to scramble off the glacier and make their way back to Laki, where they used the radiophone to call for one of Dagursson's men to come and get them. Their driver delivered them straight to the commissioner's office in Reykjavik to report the circumstances of being nearly buried alive and their incredible discovery of the subterranean laboratory.

But what they found instead was near chaos. Several hundred citizens were massed in front of police headquarters. A pretty young mother, holding onto her child's hand, was speaking stridently to the crowd through a bullhorn. Evidently, a series of earthquakes had occurred, the largest measuring 7.6 on the Richter scale. People were scared. When Dagursson saw Sam and Ryan, he herded them through the assemblage and into his office.

"I blame you for this," he said to Sam, waving a hand at the angry crowd. "You've been getting everyone's attention with your articles. Now that we've had a big quake, people think the end of the world is coming. They want to know what to do. Well, so do I. What the hell's going on, Miss Graham?"

"I haven't had a chance to check my seismograph readings," Sam said. "But someone set off explosives on Laki. We were on the icecap when it happened and felt the tremor."

"I thought your plan was to catch them, Baldwin, before they pulled their cockamamie scheme," Dagursson said with irritation.

"Look," Ryan said, "Whoever's behind this, they're serious. We've learned that much. They've tried twice to shoot us and then they blew up the tunnel to bury us alive. These people are playing for keeps. I have no idea why they're doing this, but I'd say you're lucky Sam's writing scared the tourists away. If you had a crowd of people up there right now, you'd be facing a huge evacuation and an international panic that would be a hell of a lot worse than what you've got outside here. As it is, we can continue to monitor the situation and determine if the explosions have set off any sort of chain reaction."

The commissioner stared at him. "What chain reaction?"

"It seems the Nazis gave up on their scheme to cause an eruption," said Sam. "Maybe they came to their senses, but it's starting to look more like they had something else in mind. We uncovered a major research laboratory up there, constructed secretly under the very noses of the Icelandic government. Now some other party seems to be moving on an agenda of their own. The blasts have obviously not caused an immediate eruption, but there's no telling what else might happen, any number of things, from more earthquakes to major subsidences or mudslides to lava outbursts or even flash floods from meltwater. And we can't count out a major eruption either. Just because it hasn't happened yet doesn't mean it won't."

Dagursson looked ill. "What am I supposed to tell those people out there?" he asked.

"You have contingency plans for volcanic activity," she said. "Break them out. Order people back to their homes and tell them to monitor emergency broadcast stations for instructions. Get the prime minister to go on TV and announce there's no cause for immediate alarm, that the situation is being watched closely. If I were you, I'd close the southern portion of the Ring Road and place the Laki craters completely off limits."

Ryan looked up to see a white-faced Eva standing in the doorway.

"Eva? What are you doing here?"

"Is it true?" she asked. "There's been an earthquake in the south and you're planning to close off access to Laki?"

"I think it would be the wisest course," said Sam.

"I . . . " Eva struggled for words. "I sent Jon up there two days ago to see what he could find out. I haven't been able to get in touch with him since."

"Uh-oh," Ryan stared at her. He looked at Dagursson. "You need to send someone up there to find him."

"Miss Graham here just advised me to close off the area. Now you want me to send my officers down there. Is it dangerous or isn't it? You're talking about one man. How many others should I put at risk to save him?"

"That's your job, isn't it?" asked Sam. "I mean, that's why you became a policeman, isn't it?"

Dagursson sighed. "I suppose we need to send someone anyway to try to determine if any . . . chain reaction . . . as you put it, may be underway. You're the most knowledgeable person we have on that subject. Are you willing to join my men in a search?"

Ryan looked at her quickly, knowing what her answer would be. She felt a degree of responsibility that came with her scientific knowledge of their circumstances.

Sam met his eyes, seeing something in them she hadn't seen before . . . an almost physical longing . . . and worry.

"Yes," she replied simply.

There was a commotion in the hallway, as a highly agitated Stanley Budelmann bulled his way into the office.

Dagursson threw up his hands. "Budelmann! What next? The last thing we need right now is a goddamned reporter. What the hell do you want?"

Budelmann looked around at the assembled people. The crowds out front and the earthquake he'd felt along with everyone else had convinced him that his exclusive story couldn't remain exclusive any longer.

"I want to know what the hell is going on," he said. "And whatever it is, I think it's got something to do with a certain private research center I discovered outside Reykjavik." He looked at Sam. "Are you Samantha Graham?"

She nodded uncertainly.

"Well, your father is mixed up in this somehow."

"What?"

"Maybe you didn't know he was in the country, slipped into Keflavik Airport like Elvis on the lam . . . two days ago."

Sam looked at Ryan in disbelief. "I thought he went home after we saw him."

"He must have if he came back just two days ago," said Ryan. "What are you getting at?" he asked the reporter.

"Just this. I saw Senator Graham arrive at the airport—even talked to him and he denied who he was—but I've seen him before. There was no doubt. I followed him. He joined up with Ali Akbari, the Iranian oil minister and they drove to this research center I told you about. There was a big meeting, lots of people I didn't know. Your father," he looked at Sam, "was at the center of it all. Then I discovered something pretty incredible."

Dagursson was getting annoyed. "What the hell are you talking about? What was incredible?"

Budelmann realized he was about to give up total control over his story. But it was too late to stop now.

"I . . . I took some bones out of that research lab and gave them to one of your forensic people, Dr. Leif Haarde, to study. He says they're at least a thousand years old . . ."

"The Vikings!" Sam looked at Ryan. "They took them. My dad . . ." she looked completely baffled.

"I don't know if they were Vikings or not," said Budelmann, a little miffed that his astonishing story had been interrupted. "Anyway, what Dr. Haarde determined was that the bones came from an extraordinarily old individual, well over a hundred and that they were . . . well . . . not the bones of an old person."

"You just said they came from an old person. Now you're saying they didn't. What the devil are you going on about?" Dagursson asked.

Budelmann heaved a sigh. "Dr. Haarde said he thought it must be some kind of hoax, because what he was seeing wasn't possible. The bones of a very old person that showed no signs of any age deterioration whatsoever."

The room was silent. They could hear the angry cries of the crowd outside. Sam stared at the reporter with astonishment on her face. She turned to Ryan and leaned close to him.

"All of a sudden, this is making a horrible kind of sense to me," she whispered. "One of the things my dad has been interested in for a very long time has been the science of longevity. If they've discovered something that those ancient people used somehow to extend life . . . well, dad would be all over it. It was a passion of his."

"And if he snuck into the country without telling anyone, there had to be some surreptitious reason, right?" Ryan glanced at the others, who were looking at them expectantly.

Except for Dagursson, who was already on the phone. He spoke quietly and then turned to Sam. "My men leave in twenty minutes by helicopter. You going with them?"

She nodded, but Ryan knew he had something else he had to do.

***

Ali Akbari was seething. The eyes of the frightened little man who sat across from him flitted back and forth. The man was nothing, a nobody, and he knew it. His life hung in the balance and he was ready to tell whatever he knew about the man who had hired him.

He looked again at the two men who had abducted and *escorted* him straight to Akbari's IranOil office. The men, their main job completed, now stood by the door, clearly bored. He had no illusions as to what they were capable of if he didn't cooperate.

"Tell me again," said Akbari. "Are you certain? Rashid has already set off explosives on Laki?"

The man nodded eagerly. "Yes, sir. It happened two days ago."

Mahmoud looked at the minister. "About the time the earthquake was reported. But news accounts I've seen suggest there's no danger and that the government is monitoring the situation."

Akbari swore. "I thought you said he wasn't anywhere close to carrying out his maniacal plan."

"I said we didn't know what his timetable was. We don't have good intelligence on his movements. As you know, he has many highly placed friends in Tehran."

"Damn the man. We don't have a clue what that SOB is up to. He's a loose cannon. Now this imbecile . . ." the minister waved a hand "says explosives have been set off. What if they trigger an eruption? What if lava flows cover the entire region with ten feet of rock? It'll destroy everything, the moss, the mushrooms. It could even alter the composition of the gases being vented."

"Let's not jump to conclusions," Mahmoud soothed. "We don't know if any of that will happen. Personally, I've never believed that explosives could cause what Rashid intended, and so far, it apparently hasn't. Could there be further earthquakes? Certainly. But nothing on the order of the horrendous events Rashid wants has occurred. He has failed utterly."

The man sitting in front of them looked suddenly very frightened. His eyes darted from one to the other of his interrogators. "I . . . I," he began to stutter.

"Well, what is it? Do you know something more?" asked Akbari. "Out with it, or I'll have these men flay the hide off your miserable body."

The man cringed. "Rashid was furious that more didn't happen when the explosives went off. There was no eruption, no lava or gas release, nothing on the scale he'd hoped for. He . . . he intends to move at once with an alternate plan."

Akbari raised one eye. "What alternate plan?" he asked in a low, menacing voice. "Speak up!"

"He . . . he has a small nuclear device. He intends to use it to force the eruption, to completely destabilize the rift."

Mahmoud and Akbari stared at the man in total disbelief.

"You can't be serious," said the minister, though even as he said it, he knew that Rashid was just single-minded enough and crazy enough to go ahead with such a plan.

"Where is this device?"

"I don't know, sir. I really don't, but I think it must already be in Iceland. I heard them talking like it was a done deal. That they just had to plan to be as far away from the site as possible before it went off."

Akbari slumped in his chair. He waved a hand at his guards, who at once grabbed the man and removed him from the room.

"What do we do?" asked Mahmoud.

Akbari shook his head dejectedly. "It's a complete disaster. Rashid will do anything to get what he wants."

"If he detonates a nuclear weapon . . . ." Mahmoud could barely voice the words.

Akbari completed his thought. "He'll turn all of Laki and most of southern Iceland into a radioactive wasteland. It will completely destroy the mushrooms, the moss, maybe even collapse the entire honeycomb structure, making the ventholes where the gas is created unreachable. It will be the end of everything, and the world will lose possibly the greatest discovery in the history of mankind."

"Maybe . . .," Mahmoud said, ready to grasp at any straw, "Maybe we should tell Rashid what it is that he'll be doing. What will be lost. If we just explained to him . . . ."

Akbari picked up the phone. "Anyone crazy enough to come up with something like this is beyond reason. He doesn't have the intelligence to see the import. I know him too well. He is single-minded. Nothing will stop him now."

"Who are you calling then?"

"To begin with, we can order our people to try to find Rashid and eliminate him. Maybe there's still time. Then, we'll see if the pieces can be picked up."

***

As soon as Sam and the others left, Ryan latched onto Budelmann and pulled him aside.

"You're taking me to that research center you talked about outside Reykjavik," he said.

"Christ, I don't want to go back there," the reporter said. "I was lucky to get away the first time."

But Ryan had an iron grip on the man's arm. "Just get me there," he said. "Then you can leave. I'll do the rest."

"What . . . what do you intend to do?"

"I'll figure that out when the time comes. But one thing's for certain. I'm going to find out what the hell is going on. If Senator Graham is there, then he knows a lot about this, and he's going to tell me if I have to pull his teeth out one by one. I'm tired of being pushed around, shot at and buried alive. Now his own daughter's heading back into the heart of this—and one of my employees is down there too."

Budelmann could see he had little choice. "Something I didn't mention in Dagursson's office," he said.

Ryan waited.

"They were testing something else besides the bones of the Vikings. They had big vats of a liquid. I took a sample and had it looked at by Dr. Haarde."

"What was it?"

"Haarde said it was some sort of fungus. Something they were probably trying to concentrate, but he didn't know why."

"Fungus?

The man nodded.

Ryan blinked in frustration. Could there possibly be any more mysteries?

"How well was this place guarded?"

"I didn't see any security at all. I don't think they're worried about that. Or maybe they just don't trust having security guards knowing what they're up to."

"Well, small thanks for that anyway," said Ryan. "Come on, we're wasting time. I don't like having Sam back on Laki, even if

Dagursson's whole police force is with her. There's something dangerous about that place, and I'm beginning to think it's got nothing to do with the volcano."

Barely an hour later, Ryan pulled his car off the side of the road by the gated entrance to the research center. They got out and Ryan pocketed the keys.

"Afraid you'll have to walk back," he said. "I'm going to need the car."

Budelmann shrugged. "Won't be the first time. Be careful. They may not have security, but there were plenty of people around."

Ryan pulled out his SIG. "I won't be completely alone," he said.

Approaching the building unseen in the rocky landscape wasn't difficult. He skirted the outside, checking all the rooms. No one seemed to be around, though he knew there were probably large sections he couldn't see. The laboratories also seemed deserted, except for one, where a man in a white frock was bent over a microscope.

It seemed as good a place as any to begin. The doors were locked, but it took only a moment to pick a keyhole, and he found himself inside. He stood, listening for a minute. There was the sound of humming computers and a heating system somewhere, but he had the sense that the man in the white frock was working alone.

He slipped into the room and stood a few feet behind as the man peered into a microscope until something in the way his head suddenly went still, told Ryan he'd been detected. Slowly, the man raised his head.

"Who are you?" he asked.

"I'm here to see if you have all the necessary permits to run this place," Ryan replied, moving forward.

The man stared at him with a puzzled look.

"I know. It was a poor joke. How about this?" He pulled his gun out and pointed it straight at the man. "Tell me what you're doing here."

His eyes went wide. "I-I'm just a scientist. Doing my job."

"And what would that be?" Ryan asked, holding the gun more casually. "Let's begin with this. Who do you work for?"

"I'm employed by IranOil, at least nominally. My paycheck comes through them. I've never been really clear who's in charge. When Mr. Akbari is in town, everyone defers to him, but he doesn't show up too often."

"And what do you do for that paycheck?"

"Whatever they tell me. I'm a chemist. We've been analyzing the ancient remains of bones and artifacts. We study the flora of the Laki region. Some . . . interesting things, really, but I don't know why they want these things looked at. I suspect they're searching for new products to sell." He shrugged.

Ryan considered the man. He didn't believe for a minute that he knew so little about what was going on here. His eyes wandered around the lab and came to rest on a series of large containers.

"What are those?" he asked, gesturing with the pistol.

"They contain a new substance I've been asked to study. It's a kind of fungus."

"A fungus? What's so special about that?"

"It came from Laki . . . beneath the volcano actually."

"Listen to me," Ryan said slowly. "I don't believe you're telling me the truth." He directed the gun back on the man and pulled back the trigger. It made a satisfying click.

"Sweet Jesus!" the man cried. "Don't shoot me. What do you want to know?"

"What's the real purpose of your investigations here? I'll give you one chance to get it right. Because I already know the answer."

"All right, all right! Just don't point that thing at me, okay? They believe there's something about Laki that may prolong life. The bones are from ancient people found on the volcano. They clearly lived much longer than normal and in better health. I'm supposed to find out why."

"Right answer. Now tell me what part Senator Graham plays in this."

"The senator's a fanatic about the possibility of extended life. He's in his seventies and wants to live a lot longer. He was the one who arranged the financing to create this place. The Iranians had lots of money, but they couldn't build something like this. It would have been too conspicuous. Senator Graham had the power to get it done. And he's been damned impatient. He wants results yesterday."

Ryan's thoughts whirled at the implications. Sam had told him her father was a health nut, interested in longevity. Small wonder he'd latch onto something like this. And it explained why he wanted to get Sam out of the country. He knew what was happening and why she was in real danger. But it wasn't enough to get him to stop looking for his Holy Grail.

"So what's the point of the fungus?" he asked.

"We discovered it several months ago. We found spores initially on the mushrooms that gather around the vent openings. Then we found more samples underground and began to wonder if we were looking at the filaments of a founding fungus."

"A what?"

"The filaments of a founding fungus can grow over thousands of acres and live for thousands of years. No one really knows how long they can live. The fungus spawns genetically identical mushrooms above ground. Such hyphal masses can become some of the largest and most ancient organisms on Earth."

"What's hyphal?"

"It refers to any of the threadlike filaments that form the mycelium of a fungus."

Ryan didn't know what mycelium was either, but he didn't want to go too far down this road. None of it sounded good.

"You're saying such a fungus is a single living organism?"

"Yes, it's been proven through DNA typing. Fungi break things down, cause decomposition. They latch onto a food source and release enzymes to break the substance into a mask of sugars and amino acids, which the fungi then absorb through the membranes of their filamentous hyphae. Some fungi are simple, even unicellular, but others sprout elaborate fruiting bodies packed with billions of microscopic spores."

"The ones you say can cover thousands of acres," said Ryan.

"Yes.

"I still don't see what all of this has to do with the longevity effects you've been studying."

"We still don't know what causes that. It's why we've been studying everything, from the gases released by the volcano to the mushrooms and the ancient bones." The man stared into the barrel of Ryan's gun. "I . . . I have a theory about the fungus, though."

Ryan raised an eyebrow.

"This fungus may be very old, as I said. It may not have come from here originally. Spores can float in on the wind. I think the one we're studying causes hallucinations in people, maybe other effects as well."

"And what's your theory?"

"I have no proof. But since I've been working closely with the fungus, I've sensed . . ." He stopped.

"Go on!"

"I've told no one about this. You'll think I'm foolish."

"You don't need to worry about what I think of you. Only about this." He gestured with the pistol.

"I . . . I think the fungus may be . . . intelligent."

Ryan stared at him. "What?"

"It's something I feel. A presence. Almost like it communicates with me through my mind, by giving me thoughts in the form of hallucinations."

He wondered if the man was hallucinating right now. "How old did you say it might be?"

"There's no way to know. It could be the oldest living thing on earth. Certainly old enough to have had time to evolve intelligence like man."

∗

"What was that?"

Jon Gudnasson stood rooted to the cold stone floor of the passageway, his legs spread wide, as if balancing himself on a trampoline. A severe shudder had passed through the earth.

"Felt like an earthquake," said Kraus, who held their sole flashlight. "You're the geologist. What do you think?"

Jon looked uncertain. Coming from the American Midwest, he'd never felt one before.

He'd followed the two Germans deep into the earth, hardly paying attention to where they were heading, his mind filled with fantasies about a new job and moneymaking potential. Now, he realized, he had no idea where they were. They'd taken many different branches, always, it seemed, heading deeper, as Hans, the older man, rambled on about the interesting passageways and how his father was partly responsible for creating this incredible sub world.

"We should get out of here," Jon said. "If that *was* an earthquake, there could be a danger of some of these vent tubes collapsing. And there are likely to be aftershocks." He waited expectantly for Hans to agree and lead the way out.

Instead, the German said, "I'm not sure which way to go."

Jon stared at him in disbelief. But the words barely had time to register before they felt another movement in the ground, this one preceded by what sounded like distant thunder.

"That sounded more like an explosion," said Kraus. "Look!" He pointed the light down the passage. Silt drifted down from the roof of the tunnel, followed almost immediately by a loud rushing sound.

"What was that?" said Jon.

"Sounds like rushing water."

Suddenly, a section of the tunnel floor behind them simply collapsed, disappearing into a vast maw in the earth, taking young Ernst with it.

"Ernst!" Hans cried, pointing the light into the hole that had opened up right at their feet.

But the German was gone, swept away, leaving them staring at a deep hole at the bottom of which, just where the light dissipated, they could see water rushing away out of sight.

Hans continued to stare in disbelief at the opening that had taken his friend, but Jon was already pushing him away from the gaping hole.

"We've got to get away from here!" he said. "The rest of this floor could collapse any moment."

They stumbled down the passage, the sound of rushing water and Ernst's abbreviated cry echoing in their ears. Only after both men were exhausted did they finally stop.

"Listen," said Kraus. He turned the light off and they listened in the dark to horrible sounds. It was as if the very rocks were speaking to them, a frightening collection of groaning and cracking, splitting rocks and fluids percolating away somewhere.

"This whole place sounds like it's coming apart at the seams," said Jon. "The earthquake or whatever it was has destabilized the substructure."

The two men stared at each other in the dim light. "What should we do?" asked Kraus, deferring to the other man's scientific knowledge of the region.

But Jon had no idea. He was so overcome with fear he could barely think. "There's nothing to do but keep going," he said. "We can't go back, that much is certain."

They continued on for another hour, blindly taking one branching passageway after another, with no idea where they were going. Eventually, their light began to fade.

"We're losing the light," Kraus said, his voice filled with resignation.

"Christ, what are we going to do down here without a light?" Jon almost whimpered. Then, as if to laugh at them, the light went out completely.

The blackness and silence were interrupted only by the sound of their breathing and by the occasional moaning of indefinable subterranean movements.

Jon heard Kraus grunt as he sank to the tunnel floor. "My father warned me about the dangers of this place. He said it was a honeycomb of passageways overlaying sunken vats of lava, glacial meltwaters, and something else . . . something far worse. It was what killed so many of my father's men, and it's what took away poor Ernst. I'm convinced of it." He shuddered. "He may have been the luckiest of us. At least he died quickly."

Jon fought back his growing sense of panic. "What are you saying? What could be worse than what's happened? We need to keep moving. We can't just sit here."

"You are right, my friend. We must continue on in the darkness. Though I think it will do little good. Just let me rest a bit longer. I'm not in such good shape anymore."

Reluctantly, Gudnasson sank to the ground next to him. They could still feel tremors coming through the earth. It was terrifying to feel the solid ground move beneath them in the blackness, as though they were perched on the back of some great beast.

"We must rely on our maker now," said Kraus solemnly.

"I'm a geologist . . . and an atheist," said Jon. "I don't believe in a maker, or that anyone looks out for us in this world except ourselves."

"I'm sorry for you, then," said Kraus. "But no doubt you are a good scientist. My father was also such a man. He too was a nonbeliever, though this place may have begun to change him on that score."

"What are you talking about?" Jon asked. The conversation seemed surreal given their surroundings, but talking was better than listening to the strange sounds coming from the blackness all around them.

"I will tell you a story," said Kraus. "I think there's no longer any need for you to sign a confidentiality agreement, do you?"

Jon felt the other man smile in the darkness.

"I'm a Catholic and a representative of the hierarchy of the German church. It is the church that purchased subterranean rights to the land in this place. It is the church that sent me here."

Jon stared at him in incomprehension. Despite his fears of their predicament, Kraus's soothing tone had a calming effect.

"There are unnatural things about this place," he went on. "My father told me about some of them. One of his associates was a man named Müller. Karl Müller. He'd been one of the Führer's physicians before becoming a bishop. Hitler had great confidence in Müller and sent him to Iceland to investigate the strange events my father reported. It was not until after the war that my father learned how influential Müller really was."

"What do you mean?" asked Jon.

"He wasn't just a member of the church, but an important representative of the Conference of German Bishops, very highly placed. At the same time, he was also working for Hitler. The Führer and the church had a difficult relationship. Catholics were forbidden to join the Nazi Party, you know, under threat of excommunication. But many Catholics supported Hitler, while others openly resisted the Reich. In 1941, the Nazis began to dissolve the monasteries and abbeys. But Hitler feared the increasing protests of the Catholic population, who made up a third of Germany's people. So at Müller's urging, he halted the effort.

"In return, when the time came, Müller helped the Führer gain funding for his Icelandic research and investigations through the church. All of this . . ." Kraus waved a hand, though Jon couldn't see it, "was funded by the German Catholic church."

Jon found himself listening in fascination to the incredible tale coming out of the blackness.

"In the waning days of the war," Kraus went on, "Hitler had few remaining resources. Without the backing of the church, he could not have financed my father's work."

"Why on Earth would the church care about ventholes in Iceland, for god's sake?" asked Jon.

"Because Müller had convinced the Führer that the secret to eternal, or at least greatly extended, life could be found here. And he used the same argument to persuade the church that this presented a real threat to them. My father's men had experienced what they called an 'invigorating' health effect. Hitler was convinced he'd found some sort of Holy Grail that would guarantee the success of his "master race." The church was not so sanguine. The bishops were shaken by the idea that some force other than God might ultimately control such a thing. They wanted to disprove the notion and were willing to finance Hitler's investigations in order to uphold the tenets of the church."

Jon's voice expressed bewilderment. "And what did they find out?" he asked.

Kraus shrugged. "My father thought there was something . . . some force . . . beneath the earth on Laki. Perhaps something spiritual. He found things below ground that no one had ever seen before. And his men, while experiencing the revitalizing effects of the underground, were at the same time overcome by paranoia, hallucination, and even madness. They refused to continue to work . . . ."

Kraus stopped abruptly. "I can see you," he said.

Jon realized he could also dimly see their surroundings. They stared down the passageway. Something seemed to be moving along the walls, twisting and turning and . . . glowing . . . as though phosphorescent.

"What the hell is that?" asked Jon in a whisper.

Both men stood, staring dumfounded as the approaching tentacles moved toward them like expanding blood vessels, sprouting branches and weaving a pattern along the cavern walls. The tentacles reached them and passed them by, continuing on into the darkness.

"I don't know what in the name of the Holy Virgin that is," said Kraus. "My father never mentioned such a thing to me. But whatever it is, it's allowing us to see. Let's use the light while it lasts."

They began to move down the corridor. The tentacles grew denser as they went, providing more light but also seeming to fill more of the passage. When they came to a branch vent, the entrance was completely blocked by a thick, interwoven web of the strange substance. Time and again they came to branching passageways and each time, they were given only one possible avenue to continue.

"It's as if these . . . things . . . are herding us," said Jon.

"Yes," Kraus replied. "And you notice also that each time there is a choice, we are forced to take the channel that goes lower. I fear we'll never find our way out as long as we're descending into this strange place."

But they had little choice. The tentacles lit their path, but where were they taking them?

***

Sam checked her headlamp. The Sergeant in charge of the police unit, Fridrik Stefansson, looked young and a bit unsure of what Sam's authority was. She recognized his uncertainty.

"I'm just here to offer advice, Sergeant," she said. "I think we're all going to be on unfamiliar ground."

"Yes, Ma'am," he replied. "Commissioner Dagursson said I was in charge with regard to police matters but that your experience should be taken into account on all matters related to the terrain." He lowered his voice and said, "I've never been on Laki, so I intend to lean on you, Ms. Graham."

"I'll do my best," she replied. "But you can start by calling me Sam. Everyone else seems to."

Stefansson's men carried handguns and flashlights. They'd found Gudnasson's Jeep along with two other vehicles at the Laki parking lot, but there was no sign of Jon.

"We've got a lot of ground to cover, Sergeant," said Sam. "That's *under*ground. I suggest we divide into two groups of half a dozen each. You and I should probably stay together. Do you have someone you trust to lead the other group?"

He nodded and called, "Jonsson, you'll lead six men. Miss Graham will tell you which vent to begin with. Stay in contact via radiophone. You find anyone or anything unusual, call me straight away."

"Yes sir!"

Stefansson handed a radio to Sam. "We'll keep in contact with these," he said. "They're the very best we have and should work even underground, depending on how far our groups become separated."

She nodded, took the device, and put it in her small waist pack. Then she looked at Jonsson, a strapping fellow with straw-colored hair. "Be careful," she warned. "After the explosions, we can't be sure what will happen down below." She pointed across the barren volcano. "You and your men can begin in that vent opening over there. Do you see it?"

It was hard to pick out the opening against the tortured landscape. Everything blended together in an array of brown and black rock. But after a moment, following her finger, Jonsson saw the opening and nodded.

She turned back to Stefansson and the others, motioned with her light, and proceeded underground.

Both parties carried cans of phosphorescent spray paint, which they would use to mark any branching vents or passageways. She didn't want anyone getting hopelessly lost, necessitating still another search party.

The men seemed relaxed, almost jovial, talking to one another. It was clear they didn't have much idea what to expect. To them, it was just one more search party for lost tourists. Their careless attitude made Sam uncomfortable. But she saw little point in trying to scare them at this juncture with talk of collapsing tunnels, washouts, and lava eruptions. Instead, she settled for a brief warning.

"Stay alert, please, gentlemen. Laki is a dangerous environment. Don't underestimate it."

She'd selected the tunnel she and Ryan had explored and then been trapped in. Her plan was to go as far as the blockage that had sealed them in. If Jon wasn't to be found, they would then look for new openings that might have occurred since the blasts.

She quickly realized that things were completely different below ground now. Numerous sections of tunnel had collapsed while other openings had replaced them. There was an almost constant rumbling going on, which quickly sobered the men from their jovial attitude. It was clear to anyone that the stability of this place was in question.

After a lengthy hike, Sam realized they should have come to the place where she and Ryan had first been trapped, but nothing looked the same. If not for their spraying of every new venthole they entered, they would quickly have become lost. They still might if a collapse blocked their return route.

She said to Sergeant Stefansson, "This maze has gotten a lot worse. If I had to guess, I'd say there's a slow chain reaction occurring somewhere down below."

"Chain reaction of what?" asked the Sergeant, one eye cocked questioningly.

"Collapsing ventholes, percolating forces . . . hot gas, lava, sub-glacial meltwater. You name it. I think you should make sure we still have contact with your man Jonsson."

He nodded and pulled out his radio. The rest of the men sensed a break and fell to the ground.

To Sam's relief, Jonsson replied quickly. "Been trying to raise you," he said. "Your signal is weak. We haven't seen anyone, but it's pretty queer down here. Lots of strange sounds. Making everyone plenty nervous. Also, there's some sort of . . . growth . . . along the sides of the passageway."

"What's it look like?" asked Sam.

"Sort of gelatinous. Pale in color. Seems to almost pulsate. I think it's something alive, like a plant, except I don't know how any plant could survive down here without sunlight."

Sam thought of the strange, gelatinous substance she and Ryan had seen filling the vats in the underground lab.

"All right," she said in what she hoped was a confident sounding voice. "Don't touch it. It could be toxic. Be sure to keep marking your tunnels."

"No problem there, Ma'am. We sure as hell don't want to get lost." He hesitated. "Don't see why anyone would come down here. You sure we're not on a wild goose chase?"

Stefansson took the radio from Sam. "Take it easy, Jonsson. This is a standard search and rescue. Just do your job."

"Yes sir . . . Jonsson out."

"How did he sound to you?" Sam asked.

"A little nervous maybe. This isn't exactly something we do every day. Mostly it's tracking down lost hikers above ground."

She nodded, but she hadn't liked the tenor of Jonsson's voice. There was a whiff of paranoia about it. She remembered the feelings she'd had, as though something was watching her.

They continued on. The vent grew cold and damp, as it had when she was with Ryan. She was certain they'd diverged from the path they'd taken earlier. Still, they were descending and probably getting closer to the Vatnajökull Glacier. If Jon was down here, he had to be hopelessly lost. It would be a miracle if they stumbled upon him.

Suddenly a high whining sound stopped everyone in their tracks.

"What the hell is that?" asked one of the men. "Sounds like a freaking banshee."

Sam listened to the high-pitched sound. "It's no ghost," she said. "My guess is it's a gas release. Hot gas works its way through the rock, until it finds a tiny crevice. Then it releases . . . kind of like Old Faithful in Yellowstone Park." It was as benign and comforting an image as she could conjure up.

As she spoke, the sound died away, but they could smell sulfur. That meant there was a hot spot somewhere nearby, despite the colder temperatures they'd been feeling.

One of Stefansson's men shouted, "Look!"

A split had appeared in the tunnel floor and was widening even as they stared at it. She knew what was going to happen next.

"Go back!" she cried.

The others hardly needed direction, as hot, steaming lava suddenly bubbled up through the rent in the floor.

"Mother of God!" said Stefansson.

"Come on," Sam said. "We're on the upside of it. It would be worse if we had no way to go but down. Gravity would pull the lava after us. We don't know how big a release it will be, but we've got some time." She didn't mention that the gas released by the lava might quickly suffocate them or poison their lungs in the narrow confines of the venthole.

The men scrambled up the sloping tunnel away from the lava that bubbled and poured relentlessly out of the split in the floor, like some great mass of melted fudge. The passageway grew hot from the two-thousand-degree lava, and sweat poured down their faces.

Sam realized now that what they were doing was sheer madness. They were putting all of their lives at risk by trying to save Gudnasson.

"We need to get out of here," she said to Stefansson. "The risk is too great."

"No argument from me," the Sergeant replied.

But then there was a heart-stopping rumble, as the vent ahead of them simply collapsed, blocking their way completely. They were trapped, with the ever-expanding lava inching toward them relentlessly.

Stefansson stared at the blocked tunnel. "The commissioner said you were the expert on this place, Miss Graham. I sure hope he was right."

***

Rashid followed news reports about the earthquake and the stream of aftershocks that had taken place near Laki. At first encouraged by events, he soon grew disillusioned as no evidence of massive eruptions or gas releases was reported. Indeed, the prime minister had appeared on TV to assure citizens that everything was under control.

He knew things might still change for the better, as far as he was concerned, as the blast effects percolated through the substructure of the volcano. But he was impatient. Six months earlier he'd prepared for such a moment. Making the decision had been a process, a combination of opportunity and connections coming together to form the idea. Once the idea had occurred, he'd molded it, turned it around, and looked at it from every angle. He saw nothing but possibility. He would secure a small nuclear device.

Iran had been developing a secret nuclear program for many years. The goal was to create a weapon small enough to transport easily into the heart of a western city, thus bypassing the need for a missile delivery system. Such parameters precisely coordinated with Rashid's own needs. Through his powerful connections, he'd been able to bypass the loose security surrounding the program.

All things considered, it had been surprisingly easy. He'd arranged to import the device into Iceland himself, aboard a small fishing vessel used by IranOil to transport its various operatives in and out of the country without having to deal with the nuisance of customs.

He smiled at the memory and how good it had made him feel to have used Akbari's IranOil network to effect the arrangement.

Qarawi was gone, melting away like the phantom he was, following the blasts. Once the unpleasant fellow had his money, he wouldn't be seen again. There was a market for people like Qarawi, and Rashid knew the man would do what he'd been hired for, setting the blasts on Laki. It was the only way he could ensure his future employment potential. Nevertheless, the result had been a failure.

But Rashid was not without options. Fearing betrayal at every turn, he had insisted on learning how to arm and detonate the nuclear device himself. All he needed was one other man to help transport the weapon, which now sat ready to go in a plain white van parked outside.

That the detonation of such a weapon might turn southern Iceland into a radioactive wasteland was not his concern. Indeed, it might even be a help, preventing government interference and any attempts to stop or channel the release of hydrogen sulfide gas and lava. Once things started, no one would be able to halt the release and he would be able to sit back and watch the world's climate deteriorate and the price of oil skyrocket.

He listened to one final government news bulletin on the conditions at Laki, then turned off the TV, made a quick phone call, and headed for the white van. His new toy was remarkably small and self-contained. Two men could easily carry it underground. Considerable attention had been invested in where to place the device, but in truth the damage would be so enormous that the precise location was hardly an issue. As a practical matter, it would probably be effective if simply left inside the van at the parking lot.

But he wanted more certainty than this. They would take the weapon deep underground, assuring a massive eruption.

Then he would deal with Akbari. The Iranian oil minister had been a thorn for far too long. By rights, following his successful manipulation of world oil markets, Rashid should be the new oil minister. It was a position he had long coveted.

The removal of Akbari was but a small matter compared to the triumph of strategic planning he was about to achieve.

Chapter Sixteen

Shelby Graham sat in the poolroom of the Reykjavik research facility waiting for his briefing on their team's latest medical discoveries. His thoughts turned inevitably to Sam. He was worried about her. Things were heating up since the earthquake, and he had no idea where she was. He hoped Ryan was with her at least.

He felt isolated here. Having entered the country as inconspicuously as possible, at least until that annoying *Wall Street Journal* reporter had showed up, he was now as uncertain about what to do as he'd ever been in his long and successful career. Uncertainty was a new feeling for the senator.

The idea of any sort of harm coming to Sam was something he'd feared with a sense of palpable alarm ever since he'd first held her as a baby. Nothing had ever overcome that feeling. Now, however, he was deeply troubled. For he was committed to . . . fascinated by . . . the idea of an extended life span.

He had a lot more he wanted to do in this world. He wasn't ready to leave it, the more so since his own death would essentially mean the loss of Sam. He wanted to be around to watch her and to oversee her progress in life. The rift that had come between them so many years ago had left him reeling, as Sam left for Europe and her new life. Not to have her in his life was inconceivable. He was convinced that eventually she'd come to see things more clearly, and he fully intended to be around when that happened.

He felt trapped by events. He couldn't slip out of the country now. The earthquakes had placed Iceland at the center of the world stage. Reporters were flowing into the small island nation to report on what was happening. He'd be spotted in a moment if he appeared anywhere in public. Indeed, Charlie Finlay, his chief of staff, had called repeatedly, warning him to keep a low profile. The story that he was on vacation was beginning to strain credulity at home after he missed two important roll call votes.

Ali Akbari entered along with their chief chemist, a worried-looking man in a white coat.

"Tell him what you told me," Akbari said without preamble.

"A man broke into the lab and held me at gunpoint. He wanted to know what we were doing here."

Graham's eyes went wide. "What did you tell him?"

"Anything he wanted to know," the man answered tartly. "I was staring at a loaded gun."

"Can you describe this man?"

Graham listened to the description with growing alarm. There was no question it had been Ryan Baldwin.

"What do we do now?" he asked Akbari.

The oil minister shrugged. "We continue our investigations, of course." He looked at the chemist. "You told this man about the fungus?"

"Yes. He saw the vats. I told him what we thought it was, along with my own speculations about the substance."

"Which are?" asked Graham.

"My personal belief . . . theory . . . if you will, is that this fungus might have a degree of intelligence. I told the man this, but I don't think he believed me. Anyway, I didn't tell him what else we've learned." The man hesitated.

"What?" asked the senator, a feeling of dread coming over him.

"My team decided we should have DNA tests done on the fungus-like material." He shook his head in frustration.

"What then? Out with it," said Akbari. "What did you find?"

"Nothing."

Akbari looked at the man blankly. "Make sense," he said.

"The fungus has no DNA."

The statement was met with silence.

"Don't be ridiculous," said Graham. "Every living thing has DNA. Did you repeat your efforts?"

"Yes, sir. The fungus, whatever it is, is not a living thing. It has no DNA."

"You just said you thought it might be intelligent."

"It appears to act intelligently, yes. It almost seems to communicate with people, by putting thoughts in their heads."

"You mean hallucinations?" Graham asked.

The man looked annoyed. "What's the difference? Thoughts. Hallucinations. It's all the same."

"But . . . but it moves. Pulsates. It must be alive. What inanimate object moves on its own? Something has to be animating it."

"Chemical reactions entail movement," the chemist replied. "Outside forces cause things to move as well, gravity, magnetic fields, changing temperatures, the pressure of gas releases. Any of these could be causing the fungus to pulsate."

"Stop calling it a fungus," said Graham, his frustration building. "If it has no DNA, it's not alive. It's something else."

"What?"

"How the hell should I know? Part of Laki. A manifestation of the volcano."

"Jesus!" The chemist stared at him. "That better not reach the press. They'll skewer you—or worse—they'll believe it. I can see the headlines. Volcano lives! Scientists say.

Graham wasn't concerned about the press. "What have you learned about the longevity effect?"

"Only that it's real. No question. Something gave those Vikings extended life spans. And whatever it was, it has also affected people on the ground . . . or under the ground. Some sort of vitalization takes place. We haven't been able to determine what it is."

"I want to experience it for myself," Graham said, his frustration palpable. "You haven't come up with any answers. Well, then, I want to *feel* it. I'm going to Laki."

"That's not possible," said Akbari. "Aside from the dangers associated with the earthquakes, we've learned that Rashid plans to set off a nuclear device to enhance the effects of his explosions."

Graham stared at him. "You can't be serious! It will destroy everything."

"My men are looking for him. But we believe he may already be preparing to set off his device."

"For God's sake, we've got to stop him!" Graham looked physically ill.

"There's something else," said Akbari. "The police have announced the closing of the southern Ring Road and the Laki Preserve area. No civilians are being permitted to go there."

"I'm no goddamned civilian!" Graham fumed. The thought of a nuclear explosion had placed another fear in his heart—that Sam might be on Laki herself.

***

The senator sat alone in the empty lounge of the Reykjavik facility. Akbari had bowed to his demands and left to arrange for a helicopter to take them to the volcano.

His thoughts whirled. Where was Sam? His plans for an extended lifespan had long been a dream. But if anything happened to her . . . he didn't want to live forever in a world without Sam.

He heard a sound and turned.

Ryan stood behind him. In one hand, he held a pistol, which he slowly lowered to his side.

Graham half stood, then fell back into his chair. "What the hell are you doing here, Baldwin? Why aren't you with Sam?"

"I came to find out what you know," Ryan said, moving forward.

"Where's Sam?"

"You could say she's in good hands. She's with a dozen of Commissioner Dagursson's men. Except . . . " He glanced at his watch. "By now they're on Laki, searching for an employee of mine who went there."

This time Graham stood up. "She can't be there," he said. "It's too dangerous. Goddamn you, Baldwin! How could you let her go there?"

"You've known how dangerous Laki is for some time, Senator. And despite your efforts to get Sam away from Iceland, she's still here. I don't think you give a damn. You've got your own agenda."

The senator stared at him. Ryan could see a swirl of emotions cross his face. He suddenly looked a lot older—like a man who could use a dose of longevity.

Graham's shoulders slumped. "You're right. I've chased the phantom of extended life for most of my political career. You don't know . . . . Scientists are close, Baldwin. Much closer than they were forty years ago. Then it was just a fantasy. But I still managed to get increased funding for longevity research.

"Now they're closing in on many possible solutions. Diet restriction, hormonal treatments, drugs like resveratrol, gene manipulation. Do you know they've tripled the life spans of round-worms by altering a single gene? One gene. The same with fruit flies and mice. Have you heard of GDF-eleven? It's a protein that's abundant in the blood of young mice and scarce in old ones. They concentrated the protein and injected it into old mice. It rejuvenated them, their muscle tissue, their hearts. The neurons in their brains sprouted new connections. Scientists aren't just slowing down the clock Baldwin, they're turning it back! There's a research center . . . highly classified . . . outside Reno, Nevada, where they've extended the lives of rats a dozen fold. A dozen fold! Think what that means."

"Probably means a hell of a lot of rats," said Ryan.

"It means humans could live for a thousand years!"

"Might cause some problems with the earth's carrying capacity," Ryan said. "How many children could a person have in a thousand

years?" He stared at Graham. "But of course, you don't expect everyone to live that long, do you? Just those who can afford it, right?
The cream of the crop."

"You don't understand," Graham said stubbornly. "When I
learned about the extended lives of those ancient Norse, I realized
something was happening on Laki that could be a major break-
through. This is important for the species."

"And what about the importance of Sam?"

He lowered his head. "I've worried about her every day of her
life. She resisted my efforts to protect her from the time she was in
high school. Earlier than that, even. As the child of a politician, she
was at greater risk. I thought I was doing what a father is supposed
to do. Protect his little girl."

"Well, now you've got the opportunity to really do that," Ryan
said. "For the first time, she really does need your help. Are you going
to answer that call when it's not a fantasy? When it's real?"

Akbari strode into the room. "The helicopter will be here in
twenty minutes . . . ." He stopped as he registered the presence of
the other man.

Ryan raised his pistol and pointed it at the Arab. "Why don't
you sit down until our transportation gets here?" he said easily.

***

"You may go in now, Commissioner," said the prime minister's
secretary.

Dagursson rose heavily from his chair. He'd been waiting for
twenty minutes and every second felt like a waste of crucial time.
He'd been out of touch with his men on Laki for too long.

He entered the room and stopped abruptly. The prime minister,
tall, silver-haired, deeply tanned, had discarded his jacket and rolled
up the sleeves of his shirt, revealing that the tan extended at least
that far. The man had to use either a tanning booth or coloration.
There was no other way in Iceland. In a chair in front of him sat Eva.

"I believe you two know each other," said the PM. "Good. It will save time, which we may not have a whole lot of." He turned to Eva. "Tell the commissioner what you told me."

Eva looked haggard. She hadn't slept in two days as she struggled over what course to take with the information she'd uncovered.

"In examining records of land purchases—rather—mineral rights in the Laki area, I discovered that the subterranean rights to a great deal of land have been purchased by a German holding company. After considerable digging and talking with some contacts I have in Germany, I now know who the owner of those rights is."

Dagursson waited.

"It's the German Catholic Church. Specifically, the Conference of German Bishops."

Dagursson looked stunned. "The church? Why . . . ."

The PM interrupted. He glanced at his watch. "In a few moments, I'm going to have a visitor. Which is why I called you in, Commissioner."

"Who is that, sir?"

"Cardinal Wormer from Germany."

Dagursson looked from Eva to the PM and back again. "I'm afraid I don't understand what this is all about. But I want to emphasize that I might be making better use of my time by going to Laki, where my men are right now at great risk exploring the subterranean depths . . . searching for your colleague, I might add, Eva."

A buzzer sounded on the prime minister's desk. He leaned over and pushed a button.

"Cardinal Wormer is here to see you, sir."

"Send him in," said the PM. "We'll get to the bottom of this one way or the other."

Cardinal Wormer was a lean man of about sixty with a humorless visage and eyes that shifted back and forth among the room's occupants. He moved with deliberation, as though carrying a great weight on his shoulders. The robes of his office flowed around him. A three-inch silver cross hung from his neck. He stopped in front of the PM's desk and bowed slightly from the waist.

"Good of you to see me, Mr. Prime Minister, on such short notice."

The prime minister stood and came around his desk to shake the man's hand. "A great pleasure, Cardinal. I confess I was surprised to learn of your request for a meeting. What can I do for you?"

The Cardinal lowered himself into a chair. "Perhaps it is more a question of what we can do for each other," he said.

Eva was beside herself with curiosity. "Why is the German Catholic Church buying up land rights beneath Laki?" she asked without preamble.

The Cardinal gave her a long, cold look. "That is a little-known fact. May I ask how you came by this information?"

"It's a matter of public record," said Eva. "And I poked around some more on my own."

"I see." Cardinal Wormer seemed to consider something for a moment. Then he said, "Since I was elevated to Cardinal, I am, of course, no longer a member of the German Conference of Bishops . . . though they ask my advice from time to time. Perhaps you will permit me to relate a bit of theological history."

Dagursson rolled his eyes. With everything going on, all he needed was a lesson in theology. He looked at his watch. Cardinal or no Cardinal, if this went on more than ten minutes, he was out of here.

"Christianity has a long history in Iceland," Wormer began. "Celtic hermits were the first to set foot in the frozen land, seeking a safe haven where they could worship Christ. They were driven out by Norse settlers, some Christian but mostly heathen, worshipping the old Norse gods. Iceland was constituted as a republic in nine thirty AD, based on the heathen religion. But by the late nine hundreds, missionaries from the continent . . . including some from Germany I might add . . . sought to spread Christianity among the local population.

"There was resistance to the spread of the Catholic faith and the country was on the brink of civil war. To avoid this catastrophe, the two groups agreed to abide by the decision of a man respected for his wisdom by everyone. He was the heathen priest and chieftain known as Porgeir of Ljosavatn. After a long day of meditating, Porgeir declared that the "land shall be Christian and believe in one God."

Dagursson fidgeted. "I'm sorry, Cardinal. Is there a point here somewhere?"

Wormer considered him with a level gaze. "While this decision marks the beginning of the church in Iceland, there was a . . . faction . . . that refused to give up the old Norse gods. The sagas speak of them. A group of early Norse who lived on the southern coast, in the shadow of Laki, refused to convert. They claimed that the spirit of Laki was all-powerful and would never tolerate the rise of another god."

"Excuse me, Cardinal, but isn't this all basically oral history?" said Dagursson. "We know that the sagas were largely fantasy. And in any case, what does this have to do with our current problem?"

"Fantasy? I hardly think so," said Wormer. "The church has spent many years researching this. I seriously doubt anyone knows more about the early religious history of Iceland than the German Conference of Bishops. Members of the Conference believe that those early heathens encountered something on Laki. Something that has come down to us today. Part of this history also took form during the second world war."

He paused for a moment, then continued, his face grim as if resigned to the effect his words would have. "There is a presence under the earth, a power if you will, that results in a sort of vitalization . . . call it life extension if you wish. Those early Norse may have been the first to experience it, but the Nazis also came under its influence."

The room was so silent that Eva could hear the clicking of the computer keys of the PM's secretary in the next room.

The Cardinal shifted in his chair for the first time. He placed his hands together and stared at the floor. "There is, we believe, a spiritual presence beneath the volcano of Laki, one that may have bided its time for a very long period. Indeed, it may be older than the church itself . . . perhaps many thousands of years older. But it has come awake now. It has real power and the church fears what it may mean to the future of religion as we know it."

Eva said, "You want us to believe the Catholic Church is afraid of some heathen god from a thousand years ago? Excuse me, but that's not credible."

Wormer spread his hands. "What is religion after all but a promise? A promise to believers that they will go to a better place once they leave this temporary state we live in. If the promise of everlasting life can be found here and now . . . well . . . ." His eyes shifted from one to another of the faces looking at him. "To put it another way, perhaps more bluntly, religion is born out of fear. Fear of death, fear of retribution, fear of the unknown, fear of Hell. Fear keeps the faithfuls' . . . attention . . . if you will. Remove the fear . . ." he spread his hands. "What does religion have left to offer?"

"My God," said Eva, "That's the most cynical view of religion I've ever heard."

The prime minister leaned forward. "What do *you* think lies beneath Laki, Cardinal?"

The man's eyes grew inward, as though he were seeing a vision that haunted the darkest part of his soul. "I believe it is something evil . . . something that must be resisted. The very home of Lucifer himself."

Dagursson snorted. "Why must it be the devil? Simply because it's offering something you can't? A longer, healthier existence in the here and now instead of waiting for the next life. I'm not surprised you're fearful of it taking your place. Maybe that force *is* a god . . . just not *your* god. Personally, I'm inclined to believe it's something in the natural environment, maybe something that gives a boost to the immune system. That makes as much sense as anything. Besides, we're not talking about eternal life here. You seen any of those ancient Vikings walking around lately? They died just like the rest of us are going to."

"Perhaps what you say is true," the Cardinal replied. "But this is no longer my theory alone or even that of the German Conference of Bishops. It has grown larger than that. At the end of the second world war, there was structured, in secret, a council of all major religions to study and resist this evil force."

The PM looked stunned. "You mean to tell us that religions all over the world are fearful of some spirit lurking beneath one of our volcanoes? What is Laki for god's sake? Some sort of Lourdes? If that's the case, maybe we can rebuild our economy on religious tourism."

"I am here only to warn you," said Wormer.

"Warn us? Of what?"

"Warn you that the spirit of Laki may not react kindly to interference. The earthquakes may be a sign of that. Certainly, whatever we are talking about protected the Vikings . . . for a time at least. But it drove the Nazis away with hallucinations and irrational fears."

Dagursson stared at him. "And now it may be reacting to other interference . . . from the Iranians, perhaps? Is that what you think?"

"The volcano has not been happy lately," said Wormer.

***

The small group of police officers sat on the tunnel floor, staring in horror at the bubbling lava less than fifty feet away. While more of the fudge-like mass continued to rise from the split in the passageway, the pace of the lava seemed to have arrested, as most of it was pulled by gravity away from them.

"It's stopped coming this way," said one of the men to no one in particular.

"Well that's just bloody terrific," said another. "But we're still not going anywhere. We can't go back and we sure as hell can't go down that passage. We're dead men."

Sam felt their frustration. Indeed, she felt responsible for having gotten them into this mess. Stefansson's words, that she was the expert on this place, rang painfully in her ears.

Several of the men had begun to cough repeatedly. The heat and gas from the lava were beginning to affect them. With no source of fresh air, she knew they had little time before the hot lava would exhaust the oxygen in the tunnel, if they weren't asphyxiated first by the gases.

But there was simply no solution . . . no answer. Some expert she was. They were all looking to her and they were all going to die.

"See if you can raise Jonsson on your radio," she said. "At least we can tell them to get out of here as fast as they can."

The Sergeant nodded and began to call. For all the hopelessness of their predicament, he remained calm. He was a brave man.

Then Jonsson's voice entered their blisteringly hot tunnel. Before Stefansson could declare their entrapment, Jonsson was yelling.

"Sergeant! We need help!"

Sam grabbed the radio. "Jonsson—get out of there! Any way you can. This place is too unstable. The search and rescue is canceled. We're trapped and cannot offer assistance."

There was a moment of static. Then Jonsson's reply came loud and clear. "Something's killing my men! It's these tentacles. They've overrun our position. They're all around us."

Sam and the others listened as screams penetrated their tunnel via the radio. They could hear men shouting and then gunfire.

Stefansson took the radio from Sam. "Jonsson, report! What's happening?"

"We're shooting at it!" came the reply. "But it's not helping. It's everywhere. There are only two of us left."

"How is it killing your men?" shouted Stefansson.

"I . . . I don't know. The tentacles just seem to ensnare them and cover them until we can't see them anymore. They . . . they become throbbing masses of . . . whatever this thing is. Like they're absorbed somehow."

There was another burst of gunfire, a man screamed and then the radio went dead.

They sprawled on the tunnel floor, stunned by what they'd just heard. Most of them believed they were as good as dead. Their last hope had been some sort of rescue by the other group. Now that was gone.

Stefansson threw the radio aside and asked, "Any suggestions, Miss Graham?" Most of the men were now wheezing from the depleting oxygen and the gas from the lava. They had little time left.

Sam stood and played her light across the roof of the tunnel near where the obstruction had collapsed. There had been weakness in the structure there. That meant there might be more weak sections. She picked up a rock and began hammering it against the walls on all sides. Stefansson looked at her as if she'd lost her mind.

"What the hell are you doing?" he asked.

"Looking for a weak spot." She worked her way along one wall and then across to the other side. She began reaching up as high as she could to test the roof of the tunnel.

Sweat was pouring off all of them. She couldn't guess how hot it was inside the tunnel, but it was reaching intolerable levels. Suddenly, her rock thrusts above her head were met with a hollow sound.

"There!" She yelled. "Everyone back away from this spot."

The men did as they were told.

"Now, use your firearms," she ordered. "Concentrate your fire at that section of rock where it made the hollow sound."

They all thought she was mad, but Stefansson pulled his pistol and nodded.

Bullets ricocheted around them like flies around a honey pot. It was a miracle no one was hit. But then, another miracle occurred. The section of ceiling simply collapsed and they were staring into a new vent opening that ran upward at a steep angle.

The sudden opening introduced a new source of oxygen and they all breathed deeply of the elixir, but it also gave new life to the hot lava, which began to glow more fiercely and start to issue more quickly from the hole in the floor. It began to fill the tunnel, searing its way toward them rapidly. The temperature was blistering.

"Come on!" Sam cried. "Sergeant, lift me up."

Stefansson grabbed her foot and heaved her into the new opening. Then he leaped after her, turned, and reached for the first of his men. But the floor of the tunnel, weakened perhaps by the hot lava, suddenly collapsed. The remaining police officers vanished into a cauldron of lava far below. Stefansson stared at the vacant spot that had held his men only an instant before. He'd been unable to save even one of them.

Sam crouched beside him, one hand on his shoulder. She could feel his whole body slump.

"I'm sorry, Sergeant," she said. Then, "We've got to keep going. I don't think the lava will rise through the vent—at least not quickly. We have some time."

Stefansson turned away slowly, something indefinable in his eyes. There were just the two of them now.

The venthole sloped at a thirty-degree angle, but the sides were rough and it was not hard to scramble upward. The heat continued to rise with them, like a thermal moving up the side of a mountain. But after they'd crawled several hundred yards, they could feel the temperature begin to dissipate.

"Let's rest a moment," said Sam.

They slumped to the floor. Sergeant Stefansson's eyes were blank and unfocused. He'd lost his entire command in the most horrible way imaginable. Sam could see that he was beginning to close down and realized she had to snap him out of it if they were to have any chance to survive.

"Sergeant!" She got right in front of him. "You've still got a job to do. We need to get out of here and warn the others that this whole area is dangerously unstable."

"Unstable?" Stefansson looked at her blankly. "Jonsson said something was killing his men. You heard them shooting and screaming. What the hell happened to them?"

"I don't know," she said. "But I sure as hell want to find out. Do you? Or are we just going to give up and wait to be killed by whatever got the others?"

Stefansson shook himself. His eyes refocused from the image of the horrible end his men had suffered.

"I want to know, goddamn it," he said in a low voice.

"All right. We're going to get out of here and we're going to do something about this."

***

Jon felt the fear seeping into every pore of his being. What the hell was he doing down here anyway? Damn Eva! This was her doing. She'd wanted to get rid of him. She knew she was sending him to his death. Everyone at the firm had been out to get him. It was all part of a plot.

His fear was manifest. Even Kraus could detect that something was wrong with his companion.

"What is it?" Kraus asked without looking back. They had to keep moving. Who knew how long the light from the tentacles would last?

"We can't just keep letting these things determine where we go," said Jon. "They're taking us deeper. We need to go up."

Kraus stopped. In the dim, phosphorescent light, Jon's eyes seemed to glow. They were round and panic-stricken.

"What do you recommend, my friend?" the German asked in a quiet voice.

"Why do I have to do all the thinking?" said Jon. "Any idiot can tell we're being herded like cattle. Can't you see? They want us to go lower. That's where they're waiting for us."

Kraus considered the geologist. The man was showing real signs of paranoia. Of course, fearing for their lives under the current circumstances probably wasn't exactly unreasonable. Still, it wasn't helpful to run around screaming, "We're all going to die!"

"Who, Jon? Who is waiting for us?"

"These damn tentacles! I tell you they're herding us somewhere."

"Well," Kraus continued to speak in a level tone. "I'm open to suggestions, Jon. We don't have a lot of choices here. We can't go back to where Ernst fell through, and all the branch tunnels have been covered with tentacles. We can only go in the direction left open to us. Is that not clear?"

"No, goddamn it! We're going to make our own choices from now on."

Jon picked up a large rock and threw it at the accumulation of tentacles that blocked the most recent branch passage. Then he ran at the mass and began to tear at the pulsating, gooey substance. But as fast as he tore an opening, the tentacles filled it in even faster. Soon, pieces began to stick to him.

"Stop it!" Kraus yelled. He pulled Gudnasson away from the mass of throbbing tentacles and began to rip away the pieces that had stuck to him. For a moment, he thought he might lose the battle. But the branches seemed to lose their tenacity once they were separated from the main body.

Jon slumped to the ground, shuddering, and began to help Hans pull the remaining bits away. Finally, he was free, except for being covered in a sticky sort of glue left behind.

He looked sheepish. For the moment, the paranoia had dissipated. "Sorry," he mumbled. "Guess I lost it."

Kraus gave him a smile. "For sure, we are in a tight spot. Enough to make anyone . . . lose it, as you say. When my turn comes, I will count on your help."

The words seemed to buck his companion up, but Kraus was not at all confident he'd be able to count on this man when the time came. Jon was weak and not the sort of partner he'd have chosen to face such a challenge. He helped Gudnasson to his feet.

"We must keep moving," he said. "If these things want us to go lower, there has to be a reason. The sooner we find out what it is, the better it will be. I for one would rather know than not know."

Jon nodded glumly.

The tentacles lining the cave walls were now thick as a man's arm and gave off enough light to allow them to see clearly. Indeed, the pulsating quality of the branches made them appear almost like muscular arms, flexing and extending.

"It's as though they understand what they're doing to us," Jon said, plaintively.

"I agree, my friend. There appears to be some guiding force behind them. It is not like they are simply plants. I get the distinct feeling there's a method behind every move."

"But why?" Jon asked. "Why us? What did we do?"

Hans shrugged. "We are here."

"Well, I'm perfectly willing NOT to be here. Why won't they just let us go if they don't want us here?"

"Perhaps that is too advanced a way of thinking. Beyond them. Like fire ants faced with some animal digging into their hill. The ants would rather the creature not do that and go away. But they're not going to leave it alone. They will attack and keep on attacking until they kill it."

"Jesus!" Jon said.

"Jesus has nothing to do with it," replied the German.

Jon just stared at him.

"Whatever we are facing," said Kraus, "it is the opposite, the antithesis of Christ. It is why the Conference of Bishops has invested so much of itself in trying to determine what is really down here."

"You're talking nonsense. Fire and brimstone, end-of-the-world fantasy. If you think Lucifer is down here somewhere, you're even crazier than I thought."

Kraus considered him. "It is your belief then, that all this is simply the result of some natural phenomenon?"

"Yes," Jon said stubbornly.

"Well, I certainly hope you are right. In any event, we must keep going—wherever it is that the tentacles wish us to go—I see no alternative."

They stood and began to trudge slowly along the tunnel, in the only direction open to them, lower. Each man retreated to thoughts guided by his own beliefs. Kraus relied upon faith and prayer. Jon, with little to support him other than reason, couldn't suppress the fear. And as they moved lower, the paranoia returned.

***

Professor Hauptmann gazed upon the pile of student papers and scowled. Students seemed to get dumber every year. It was a wonder his own mind hadn't atrophied from having to read such drivel.

He got up, paced around the desk to his office door, closed it firmly, and locked it. He was due for student advising in half an hour. To hell with them. He had more important fish to fry.

He took a pair of white linen gloves out of a box and pulled them on. Then carefully, almost lovingly, he unlocked a drawer in his desk and removed an ancient ledger. He laid it gently on top of the desk and opened the book.

This was his latest discovery, mined from the extensive archives of the university. It was a copy of the Heimskringla, the Icelandic sagas of the Norse kings that explained in pagan terms how the world was created.

He was familiar with the text, of course, written down by Snorri Sturlason, poet, lawyer, and lawspeaker of the Althing in Iceland in the late twelfth and early thirteenth centuries. It had long been known to scholars, and of course no one agreed as to what extent the text was accurate. Like all of the sagas, it related epic events that had occurred hundreds of years before they were recorded.

He knew the tortured early history of the work. The original manuscript was not known. The oldest extant copy of the Heimskringla was believed to have been written about 1260. In the sixteenth century, it was in Norway. It moved to Copenhagen in 1633 and was destroyed by the fire of 1728. By then, fortunately, it had been copied several times.

It was one of these early copies that had come to the university, though no one seemed clear on precisely how. No matter. What was important was that he, Ernst Hauptmann, historian extraordinaire, had made a significant discovery. Once his findings were published, he would become famous. No doubt about it. For now, however, there was wondrous fantasy in knowing something no one else in the world knew.

After years of studying the ancient book, he'd become increasingly frustrated by a break, an unexplained gap in the narrative. The gap was well known to experts. It made no sense. A line of text simply stopped and when the page was turned, the next line did not follow in context. None of the other extant copies of the Heimskringla contained the gap, suggesting something unique about the university's copy.

Numerous scholarly papers had been written about this phenomenon, trying to explain the gap. But none had ever done so to Hauptman's satisfaction.

The pages were of ancient vellum. The finest goatskin. Very delicate now, and it was necessary to handle them oh so carefully. Which was why no one had ever discovered what he had. To his carefully gloved hands, the page he had turned so many times seemed slightly more dense than the others. It was an almost indefinable thing. But one day he had decided to see if his suspicion might be accurate.

Using a special chemical bath and a commercial steamer, he spent long hours very gently treating the page. If anyone ever learned what he'd done, he might well have been refused permission to ever handle ancient texts again. Such treatment was sacrilege. He'd worked only on weekends, his office door locked and barricaded. Ever so slowly, an edge appeared where there had once been but a single page. It took three months to totally separate the pages.

But at last he was confronted with something extraordinary. Several completely new, never before seen, pages of text, deep in the heart of the Heimskringla that had been stuck together for centuries.

The first of the newly discovered pages was a continuation of the previous text and of little interest, mentioning mundane events in the life of one of the more obscure kings, as it did in the other extant copies of the rare book. But now there was an explanation for the famous gap. For the newly revealed pages had never before been seen.

The pages stunned him. It had taken many months to fully translate and understand them. The text further related the story of Amma, the Norse Holy Woman or shaman who had lived with her clan on the southern coast of Iceland in the tenth century. This was the same Amma about whom Hauptmann had previously found an unknown saga, in which the old woman related how unrest had come to her clan after many years of peace.

Now, Hauptmann read, his face inches from the aging vellum, as Amma related how her clan had come under attack from *strange beasts that creep upon the tunnel walls.*

The fears that infected Amma and her family leaped from the page. Their terror drove them underground. Paradoxically, they attempted to escape from the gods of Laki by retreating even further underground.

Their solution to the problem facing them seemed irrational. If the beasts came from beneath the Earth, why go lower still to escape from them? Amma's words grew increasingly paranoid as it became clear she was growing delusional, insisting that her family go ever deeper in order to escape what obviously emanated from the depths.

Here they were attacked by the *beasts* that crawled the walls. She told how their greatest warrior, Afastr, fought the strange attackers and how, for a time, they broke through to a lower level.

At this point in the incredible tale, Hauptmann paused, as he always did. For he didn't understand what Amma said next. He had translated the passage and translated it again, but still it made no sense. His best interpretation was that the clan had come upon:

A hole at the center of the earth. A hole filled with stars.

He shook his head in frustration. The words were inscrutable. Had Amma succumbed completely to delusion? It seemed likely, except for the fact that the Holy Woman went on to finish the narrative seemingly in control of her thoughts. She told of returning from the depths and of a pact between the family members to seal themselves in and die as one, on their own terms.

Ernst stared at the ancient pages of vellum. He needed to talk to someone. To Sam. They had been friends and sometime colleagues for many years. Her insights concerning the volcano of Laki were profound. Perhaps the strange words of Amma would mean something to her.

But he'd been unable to contact her. He was not completely cut off in his ivory tower. He knew what was happening, that the earthquakes had caused significant damage and even panic among some in Reykjavik. He hoped Sam was all right. There was no one else he could talk to about this. Not if he wanted to keep his academic and publishing intentions intact.

Someone must know where Sam was. If he could only find her friend, what was his name? Baldwin. Maybe he should go to the police, claiming he was worried about them. Yes. That was it. The authorities would know. He'd read in the paper that Sam had been detained. Maybe they still had her in custody. They would know where she was.

Chapter Seventeen

The Oval Office
Washington D.C.

Charles Finlay, Chief of Staff for Senate Majority Leader Shelby Graham, waited anxiously for entrée to the Oval Office. He knew why President Thurman had summoned him. He knew exactly what the President was going to ask him. What he didn't know was the answer to the question.

The secretary looked at him. She'd said something he hadn't registered. "You may go in *now*, Mr. Finlay."

He hated the new headphones used by the President's aides. They were all wired in together. No buzzer, no office intercom. Just a headset and a silent communication. He preferred to hear when a message was being transmitted, instead of this sudden, silent directive.

The President met him at the door. There were two other men sitting on the sofa in front of the fireplace. Finlay recognized both of them: Grant Lyndaker, Secretary of Energy, and Prescott Carlisle, the President's Science Advisor.

"Charlie," said President Thurman. "Good to see you. Thanks for coming over."

"My pleasure, sir. Always at your disposal."

The President was a Republican. Family money had essentially purchased the office for him six years ago. He liked to pretend he'd worked his way up, and in a sense he had, from mayor of Cincinnati to congressman to senator. But the money scared off any real competition. He'd never had an opponent who garnered more than thirty percent of the vote.

"I wasn't happy about my education bill, Charlie," President Thurman said, immediately broaching the question Finlay had anticipated. "We knew it was going to be close in the Senate. Frankly, I find it inexplicable that Senator Graham missed the vote."

Finlay sat across from Lyndaker and Carlisle, nodding briefly to both men. "Sir, I confess it's as much a mystery to me as it is to you. The senator has taken some personal time lately. I think it has something to do with his daughter, but I really don't know. I believe he may be out of the country."

"Damn right he is," said the President. "I had to set my people to find out where he went. He's in Iceland. You trying to tell me you knew nothing about that?"

Finlay squirmed. Shelby hadn't taken him into his confidence. It was clear, however, that the President knew a great deal more about what was going on than he did.

"I confess, Sir, I didn't know where the senator was."

The President cocked his head at the other men in the room and raised an eyebrow. "So you're out of the loop, eh, Charlie? Hard to be a Chief of Staff sometimes. Have you at least heard about the earthquakes in that country?"

"Of course, Sir." The news had gone worldwide very quickly.

The President sat in an oversized wing chair and crossed his legs. He picked at an imaginary spot on his pants. "Why don't you bring Mr. Finlay up to date, Grant," he said.

"Since the first quake in Iceland," said Lyndaker, "we've been recording the aftershocks. Quite a few. Actually, they've been almost continuous. Indeed, we've confirmed a worldwide confluence of seismic activity all seeming to radiate out from Iceland."

Finlay's mouth broke into a frown. "That would seem highly unusual," he said, a baffled look on his face.

"The U.S. weather service has also recorded unusual weather patterns and temperatures," Lyndaker went on. "Something seems to be precipitating a rapid change in the normal cycles across the Northern hemisphere. Our temperature gauges have recorded fluctuations as well in oceanic temperatures and levels."

Finlay was well aware of the many possible causes of climate change. "Has there been the collapse of a major ice sheet somewhere?" he asked.

"Our first thought. We checked satellite pictures, however, and there has been no such collapse. Both the seismic activity and the unusual weather phenomena seem to be focused in the deep ocean off Iceland." He looked at the President, who nodded almost imperceptibly.

Science Advisor Prescott Carlisle took over. Finlay knew Carlisle by reputation only. He'd been a highly regarded astrophysicist before coming to work for the President. He was a stooped, bookish-looking fellow wearing a traditional dark blue suit with a shirt open at the collar. Maybe advisors didn't have to wear ties as Cabinet members did.

"We've also detected a surplus of particles from space invading Earth's atmosphere," Carlisle said. "Electrons in higher numbers than usual, as well as two unexpected patches of high-energy protons."

Finlay looked from Carlisle to the President and back again. His confusion was evident.

Carlisle continued. "The Earth is being bombarded with high-energy cosmic rays from an undetected source. No one knows where these rays come from or how they are generated. Many different theories have been put forth: pulsars, shock waves from supernovas, even dark matter. Finding a specific source is almost impossible because the magnetic fields of the Earth and the galaxy mix up the flight paths of the particles, almost like they were scrambled in a Mixmaster, making it impossible to trace their trajectories back to the source."

"Let's try to keep it simple for us non-eggheads, Prescott," said the President.

Carlisle tilted his head slightly. "We believe the excess protons may be produced near a black hole. The electron spike could come from a nearby pulsar or microquasar. Another possibility is that the electrons were created by dark matter."

"Dark matter?" asked Finlay.

"Dark matter is believed to make up eighty-five percent of the universe's mass, though we really don't know *what* it's made of." Carlisle hesitated, looking at the President. "Here's where it gets a *little* complicated. One prime candidate for dark matter includes WIMPs—weakly interacting massive particles. Two WIMPs colliding would produce a peak in the electron energy spectrum. Such a bump in the spectrum creates a signature that would emerge if a WIMP known as a Kaluza-Klein particle was a primary dark matter component."

"You're losing me, Prescott," said the President.

"Sorry, Mr. President. Let me just say that if Kaluza-Klein particles are real, they would owe their existence to 'additional' dimensions beyond the three we are familiar with. The particles would travel in the extra dimensions, but collisions would cause electrons and positrons to spit out and travel through our ordinary dimensions where they can be detected."

"Frankly," Lyndaker interrupted, "we were wondering what Senator Graham might know about all of this, Charlie."

Finlay looked from one man to the other. "Gentlemen, I've known the senator a long time. He's a smart guy, but he knows as little about—what did you call them—Kaluza-something particles, as I do. Why would you think otherwise?"

"Because," said the President. "As near as Prescott's eggheads can determine, the cosmic bombardment seems to center along the Mid-Atlantic Ridge, seemingly connecting with the recent volcanic activity in Iceland. It's a fair coincidence, wouldn't you say, that this is where Senator Graham appears to have decamped just as his vote was needed?" He leaned forward, his dark eyes boring into the bewildered face of Charles Finlay. "What the bloody hell is your boss up to?" he asked.

"I really don't know what to say, Mr. President."

Thurman stared at him, trying to read whether he was telling the truth. Then he looked at Carlisle. "I want you to put together a team, Prescott, go to Iceland and find out what in blue blazes is going on."

"Yes, sir. Uh, what about the government over there?"

"I've talked with their prime minister. He welcomes our assistance. I guess the whole place is in a panic. First the financial crisis and now earthquakes, eruptions, I don't know what all. You'll get complete cooperation. PM's worried about reelection."

"And what about Senator Graham?"

"He's already missed the vote on my education bill, so who gives a shit about him? If he's connected to this in some way, I'll nail his hide up on the wall of the Lincoln bedroom. You hear from him, Charlie, you can tell him that. Son of a bitch is getting senile if you ask me. I think his incessant exercising and preening about his physique and all the bloody vitamins he takes was just an effort to mask his mental decline."

Finlay looked shocked. The senator's fixation on health and longevity research was well known. The man had been at it for forty years. But his chief of staff was now as curious as the President as to what his boss was up to. He stood up.

"I'll certainly pass your message along, Sir, if the opportunity presents itself."

"You run across the man, you have my permission to piss on him!" said the President.

***

Ali Akbari considered the man who had invited him to sit. Then he focused on the gun the man held. He sat.

"What's going on?" he asked Senator Graham. "Who is this?"

Graham waved a hand. "Ryan Baldwin. He's . . . uh . . . an employee of mine."

"Clearly you aren't paying him enough," said Akbari. "Would you like to work for me, Mr. Baldwin? I'll pay double whatever the senator is paying."

"So far, no one's paid me anything," said Ryan. "Though the senator has threatened to destroy my business."

"What business would that be?" Akbari asked.

"Thermal energy."

The Arab stared at him with a puzzled expression.

"Mr. Baldwin tends to abide by his own rules," said Graham. "He's an . . . independent contractor."

"I don't understand," said Akbari. "What do you want?"

"Right now?" Ryan looked at his watch. "Right now I want to go to Laki."

Graham sighed. "I hired him to protect my daughter. She's on the volcano."

"Ah," Akbari smiled as if some great truth had finally been revealed. "The annoying Miss Samantha Graham. Hmm. Perhaps we should join forces." He looked at Graham. "Does he know about Rashid?"

The senator shook his head.

Akbari looked like he felt more in control now. "We may be on the same side at this juncture, Mr. Baldwin. You wish to protect the senator's daughter. We wish to . . . dissuade . . . Rashid from his rash course of action."

A light went on in Ryan's head. "You're the Iranian minister of oil," he said. "I thought you looked familiar. Somehow I don't see us being on the same side of much."

"Actually, if you wish to protect Miss Graham, we may be. Rashid is something of a rogue in the energy business. Not unlike yourself. He plans to set off a nuclear device beneath Laki."

Ryan stared at the Arab. His mouth had turned desert dry. He felt a cold finger of sweat trace slowly down his side. The Iranians had already destabilized Laki. Now, it appeared, they were about to up the ante.

"Are you all completely insane?" he asked.

"There's a great deal at stake, Mr. Baldwin," said Akbari. "Perhaps the future of the human race will be affected by what's happening on Laki. The senator understands. He's been a longtime advocate for longevity issues."

Ryan shook his head. "I think the longevity thing is a red herring. It all comes down to money with you guys in the end."

"Money will be made, no question about it. But I admit I wouldn't be averse to living for a thousand years. Would you? Rashid, on the other hand, is only interested in money. By causing Laki to erupt he hopes to alter world climate, making it much colder, thus increasing the value of his oil holdings."

"And yours, I would imagine," said Ryan.

"The plan is a fantasy. It will never work. But it does stand a good chance of destroying whatever is causing the longevity effect. The senator wouldn't like that. I wouldn't like that. The government of Iceland wouldn't like it if their popular tourist destinations in the south were to be made radioactive for thousands of years."

Akbari looked up as they all heard the arrival of the helicopter. He cocked an eyebrow at Baldwin.

"I don't know which of you is crazier," said Ryan. "But once we're on Laki, I suspect we'll find out."

***

Ryan stared down at the blasted landscape below. It looked different from the last time he was here. Now, steam vented from a hundred different locations. A new lava flow had emerged and begun to flow down the western slope. It moved like a river of liquid butterscotch, golden in color, as it wound its way into the valley.

Sam was somewhere down in that haunted landscape, along with a dozen police officers, Jon Gudnasson, and maybe even a lunatic named Rashid. Soon, the United States Senate majority leader, the Iranian minister of oil and one very tired ex-Secret Service agent would be added to the mix.

"Hard to believe anything could be alive down there," said Graham, staring at the chaos below. "Let alone beneath the surface."

"She's alive," said Ryan. "She knows this place better than anyone. Sam's got your blood in her veins, Senator. She's too stubborn to die."

"I hope to God you're right, Baldwin."

The pilot circled several times. He didn't like the idea of landing, period.

"Impossible to tell what's on the surface," he said. "There could be hot spots all over the place. We touch down on some lava that's cooled just enough to look like rock and this baby will explode like the goddamned space shuttle."

Ryan stared off to one side. "How about over there—by the parking lot. I still see some vehicles down there and they haven't caught on fire. Should be safe enough."

The pilot grunted, but he began to maneuver toward the opening. The chopper was being buffeted by thermals caused by the variations in heat below. Twice he touched down but was blown to one side before he could cut the engines.

Finally, they touched hard and the pilot throttled back. They were down.

"Get the hell off if you're going," he said. "I'm not staying here."

Akbari grabbed the man by the arm. "Take off and hover nearby until your fuel runs low. If we're not back by then, go refuel and come back."

The man started to protest.

Akbari said, "I will pay you one million dollars if you are here when we need you."

The pilot stared at him for a long moment, evaluating the seriousness of the offer. He knew the Iranian was filthy rich.

"I'll be here," he said.

***

Sam stood at the base of yet another venthole and stared up into the darkness. Sergeant Stefansson was up there somewhere. He'd insisted on checking the newly discovered vent himself. Very chivalrous and all that. She knew she should have done it, since she was more at home down here.

But something held her back. She was having those feelings of paranoia again. Almost overwhelming. Like a premonition that something bad was going to happen.

So Stefansson had gone first. He'd been out of sight for almost ten minutes now. She tried calling to him, but there was no reply. It wasn't all that surprising. The noises on Laki had grown from a vague background hum, like distant roadwork, to what now seemed an ever-present, if muted, din. Sudden gas releases like whistles, the crackling of bubbling lava . . . and other sounds. Indefinable ones. Like movement, but not of subterranean forces. More like some . . . thing. Almost—she thought she could hear voices.

Once she could have sworn she heard someone crying. The distant wailing was terrifyingly real, and it sent chills down her spine. She tried to convince herself it was just another gas release, but she didn't believe it.

She played her light down the vent behind her, in the direction they'd come from. Her eyes had been playing tricks, like her ears. She couldn't trust any of her senses. She was sure she was hallucinating.

She tore her eyes away finally and looked back up the venthole. She called to Stefansson as loudly as she could, but there was no answer.

"To hell with this!" she said out loud.

She began to climb up the hole after the Sergeant. If not for gravity, she would have had little sense of direction at all. Going up, at least, seemed preferable.

She climbed for several minutes. The sides of the vent were warm, but the going was easy enough. She stopped when she heard the strange wailing again. What the hell *was* that?

Then she saw something moving ahead. Stefansson.

She climbed quickly until she reached the dim figure. "Why didn't you answer when I called?" she asked, breathlessly.

She brought her light up and froze, as it played on Stefansson—or what she had thought was the Sergeant. For he was now a virtual part of the wall, covered in the strange tentacles. They grew out of his face and encircled his body. Sam stared into his sightless eyes. She could see tiny branches, like blood vessels, growing inside the whites of his eyes and even moving just under the surface of his skin.

She screamed and dropped her light. It fell a long way down the tunnel. She gasped for breath, her heart beating like a sledgehammer. She had no idea what had happened to the Sergeant, but he was clearly beyond help.

She was alone down here now. In the dark with no light. The distant wailing carried up the tunnel and she heard a sort of creeping sound, as though something were crawling over the Sergeant's body.

Her fear was unlike anything she'd ever experienced. For several minutes she simply froze, unable to go forward or back. The blackness was like an enormous weight, her imagination crafting all manner of horrors. Finally, through sheer force of will, she began to move forward, slipping past Stefansson's body an inch at a time.

There was nothing behind them but lava. She had to get around her friend's body and hope that whatever had overcome . . . or devoured . . . him wouldn't attack her as well.

She felt a prickling sensation as she edged past him. Once by the horrific mass of tentacles that engulfed what had been Stefansson, she scrabbled up the tunnel, too terrified to do anything but crawl ahead in the darkness.

After perhaps a hundred yards, she stopped out of sheer exhaustion. The tension and stress were draining. She slumped to the ground, feeling completely debilitated.

She needed to get a grip on herself, goddamn it. She was no simpering, helpless female. That was the antithesis of who she was, and it angered her to feel this way. She thought of Ryan and wished he were here, realizing with a start how firmly he'd inserted himself into her feelings. She remembered his face when she'd agreed to go with

Dagursson's men. Something indefinable in it. Worry? Right now, she would have given anything to feel his strong arms around her.

Her head jolted upright. There was the strange wailing again. This time it seemed closer. She turned her head from side to side, trying to pinpoint where it was coming from. It was somewhere ahead. God, what she would give for a light.

She had to move. Anything was better than sitting here in the dark. Slowly, she forced her feet forward. They felt encased in lead. One hand after the other gripped the sides of the tunnel. Only by concentrating on moving, putting everything else out of her head, was she able to function.

After a few minutes, she realized she could see again. The tunnel walls pulled back to reveal a larger space, like a natural cavern. Far above, a source of light filtered down. New tunnels branched off in all directions. She had no idea which way to go, only that she had to keep moving. In spite of what every fiber of her being was telling her, she headed toward the wailing. It was a goal, the only one she had. She had no desire to confront whatever was making that awful sound, yet something compelled her.

The horrifying lament rose and fell, occasionally resembling a whimper, then someone laughing. She began to wonder if it existed only in her mind.

Then, suddenly, the sound was close. Her body very nearly ceased to function, so quickly had the strange cry gone from a distant goal to a presence that felt alive and very near. Only it had changed from a wailing to something now much more like language.

She turned her head and saw an object on the wall beside her. It was almost as large as she was and looked vaguely human, but was covered with a spray of fine tentacles that she now realized covered the walls like tiny blood vessels. The figure was large, bloated-looking, but it resembled . . . a woman.

It had stringy, grayish hair and pale skin. It was possible to see an expression . . . sort of . . . on the face. The tiny tentacles penetrated the body and pulsated. Despite their small size, they looked very old, like varicose veins long established.

Then the thing spoke.

Sam's heart leaped straight into her throat. Here, deep underground, this strange entity attached to the wall appeared to be trying to communicate with her. It was madness. At first, the words were unintelligible, resembling the eerie wailing she'd heard earlier. But then she realized that the tone was almost familiar. Whatever this thing was, it spoke in ancient Norse, a language Sam knew only bits and pieces of. She needed Dr. Hauptmann.

She racked her brain for a few words. Then, when she tried to speak, her mouth was as dry as sand and her voice cracked. "What *are* you?" she asked.

The voice answered in a stream of words she couldn't understand. She tried again. "*Who* are you?"

The mouth opened and shut. The thing pulsated. Sam could see tiny bits of tentacles expanding beneath the surface of the skin, if it could be called anything remotely like skin.

The mouth opened again. This time, like the release of a bit of vented gas, the thing said, "Ammmmaaaaaa."

Chapter Eighteen

The General entered the main cabin of Air Force Two. The plane had been commandeered from the Vice-President for this mission. The rear of the aircraft contained banks of computers and a military command center. No one who worked in this section entered the civilian cabin without express permission.

Not that the President's Science Advisor would have cared. Prescott Carlisle was too absorbed by the papers in front of him to even think about such mundane matters. He had a world of details to attend to and very little time. The Vice-Presidential plane offered the ability to work while traveling and maintaining instant communications with anyone in the world.

A dozen others shared the passenger cabin with him. The men and women relaxed comfortably in their lounge-like seats, all of them hard at work, studying their briefing papers. It was probably the most talented bunch of scientists ever to fly anywhere together in the history of the world. Others would join them at their destination.

The General stopped at Carlisle's seat and waited until Prescott looked up. "I have confirmation, sir," he said. "Most of what you requested was on hand at the U.S. military base in Frankfurt."

Carlisle grunted and scanned the requisition list. It was long and at the top were the most urgent items: two full-size buses that would house the personnel and equipment necessary to their mission. The vehicles were highly specialized command centers that had been used in the past to deliver on-site scientific expertise anywhere in the world.

Prescott reached over to the seat beside him, where a map of Iceland lay open. "You ever been to Iceland, General?"

"No sir. Can't say I've had the privilege."

"Well, it's one forbidding goddamn piece of landscape, if this map is at all accurate. Few roads, only one major airport, population density outside of Reykjavik that wouldn't rival a goat herders' convention in Chile."

He stared at the map. "Place we're going, Laki, is at the end of a dead-end spur that cuts off from the Ring Road. Bloody road crosses several rivers. And I mean without bridges, General. It's a freaking miracle they don't expect me to go in by reindeer."

The General smiled. "It is a tad remote, sir. But we'll get you there."

"It's not me I'm worried about. It's the equipment. What if our buses get bogged down in those rivers, for God's sake?"

"You're to be accompanied by members of the Icelandic armed forces, sir. They'll have heavy halftracks capable of pulling the buses through if they get mired down. It's all been planned for."

"Have you received clearance for the C-17s to land at Keflavik airport?" Carlisle asked.

"It's all arranged," the General said soothingly. He was used to dealing with civilians. "Soon as the C-17s touch down, the buses will offload and we'll be on our way."

"We're on schedule to meet them there?"

"Precisely, sir. To the minute."

The President's Science Advisor continued to worry. It was his job, and one hell of a lot was riding on him being successful. He searched the General's face for reassurance, then gave him a weak thumbs up.

***

Jon crouched beside a boulder jutting out of the side of the vent they'd been trudging down. His wits were almost totally frayed. The

paranoia was firmly rooted. His heart lived in his mouth, antici-
pating the next horror they were sure to come upon.

He stared at Kraus. The man was an idiot. The German had
moved forward toward the edge of what appeared to be a great sink-
hole. A vast wind had come up, blowing so hard it made it difficult
to walk against as they had moved down the tunnel.

A wind here, so deep beneath the surface, was completely inexplicable and, having no explanation, they avoided talking about it.

But then they had reached the opening. The tentacles that provided them with light had continued to grow in size. Now the arm-
sized coils, like thick electrical conduits, covered the vent walls. They
snaked over the edge of the precipice in front of them and disappeared into the void from which the wind was coming.

The gale-force blast whipped out of the opening, and Kraus's
hair blew straight back as though slicked down like some fifties
crooner as he struggled to the edge.

He wanted to see what was down there. Curiosity had overcome
his fear, at least for the moment. He looked back briefly to see Jon
cowering behind the boulder. Good. The man was useless . . . hopelessly mired in some paranoid trauma. He felt it too, but relied on his
faith to keep going.

Kraus grasped a sort of stone barrier at the edge of the opening
and pulled himself forward. The wind was incredibly strong. Slowly,
he pulled his head even with the ledge and looked down.

What he saw simply didn't register at first. Certainly not in any
rational sense. Perhaps he was becoming as paranoid as Jon. He had
to be hallucinating. Holding tight to the stones with his left hand,
he raised his right to try to shield his eyes from the incredible blast
of wind.

"What is it?" Jon cried from behind his boulder. "What do you
see? Is it a way out?"

Kraus ignored him. He couldn't have answered if he'd wanted to.
For he had no idea what he was looking at.

The swollen tentacles poured over the sides in a mass and disappeared into the void. The pulsating light that had been guiding the

two men in their nightmarish journey through the venthole disappeared as soon as the branches plunged into the opening, as though every bit of energy in the tentacles was suddenly drained away.

But something else was also dissipating. Kraus felt his fears and barely controlled paranoia fall away. The knot in his shoulders relaxed. His mind slipped into a state of peace and tranquility. He felt completely content and happy to be where he was. Warmth seeped into the very heart of his being.

He stared down into the darkness. The wind whistled out of the depths, and he wondered if there might be some sort of vent to the outside that allowed the wind to roar through the tunnel. If so, then it could be a way out. But how could they fight the nearly hurricane-force wind? And how could they begin to climb down the sides of the opening?

It would be a journey into blackness. Even so, he felt not a tremor of concern. It was wonderful just to be here. To feel so . . . perfect. He looked back at Jon. Poor bastard. If he only knew.

He squinted against the wind. There was something down there. Something that made no sense. All was blackness . . . except . . . he could see pinpoints of light. Thousands of them.

Almost . . . like stars.

***

Ryan put his pistol in his jacket pocket. No need for it now. Whatever lay ahead, they would have to face together. Akbari. The senator. The Secret Service agent.

Ex-agent. Lately, he'd almost forgotten that.

"Where do we begin?" asked Graham. He wore slacks, dress shoes, and a lightweight nylon jacket. Ryan knew the man was in good physical condition. Evidently, part of his lifelong quest to extend life had been to take care of the body he had. To give science as long as possible to come up with the answer he so desperately wanted while he was still in relatively good health.

Akbari grunted in response. He seemed soft, a little pudgy. But at least he was younger than the senator, maybe fifty years old. He was already peering into the various vehicles now abandoned in the parking lot.

"No way to tell if one of these belongs to Rashid," he said. "But I'd bet on it. He's down here somewhere. He was in a hurry to put his foolish plans to work."

Ryan stared across the fire-blasted landscape. Which way to go? Sam was somewhere down below, along with Dagursson's men, maybe Jon, and a lunatic with a nuclear weapon.

He turned on his heel. "Come on," he said and disappeared into the first venthole he saw.

It was warm underground. It had been nothing like this before. The temperature of the entire mountain seemed to be rising. And there was a near-constant background din. Things were moving and shaking beneath Laki, as if the whole place were coming apart at the seams. If he'd been willing to wait, Rashid might not have needed his backup plan.

They kept close together. Periodically, Graham called out Samantha's name. His voice sounded pathetically small in the tiny circles of light their flashlights threw.

Still, Ryan knew if the senator hadn't been calling, he'd have done it himself. He remembered Sam telling him how this place was an enormous maze—ten thousand years of ventholes was how she had put it. How in God's name were they going to find anyone?

Chapter Nineteen

Margret found Sahar coming out of her chemistry class. She wasn't the last one out of the room this time, and she was actually talking to another girl. She smiled when she saw Margret and said something to the girl, who went ahead on her own.

"A new friend?" Margret asked.

"Maybe," said Sahar. "I didn't see you at lunch today."

"I need to talk to you, Sahar. Can we go somewhere?"

"Okay. I just have study hall next. Want to go to the library?"

Margret stopped when they entered the library and stared. It was totally different from when she was a student. Then, books lined the walls and there were large, wooden desks to work on. Now, the books were mostly gone. In their place was row upon row of computers lined up in little cubicles in place of the large wooden desks.

"Wow!" she said. "Doesn't anyone use books anymore?"

Sahar smiled. "Sure. They're mostly back in the stacks though. No card catalogs either. You find what you want on the computer and then ask one of the librarians to get it for you."

Margret just shook her head. They went over to the single remaining desk that didn't have a computer on it. There were only two other students in the room, at the far end.

"I need to tell you some things, Sahar. And I need to apologize to you."

Sahar looked puzzled. "What for?"

"I'm not a teacher's aide, Sahar. I'm a police officer."

The girl's eyes went wide.

"I apologize for lying to you. It had to be done. And for what it's worth, after you hear me out, I'd still like to be your friend."

Sahar seemed to close down, like she knew in some strange way what was coming.

"Things are going to be a lot better for you, Sahar. You probably noticed that Sven and Nils have not been in school the last couple of days. Well, you can get used to that. They are never coming back."

"Never coming back? Why?"

"Because of what they did to you. Yes. I know about it. I've seen the picture, and you can be sure that no one else will ever see it. For all practical purposes, Sven and Nils have been expelled. But no one will know why. And none of the other students will know what they did to you. In fact, it's part of their punishment. They understand if they ever mention what they did to anyone, they'll go to jail."

Tears started to flow down Sahar's face. Margret reached over and took her hand. "What happened to you should never happen to anyone. But you're safe now and you can at least begin to try to stop thinking about it. I want you to talk to one of the counselors. She's a very nice lady who understands what happened and is very sympathetic because she once went through something very similar."

"My . . . my father doesn't believe we should talk to others about our problems. That it is private."

"Well, sometimes it's necessary. And this is one of those times. Your parents don't have to know about it. Your sessions with the counselor will be informal and she'll tell no one about them."

"Will I ever see you again?"

Margret smiled. "You can't get rid of me that easily. I'll stop by the school regularly to have lunch with you and see how you're doing. Maybe we can get together outside sometimes too. One thing I didn't lie to you about, Sahar, is that I really do want to be your friend."

Sahar seemed to be trying to absorb everything. "Is it true?" she almost whispered. "Sven and Nils . . . are gone?"

"From your life—forever. I give you my word on it."

The smile that emerged and grew from Sahar was almost beatific. She could be a girl again.

Chapter Twenty

Prescott Carlisle stood off to one side of the parking lot at Laki and surveyed the activity going on around him. The two large buses were pulled up at right angles to one another. A generator hummed loudly and men were snaking cables between the two vehicles.

Thus far, things had gone more smoothly than he could have hoped. The C-17s had arrived on time as the General had promised, along with a contingent of specialists and scientists stationed at the U.S. base in Frankfurt.

The inside of each bus looked like a NASA launch center with banks of computers, technicians, volcanologists, seismologists, physicists, and military grunts who sprang into action whenever any of the scientists needed something. The computer network equipment was state-of-the-art, capable of simulating abstract models of a whole range of systems. They would rely upon such simulations for much of their analysis.

All in all, it was a very efficient-looking operation and Carlisle grunted in approval. Most of the military people and a smattering of the technical assistants had been provided by Iceland's prime minister. This was a joint venture, so to speak, between Iceland and the United States, with a handful of German specialists thrown in.

Dagursson came over and stood beside Carlisle. He was just a little in awe at the incredible might of U.S. technical prowess that had suddenly been brought to bear in his homeland.

"Have your people detected any radio transmissions?" he asked.

Carlisle snorted. "Not bloody likely. One drawback to all this equipment is the amount of interference it causes. Right now, I'm counting ourselves lucky to have gotten the vehicles here in one piece. There are hot spots all over this place. One tire in the wrong place and POOF!

"We're getting some pretty strange readings. Cosmic particles are going through the roof. Our people have detected some sort of vast chamber or void located far beneath the surface. We haven't figured out what it is yet."

Dagursson stared at the bleak landscape. Steam vented from a dozen holes. A semi-permanent lava flow oozed from the western slope and meandered away into the distance.

He was beside himself with indecision. A dozen of his men were out there somewhere, along with Sam, maybe others. There was no way to tell where they were. To send more men below in this violent landscape without any idea where they were going or what they might encounter would be folly and risk many more lives.

"Have there been more earthquakes?" he asked.

"Nearly continuous. Mostly aftershocks, but there have been two quakes that came close to 7.0 on the Richter scale. The entire region is experiencing massive destabilization. Frankly, I'm not at all sure we're safe here. God knows what it must be like underground."

A young, nerd-looking scientist emerged from one of the buses and came over to the two men. He carried a computer readout.

"I think you should look at this," he said.

Carlisle took the readout and stared at it. Dagursson saw his face darken. "You double-check this?" he asked.

"Yes, sir. It's under the entire region, not just Laki. Biggest chamber any of the volcanologists have ever seen—or even speculated could be possible."

"What is it?" asked Dagursson.

"We've detected a magma chamber far beneath the surface," Carlisle replied. "Miles down." He cursed softly under his breath and turned to the technician. "This can't be right," he said. "Run the tests again. And perform a sensitivity analysis."

The man nodded and went back into the bus.

Dagursson stared at Carlisle and waited.

"If these figures are correct," Carlisle said finally. "We could be a lot less safe than I thought. The magma chamber is huge. It could hold thousands of cubic miles of magma. That would make it a supervolcano."

"A what?"

"Only three or four have ever been discovered. Massive volcanoes that caused enormous destruction at some point in past geological history. Yellowstone is such a volcano. It last erupted about six hundred thousand years ago. Its magma chamber is over five miles deep. It will eventually erupt again once the magma chamber fills up, quite possibly destroying much of North America and perhaps life as we know it on earth. You remember the term 'nuclear winter'?"

Dagursson said, "The idea that a nuclear war would raise so much dust into the atmosphere that it would block out the sun and destroy plant life."

Carlisle nodded. "This would be a volcanic winter. Same principle. The magma chamber of a supervolcano could erupt in a blast thousands of times larger than Mount St. Helens."

"Isn't there any way to determine how close such an eruption might be?"

"It's an inexact science, but certainly clues would include large amounts of seismic activity, evidence of destabilization in the region, perhaps weather or temperature changes in the ocean."

"Correct me if I'm wrong," said Dagursson, "but isn't that precisely what's going on here?"

Carlisle rose up from his normal stooped position and looked the police commissioner in the eye. "Precisely," he said.

***

Dagursson returned to his office in Reykjavik. There seemed little he could do on Laki. His best men were still inside the Earth somewhere. Sam, with the most hands-on experience with the volcano, was down there with them. If any of his men were still alive, it was likely because of her presence.

He'd considered long and hard going down into the ventholes on his own, but he'd almost certainly have become lost, which would do his men no good at all. At least here, in his office, he could monitor the situation, keep in touch with the prime minister, and begin to organize some sort of relief effort, if any information or contact from his men was forthcoming.

He looked up to see an unfamiliar face in his door.

"Can I help you?"

The man moved forward. "I am Ernst Hauptmann," he said. "I was told you might be able to assist me. I'm looking for Miss Samantha Graham."

Dagursson leaned back in his chair. "You're the professor with the theory about the Nazi plot to cause an eruption on Laki."

Hauptmann looked pleased that his reputation preceded him. He sat in a chair facing Dagursson. "I must speak with Sam—Miss Graham. I have new information about Laki. I read in the paper that she'd been detained."

"Miss Graham's whereabouts are currently unknown. She is somewhere beneath Laki, along with a contingent of my men. They were conducting a search and rescue."

Hauptmann's face showed sudden concern. "I've heard about the earthquakes. It cannot be safe to be down there now. What are you doing about it?"

"Perhaps if you told me what you wanted to ask Sam, it would help me determine what to do. I've been trying to decide if a rescue to find the rescuers is in order. But I don't want to risk more lives in a fruitless effort."

Hauptmann stared at him, his bushy eyebrows going up and down furiously. He spread his hands in a gesture of helplessness.

"My research is largely speculative. I've uncovered new information from the sagas—about the early Vikings who lived on the volcano. Few take the sagas as gospel. There is much interpretation involved. That's why I wish to speak with Sam. She knows as much about that lonely place as anyone."

"Not so lonely these days," said Dagursson. "Counting my men, Sam, a couple of dozen military types, and God knows how many scientists, Laki is more populated than Grandagardur Street on a Friday night."

There was a timid rap on the open office door and both men looked up to see Sahar, accompanied by a middle-aged man with a large mustache.

Dagursson stood up, surprise showing in his face.

"Sahar. What are you doing here? Is everything all right?"

The girl stepped into the room, looking around. "I . . . I wish to speak to you about something. Margret said I could talk to you . . . about anything." She turned slightly. "It's about the volcano. This is my father. He would prefer to speak in English, if that is possible."

"All right. Come in." He shook hands with the girl's father.

The man looked uneasy, but he acknowledged Dagursson with a slight nod. "My name is Hassan." He glanced at Hauptmann. "This is a private matter," he said.

Dagursson started to say something to Hauptmann, but the professor interrupted him.

"If this is in regard to Laki, it could be important for me to hear," he said.

Dagursson watched as Sahar and her father sat and then said, "You are probably aware of the earthquakes that have happened. A number of people may be trapped on Laki. Professor Hauptmann and I have been discussing this. Any information you may have could be vital in saving lives, and I believe Professor Hauptmann needs to hear it. I can assure you, we will be discreet."

Hassan stared at Hauptmann a moment longer, then seemed to dismiss him.

"First," he said. "I know about your intervention with regard to my daughter. Sahar is a good daughter and after she spoke with a woman counselor at the school, she felt the need to tell me what happened." He hesitated, looking about the room. "This is not easy for me. I believe in keeping family . . . things . . . in the family. I do not believe in counselors . . . but . . . ."

"But in this case, Sahar needed someone to talk to," said Dagursson. "And now, I believe, she can talk to you as well. That is very good news, I think, for everyone."

The man nodded. "I am grateful for what you did for my daughter. Her mother and I had thought something must be wrong, but we assumed it had to do with her inability to make friends. This . . . situation . . . could not continue. I tell you now," his voice tightened and his body seemed almost to vibrate. "If I knew where these boys who did these things were, I would kill them with my bare hands."

"As police commissioner, I would have to arrest you if you did," Dagursson said. "As a father myself, I'd probably want to help you."

Hassan nodded. "I wish to repay this debt."

"You don't owe me anything. I was just doing my job. Frankly, it was one of the most rewarding things I've been able to accomplish in a while."

Sahar sat silently, saying nothing. Dagursson wondered what was going through her head. But her hand reached out and took her father's and their eyes met. Hassan's eyes were moist.

"Nevertheless," Hassan said, "I repay my debts, and I think you will find what I have to say interesting."

Dagursson and Hauptmann waited.

Hassan took a deep breath. "I have worked for the same man for almost fifteen years, as a personal assistant. We have traveled to many countries and I have done whatever was asked of me. There were things about this man I grew to dislike over time, but . . . I needed the job."

He looked briefly at Sahar. "The man's name is Rashid."

The name meant nothing to Dagursson. He looked at Hauptmann, who shrugged.

"Rashid is very wealthy, though he does not pay his employees particularly well. For some time, I have known that he has been intensely involved with an effort to set off explosives on Laki. I do not know why he wanted to do this and I did not like the idea very much but did not see how setting off explosives in such a remote area would cause any problems."

"We believe those explosions may have begun the process that led to the earthquakes," said Dagursson.

"I realize that now, and I am sorry I did not report it earlier. But now I have learned something else . . . something almost impossible to believe. Rashid intends to set off a nuclear explosion on Laki."

Dagursson had been leaning back in his chair. Now he came forward with a loud thump and stared at Hassan. Hauptmann's eyebrows were working a mile a minute.

"Mother of God!" Dagursson said. "Would such a thing be possible?"

"I have worked for this man, as I said, for many years. He does not tell me everything, but I know pretty much what goes on. There were communications over a six-month period leading up to the delivery of the device. I did not understand everything at first. But later, I began to put it together."

"Do you know when this is going to happen?"

"I do not know when it will happen, but I believe the process is underway."

Hassan stood up, still holding Sahar's hand. "What you do with this information is up to you. I believe I owed you a debt, but more than that, I cannot be any part of something such as this—that may kill many innocent people. Again, I thank you for helping Sahar."

Sahar smiled widely at her father and then transferred some of the wattage to Dagursson.

"Thank you," she beamed, and they left.

***

Cardinal Wormer sat at the head of a heavily carved oak table in an elegant, church-owned chateau in the woods outside Berlin and listened to the debate raging around him.

Rabbi Levitz was the most forceful. "We must do something!" he said. His long beard was sprinkled with gray and reached nearly to the center of his chest. "We've debated, some of us, for thirty years, and our predecessors for another thirty before us. Laki was contained, or so we thought. But not anymore."

Wormer had been chair of the highly secretive religious council for more than a decade. Though the endless theological discussions resulted in precious little concrete action, he had plans. His control of the group would continue to augment his influence inside the church. He was an ambitious man with an eye to rising in church hierarchy. The idea that Laki was some sort of god or devil he had long dismissed. But he'd used the argument . . . religiously . . . to buy the attention of the prime minister and to manipulate the members of his group. Fear was a very useful tool in the business of self-promotion.

However, what the Rabbi had said was true. Things were getting out of hand. Laki was in the news daily now. Earthquakes, lava flows, scientists reporting unusual seismograph readings and still stranger findings of cosmic energy, quasars, and dark holes. Most of the information was difficult to understand, vague, abstract, and occasionally frightening. The world press was eating it up.

Wormer considered the other members. It was a volatile group, a dozen representatives of the world's major religions. The organization first came to the table shortly after the Second World War, when Karl Müller contacted leaders and suggested that something unnatural was happening beneath Laki. Since then, appointments to the council had been handed down secretly.

Each member took his position seriously. Wormer suspected most reported to their church elders, though it was hard to say how many others knew of the group's existence. It couldn't be many.

The suggestion that life-enhancing effects were emanating from the volcano had at once been seen by members as a threat to their very existence. Why should followers obey the tenets of their faiths in exchange for their promised reward in the afterlife if Laki was offering eternal life here and now?

Bishop Müller had been a believer in the longevity effects that had so intrigued the Führer. But like Fritz Kraus, he'd grown fearful of the strange events that went on underground, the visions, and hallucinations. One day, Kraus had shown him the chrysalis in the underground laboratory.

From that moment on, Müller had believed that whatever was happening on Laki was a manifestation of the supernatural. Whether good or evil, he had no idea, though he leaned toward the latter. He had agreed with Kraus that the underground research lab should be shut down.

But Müller never lost his fear of the unknown forces that existed beneath the volcano. What he did know was that they represented a threat to the German Catholic Church and to all world religions. So he undertook to create the council in order to find some way of reacting to this force . . . religious entity . . . Devil or God. Whatever it was.

"I have no doubt that you are correct," Cardinal Wormer said to the Rabbi. "For the past two years, as reports of seismic events have increased, I, too, have been worried. For more than sixty years, we've contained Laki, but now . . . ." His hand fell gently upon the cross that hung from his neck. He had to fight back a laugh at how gullible the others were. He would use their silly fears to his own ends.

Ayatollah Majd, the Shia cleric, stirred in his black robes at the foot of the table. He was a soft-spoken man but had proven his great wisdom in the past.

"I do not believe *we* have contained anything," he said. "What Laki represents is inscrutable. We don't know if the volcano is a manifestation of the Holy One or some power altogether unknown to us. Perhaps we are not meant to know. However, recent events certainly suggest the spirit of Laki is no longer content. The question remains, what is our reaction going to be?"

"We must do nothing!" said Maharishi Brahmachari, the Hindu leader. "It is presumptuous to believe we have such power. Laki, in whatever manifestation, acts in ways we cannot understand. We must watch and wait."

"And if Laki decides to reveal the secret of life . . . of extended existence . . . here and now?" asked the Rabbi. "What do we tell our constituents?"

Cardinal Wormer rolled his eyes. "So . . . we are calling them *constituents* now, my friend?"

"You know what I mean," the Rabbi said petulantly. "We are expected to provide answers."

Wormer sighed. "Most of the world thinks Laki is simply a volcano, perhaps struggling to come to life. For now, it is nothing unusual, and I doubt that even the histrionics of the press will change that."

"And if there is a revelation?" asked the Maharishi.

"Then we must offer a united front. The leaders of all our churches must make a joint pronouncement."

"Saying . . . what? That we accept the revelation of a new God? That we will kowtow to some . . . *thing* . . . beneath a volcano? That we encourage our flocks to worship this being and to give up our own beliefs? Is this what you seriously offer us?" The Maharishi shook his head. He stared at the Cardinal, whose enjoyment of the trappings of power was well known to all of them. "This will not do your reputation in your own church any good," he said.

Wormer knew the Maharishi's take on the matter was shared by the others. They believed that all of their career paths might rest in the hands of the unknown. Wormer was alone in his feeling that Laki was nothing but a volcano. His realism would lead to his elevation in the church once Laki subsided in its fury, provided he played his cards right. He had to keep his colleagues' fanciful notions alive for the time being, however.

"Talk, talk, talk," said Rabbi Levitz. "It's all we ever do. For sixty years, we talk."

"Maybe this time," said Wormer, "Laki will be the one to talk . . . and all we will be able to do is listen."

***

Sam sat at the foot of the chrysalis that called itself Amma. For many hours, she had tried to absorb the occasional words . . . pronouncements she had come to think of them . . . that emanated from the bizarre presence. The voice had a disembodied quality. Though the mouth opened, the sound seemed to come from another place. Sometimes it was the high wailing that she had first heard. Others, it was much more human-like.

Her ability to understand the ancient Norse language had been almost nonexistent at first. But then she began to more fully comprehend the words, as though she had somehow received an immersion course in the language. Still, she wished Hauptmann were here.

She understood now that the thing was, in fact, Amma, the tenth-century Norse shaman described by Hauptmann. The volcano had the ability to absorb things . . . people . . . and was able to keep them alive. That this could be possible troubled her deeply. She was a scientist after all and didn't really believe in God. Certainly, Laki had done strange things to her, given her visions, made her paranoid. But up to now, she had tried to tell herself it was the effects of volcanic gas or her own personal lapses.

She stood suddenly and shook herself. The ground was rumbling again. She peered into the face of the frozen entity on the wall beside her. It appeared to be asleep or at least no longer aware of her. She considered touching it, remembering the vision that had come to her and Ryan after touching the skull in the cave. But she couldn't bring herself to touch the chrysalis.

Amma had told her many things. Sam now knew what Laki was, or at least what Amma thought it was. That knowledge brought a chill to her very core, so that she could barely function if she thought about it too deeply.

What she wanted most was to get out of here. To return to the world of the living, to sunlight, to a place where what she saw and what she heard made any kind of sense. To be so totally alone down here was almost too much to bear. She wanted to see Ryan again.

But which way to go? The large cavern with its many branching tunnels provided too many choices. It was like a hall of mirrors, each

tunnel the same as the next. She moved forward out of simple indecision. It was better to move than to remain still.

After a time, it seemed the tunnel she'd selected began to
descend. She stopped, again indecisive. Then she heard voices. Not
the wailing that Amma had made, but real, human voices. They
were coming toward her, and in a moment, she stared as two men
appeared out of the gloom.

They looked as lost as two little boys, and about as filthy. One
had some sort of slick, gooey material all over his clothes. The
other man also had some of this and his hair and clothes were
completely disheveled.

Jon Gudnasson stared at Sam as though she were a ghost. "Who
are you?" he asked. And before she could answer, "Do you know how
to get out of here?"

She shrugged. "My name's Samantha Graham. I came down
here with a group of policemen to look for a man thought to be lost,
named Jon Gudnasson."

"That's me," said Jon, suddenly hopeful. He looked around.
"Where are the police?"

"All dead."

Both men stared at her.

"What happened?" asked Kraus.

"They were attacked by some . . . thing . . . down here," Sam said.
"The others were killed in a sudden lava outburst. I lost my light and
have been stumbling around ever since."

"I know who you are," said Jon. "You're the volcanologist
who's been telling everyone that Laki might erupt." He glanced
around uneasily, searching for more of the tentacles. "Seems you
got that right, at least. You're supposed to be some sort of expert
on this place," he said accusingly. "How the hell do we get out of
here?"

"Sorry. I'm completely turned around. I have no idea which way
is out."

Kraus was nodding. "Our stories are remarkably similar," he said. "This place is destabilized and unnatural. Have you seen the tentacles?"

She nodded. "Ryan and I first saw them in a sort of underground laboratory near the glacier. They seem to be everywhere. I don't know what they are or where they come from."

"I don't know what they are, either," said Kraus. "But I know where they come from."

She stared at him.

"Where?"

"I'll show you. It's only a little way back down the tunnel."

"Don't be crazy!" Jon said. "We can't go back there."

"I fail to see what difference it makes," said Kraus. "We don't know which way is out. One direction is pretty much as good as another. If this woman is an expert, as you pointed out, she needs to see what we found."

They headed back down the tunnel the two men had emerged from. Jon grumbled, but no way was he going to remain behind alone and wait for them to come back.

After a few minutes, Sam saw the tentacles appear once again on the walls. They grew quickly in size and soon gave off enough light to see by. Then she became aware of a growing wind.

"That's really weird," she said. "There shouldn't be any wind down here."

"None of this stuff should be down here," said Jon grumpily. "But it is."

Then the wind grew to gale force and the three had to fight their way along the tunnel. Kraus led the way with Sam at his heels. Jon fell back, in no hurry to revisit their last encounter.

Finally, they came to the strange hole that disappeared into the Earth. Kraus, his hair plastered back by the wind, shouted to be heard. "That's where your tentacles come from," he said, pointing. "Take a look."

Sam needed no invitation. She fought closer to the opening, actually holding onto the cable-sized tentacles that now lined the tunnel. She pulled herself to the stone wall and stared down into the maelstrom.

What she saw was a vast blackness. An emptiness. The tentacles slipped over the side and disappeared into the depths. The darkness was so deep that it gave her vertigo. It was like staring into all bottomless eternity.

"What is this?" she shouted.

"Looks like a hole in the Earth, if you ask me," Kraus said.

Chapter Twenty-One

If he'd done this rationally, Ryan thought, they might have had a better chance of finding Sam . . . or anyone for that matter. But what was rational? Should he have tried to return to the underground research lab? The tunnel he and Sam had taken together was now blocked from the explosives meant to seal them in.

He tried to think what Sam would do. She had no idea where Jon had gone. But one thing he knew for sure. She would have figured out pretty quickly that Laki was destabilized and much too dangerous for anyone to be there. So by now she'd be looking for a way out to save the lives of herself and the police officers with her. She would avoid tunnels that seemed to go farther underground.

He looked around. Everything seemed different below ground than it had before. To begin with, the sounds were terrifying—subterranean movements, whooshing sounds of gas releases or perhaps glacial meltwaters. They regularly heard cave-ins, as pieces of ventholes collapsed. No tunnel could be relied upon to provide them with an assured retreat.

After two hours of more or less blind stumbling about, Ryan knew they were irretrievably lost. They were supposed to be looking for Sam, but it was just as likely she'd stumble upon them as the other way around.

"Can we take a rest?" asked Senator Graham.

Ryan nodded and the three men sank to the ground.

"You any idea where we are?" Akbari asked.

"Underground?" Ryan replied helpfully.

"Great."

"Look. There's nothing we can do but stumble around and hope we find someone."

"If we're down here when Rashid sets off his little toy, we won't have anything at all to worry about," Akbari said, looking defeated. "What a waste."

Ryan considered the Senate majority leader, sprawled out on the ground, his clothes unkempt and dirt-covered. He looked completely drained. Much of this was his fault, and Ryan felt no sympathy for him. "Feeling any of that revitalization stuff yet?" he asked.

Graham glared at him. "You can make fun if you wish. I've heard it all before. My colleagues have joked about Graham's 'youth' movement for nearly all of my forty years in public service. They all laughed at my support for longevity funding. But what I was pursuing made as much sense as what most of the rest of them fought for, increased military spending, support for one corporate boondoggle after another, cuts in taxes."

"Whereas you were going straight for the Holy Grail, right? Gave you a sense of superiority, I bet."

Graham looked bleak. "Wait until you're an old man," he said. "You'll see things differently. You'll reach a point where you'll do anything for a few more good years."

"I don't know," Ryan said. "Every additional year I'm on this planet, I think I won't miss it too much when the time comes. I think God may actually have a plan—to make us sick of it all just about the time our number is up. Perfect biological timing."

"God has nothing to do with it," Graham said forcefully. "If our life clocks were meant to be permanently set, what would be the point of science? We've doubled our life spans in just the last century as a result of science and medicine. There is no set limit. Only our own cognitive abilities will determine how far we can go."

Ryan looked at Akbari. "What about you? You're a Muslim. I thought you fellows believed that everything was preordained or written down somewhere."

"So it is," Akbari replied. "But we can't *know* what is written. We can safely assume that whatever we do is part of God's plan. Perhaps He *intends* for us to achieve immortality."

There was a sudden, long, shuddering sound, as if the massive engines of an ocean liner were straining to comply with her captain's call for more power. It was hard to know where the sound came from, though it seemed to be far beneath them.

"Jesus!" Graham said in a low voice. "Place sounds like it's alive." He looked at Akbari. "You think Rashid . . .?"

"Relax, my friend," Akbari said. "We'll never know if Rashid sets off his device. We will rest in oblivion, and you will have no more concerns about longevity."

***

Dagursson and Professor Hauptmann stared down from their helicopter at the ever more crowded Laki parking lot. The news of Rashid's nuclear threat had been enough to convince the commissioner that he needed to be back on site. His men were here, still alive he hoped. Maybe he couldn't stop this crazy Arab, but he was prepared to do anything necessary to try. Half of his nation, maybe more, could be rendered permanently uninhabitable if this lunatic succeeded in his plan.

The pilot pointed to an open area near where Carlisle's buses stood. "Looks feasible—barely," he said.

If possible, Dagursson thought, things had deteriorated even more since he was last here. There were now several lines of lava emerging from the volcano and wending their way lower. Two showed signs that they would soon merge, cutting off the parking lot from the highway.

Carlisle and several of his scientists emerged from one of the buses and stared up at them. Slowly, fighting the thermals, the pilot brought the aircraft to a rocky landing.

As the blades slowly wound down, the pilot suddenly said, "Christ, will you look at that?"

Across the valley floor, near the next volcano in the Laki chain, a vortex of motion had appeared.

"It's a goddamned tornado," the pilot said.

They watched as the windstorm grew in size, pulling up dust and dirt from the bleak Laki hills, taking on the color of its surroundings.

"You ever heard of a tornado in Iceland?" Dagursson asked Hauptmann.

"I think anything will be possible here," the professor replied.

They got out of the helicopter and went over to stand beside Carlisle and his men, who were also staring at the tornado.

Dagursson said, "Mr. Carlisle, this is Ernst Hauptmann from the university. He's been studying Laki for many years, its history as revealed in the sagas and that of the Vikings and Nazis who both lived and worked here."

Carlisle nodded. "We'll take all the help we can get." He shook Hauptmann's hand, then looked back at the tornado. "Look at that damned thing. We've already had marble-size hail and the most incredible display of northern lights I've ever seen. Now this." He looked back at Hauptmann. "Maybe you can tell us if we're in its path?"

Hauptmann shrugged. "The thermals here must be all over the map. Impossible to tell which way it will go."

But even as he spoke, they could see the windstorm begin to die down and move away down the slope.

"Too many competing weather systems," Hauptmann said. "You see? It's breaking apart. The surrounding thermals are pulling it in different directions."

Carlisle grunted. "Come inside," he said.

It was Dagursson's first excursion inside one of the buses. They were well insulated and as soon as the doors were closed behind them, the constant sounds of Laki under duress were replaced by the whir of computers and the sounds of men going about their duties. It was surprisingly spacious. Technicians sat at computer stations or watched readouts in comfortable swivel chairs. The walls were lined with equipment, the function of which Dagursson had no conception.

"Learned anything more about your magma chamber?" he asked.

"We've detected a lot of electrons and positrons, probably emanating from the chamber and probably spun out by Kaluza-Klein particles. At least that's our working theory. No one really knows if the particles are real. If they are, they operate in another dimension."

Dagursson stared at him. He felt as though he needed to go back to college and get a few advanced degrees. "Let me try to understand this," he said. "If the electrons and . . . positrons? . . . are coming from the magma chamber and are spun out by these Kaluza-Klein particles . . . then, what? You're saying the chamber could be another dimension?"

Carlisle spread his hands. "You said it as well as I could."

"What the hell would be the consequences of that?" Dagursson asked.

The scientist looked at Hauptmann. "You got any thoughts about any of this, professor?"

Hauptmann had been staring at the banks of computers like a kid in a candy store. He turned his attention to Carlisle. "I believe my offerings will be less on the scientific side and have more of a . . . uh . . . supernatural slant."

"Hell," Carlisle said, "That would be a refreshing change from the sorts of far-out theories we've been batting around."

"Very well. The sagas speak of something that I interpret as a *hole at the center of the earth. A hole with stars.*"

Carlisle's mouth fell open. "You're telling me there is a description of our magma chamber from a thousand years ago?"

The professor nodded. "It came from a holy woman, a sort of shaman, if you will, whose clan was engaged in some sort of fierce battle underground."

"Battle? Battle with what?"

"That's not clear."

"Son of a bitch!" Carlisle said in a loud voice. For an instant, every scientist on the bus looked at him. "I could use some goddamned answers here!" he said, almost petulantly.

"Listen," Dagursson said. "We've got another little problem." He proceeded to relate what he'd learned about Rashid and his plans.

Carlisle's face grew longer and longer as he realized that everyone on Laki was likely in even more danger than he had thought.

"And where is this lunatic?"

"We believe already below, placing his device . . . or possibly he has done so and has already left. He wouldn't want to be anywhere nearby when it goes off, not if he hopes to collect on his oil futures."

"What next?!" Carlisle exploded.

"Perhaps," said Hauptmann, staring again at the incredible array of machines that surrounded them, "You have some way of detecting the presence of plutonium?"

Carlisle's face lit up. "We can detect the hell out of just about anything with the equipment we have here. Maybe not another dimension . . . but just about anything else."

He moved away and began to consult with several technicians.

Maybe, Dagursson thought, he'd soon have some idea where to go in the maelstrom that was Laki. He'd not forgotten about his men . . . or Sam.

***

Abdul Rahman, selected by Rashid to help carry his device into the depths of Laki, was unhappy.

"We are deep enough," he said. "Listen to this place. It is coming apart. You probably do not even need this thing. I say we get out of here while we still can."

"Just a little farther," Rashid coaxed. He needed Abdul. He couldn't carry the device by himself. "The lower we place it, the more damage it will cause. And," he said, "the more I will pay you."

"It will do me no good if I am dead," Abdul said, but he kept on. Mostly, he was worried that they wouldn't be able to find their way out. But Rashid faithfully sprayed paint from a can at each new tunnel entrance.

Finally, they entered a venthole that seemed different from the others. From somewhere deep within, they felt a breeze blowing in their faces. A warm breeze, like something from the tropics.

"This is good," said Rashid. "Warm air must be coming up from deep thermal energy, a magma chamber perhaps. The closer we get this thing to it, the more likely our blast will do the sort of damage we want."

"By the Prophet, a nuclear bomb will blow this whole place to bits, evaporate it, turn magma into radioactive debris and fallout," said Abdul. "No telling how far away we should be when that happens. It better be a long, long way."

"It will be," Rashid promised. "The timer can be set for as much as twelve hours. We'll be back in Reykjavik. I already checked prevailing weather patterns. Any radiation will be blown away from the city, toward the British Isles, along with the sulfuric acid expelled by Laki.

"Let's rest a moment," he said. The device weighed more than a hundred pounds and though it had convenient handles, it was still a heavy burden. They halted and put it down.

Rashid shone his flashlight onto the tunnel walls. There was something on them, small, vein-like projections that seemed to pulsate slightly. He played the light down the passage and could see the veins or whatever they were growing larger.

He left his helper where he was and followed the strange tentacles. It was very curious. They seemed to almost glow. He turned his light off and could still see a phosphorescent shimmer coming from them. The farther he went, the larger they grew. Intrigued, he wanted to keep going but was afraid Abdul would scamper away if left alone. He went back and spoke to the man.

"Not much farther. I think we are close to something."

"What?"

"I don't know, but I think we must be close to the heart of Laki. When we set off the device, the mountain will get a dose of what *real* power can do."

They continued on for another ten minutes, the tunnel growing steadily warmer and the breeze stronger. Finally, Rashid ordered a halt.

"This will do," he said, to the obvious relief of his companion. He knelt beside the device and began to go through a checklist.

"Hold the light closer."

There were a number of steps that had to be taken to set the timer and activate the device. At last, everything was ready. Rashid engaged a final, digital command and they watched as the timer began to count down.

The moment the button was activated, there was no longer any way to stop the process. They were committed. Rashid stood up. "All right," he said. "Time to leave, my friend."

Abdul turned immediately, then stopped dead in his tracks. In front of them, filling the sides of the walls, the strange, tiny tentacles had suddenly grown much larger. Before their eyes, the things throbbed and pulsated, as they grew to the size of a man's arm.

The tentacles were also now moving along the walls at greater speed. The two men gaped at the strange phenomenon as it pulsed forward to the last branching tunnel they'd come through and began to fill the opening that was to be their escape route.

"What's happening?" Abdul cried in an anguished voice. "It . . . it's blocking our escape."

Rashid raced forward, only to stop and stare at the tunnel exit. It had been clearly marked with their spray paint. Now, it was completely filled by the tentacles.

The two men stared at the pulsating mass of tentacles that blocked their path. Then, almost comically timed, they turned and looked back at the device they had set in the tunnel.

"Mother of God," said Abdul. "We'll never find our way out of here."

Rashid was inclined to agree with him. The tentacles had left them a tunnel to follow, but it wasn't the one they'd come in with. They'd have to trust to random luck to get out now. And the clock behind them was ticking.

***

Prescott Carlisle stood on a small rise thirty yards from his two humming buses and stared at the strange landscape that surrounded him. To the west, a pair of lava flows slowly made their way down the slope. It seemed probable that at some point they would join, cutting the Laki road and stranding the vehicles in the parking lot. Off the north rim, two mini-tornadoes danced around one another, sucking debris into the lower atmosphere.

"Incredible," said the young scientist who stood beside him. "We must be seeing phenomena that no one else has ever witnessed."

"Don't want to witness it," Carlisle grunted. "Who the Christ knows what will be next."

The tornadoes suddenly collided with one another, the competing forces breaking them apart. The debris from both collapsed to the ground in a pile of loose shale and volcanic dust.

Another scientist made his way up the slope to where they were standing.

"Call for you, sir," the man said. "Priority One."

Priority One was the President. Carlisle sighed and headed for the bus. Inside, the normal hum of conversation among the technicians died abruptly upon his entrance. He knew they were worried about conditions and had been discussing matters among themselves. These were not military personnel, and though they had signed on for potentially hazardous duty, Laki was turning out to be something more than they'd bargained for.

He ignored them and moved to the rear of the bus, where a small partition separated his tiny office from the rest of the space. He sat heavily and picked up the special phone that connected only with the leader of the free world.

"Yes, Mr. President," he said.

"Prescott? What in the Sam Houston is going on over there? Our weather people say they're seeing things never before recorded in the North Atlantic. Water temperatures have increased three degrees a hundred miles off Iceland's shores. That is unprecedented."

"Yes sir. It certainly is. Conditions here are unpredictable. We've had many unusual weather phenomena. I believe it's at least partly caused by thermals from all the hot spots. There's a huge magma chamber below us. It may connect somehow with ocean currents, causing the water to warm." He lowered his voice. "My people may be in some danger. Lava flows are threatening to cut us off from the main road."

There was a moment of silence from Thurman. "Can you relocate out of danger?" he asked.

"No place to go really," said Carlisle. "Our equipment requires that the buses be on level ground. The parking lot here is the only available place."

"Maybe you should get the hell out of there while you can," the President said.

"I don't really consider that an option, Mr. President. Whatever is happening here could affect all of Iceland. Maybe the entire world. We need to do our work."

"Understood." There was another pause on the line. Then the President cleared his throat. "Ah . . . reason I called, Prescott, is because of something else. We've been contacted by a number of religious leaders in the past twenty-four hours."

"Sir?"

"Bunch of looney-tunes if you ask me, but they seem to have formed some sort of consensus . . . Christ, that's got to be a first . . . that what is happening in Iceland has . . . religious implications."

"Excuse me, Mr. President, but what the hell does that mean?"

"Not sure I understand it myself. But several have suggested that some sort of underground connection may exist between what's going on with your magma chamber and volcanoes in their own countries."

Carlisle pulled the phone away from his ear and stared at it. A collection of bible thumpers was all he needed. "Uh . . . could you expand on that for me, sir?"

"Seems that volcanoes across the globe have been experiencing events. Vesuvius, Etna, Damavand, Merapi in Indonesia, some in South America, the Aleutians and the Pacific—a trail of them really, right around the world. Increased lava flows, steam events. Even a number of volcanoes thought to be completely dormant are showing increased thermal activity. Yellowstone is acting up, for God's sake. It hasn't erupted violently in half a million years. You have any thoughts on this, Prescott?"

He was silent, considering it. Could it be possible that the huge magma chamber they'd detected was somehow connected deep beneath the earth's surface with other hot spots? Yellowstone also had a deep magma chamber. It seemed nearly impossible, yet they were dealing with the unknown here.

"I'm afraid I simply don't know, sir."

"Well, I'm getting a lot of pressure on this end, Prescott. The world press has been eating this up. Iceland is front-page news in every city in the world. Hell, I had a call from the Pope, worried about Vesuvius." Thurman laughed. "I told him things were under control but he could certainly pray on it."

"Good you can take a light approach, Mr. President."

"Don't misunderstand me," said Thurman. "I also had a call from some German Cardinal, a whack job by the name of Wormer. He said some secret council of theirs . . . wouldn't specify . . . damned religious zealots . . . has been studying Laki for sixty years. Sixty years! Says there's something *evil* down there. I nearly hung up on him. But no one can cause trouble quicker than a mess of Catholics. I don't need the Vatican breathing down my neck."

"Yes, sir. I imagine that would be trying."

"Frankly, it would be helpful if you could think up a response for them. Something I can feed them . . . you know . . . calm them down."

Carlisle breathed evenly. What next? "I'll see if I can come up with something, Mr. President," he said.

***

Sam led the way through a maze of tunnels. They had no idea where they were, except that it was far enough from the strange hole that the wind had now retreated to little more than a warm breeze. Continuing blindly on was a form of insanity only slightly less crazy than staying in one place would have been.

She was having trouble accepting what Kraus and Jon had just shown her. Literally, a hole at the center of the earth. Except she knew it wasn't that. Amma had suggested something else entirely. Communicating with the strange apparition, or chrysalis or whatever it was, had been illuminating and terrifying at the same time.

Amma spoke in ancient Norse. That Sam had understood what she said was mystery enough. But had she really understood? The mind-set of a thousand-year-old Viking was so far outside Sam's own reality base that she couldn't be sure of the specter's real meaning. Everything the old woman said was based on a worldview that included the supernatural, Norse gods and mystical and spiritual claptrap that was utterly foreign to Sam.

She wondered if the holy woman was speaking for herself or for someone . . . or something . . . else. Amma clearly believed that Laki was a god. Was the old woman being used as a mouthpiece for that god? Was she some sort of burning bush, passing on the ruminations of a higher being?

There was no way to know. But Sam had the sense that when Amma spoke of a *hole at the center of the earth* she was really talking about God . . . the spirit God, Laki. Of course, Sam had actually *seen* that incredible hole. It was real enough, if incomprehensible. Perhaps

Amma was referring to some sort of religious whole or center. It was all too frustrating to think about.

"We're not getting anywhere," Jon whined. "We're going in circles."

"Maybe," Sam replied. "But it doesn't do us any good to just sit down in one place and die."

"I agree," said Kraus. "We can only continue on and trust in God to deliver us from this place."

Sam stopped in her tracks so suddenly that Jon, who'd been following on her footsteps, ran into her.

"What?" he asked.

She raised a hand. "Shh . . . listen."

They could hear Laki, its bubbling lava, gas releases, and subterranean movements. But there was something else.

"That's a voice," Kraus said. "A human voice."

They listened, hands cupped to their ears. Sam was pretty sure it wasn't the wailing of Amma. It was distant, but there was something familiar about it. Then they heard it again. Closer now.

Sam's heart thumped in her chest as she heard, "Sa-MAN-tha!"

The others looked at her. Over and over, the voice repeated the cry. It was coming closer and getting louder and finally Sam knew with absolute certainty who it was.

She started forward, first at a trot, then a run. "Father!" she yelled.

The voice stopped for a moment, then began with renewed fervor, and the two closed on one another rapidly.

Then she was being held by her father, tears streaming down his face.

"Sam! I thought I'd lost you forever. You're okay."

"As okay, I guess, as any of us can be down here," she said. She looked past him and saw Ryan, a huge grin on his face. She slipped out of her father's grasp and fell into Ryan's strong arms.

"I knew you'd be all right," he said softly. "You're too damn stubborn to die." He squeezed her tightly and looked past her at Jon and Kraus.

"I'm glad to see you too, Jon." He nodded at the other man. "How many more are down here?"

Sam pulled back from him. "Dagursson's men are all dead, Ryan, a dozen of them. We were mad to come down here. This place is too dangerous. I was a fool to let them come. I'm responsible for their deaths."

"No," he said. "You were just trying to help, to find Jon. You couldn't know how bad it would be."

"Do you know how to get out of here?" asked Jon, almost pleading. Ryan shook his head. "We're as lost as can be."

"Well, if one direction's as good as another," said Sam, "I think we should show you what we found back there." She gestured behind them.

""I agree," said Kraus. "The more people who can confirm what we've seen, the better. The only question is if you think we can find our way back to it."

Jon started to protest, then stopped. What difference did it make which direction they went?

"We just need to follow the breeze," said Sam. "At every juncture, we take the passage with the most wind coming from it."

Ryan gestured at Akbari, who up to now had remained silent at the back of the group. "This dour-looking fellow is the Iranian minister of oil, Ali Akbari. He and your father have been in this from the beginning, Sam. For what it's worth, they . . . agreed . . . to come look for you."

She stared at her father. "All of this is because of your interest in something the Vikings found that extended their lives, isn't it?

Graham looked more tired than regretful. "I'm sorry, Sam. It's the cause of my life. I had to know if it was real."

She looked at him for a long moment. "I found one of those Vikings. Still alive after a thousand years, but I doubt you'd want to change places with her." She waved a hand dismissively at his astonished look.

"Come on," she said. "One mystery at a time."

The little group fell in behind, as she began to retrace their steps. Ryan walked beside her, close enough that they could speak without the others hearing over the background din of Laki.

"Were you serious?" he asked. "You found a Viking alive after a thousand years?"

She glanced at his face for a moment. She wanted to burn it into her memory. She'd thought she'd never see him again. "It was Amma. You remember? The Norse holy woman Hauptmann found in the sagas."

His face showed disbelief.

"After all these years? You're saying your father was right—there *is* something keeping them alive?"

"I'm not sure *alive* is the right word. We did see their bones after all, remember? Or at least someone's bones. Anyway, it hardly seems like much of an existence. She's some sort of . . . thing . . . hanging on a wall like a damn bat. She speaks in this disembodied wail, like an automaton."

"You *spoke* with her?"

"Her . . . it . . . a cocoon. I don't know what to call what I saw. She spoke in ancient Norse and yet I understood what she was saying. How can that be? I don't even like to think about it. I was all alone in the dark with this disembodied creature trying to communicate with me. Only I didn't sense that it was really Amma, you know? It was more like something else speaking to me through her."

"It must have been awful." He put one hand on her arm. "What did the thing say to you?"

"That we were trespassing. That we weren't wanted down here. Amma believes Laki is a god. Or maybe she's part of Laki herself now, absorbed, somehow, by the volcano. My overwhelming sense was that we shouldn't be here. I don't know, maybe it was the paranoia returning. Maybe whatever it is tries to get rid of us by making us feel paranoid."

She paused at a branching of tunnels. The wind coming from one was much stronger now and there was no question which way they should go. The walls were thick with the arm-sized tentacles, throbbing and glowing. After two more branches, she sensed they were close.

Jon began to hang back. He wanted nothing to do with the strange forces they'd encountered. But Kraus seemed energized.

"We're almost there," the German said, a strange look in his eyes. "I can feel it."

The wind became fierce, forcing them to lean into it.

"This is too weird," Ryan said. "How can there be wind down here? Where's it coming from."

"You'll see," said Sam.

They rounded a turn in the passage and came to the boulder behind which Jon had cringed earlier. Kraus, too, held back now. He'd experienced the hole. It had made him feel strangely invigorated and content. Peaceful. He'd resisted an almost overwhelming desire to throw himself into it. This time, he feared he might not be able to resist.

Akbari and the senator also held back. Sam could see her father's intense face. He was fascinated by what they were experiencing but fearful at the same time.

"Be careful," he said, as Sam and Ryan fought their way toward the opening.

Then they were side by side staring into the abyss. The wind whipped their hair back and even rippled the flesh on their faces. The coils of tentacles disappeared into the depths.

"God almighty," Ryan said. "What is it?"

"Kraus said it looked like a hole at the center of the earth," said Sam.

"But there are lights down there," Ryan said, incredulity in his voice. "Pinpoints of light—like stars."

From behind them, over the wind, they heard a voice.

"It's beautiful. Peaceful. It feels like . . . harmony." Akbari had come up to hold onto the rock wall beside them. His hair was plastered back on his head, his eyes large and unblinking as they stared down into the opening.

"Beautiful," he said again, and then, before Ryan or Sam realized what he was doing, the Arab vaulted over the stone wall and threw himself into the hole. His body spun around, seemed to float between worlds. Then, with a flash of light, he was gone.

"Jesus . . . God . . ." Jon whimpered.

The senator came closer too and stared at the space that had been occupied by Ali Akbari. "What happened to him? Where has he gone?"

"Get back," Sam cried. She and Ryan pushed themselves away from the edge and pulled the senator back to where Jon and Kraus were standing.

"It's a trap," Jon shouted. "It wants us to come closer, then it makes us jump in."

"Ryan and I didn't jump in," said Sam. "Kraus didn't jump in."

"I thought about it," said the German, his face sober. "It took hold of me. I had to resist with every ounce of my strength."

"For all his flaws, Akbari was a deeply religious man," said Senator Graham. "Perhaps he was more affected by this place than the rest of us. More open to whatever may have called to him."

"Yes," Kraus said. "I felt something call to me as well. The temptation to follow it was very strong."

"So what do we do now?" Jon asked.

"We've got to find a way out of here," said Sam. "We need to be able to talk to people outside, tell them what we've found, determine if anything can be done. Dagursson must be working topside with the authorities." She stared blankly at the various passageways.

"Look," Ryan said, "You followed the tentacles here, right? They got larger the closer we came to the hole. Well, then, let's follow them out. What can we lose? Maybe they'll lead us to the surface."

She could think of no reason why the strange, living fingers should lead them to the surface, but she didn't have a better idea. They began to follow the tentacles. The farther away from the hole, the smaller they grew. Their little group traipsed along what seemed like miles of ventholes. They passed fresh signs of collapses and blockages but each time, the tentacles simply meandered off in a new direction.

The strange growths decreased in size steadily, until they were like veins, crisscrossing the passage walls, percolating outward as the faintest of lines.

"This is what they were like when Jonsson, one of Dagursson's men, first encountered them," said Sam. "He said they pulsated. I told him not to touch them because they might be toxic." She laughed bitterly. "They were toxic all right. They killed Jonsson and all his men."

"Maybe we shouldn't be following them," Jon said nervously. "If they killed the policemen, they can do the same to us."

Sam started to reply then stopped. "There's something familiar about this place," she said.

They all stopped and looked at her.

"What is it, Sam?" Ryan asked.

"I think . . . I've been here before. I recognize the way these vents come together here."

"It all looks bloody the same," said Jon. "How can you possibly tell?"

"I don't know. Something I feel. I think this channel on our left will lead to Amma."

"Well, the tentacles go that way, so we might as well follow them and see," Ryan said.

Sam wasn't sure she could trust her own senses. She'd been alone and in the dark, until she'd reached the great cavern that had provided light. That light had to come from the surface, so they were going in the right direction. They had to continue.

When they reached the cavern, it was as if a great weight fell from their shoulders. They could see once more, without artificial light or the pulsating glow of the tentacles.

"Were you here?" Ryan asked.

"Yes. Amma must be close." She noticed an opening in the side of the cavern she hadn't seen before and went over to look at it.

"There's something in here," she said.

He came over beside her and played his flashlight into the opening. He took in a sudden, sharp breath. Sam grabbed his hand tightly.

"More of them," She whispered.

The space was filled with the strange chrysalises. They lined the walls, dripping and shiny in the light.

"There must be dozens of them," she said in a hushed voice.

"More like scores," said Ryan. "Maybe this is where the rest of the Vikings, the Nazis who disappeared, even Dagursson's lost tourists ended up."

Suddenly, they heard the strange wailing sound again. Sam whirled around.

"What's that?" asked Jon, his voice edging near panic.

Sam moved away from the opening and toward a more familiar venthole.

"It's Amma," she said to no one in particular. Her heart was pounding. She had little desire to encounter the Viking woman again. Still, she had more questions about this place. Maybe Amma could answer some of them.

Then she once again stood beside the terrible apparition attached to the wall. The Norse woman looked the same. Her stringy gray hair hung down and appeared to shimmer from the glue of the chrysalis.

The others came up beside her and gaped. The wailing had subsided, but Amma's mouth continued to open and close.

Senator Graham moved next to his daughter. He stared at the figure as though seeing his own personal demon.

"This is the Viking woman?" he asked.

Sam nodded. "She calls herself Amma, which was the name Hauptmann found in the sagas. She lived in the tenth century. If what we're seeing is really her, she would be over a thousand years old."

Something fired in the senator's eyes. He was face to face, at last, with what he'd been searching for all of his adult life. He reached out a hand, hesitated, then touched the strange figure.

Amma's eyes opened wide and Graham stared into them as though they might somehow hold the answer to his search for the Holy Grail.

"How . . . how have you lived so long?" he asked.

"Laki," came the one word reply. Then Amma said a spray of words.

"I don't understand what she's saying," Graham said.

"Just wait," said Sam.

Amma continued to speak in ancient Norse. After a few moments, they suddenly realized they could understand the words.

""How is that possible?" Ryan asked in a whisper. "I don't understand ancient Norse."

"It happened to me before," said Sam. "Somehow, we are meant to understand."

Graham leaned closer to the chrysalis. "How have you lived so long?" he asked again. "Is it something here? Something you eat? The mushrooms? Is it the air? The volcanic gas? What made it possible for you to live for a thousand years?"

"Laki," came the single word answer again. Then Amma said, "Laki needs me."

There was an air of pride in the old woman's voice.

"I speak for Laki," she said. "In return, Laki allows me to live . . . forever."

"You call this living?" asked Graham, a note of horror in his voice. "Frozen to a wall, alone in a black cavern?"

"I am not alone," Amma said. Her eyes were like two sightless orbs, but they moved, turning toward the opening where the other chrysalises hung. "My clan is all here," she said. "Skari is here. He was the first to meet our god. Those of us who resisted, died in our chamber underground. But those who accepted him will live forever. Laki is God, but he asks nothing of us. We have free will," she said.

"Jesus," said Jon. "Free will?"

Kraus moved next to the senator. His face was filled with suspicion and disbelief. "What does your god give you in return for your free will?" he asked.

"Eternal life," said Amma.

"This?" Kraus said in disbelief. "If this is eternal life, it is in hell."

"Laki does not care what we think," Amma said. "Laki wishes only to be left alone."

Sam turned to her father and put her hand on his arm. "Is this what you've been in search of for forty years?"

"No." The pain in her father's eyes was palpable. "I want no part of this awful thing. Death would be better than this."

***

The shock of their confrontation with Amma weighed on all of them. It seemed to sap their will to continue. They moved back into the light of the cavern and rested. Senator Graham, especially, was subdued. He moved away from the others and sat on the floor, his head in his hands.

Ryan sat with Sam, their bodies touching, seeking comfort in their shared warmth.

"I think your father may finally be ready to reconsider his long quest for longevity," he said.

"Seeing Amma was definitely a shock to him. Not exactly what he had in mind when he contemplated extended life. He hasn't spoken to me or anyone. I don't know how, or if, he'll come out of this."

Kraus sat next to them. He looked completely drained by their encounter. "I don't understand what that thing meant," he said.

"How so?" Ryan asked.

"Amma said that they bargained with Laki, that those who accepted what the volcano was, a living god, were given eternal life. But she also said that Laki didn't care *what* they thought, that it only wanted to be left alone. For sure, it is a contradiction. They had to accept Laki in order to be given eternal life—to be saved. But at the same time, Laki just wanted to be left alone. It—Laki—God, whatever you want to call it, cares yet doesn't care."

"Sounds like your typical god to me," said Ryan. "Full of contradictions. Many religions tell us that God loves us, even created us in his image. But then we're presented with a perfect conundrum—we're given free will, so we can reject him if we want. Thus God, who supposedly loves us, is perfectly willing to let us suffer and die and go to Hell. He's the one who creates the parameters. We can believe in him and receive paradise or we can reject him and go to Hell—at least in the traditional Catholic tradition. It's up to us, except we only have two choices, the two *he* is willing to give us. That's some kind of tough love, all right."

He looked at Kraus. "What I think, if God actually exists at all, is that he's simply lost interest in his creation. How can he allow us to suffer such torment if he loves us? That's no definition of love that I accept. I understand you are a religious man. I bet I can guess what your response to all this will be."

Kraus raised an eyebrow. "Indeed?"

"You'll say that we have to accept what God does on faith. We can't understand his higher purpose. Well, that's a cop-out in my opinion. Because you can't explain why God has abandoned us, you fall back on, 'Oh, well, we really can't understand him.'"

"But that's true," said Kraus.

"Bullshit," said Ryan. "What's true is what Amma said. Laki doesn't care what we do. He just wants to be left alone. Laki wants to be left alone so much he makes us paranoid to try to get us to go away. If he created us, it was an afterthought. Probably one he now regrets."

"God gives us free will so we can be more like him," said Kraus. "So we're not mere automatons, figures of clay that have to do what he says. We can make our own decisions."

"Maybe so," said Ryan. "But if that's the case, why didn't he give us a little more strength of character before setting us loose? He made us, after all. He could do whatever he wanted. But he deliberately made us imperfect. And that's being generous. If you look at all the horrors of human frailty on exhibit in the world, an argument can be made that he didn't just make us imperfect, he made us weak and vacillating and self-absorbed and cruel . . . the list goes on. Why couldn't he have made us better to begin with?"

"There is evil in the world," said Kraus. "God must deal with the devil."

"Oh, give me a break," Ryan waved his hand at Kraus. "You religious types always have some way to excuse the evils of the world. If God isn't stronger than the devil, then he's not really God, is he?"

"Well I for one don't believe in God," said Jon. "This horrible place is proof, as far as I'm concerned, that there is no God, period. And this conversation isn't getting us out of here. Will someone, please, for Christ's sake, talk about that!"

Sam stood up. "Jon's right. We can debate all this later in the comfort of our living rooms. Provided we live so long." She stared up at the light filtering down from above. "I think I see a way out of here. It won't be easy, but we can do it. Let's not waste any more time."

***

It took two long hours to clamber out of the cavern. They emerged to find a world gone haywire. They were below the far western rim of Laki, an area where Sam had spent little time, perhaps a three-hour hike back to the parking lot.

They gaped at the surrounding landscape. The surface of Laki resembled something out of Dante's Hell. The sky was black with boiling clouds that raced across the firmament. Mini-tornados seemed to be everywhere, forming instantly, raising black spirals of dust and loose rock, only to collide with one another and collapse.

One of these appeared ready to descend on them. There was no way to outrun the phenomenon. They looked around wildly for shelter. Then the storm collided with another and both dissipated, leaving them covering their heads as rocks and dust fell on them.

"Look at those lava flows," said Ryan. "There must be half a dozen of them. We're going to have our work cut out finding a path through them."

Even as he spoke, the ground a hundred yards away heaved and split open and a new flow emerged. The liquid rock began to pour toward them.

"Come on," he said. "Time to get the hell out of Dodge."

"More like time to get the hell out of Hell," said Sam, contemplating their fiery surroundings.

Their path across the tortured surface of Laki might have been an exercise in avoidance training. It seemed every avenue they took led to another obstacle. They followed a circuitous route that took them much longer than they'd expected. When at last they saw the parking lot, the little group gave out a small cheer.

Jon raced ahead, crying out as figures began to emerge from the two buses, their faces incredulous that anyone could have survived and emerged from beneath Laki.

Ryan and Sam made their way up to Professor Hauptmann, who beamed at them.

"I had given up all hope for you," he said. He gave Sam a bear hug and grasped Ryan by the shoulder.

"But why are you still here?" asked Sam. "This whole place could collapse into a great cauldron of lava. It's beyond dangerous."

Hauptmann nodded. "Believe me, the thought has crossed all of our minds. Let me introduce you to Mr. Prescott Carlisle. He works for the President of the United States and has come here with all this marvelous equipment to try to help."

Incredulity in his voice, Carlisle said to Ryan, "I remember you. I met you once when you worked for our previous President. Glad to see you made it out safely." He nodded to Graham. "Senator. Glad you're safe too, though I think the President may have some questions as to why you are here."

Graham simply stared blankly at the distorted landscape. With the loss of his dream of extended life, at least in any credible form, his political career appeared to hold little interest for him anymore. He was still very much in a state of shock over their experiences.

"Perhaps," Carlisle continued, "You can tell us something about conditions underground. We have reams of technical data but no first-hand information."

Sam related what they'd encountered beneath Laki. She left nothing out. When she was finished, Hauptmann stared at her with wide eyes.

"Amma exists?" he asked in an awed whisper. "The sagas are true." He seemed overwhelmed by the news.

In turn, Carlisle filled them in on what was happening not only on Laki but also around the world.

It was Sam's turn to be incredulous. "Volcanoes all over the globe are erupting?" she asked, unable to get her mind around the unimaginable concept.

"Yes," Carlisle said. "And what's worse, religious leaders appear to believe that it's because of Laki that something spiritual is happening here." He spread his hands. "It's hard to fathom what may be going on in their heads. The President is at a loss over how to react."

"Join the club," said Ryan.

"One more thing we haven't told you." The President's advisor met their eyes with his own hard, blue orbs. "An Arab by the name of Rashid may have planted a nuclear device beneath the surface with the goal of completely destabilizing Laki."

It was the first time Sam, Kraus, and Jon had heard this. But it was hardly news to Ryan. "I know," he said. "Akbari told me, and the senator also knows. They were concerned about what it might do to their longevity investigations and were desperate to stop him."

"You might as well come inside," said Carlisle. "I want to hear first-hand what you think is going on here. And perhaps we can tell you a thing or two."

They crowded into his tiny office, spilling out beyond the partition that separated it from the rest of the bus. Carlisle gave his chair to Sam and stood in front of a bank of computers.

"So," he began, "Do any of you have an opinion on Laki? Is it some sort of natural phenomenon or does the religious community have a leg to stand on? I told the President I'd get back to him with something for him to feed the holy rollers and frankly, I could use some input."

Ryan shook his head slowly. "When I stared down into that . . . whatever it was . . . hole at the center of the Earth, I had no idea what I was looking at. It was like staring into a miniature universe. One that seemed to suck the light and energy out of the tentacles and anything else that got too close—including poor Akbari." He looked at Sam. "And what were those stars?"

She stared at the floor as though she might see right through the bottom of the bus. "Before I talked with Amma, I would have said it was some sort of natural phenomenon, a magma chamber maybe. But we actually met and conversed, if you can call it that, with a human being who has lived for over a thousand years. There's no question what Amma thinks Laki is. A god, pure and simple."

Carlisle said, "According to our measurements, Laki has an enormous magma chamber deep in the Earth. You could have been looking into that. The stars you mention might have simply been hot spots. Or . . ."

"Or what?" Ryan asked.

Carlisle looked uncomfortable. "You *could* have been seeing electrons spinning off from Kaluza-Klein particles in another dimension."

The silence in the tiny space was heavy. Kraus was the first to speak. "Another dimension," he said, almost to himself. "I guess that could be one definition of God."

One of the technicians peered around the partition and said, "We got a real good fix on the Pu-239, sir. Uh . . . and you might want to come outside and talk to the military staff. They picked up two men who were coming out of a venthole."

"Who are they?"

"Don't know, sir, but they appear to be foreign nationals . . . and they're pretty nervous about something."

Chapter Twenty-Two

Outside, half a dozen soldiers kept an eye on two distraught-looking men. To Ryan's eye, they were obviously of Arab descent and he realized with a start that the older man was probably the one Akbari had called Rashid.

He went over to the officer in charge.

"Where did you find them?" he asked.

"We were doing a perimeter check," said the sergeant. "We do one every hour, looking for new lava flows or other disturbances, trying to determine if the road's in danger of being cut off. These two," he gestured at the men with his thumb, "came barreling out of a venthole like they were being chased by demons from hell. When they saw us, they took off down toward the parking lot. We didn't know who they were, but they were sure acting suspiciously. So we went after them, and . . . here they are. Haven't said much, except to repeat that we have no right to detain them."

"Mind if I talk to them?"

"Be my guest. The older one speaks English well enough. The other one hasn't said a word, just looks at his comrade and keeps checking his watch."

Ryan went over to the figure he believed was Rashid. The man sat on a rock. He was clearly agitated, his dark eyes darting about the wild landscape. When he saw Ryan, he stood up.

"You can't keep us here," he said. "This place is too dangerous. We're just civilians. Tourists who got lost. As foreign nationals we demand to be taken to our embassy in Reykjavik at once."

Ryan stared at him. "I know who you are," he said. "Your name is Rashid and you've been attempting to blow Laki up with a nuclear weapon."

The Arab's face registered a combination of surprise, fear, resentment, and superiority all at once. He glanced around. There was no one within earshot. In a low voice, he said, "Take us out of here and I will pay you one million dollars."

Ryan ignored the offer. "How much time do we have?" he asked.

The Arab started to plead ignorance to the question, then thought better of it. He looked at his watch. "In less than three hours, this entire place will be vaporized. Laki will erupt in a massive explosion. All southern Iceland will become a radioactive wasteland. Believe me, you don't want to be here when that happens anymore than I do."

"You're going to take me to where you left the device," Ryan said.

"Are you mad?" asked Rashid. "We were lost down there, wandering from venthole to venthole. I couldn't find it again if I wanted to. Even if I could, it would make no difference. The device can't be disarmed once the timer's been set."

Ryan stared at him for another moment, then turned and said to the sergeant, "Keep an eye on them. Under no circumstances are they to be allowed to leave here."

Then he turned abruptly and went back to the bus.

Carlisle, Sam, and Hauptmann were consulting in Carlisle's tiny office, staring at a sheaf of computer readouts. Sam looked up as Ryan came in. "They've got a fix on the nuclear device, tracing the plutonium. It's in a deep venthole, and it looks like a new opening has occurred just in the last hour that may give us a more direct route to it—with the small proviso that it's not already filled with lava," She said. She grabbed his arm. "We've got to go get it."

He took a deep breath. "One of the men brought in by the military people is called Rashid. He's the one behind the nuclear device and he says it can't be disarmed. That there's no way to stop it."

They all stared at him. "Do you believe him?" Sam asked.

"I believe he's scared as hell. Offered me a million bucks to get him out of here, for Christ's sake. He understands he's not going anywhere. His only chance to survive is to disarm the device. If he's not even willing to try, it probably means it can't be done."

"Jesus!" said Sam. "How much time do we have?"

"Less than three hours."

"What are we going to do?"

"I don't think there's any way we could get clear of a major blast in the time we have left. The roads are poor and the disruptions, earthquakes, and lava flows would slow us even more."

"What about calling in helicopters?"

"Atmospheric conditions make communications with the outside iffy at best. And these crazy thermals and tornados would be nearly suicidal for aircraft. Anyway, I heard Akbari offer a million dollars to his pilot if he came back for him. I haven't seen any sign of the man. He's probably too scared to come back. Besides, we'd need a fleet of choppers to take everyone out. There are at least fifty people here on Laki."

"So you're saying . . . there's nothing we can do?"

"Our only hope is to find the device and try to disarm it. Maybe Rashid is lying or wrong about that. I don't see any alternative."

***

Cardinal Wormer fidgeted nervously. He'd never had a private audience with the Pope before. Indeed, he'd met the pontiff only as part of a group of cardinals. To be summoned as he was for a meeting at the Vatican would normally have been the greatest honor of his life—one that he would have endeavored to manipulate to his own best interests in whatever way possible.

But he knew he wasn't here to have coffee and a theological chat. The entire world was in an uproar over what was going on in Iceland and over the outbreak of convulsions in volcanoes everywhere.

Vesuvius itself was just over a hundred miles away and had been belching steam for days. Still, he believed this could be his moment. Somehow, the Pope knew of his connection with Laki and was seeking his advice. It was perfect.

A young priest in a plain, black robe approached and nodded to him. "His Holiness will see you now," he said.

The pontiff stood before the open balcony that looked out on St. Peter's Square. He looked much older than Wormer remembered. Rumors of his declining health were evidently correct. This, too, did not displease the Cardinal. Only when Popes died did real upward movement occur in the Vatican hierarchy.

Standing next to the pontiff was the papal Secretariat, Demetrio Ricci. Ricci's position was one that Wormer had long considered appropriate for himself. It would place him at the seat of power.

Dark-skinned with a beak nose and pockmarked face, Ricci was known to be a no-nonsense hardliner. His presence was proof, if any were needed, that this was not a social call.

Wormer knelt before the pontiff and kissed his ring, then rose at the Pope's uplifted hand. "Come here, my Cardinal," he said, gesturing to the window.

Wormer moved forward, puzzled.

"Tell me, what do you see?"

He stared out the window. "Your Holiness, I see the great square of St. Peter and . . . uh . . . many of your subjects. I . . . that is all."

"Raise your sights, Cardinal," said the pontiff. "On the horizon, even at such a great distance, you can see clouds of steam rising from Vesuvius. My advisors tell us that a full eruption may be imminent. We are aware of the activities of your . . . organization . . . that has for decades concerned itself with a certain volcano in Iceland. Surely you didn't think your group was unknown to us?"

Wormer swallowed heavily. He'd long suspected as much and wondered momentarily which of his group had been a spy for the Vatican. Members swore an oath to tell no one of their activities. But he was well aware that no one could renege on an oath more quickly than a high member of the church. There were many ways to receive dispensation for breaking an oath. Reporting directly to the pontiff was one of those ways.

"Your Holiness, I'm honored by your interest. For sixty years, our members have studied the unusual case of Laki. Until recently, there has been little to report. A fascinating history, to be sure, dating from the time of the Vikings and including the efforts of the Nazis, as well. But for the most part, our meetings are typically theological in nature, along the lines of how many angels can dance on the head of a pin. I would not have bothered Your Holiness with such trivia."

"Trivia," said the Pope. He stared out at the clouded horizon and shook his head. He looked tired and old.

Ricci cleared his throat. "What His Holiness would like to know is why the volcanoes are threatening his subjects. We have prayed on this without success. Do you truly believe there is another power involved here? One that threatens the Holy See?"

"There can be no power greater than that of the Holy See," said Wormer quickly.

"Heartwarming to hear it," said Ricci. "Perhaps you can tell us, then, precisely what we are dealing with."

This is not going well, Wormer thought.

"Your Holiness, there is an interesting history, as I said. The ancient Vikings believed Laki was a god, one that seemed to have the ability to prolong human life. The Third Reich followed up on this and experienced many unusual phenomena during their time in Iceland. The German Catholic church felt it was in our—excuse me—in your Holiness's interest to try to determine if there was any truth to the claims of longevity, since it was felt this could prove to be a challenge to the authority of the church."

Ricci exchanged looks with the Pope. "Good of you to try to protect the church under your own auspices," he said. "Save us the undo worry."

Wormer didn't care for the way the papal Secretariat appeared to have taken over the job of questioning him.

"Evidence is sketchy. It has been so for decades," Wormer said. "However, it certainly seems that Laki's reach has recently been extended. It was my intention to request a meeting with His Holiness at his earliest convenience to discuss new developments. Unfortunately, events overtook us, and I am here now at the request of His Holiness."

"No one can question the ultimate authority of the church," said the pontiff. "Yet clearly, something of note is occurring in Iceland, something that is affecting the entire world. Press coverage of events has been extensive, and many have speculated on the connection between Laki and recent volcanic upheavals around the globe. Perhaps it is purely geological in nature. We are not without our own scientists. They tell us that the volcano Laki may have an underground magma chamber that could connect with a magma vault, if you will, that encircles the entire earth."

"Yes, Your Holiness, I have heard this as well."

"More concerning is this question of extended life. Here we are entering the purview of our Lord God. He alone controls the allotted three score years and ten. We are of the mind that such a claim must be nipped in the bud."

"Perhaps, Your Holiness, Laki will do this for us. I understand massive lava flows have begun. If this continues, they could blanket the volcano, covering and burying whatever may be causing the longevity effect. It could, after all, simply be something of a scientific nature, a plant, perhaps, or a mixture of volcanic gases that may have some slight effect on the human immune system. Blown out of proportion by those eager to believe there may be a Holy Grail."

The pontiff smiled. "We're inclined to agree with this interpretation. Nevertheless, we are concerned for our people living in proximity around the globe to these volcanic incidents. We have decided to send a delegation of cardinals to Laki to pray on the matter . . . in close proximity to the problem."

Ricci said, "By sending cardinals, we show the seriousness with which we take the issue. This will be done in the open, with full knowledge of the world press. So that our congregants can see that their pontiff is concerned and willing to take on any false gods."

"A most worthy approach," Wormer said, breathing a sigh of relief that he was evidently not going to be taken to account or even demoted for keeping the existence of his group a secret.

"We have selected you," the pontiff added, "to lead this delegation."

Wormer nearly choked. "You . . . your Holiness . . . I've been following accounts in the press. Iceland is a dangerous place right now and the volcano even more so. It would be a very risky undertaking."

"All the more reason to show the power of our prayer, I'm sure you agree," said Ricci. "Everything is arranged. His Holiness's personal plane has been put at your disposal and is prepared to leave at once. Ten cardinals have been selected from among those who happened to be visiting the Vatican. They await only your expertise, Cardinal Wormer."

***

"You can't do this! It's too dangerous." Senator Graham spoke more forcefully than he had since his meeting with Amma. Indeed, the thought of danger to Sam seemed to have brought him back to reality. "I won't allow it."

Sam sighed and took her father's hand. "I have to go. Don't you see it's our only chance? I know this place better than anyone."

"You're all I have left," Graham said.

"Sam is right, Senator," said Ryan. "I don't like the idea of her going down there anymore than you do. But she could be crucial to our finding Rashid's device. If she stays here and we fail, we're all going to die anyway."

Carlisle appeared with one of his youngest looking scientists. "This is Andy Pryne. He's the most knowledgeable man I have with regard to nuclear technology. He's volunteered to go with you to help defuse the weapon if you find it."

"We have to find it," Ryan said. "And there's no more time to waste. We've less than three hours. Your men have shown me the new vent opening they think will lead more or less directly to where Rashid left the thing."

"I will go too," said Hauptmann.

Sam looked at him. "There's no need, Ernst. What can you do?"

"I wish to meet Amma," he replied simply. "There is much I want to ask her . . . about the sagas and what happened to her clan."

"There won't be time for that," said Sam.

"There will be time after the bomb has been defused. If we fail in that, then . . . nothing really matters does it?"

"I might as well come along too," said Dagursson. "My men gave their lives down there. I want to know why."

They moved quickly to the new vent entrance. Carlisle handed Ryan a computer printout showing the supposed location of the bomb and the new passageway they hoped would lead to it. Andy Pryne had a backpack filled with specialized tools. Each of them carried a powerful flashlight, drinking water and, as an afterthought, food. Even if they were successful, the changing conditions under- ground could block their retreat. They could become lost under- ground once again.

Sam led the way into the new opening.

"Be careful what you touch," she said. "The sides are still warm. There could be hot spots anywhere."

"Are we likely to encounter a new lava flow?" asked Dagursson.

"I'd say we're likely to encounter just about anything. I've given up trying to predict what Laki will do next."

As if to reinforce her point, the decibel level seemed to ratchet up as they moved lower. Small quakes rattled the ground beneath their feet and their nerves as well. The smell of sulfur in the air was strong. Every few minutes they heard what could only be interpreted as the collapse of distant ventholes.

"It'll be a bloody miracle if we manage to find our way back through this same tunnel," said Ryan. "You were right, Sam, when you said this place is like a Swiss cheese. If we get a big enough quake, the entire subsurface might just pancake like the Trade Center on 9/11."

She nodded grimly. "Hard to imagine what might happen if Rashid's device detonates. I suppose it could even open up the hole we saw, or magma chamber or whatever it is. All of Southern Iceland—hell, the entire country might disintegrate in a catastrophic eruption. Only consolation is, we'll never know if it happens."

Hauptmann puffed along beside them. He was not in the best of shape, but he was driven by his fierce intellectual desire to know what Amma knew.

To Sam he said, "You have no doubt? Amma believes Laki is a god?"

"Yes, or maybe one of many gods. The Vikings had quite a few, as you know, Odin, Baldur, Asgard, Thor. It's a long list. I don't know exactly what Amma thinks, but my impression was that she considered Laki perhaps the most important of them all. All powerful."

"She knew about the *hole at the center of the earth*," said Hauptmann. "It was in the sagas. Did she say anything about that?"

"No. My sense was she was there to tell us that Laki wished to be left alone. That her god wanted nothing to do with us."

He stared at her. "So Amma is the voice of God?"

She raised and lowered her shoulders. "It struck me that something was speaking through her. But I could have been wrong. I was pretty damn paranoid the whole time. Speaking to that apparition glued to the wall in that black passageway would have made anyone paranoid."

The smell of sulfur continued to grow stronger and seemed to be wafting toward them on an increasingly strong breeze.

Ryan said, "This breeze must mean we're getting closer to the hole." He pondered the computer printout Carlisle had given him, then looked at his watch. "We can't get distracted," he said. "We've less than two hours."

Pryne stopped and shook his pack off. He consulted a radiation detector.

"We should be getting near it," he said.

"Unless you're simply detecting background radiation," Sam suggested. "Who the hell knows what could be coming out of that hole. Your boss suggested there was some sort of cosmic radiation, right? And they didn't know where it was coming from."

Pryne shrugged. "Not the same thing. Elements thrown off by Kaluza-Klein particles, for instance, have a different profile. There's no question the readings I'm getting are from the device."

The passage they were using began to intersect with other new openings. In each instance, Pryne was able to direct them according to the strength of his readings.

"I'm surprised Rashid went down this far," Dagursson said. "It would hardly seem necessary."

"He's a fanatic," said Ryan. "He wanted to assure himself of the greatest possible effect."

Suddenly, the walls of the vent seemed to shudder. They all stood stock still, waiting for they knew not what. Then a part of the vent collapsed, opening up yet another passageway. The wind coming from the new opening was much stronger.

Pryne said, "My readings are going off the chart. We must be very close. Take the new opening."

Again, Sam led the way and after going less than a hundred yards, they saw it. The device sat on the passage floor. It was about four feet long and oval-shaped. As they approached, they could clearly see the timer ticking off their precious remaining seconds on a red digital counter.

Pryne went to it immediately, took off his pack, and began to examine the strange object. The others gathered around, a little in awe at being so close to a nuclear weapon.

"Guess we're at Ground Zero," Ryan said. "If we don't figure this thing out, we'll never know what hit us."

"Can you stop it?" Sam asked Andy.

"Don't know," he grunted. "It's a complicated mechanism. Could even be booby-trapped to go off if it's tampered with. This will take a while."

The others slumped to the ground and watched as Pryne studied the weapon.

"I'm of no use here," said Hauptmann. "Sam, you said the breeze came from the hole. I wish to see it."

"Why not?" she said. "I'll go with you. We just have to follow the wind."

"I don't think we should split up," said Ryan. "What if there's another tunnel collapse? We might not be able to get back together again."

"I have another reason for wanting to find the hole," Sam said.

"What?"

She met his eyes, something indefinable in them, but she refused to say more and looked away.

"All right, all right. But someone should stay with Andy in case he needs an extra pair of hands." He looked at Dagursson.

"I'm about as useful here as Hauptmann," said the police commissioner. "And I'd like to see this so-called hole too."

"Guess that leaves me," Ryan said. "Be careful."

Sam leaned over and gave him a kiss. "Don't worry. Either we come out of this together or we don't come out at all. If the end result is bad, we'll never know it."

**

President Thurman was meeting with his Joint Chiefs of Staff and with the head of Homeland Security, Alexander Pinkerton.

"We've got volcanoes all over North America acting up," Pinkerton said. "Mount St. Helens, Popocatepetl in Mexico, Mount Redoubt in the Aleutians, hell, even Yellowstone is suffering an earthquake every hour. There are at least fifty active volcanoes in the United States."

"Well what the hell are we doing about it?" demanded the President.

General Magneson said, "We've mobilized the Reserves in all fifty states, in the event one of these things really goes off, though most of the volcanoes are located in the Aleutians. Emergency broadcast systems have been activated, but . . ."

"What? Spit it out, General."

"Sir, all we can really do is prepare for a catastrophe. There's nothing we can do by way of prevention, if you see what I mean."

The President stood up, went over to the window of the Oval Office, and stared out at Pennsylvania Avenue. He nodded at the mass of humanity just beyond the gates.

"They probably wouldn't agree with you," he said, staring at a sea of signs calling for prayer as a way of dealing with the challenge facing humanity. "The religious nuts are out in force. There's even been a call to impeach the godless chief of state in order to appease the volcanoes."

"Yes, I heard that, Mr. President," said Pinkerton. "It came from Jonathan Harney, 'Hatchet' Harney, the televangelist. No one gives a damn what that idiot says."

Thurman turned back to the table. "I give a damn! That's *me* they're talking about. Has the whole world gone crazy? The Pope's been calling me three times a day. Wants to know what I'm doing about the evil that lurks beneath Laki. He says he's taking matters into his own hands, arranging a delegation to go to Iceland to pray, for Christ's sake."

"Probably can't do any harm," General Magneson muttered.

Thurman stared at the General, but before he could say anything, an aide entered the room and went round to the President.

"Sir, you have a call from your Science Advisor."

The President picked up the phone and put it on speaker so everyone could hear. "What the hell's going on now, Prescott?"

The voice was sketchy, bleeding in and out, then firmed up. "Mr. President, I've been trying to get hold of you. Our communications are not good here. We've got all kinds of atmospheric disturbance—cosmic particles are going through the roof, mini-tornados all around, lava flows, everything but the Second Coming."

"Yes, yes, tell me something I don't know, Prescott. We've got our own problems on this side of the world."

"Well, here's something you probably don't know, sir. We have firm evidence that a nuclear device has been set to detonate beneath Laki in less than two hours."

The silence in the Oval Office was thick.

"Why . . ." The President had trouble with the words. "Why would anyone want to do that?"

"Something to do with the Iranians, sir. Near as we've been able to figure from what Senator Graham has told us, they were trying to set Laki off to somehow affect the world price of oil."

Thurman said, "Senator Graham is there with you?"

"Yes sir. He and his daughter have . . . uh . . . actually been helping us track down the perpetrators. We have two of them in custody, as a matter of fact. Main guy is called Rashid, but they aren't being cooperative, except to tell us that in two hours we'll all be incinerated and there's nothing anyone can do to stop it." There was silence on the line for a moment. "So, this may be my last communication, Mr. President. We have a team underground searching for the device. But even if they find it, it's highly unlikely in my opinion that they'll be able to deactivate it."

"Can't you get out of there, Prescott?"

"No, sir. Lava flows have cut us off. In any case, there's not enough time. I hope you'll give commendations to all of my people, Mr. President. They've worked hard and put their lives on the line."

Thurman looked completely drained. "We'll do what we can on this end, Prescott. God be with you."

But the line had already gone dead.

Chapter Twenty-Three

Sam led Hauptmann and Dagursson toward the source of the ever-growing wind. As they grew closer, they had to lean more and more firmly into the gale.

"I have never experienced such a thing," said Hauptmann. "Where is it coming from?"

"You'll see soon enough," Sam replied. She was getting used to the incredulity of those she led to the hole. She glanced at Dagursson. "Would you say you are a religious man, Commissioner?"

He shook his head. "Never could take to it. Probably a cop's mentality. You see enough bad stuff and you begin to question what the point of God is if he won't do something about the mess once in a while, you know?"

She nodded. "Good. Ernst I know is a nonbeliever."

"What difference does that make?"

"Perhaps none. But the hole seems to take hold of true believers more powerfully than others. Akbari was one who couldn't resist. Kraus said he came close to being pulled in as well. They were both religious men. Ryan, my father, Jon, and I were not tempted, and we are all non-believers."

Dagursson seemed startled by the information. "You talk as if this hole were intelligent . . . scheming, somehow, against us. Do you have any idea how crazy that sounds?"

She had no answer for him. When they reached the opening, the wind was once again overpowering. Everything was as it had been. The throbbing, arm-sized tentacles poured over the edge of the hole and disappeared into the depths.

Dagursson fought his way to the stone wall and peered in, his thick silver hair plastered back against his head. The others came up beside him, grasping one another against the gale, but also against the possibility that one of them might be tempted to throw himself in as Akbari had.

"Incredible," Hauptmann gasped. "It is Amma's hole at the center of the Earth. Just as she described it. A hole with stars. The sagas were correct."

"Correct, yes," said Sam. "But what *is* it?"

As they stared into the depths, the pinpoints of light that appeared to be stars began to coalesce. Soon, they were swirling into patterns.

"My God," Dagursson said. "Look. They're forming . . ."

"Galaxies," Hauptmann said softly, his voice almost disappearing in the wind.

The stars had begun to come together into shapes. Familiar shapes . . . clusters that looked like spiral galaxies, one that had the appearance of a butterfly, others that appeared to be colliding, pulling each other apart like taffy being spun out.

"What are we looking at?" asked Dagursson in a voice filled with awe. "It . . . it's almost like being in a planetarium. As though someone's putting on a show for us."

"I don't think so," said Sam. "I think what we're seeing is real."

The others managed to tear their eyes away from the incredible spectacle long enough to stare at her.

"Carlisle said something I didn't completely understand," she went on. "Something about cosmic particles bombarding us, about Kaluza-Klein particles and another dimension. That's why I wanted to come back here, to see it again. I think we're looking into the heart of the universe. Some sort of portal to another dimension."

"How can such a thing be possible?" asked Hauptmann. "It is contained. How can the entire universe be contained in a hole in the ground?"

"Maybe it's not contained," Dagursson said. "At least not in any way we can identify with. Maybe we're seeing into another dimension . . . like a window. We're being offered a view through a window into another universe."

"But why? How?" Hauptmann asked. "For what reason?"

For this, no one had a reply, but Sam said, "I don't know what it all means . . . but it just might represent salvation for us."

Before anyone could think of something to say to this, she added, "Come on. I want to return to Amma. Ernst, you said you wished to ask her questions. Well, so do I."

Sam felt as though she were actually beginning to know her way around this nether world. It took only a few minutes to find their way to Amma's side. The gruesome sight of the ancient woman was no less heart-stopping than it had been the first time she encountered it.

Dagursson and Hauptmann held back, unable to absorb what they were seeing.

"It's all right," Sam said. "It won't hurt you. This is Amma, Professor. She'll answer your questions . . . at least if you understand the answers."

But for the moment, Hauptmann appeared to have forgotten the questions. He peered at the strange apparition, reached out one hand, and touched it. Amma's eyes opened abruptly and the professor backed away quickly.

He stared at Amma for perhaps a full minute before finally finding his voice. "What . . . what happened to your clan?" he asked.

Amma responded in her disembodied voice with a stream of words in ancient Norse.

Hauptmann turned to Sam. "She speaks too quickly. I cannot understand her."

"Wait," Sam said. "You'll begin to understand."

And indeed, almost at once, Hauptmann realized he was starting to comprehend what the figure was saying. Again, he asked, "What happened to your people?"

"They are all here," came Amma's reply. "Even Skari."

"They were absorbed, as you were? By what?"

"We are not absorbed. We are one . . . with Laki," said Amma.

"What is Laki?"

Amma's eyes seemed to roll back in her head, as though she were entering a trance, though truth be told, the entire setting was as surreal and trancelike as anything any of them had ever experienced.

"I . . . am . . . God," said the figure.

They all stared at her. If this was the answer they might have been expecting, it wasn't one they were prepared to accept.

"But you are Amma," Hauptmann said.

"It is the same," said the voice.

"Does . . . does your clan worship Laki?" Hauptmann asked.

"We revered him . . . in our other lives . . . feared him at first. We shut ourselves off, buried ourselves alive. To us, our deaths were real, and we mourned as each of us passed. But then we were reborn here."

"You call this a rebirth?" asked Dagursson. "A living hell would be more like it."

"What do you want?" Sam asked. "What does Laki want of us?"

"Nothing," Amma replied.

"Do you want us to worship you?" Hauptmann asked.

"No."

"But why are you here? Why are we here?" asked Sam.

"I am here because I am here," said the voice of Laki. "You are here because of me."

"You created us?"

There was a long silence. Amma's eyes rolled back down out of her forehead and stared at them. "It was nothing," she said.

"Jesus!" Dagursson said.

"Then why did you do it?" Hauptmann asked softly. "We were not created for a reason? For a purpose?"

"It was nothing," the voice repeated. Then Amma's eyes closed once again, and she seemed to go to sleep.

"So," Hauptmann said in a small voice. "We are nothing."

Sam put one hand on his shoulder. "Isn't that what you always believed, Ernst?"

"I do not believe in God, or that we have some higher purpose. But I always believed we might, someday, evolve into something . . . better." He rubbed his eyes. "I would have preferred that we rose from the depths to become what we could become. On our own merit. Not this. Not that we were created . . . for no reason. For what? A whim? A mistake?"

"We are nothing," Dagursson repeated, shaking his head.

"Perhaps," Sam said softly. "Perhaps that is all there is. But even so, we may be able to make use of Laki. We may be nothing to it, but it may be everything to us."

Hauptmann looked at her blankly, but Dagursson seemed to take her meaning.

"Yes," he said. "You're right." He looked around. "We need to get back to the others."

***

They found Andy Pryne still huddled over the device, a series of inscrutable tools spread out before him on the passage floor. Ryan sat next to him, ready to assist at a moment's notice. When he saw Sam, he leaped to his feet and greeted her with a bear hug.

"I was worried," he said. "You were gone too long." He looked past her at Professor Hauptmann. "Did you get the answers you were looking for?"

Hauptmann merely shook his head and slumped to the ground. Dagursson did the same.

"It wasn't what we expected," said Sam. "Amma considers herself one with Laki . . . and she considers Laki to be God. But he's not the sort of God you or I might envision."

Ryan looked puzzled. "How do you mean?"

She sighed. "Amma says Laki created us, but doesn't care what we do, doesn't want us to worship him. He would rather that we just went away. He said that creating us was nothing."

"Nothing? But then, why bother?"

"I do not believe that thing is God," said Hauptmann. "The devil maybe."

"We saw something else," said Sam. "Something you and I didn't see before. When we looked into the hole, the pinpoints of light? They began to coalesce into the shape of galaxies. Oh, Ryan, it was like looking into the center of the universe. I . . . I have no explanation for what we saw."

"Perhaps it was Carlisle's other dimension," said Dagursson. "That makes as much sense as anything."

"Which is why we came back as fast as we could," said Sam. She looked down at Andy. "How much time do we have?"

He sat staring at the device, his shoulders slumped. "Not enough," he replied. "I can't figure out a way to disarm it. It seems that Rashid may have been right. The damn thing's impregnable once the counter is started."

She knelt beside him and looked at the counter. It showed less than ten minutes left.

"So little time," she said. "We have to hurry."

"Yes," said Dagursson, standing up abruptly. "There's not a moment to waste."

"What are you talking about?" asked Andy. "I tell you, there's nothing we can do."

Ryan stared at Sam and Dagursson. "Maybe there is," he said. He picked up one end of the device and Dagursson picked up the other.

"Follow me," said Sam.

"I don't understand," said Andy. "Where are you going?"

But the others were already heading down the passage. All Pryne and Hauptmann could do was follow.

Sam moved as quickly as she could. She knew which way to go. She just didn't know if they would have enough time.

Ryan read out the digital numbers as they went. "Seven minutes left. Hurry!"

They raced down the passage with their deadly cargo as fast as they could go. The device was heavy and unwieldy. Several times they bumped into the cavern walls and nearly dropped the thing.

"Be careful!" said Andy, as if bumping the device might somehow shorten the few minutes they had left. "Where are we going?" he cried again in exasperation.

"To the hole," Sam shouted back. "We're going to throw the bomb into the hole."

"What bloody good is that going to do?" asked Hauptmann. "You're talking about a nuclear weapon, for Christ's sake. It will destroy half of southern Iceland. Throwing it into a hole won't help."

"Maybe . . . " Andy said, a light coming on in his head. "Maybe it will. If Carlisle is right. That the hole is another dimension."

Ryan's muscles burned with the effort. The device was awkward to carry and footing in the tunnels was uneven. Sam's flashlight flickered against the walls, making it hard to see obstructions on the passage floor. He tried to read the digital counter as it bobbed up and down with their movement.

"Four minutes!" he cried.

Then they were pushing against the wind, struggling past the giant boulder and right up to the strange opening in the earth. Dagursson and Ryan lowered the device heavily to the ground, staggering and gasping for breath from their effort. Ryan wasn't at all certain his burning shoulders had enough strength remaining to lift the device one more time. He stared at the counter.

"Ninety seconds!" He peered into the hole and caught his breath against the wind and against the incredible sight of galaxies spinning so close he felt as though he might reach out and touch them.

It was a mind-numbing vision. Here in the heart of an active volcano on an island in the middle of the cold North Atlantic Ocean was something too inexplicable to be believed. In the flickering light, they looked a little like demons themselves, wide-eyed, dirt-and sweat-covered from their efforts, their eyes flicking from one to another as if seeking some respite from their collective nightmare.

Mutely, Ryan and Dagursson struggled to lift the weapon up. The object felt heavier than it had. The resistance of the gale-force winds made their job all the harder. Then Hauptmann put his hand on the bomb, pressing against them.

"Wait!" he said. "We need to think about this. We need to think what could occur if such a thing were to come into contact with another dimension. Anything might happen. We could cause a rift in space or time. We might destroy not just Iceland but the whole bloody world."

The weight of the German's hand was enough to force Ryan and Dagursson to lower the device to the ground once again. They slumped beside it, their shoulders quivering.

Sam looked into Hauptmann's eyes. He'd been her mentor for many years, and she valued his insight, the strength of his mind. For an instant, she wondered if he could be right. Then Ryan's voice brought her back to the moment.

"Twenty seconds!" he cried.

"We have to do it, Ernst," she said. "We don't know what will happen if we throw it in. We do know what will happen if we don't. We have to take the gamble."

Slowly, painfully slowly, Hauptmann removed his hand from the device.

"Eight seconds!" Ryan cried.

Sam leaned in and lifted with the two men. The weapon teetered on the edge of the rock wall. She saw the counter register three seconds, as it toppled into the void.

They all grabbed on to the wall and peered after it. The device began to spin counterclockwise. There was a momentary flash of light, but it instantly turned to blackness, as though absorbed completely by the emptiness of the swirling galaxies below. Then Rashid's climate changer was gone.

They collapsed together on the passage floor and stared at one another.

"Damn," said Ryan. "We're still here," and he began to laugh with relief. In a moment, they were all laughing.

"So," Hauptmann said. "I was wrong. Thank God I was wrong." Then, after a moment, he added, "Though I believe God had nothing to do with it."

"No. He had something to do with it," said Sam. "If he exists at all that is. He made this hole or other dimension or alternate universe. Whatever it is. Without it, we'd all be dead now. We may be nothing, but I think Laki controls what happens to us more than we know. Maybe more than he knows."

***

Prescott Carlisle watched as the exhausted group of four stragglers crossed the barren, seemingly demented landscape of Laki to the parking lot. One of his men had informed him that Sam and the others had reemerged from the underground and Carlisle had immediately rushed outside to greet them. Senator Graham was close behind him.

Graham went straight to Sam and latched onto her as though he'd never expected to see her again.

"What happened?" asked Carlisle.

"A miracle," Hauptmann replied.

"I don't know what to call it," said Sam. "Maybe Ernst is right. Andy couldn't deactivate the device. Time was running out, so we carried it to the hole and threw it in."

"You threw it into the magma chamber?" said Carlisle, his voice filled with disbelief.

"Call it whatever you want," said Sam. "It's not like any magma chamber I've ever seen. Anyway, we'd run out of options, so we took a gamble."

"But what happened to the bomb?"

"Obviously, it didn't explode. It simply disappeared, as though it was completely drained of energy somehow."

Carlisle's face took on an indefinable look. He shook his head slowly and stared out at the dark clouds surrounding Laki. "Maybe not completely," he said finally.

The others gave him a puzzled look.

"I had a call from the President a few minutes ago. How long since you threw the weapon into the chamber?"

Sam looked at her watch. "About an hour. We made good time coming back."

"Yes, well, what the President said may be difficult for you to accept."

Again, there were blank faces.

"What are you going on about, Prescott?" Ryan asked.

"The President informed me that an hour ago seismographs and satellites recorded a thermonuclear blast in the Southern Ocean about one hundred fifty miles off the coast of Antarctica. His people pinpointed the location as almost precisely the opposite side of the globe from Iceland."

There was a moment of stunned silence, as Carlisle's words sank in.

Ryan was the first to find his voice. "You can't seriously be suggesting there's a connection. That's absurd. It has to be a coincidence. Some other nation must have set off a bomb. There are plenty of countries suffering from nuclear envy that have no place to test their devices on land. Someone must have conducted a test in the Southern Ocean."

Sam looked at him. "You know what the odds are that something like that would occur at the precise moment we threw our weapon into Laki?"

"You're saying our bomb traveled all the way through the Earth, a distance of eight thousand miles, and just popped out the other side?" Ryan's incredulous look reflected what the other non-scientists were thinking.

"I think Miss Graham is correct," said Carlisle. "We must go on the assumption that the explosion was from your device. No one's saying it traveled through the Earth's core. You say it disappeared or seemed to be drained somehow. Well, there's another possibility. That it passed through some sort of portal to another place. Another name for such a portal would be a black hole."

Dagursson stared at Carlisle in disbelief. "I'm just a simple cop," he said. "I know nothing about all this scientific mumbo-jumbo. Maybe such things are possible. God knows I've seen things here I never would have believed without seeing them with my own eyes. But this . . ." He just shook his head.

"There are plenty of bizarre theories," said Hauptmann, "regarding extra dimensions of space-time, dark matter, and black holes that could destroy the Earth . . . from the inside out, so to speak. Here's just one example that you may have heard about. The world's biggest physics experiment is known as the Large Hadron Collider. It was designed to smash protons together in a search for particles created during the first trillionth of a second of the so-called Big Bang."

"Even I've heard of that," said Dagursson.

"Yes," the professor continued, "but have you also heard that all the problems they've had with the collider breaking down may be the result of the device being sabotaged by its own future?"

Dagursson's look clearly showed that this was beyond his limited purview.

Hauptmann nodded. "The Higgs boson, sometimes called 'The God Particle,' was actually detected only recently by physicists. One theory these scientists had was that the Higgs boson would be so abhorrent to nature that its creation would cause ripples backward in time and stop the collider before it could make one."

"The classic case of a man going back in time and killing his grandfather, thus preventing his own birth," said Sam.

Hauptmann nodded approvingly.

Carlisle had been listening intently. "A good explanation, as far as it goes," he said. "By the standard rules of physics, the Higgs is responsible for imbuing other elementary particles with mass. Some theorists have predicted that any machine designed to produce the Higgs boson would have an endless run of bad luck. No reasonable explanations could account for it . . . only that the past was forbidding it."

"I'm way out of my depth," said Ryan.

"Just one further point," said Carlisle. "One theorist actually suggested that this might almost be a model for God. And that God would not like Higgs particles and would attempt to avoid them. In fact, there have been a number of utterly inexplicable mishaps to the collider program. Just in 2008, after the CERN collider was turned on, a connection between two magnets vaporized, shutting the thing down for a year."

"A model for God," Senator Graham said in a quiet voice.

"This is not entirely a new concept," said Hauptmann. "In 2000, there were concerns that the Relativistic Heavy Ion Collider at Brookhaven might create black holes. But the fears soon moved on to the danger posed by hypothetical particles called strangelets. Some said strangelets could transform the Earth instantaneously into a dense, completely dead lump."

"All this speculation is doubtless a great game for you physicists and scientists," said Ryan. "But what does it tell us about what happened to our bomb?"

"Only," said Carlisle, "that the universe is a strange place. Your weapon may have passed through a black hole. But if it did, it still had to go somewhere, the other side of the galaxy, another dimension, the past or future . . . or off the coast of Antarctica. Who can say? The random nature of quantum physics is such that there will always be a tiny, non-zero chance of anything happening, including a collider that spins out man-eating gargoyles."

"Einstein once wrote that the separation between past, present, and future is only an illusion," said Andy Pryne.

"Well . . . that's certainly helpful. Thank you, Andy," said Carlisle irritably. "If I might bring this discussion back to the present for a moment. There's something else the President told me. Reports have begun to come in that there may be tsunamis moving across the world's oceans from the blast. It's too early to be sure, but ships at sea report large swells in the Southern Ocean. The first nations to be affected will be in South America, Australia, and New Zealand. Several of our Navy ships are heading to the area of the blast to test for background radiation and . . ."

Carlisle stopped in mid-sentence, his mouth open. "Oh . . . my . . . God," he said.

The others whirled around to see what he was staring at. All the talk about black holes, other dimensions, and strangelets had them jumpy enough to expect to actually confront man-eating gargoyles. In fact, what they saw was so incomprehensible given their current panoply of problems that their reactions were muted with disbelief.

Marching along the rim, above Laki's distorted landscape, were perhaps a dozen men dressed in red robes. Periodically they stopped and engaged in a series of mumbled chants.

"What in the name of god . . .?" asked Sam. "Are those what I think they are?"

"I can't believe it," said Carlisle. "The President warned me, but I've had too much on my mind to think about it."

"Warned you about what?" asked Ryan. The strange sight looked like something out of Monty Python's Flying Circus. He remembered the comic group's mantra: *And now for something completely different.*

"President Thurman told me that the Pope was going to send a delegation to Laki to pray. An attempt to get the volcanoes erupting around the world to shut down."

"The Pope?" Like Ryan, Sam was having trouble making any kind of sense out of what she was seeing.

"Near as I understand it, religious leaders formed a secret organization that has been tracking events on Laki since the Second World War," said Carlisle, his own disbelief evident. He stared at the red-robed men as they began to come down off the rim and approach them.

The man in front of the group had eyes that were fixed and humorless. He looked younger than the rest of his fellows. Indeed, the others appeared much too old to be wandering about the devastated landscape of Laki. When they reached the parking lot and the buses, the group stopped and their leader spoke to Carlisle.

"I'm Cardinal Wormer," the man said. "We are here to help."

Chapter Twenty-Four

The Oval Office

Washington, D. C.

President Thurman frowned at the uniformed figure standing before him. "Run that by me again, Admiral Crouse," he said.

"Sir, we have lost touch with our destroyers in the area of the Southern Ocean where the thermonuclear blast was detected."

"Lost touch. You mean the blast disrupted communications?"

"No, sir. We figured out long ago how to maintain proper communications during the magnetic disruptions caused by nuclear blasts. This is not a communications problem."

"What is it then?"

"We cannot raise our ships by any means, radio, data links, radar, satellite . . . it's as though they simply disappeared."

Thurman swiveled his chair around and stared out the window. The lunatic fringe was out in force this morning. He could see signs bobbing up and down beyond the fence and was glad they were far enough away that he couldn't read them.

Crouse fidgeted. "Sir, one of our AWACS planes is en route to the Southern Ocean. We expect their initial report momentarily. I took the liberty of ordering it delivered to your office the moment it comes through."

"Could the ships have been destroyed by the tsunami?" asked Thurman.

"That far out to sea, it would seem unlikely, sir. The tsunami would be detectable only as a swell. I suppose there could be the possibility of a rogue wave. We're in uncharted territory, Mr. President."

The President's personal secretary came in. She gave him a weak smile. "Sir, you have another call from the Pope," she said.

"God, won't the man give it a rest?" He swiveled back around to his desk and picked up the phone. Much as he would have liked to ignore the call, Catholics made up a large part of his constituency.

"Good morning, Your Holiness. I hope you have some good news for us. Has Vesuvius quieted down?"

He listened for a moment. "I see. Well, that is very good news, indeed. We'll all be waiting to hear the results. Please inform me as soon as you know anything. Yes. Thank you, Your Holiness."

He placed the phone gently in its cradle and shook his head.

"Some good news, sir?" asked the Admiral.

"Oh, very good news. The pontiff's delegation is in Iceland and praying a mile a minute. All our problems should soon be over. His Holiness just thought I'd want to know."

The Admiral smiled. "Good to have all the help we can get," he said. He looked down as the beeper in his pocket went off. Almost at the same moment, the secretary came back in, followed by one of the Admiral's aides.

The aide handed a piece of paper to the Admiral without saying a word, then stepped back. Crouse perused the document for a moment. His face turned white.

Thurman said, "What is it, Admiral?"

"I . . . I don't know quite how to put this, Mr. President. The AWACS reports that the Southern Ocean is . . . disappearing."

Thurman stood up. His hands gripped the edge of his desk, his knuckles turned bone white. "What the hell are you talking about?"

"According to the aircraft, as they approached the area where our ships were supposed to be, the ocean began to swirl in a sort of enormous whirlpool, hundreds of miles across. Near the center of the whirlpool, the ocean simply flows into a black hole and is . . . gone. The AWACS says coordinates from the destroyers before contact was lost suggest they may have been sucked into the vortex."

The President sank slowly back into his chair. His secretary, Admiral Crouse, and the aide all stared at him, waiting for a reaction. But Thurman had no idea what to do with the information he'd just been given. The man he relied upon in such instances, his science advisor, was three thousand miles away in Iceland.

"Martha," he said finally. "See if you can raise Prescott Carlisle for me." His face darkened. "Maybe His Holiness is taking the right approach after all."

***

Wormer joined the others as they all crammed into Carlisle's little office space at the back of the bus. The rest of the cardinals remained outside, continuing their fervid prayer assault on Laki.

"Exactly how do you plan to help in this situation, Cardinal?" Carlisle asked.

Wormer sat back in the comfortable console chair that had been offered to him. He enjoyed being the center of attention. His initial fear of being in Iceland had given way to a more palatable scenario. If things went well, he'd begun to see a path to the papacy itself coming from all of this. The world would be eternally grateful if he defused the tense situation on Laki.

"My charge from His Holiness is to do whatever I deem necessary to help deal with this situation," he said. "I represent a council of religious leaders from around the world who have been studying Laki for more than sixty years. No one knows more about this situation."

Carlisle stared at him as though he were some sort of lunatic. "I take it then," he said, "that you understand the scientific ramifications here. The bombardment of cosmic rays, the Higgs boson, the extra dimensions of space-time, strangelets . . ."

Wormer waved a hand. "The only ramifications that matter have to do with God and the power of prayer," he said. "That is my charge from His Holiness, and I expect full cooperation from you."

"Cooperation to do what?" asked Ryan with real curiosity.

"To get to the heart of the matter," said Wormer. "We will take our prayer beneath Laki. I for one do not accept what many seem to believe, that we're dealing with some sort of god. It is merely a natural phenomenon, perhaps gone out of control, but that is precisely what the power of prayer is meant to deal with."

Dagursson said, "I'm sorry, Cardinal, but I can't allow you to go underground. As police commissioner, I'm the one ultimately in charge here. You don't seem to realize how dangerous Laki is. We've got earthquakes, tunnel collapses, poisonous gases, an enormous and unpredictable magma chamber . . ., or perhaps something even worse. Have you looked at the skies outside? Those boiling, black clouds, the tornadoes? Believe me, it's ten times worse beneath the surface. I can't be responsible for the deaths of a dozen cardinals. That's the last thing we need."

"I understand your predicament, Commissioner. I really do," said Wormer. "But I answer to a higher authority. Do not underestimate the power of prayer."

Dagursson considered the man in front of him. He was either a complete fool or a religious zealot. He wasn't sure there was a difference.

"When it comes to Laki, Cardinal, I am the only higher authority that matters. I have the final word. Not only will I not allow you to go underground, but I have to insist that you and your fellow cardinals leave Laki at once. All of southern Iceland is currently off limits to civilians."

Wormer gave him a withering look. "I am *hardly* a civilian," he said.

"You are in my eyes. I assume you came here by helicopter?"

The cardinal nodded tightly.

Dagursson said, "Ryan, I'm putting you in charge of making sure the cardinals get safely away."

"Are you deputizing me?"

"Not necessary. I have the authority to appoint anyone I want." He stood up. "Cardinal, you will accompany Mr. Baldwin back to your chopper."

A breathless young soldier suddenly burst into the room. "Sir," he said, addressing Carlisle.

"Yes, what is it?"

"The two foreign nationals have escaped."

"What?"

"The man named Rashid and his partner requested a meeting with you. Two of our men accompanied them and as best we can determine, that's when it happened. The bodies of both soldiers have been found poorly hidden in a gully."

"Goddamn it!" Carlisle looked apoplectic.

"It doesn't make any sense," said Ryan. "Where can they go?"

"Evidently they saw the cardinals' chopper arrive," said the soldier. "That probably gave them the idea. It took off moments after we found the bodies. Rashid and his partner must have forced the pilot to fly them out."

Wormer stood up. "So. You see, Commissioner. The Lord works in mysterious ways. It appears you are stuck with us." He nodded and exited the bus.

Dagursson and the others stood frozen in indecision.

"We might have used that chopper to get everyone evacuated," said Ryan. "It would have taken eight or ten trips, but it was at least a chance."

The commissioner went over to Carlisle's communications man. "I'll try to get the chopper intercepted," he said, but as the radio officer began to work his dials, he suddenly raised his hand and motioned to Carlisle.

"Priority One," the radio operator said. "President Thurman for you, sir. He says it's urgent."

Carlisle wondered what could possibly come next. He took the phone, stared at the others gathered around expectantly and told the radio operator to put it on speaker. They were all in this together. "Yes, Mr. President?"

"Prescott, I have more bad news, I'm afraid," came Thurman's voice.

"Only kind we seem to have, sir. What is it?"

"It appears some sort of hole or vortex has opened up in the Southern Ocean. We believe it has swallowed several of our destroyers and according to the AWACS we have on site, it appears to be growing, swallowing a thousand square miles of ocean so far."

Carlisle's face registered shock. "Do you know the coordinates for this vortex?" he asked.

"I suspect you've guessed, Prescott. It appears to be centered where the nuclear blast took place. You have any idea what's going on?"

Carlisle seemed unable to speak for a moment. Finally, he said, "The worst scenario, Mr. President, is that some sort of black hole has been opened up by the nuclear blast combined with the space-time distortion that apparently caused it to be transported to the Southern Ocean."

There was a momentary pause from the speakerphone. "I don't have a damn clue what that means, Prescott. I want to know what the bloody hell we can do about it."

"I'm sorry to say, Mr. President, that I believe the answer is nothing. Scientists have speculated about this sort of possibility for years. It was debated fiercely when the Hadron Collider went online. Some thought such a thing might happen. No one knew if it could, but one thing everyone agreed upon was that if it did, there'd be no way to stop it from continuing to its natural conclusion."

A heavy pause emanated from the phone. Finally, Thurman said, "And what would be its natural conclusion?"

"That the hole would continue to absorb the Earth until it was completely gone."

***

Sam and Ryan sat outside the bus and watched the tumultuous skies above the volcano's rim. Even though it was mid-day, it was dark from thick, boiling clouds being tossed around by thermals rising off the numerous streams of lava.

Most of the others had drifted away following Carlisle's talk with the President. To see the President's science advisor so completely discouraged seemed to drain the energy out of all of them.

They had coffee and microwaved sandwiches from the tiny closet on the bus that served as mess hall. It had been turning out a steady stream of Meals Ready to Eat, Laki style, for the assembled scientists and military personnel.

Ryan looked at Sam with concern. She appeared tired. "How are you holding up?" he asked.

She smiled weakly and held up her sandwich. "Sitting up and taking nourishment." She took a bite and chewed disconsolately. "What do you think it all means? Do you really think it's the end of the world? Of our species?"

"I don't know. Humans never seem to believe they'll come up against something for which there is no answer . . . no solution. But that sure sounded like what Carlisle was suggesting. How the hell can we do anything to stop a black hole from consuming the planet? We don't even really know what a black hole is, much less how to deal with it. Maybe . . ."

"What?"

"Maybe, Wormer's course is the only one left to us. Prayer."

"He said he didn't believe Laki was a god. So who's he praying to, for Christ's sake?"

"His own god, I would presume."

"Maybe a prayer to Laki would be more appropriate. Look, we both saw what was in that hole. I don't have any more idea what we were looking at than you do, but it couldn't be any more inexplicable than a black hole eating the damn Southern Ocean. Two inexplicable things like that have to be related. Amma told me what *she* believed, that Laki is God. Well, you're looking at one atheist who's come around. No way is Laki simply some natural phenomenon, like Wormer said."

"I guess I agree with you. But I don't know what good it does us."

"Only this. We know we can communicate with Laki through Amma. Maybe it . . . he . . . doesn't realize what he's doing. Why don't we tell him? Ask for his help."

"If Laki is God, then he knows what he's doing, by definition," said Ryan. "What you're really saying is let's go pray to him—just like Wormer."

She blinked, said nothing.

"Sorry to interrupt," a man's voice interrupted.

They looked at Cardinal Wormer.

"I'm taking my people underground," he said. "I wanted you to know. I don't really see any way that you and Dagursson can stop us. What are you going to do, beat up a dozen elderly cardinals? That would probably go over even worse in the press than our getting killed."

Ryan nodded. "I've been coming around to your way of thinking, Cardinal. I'll talk to Dagursson. Then, maybe we can all go down together. A full frontal prayer assault." He shrugged. "For what it's worth."

"You will see," said Wormer. "Sometimes prayer can be worth a great deal."

"Perhaps you're right," said Ryan. "What have we got to lose?"

"Maybe a hell of a lot," said Sam. "Our lives, to begin with. It's a horrific decision, Ryan, to take half a dozen souls down there again. For no better reason than to pray. What's wrong with praying on the surface, for heaven's sake? I thought the whole point of prayer was that it worked anywhere—because God is everywhere."

"Sometimes," said Wormer, "God likes to see a little effort on the part of his supplicants. He likes us to pray in church, for example, or to go on pilgrimages and the like. It's a show of faith."

"I've already been responsible for the deaths of a dozen policemen beneath Laki," said Sam. "Laki was once the focus of my entire professional life. Now, I see it in a completely different light. It simply frightens me to contemplate going underground again. If you'd been there, it would scare you too, Cardinal."

Wormer gave her the self-righteous smile he bestowed upon all poor nonbelievers. "God will not forsake us," he said.

Ryan said, "What the hell, Sam. Maybe the Cardinal's right. Hasn't Laki always shown us the way out of that underground maze so far? If he wanted to destroy us, he's had ample opportunity to do so."

She looked at him. "He showed you and me the way out, if you want to put it that way. He didn't show Dagursson's men the way in time to save their lives. He didn't show Akbari. And look what happened to Amma and all the others in that cave down there. Do you really want to risk spending eternity glued to a wall like them? For what? To pray? You're asking a lot from a barely reformed atheist."

"Your efforts will be doomed to failure," the Cardinal warned, "If you plan to pray to some Viking, heathen god. You must pray to the one true God."

"Must be nice to have utter certainty who that is," said Sam archly.

Ryan shrugged. "I can't argue with what you're saying, Sam. But if we've come around to even contemplating the existence of some sort of deity on this volcano, then I think we must also contemplate a non-scientific approach. Irrational as prayer may seem to a scientist, it's really all we have left."

Sam's emotions played openly across her face. She was wracked with indecision. But the disappearance of the Southern Ocean was a clear sign they were operating on a new plane. The planet had begun to disappear. In the face of that, how could the potential risks not be worth the effort?

"All right," she said in a resigned voice. "I always wondered if I'd stand by my principles when faced with death and not go running off to church begging for salvation. None of us atheists ever know for sure what we'll do until that time comes. But I suppose we'll go. I just hope Laki doesn't suspect me of being insincere when the time comes."

***

It took half an hour to convince Dagursson of their plan. He wasn't a happy camper, but he gradually came to accept that with Ryan lined up against him, he wasn't going to be able to single-handedly beat a dozen cardinals into submission. Still, he insisted that Wormer select only the four physically strongest of his people to go underground. The rest could continue their prayers from the rim.

Meanwhile, Laki was beginning to show signs of not waiting around for anyone, delegation or no. Carlisle's scientists had detected something rising in the magma chamber.

"What is it?" Ryan asked, staring at a series of computer-generated graphs that clearly showed something expanding far below.

"We haven't been able to analyze it," said one of Carlisle's whiz kids. "Doesn't seem to profile like magma, but we can chart its movement all right. Our projection is it'll reach the surface in twelve to fourteen hours if it maintains its current rate of expansion."

"Terrific. Another timetable," Ryan said. "We barely beat the one for Rashid's little toy. I don't like our chances the second time around."

They gathered at the venthole opening that Sam had used to lead the others out of the subterranean maelstrom. Barring any new tunnel collapses, it would offer the quickest route back to the hole and Amma.

Sam tried to give the cardinals some idea of what to expect. "You're about to enter a world stranger than anything you've encountered before," she said.

"Stranger than the Vatican?" asked one of the cardinals with a slight smile.

"I should think so," Sam said, though she acknowledged the humor with a quick smile of her own. "Strange . . . and dangerous. We've already seen what might be considered a view into another universe and spoken with an entity that is over a thousand years old."

The men in robes looked startled at this news. Only Wormer seemed unconcerned. His agenda had more to do with church hierarchy and his own place in it than with inexplicable mysteries.

"There is nothing that will not bend to prayer," he said piously.

"Right," said Sam.

She and Ryan would lead the group. Dagursson insisted on coming along to offer extra protection to their elderly charges. Hauptmann was too tired to engage in another long underground adventure. He and Kraus would remain behind. Jon continued to be paranoid and was so frightened he would be of no use to anyone. No scientists would accompany them either. This was not a scientific expedition but rather a roving prayer mission.

As they entered the venthole, an unusual quiet descended. The background din they'd become used to receded. In an eerie way, it was almost as if Laki were welcoming them.

Ryan moved up beside Sam. "I'm having second thoughts about taking them to the hole itself," he said in a low voice, "given the effect it seems to have on those who are overtly religious. If this group doesn't qualify, I don't know who would."

"I've been thinking the same thing," said Sam. "Wormer wants to pray to his own God. I have no problem with that, but I don't think they'll have a clear idea of what they're dealing with if they don't actually see the hole . . . *see* what is at the heart of Laki."

"All right," Ryan conceded, a bit dubiously. "We'll just have to try to keep close tabs on them once we get there. I'll mention it to Dagursson." He glanced back at the cardinals. "They're not the most sprightly bunch. We ought be able to corral any that seem inclined to jump in before they can actually take the leap, like Akbari."

Sam looked behind them. "I don't trust Wormer," she said softly. "There's something about him that makes me uncomfortable."

"You mean besides being a pompous ass?"

"Sort of."

"He does seem pretty wrapped up in himself. I get the sense he'd like nothing better than to take Laki on, to prove it's a false god."

"And by doing so, show himself off in the best light to his fellow cardinals," said Sam.

"Sounds almost political, doesn't it?"

She looked at him. "You thought that too? Like he's on a mission, not to quiet the volcanic activity but to promote himself."

"There are ambitious religious leaders," Ryan said.

"Most of them, from my experience. Anyway, we can't forget our own purpose here, which is to try to speak to Laki through Amma, and ask for his help."

"Talk to a volcano." He shook his head. "I never could have imagined such a thing a few days ago."

"You two seem thick as thieves," said Wormer, moving up beside them. "Anything I should know about?"

"To be honest, Cardinal," Ryan said, "we're a little concerned about your group's reaction when you see some of the more bizarre aspects of this place."

Wormer looked around. They were moving deeper into the venthole, but so far nothing seemed out of the ordinary.

"Place appears normal enough to me," he said. "If anything, it seems quieter down here than it did on the surface. I don't know what all the fuss is about. We're dealing with a natural phenomenon here. Certainly there will be hot spots, maybe even earthquakes, but beyond that, I think you're exaggerating. I intend to put this absurd notion of a volcano as deity to rest once and for all."

There was a sudden rumbling, the first they'd heard since moving underground, almost as though Laki were displeased at the cardinal's words. For the first time, Sam thought Wormer looked nervous.

"What was that?" he asked.

"Just Laki talking to us," said Ryan. "Better than an eruption, trust me."

Wormer turned to his fellow cardinals and said something in Latin. Immediately, they began to chant. Sam saw Wormer moving his own lips silently. She rolled her eyes at Ryan.

The wind began to pick up, indicating they were on course. Dagursson came forward and took Wormer's place next to Sam and Ryan, as the cardinal fell back with the others.

"We've got to watch these characters when we reach the hole," Ryan said. "God knows what they may be capable of once their prejudices are confronted by the unknown."

Dagursson nodded. He seemed lost in thought. "I have to say that my own preconceived notions have been shaken more than a little by all of Carlisle's and Hauptmann's scientific talk. I don't know what to think anymore, whether we're dealing with basic science here or some religious Second Coming. But this place makes my flesh crawl. Until that rumbling we just heard, it's been a lot quieter than the last time around. What the hell does that signify?"

"Maybe things are subsiding a little," said Ryan.

As if in response, there was a sudden, loud shriek that made everyone jump.

Over the din, Wormer said, "Mother of God. What was that?"

"Just a gas release," said Sam, more confidently than she felt. "When pressure releases suddenly, it can make an incredible racket."

The shrieking went away quickly but was replaced by a distant wailing that went on and on and that Sam recognized as Amma's distant cry. The wail had a different quality from the one she'd heard before. This seemed more like a cry of despair.

The cardinals showed signs of increasing nervousness at the strange sounds. Unconsciously, they had grouped more closely together. Wormer tried to reassure them, though he seemed tense himself.

"I hope none of them drop dead from a heart attack," said Dagursson. "My own heart's beating like a sledgehammer."

Now the wind was getting very strong, as they neared the boulder that stood opposite the opening in the earth.

"Watch them," Ryan reminded Sam and Dagursson. "If I had a bloody rope I'd tether our religious fanatics to the boulder, or at least to each other."

Then they stood before the opening. The wind whistled up from below, the cable-like tentacles throbbing as they disappeared into the depths. The elderly cardinals, with the exception of Wormer, seemed not to possess the strength to approach the hole against the gale.

Wormer fought his way forward with Sam and Dagursson to the edge of the stone wall and peered in. What he saw froze his features into a mask of incredulity.

The swirling stars and galaxies seemed even closer than Ryan remembered. It felt as though he could literally reach out and grab them, and he wondered if this had something to do with the expansion in the magma chamber.

"Look out!" Dagursson suddenly cried.

Ryan felt rather than saw the movement next to him, as the cardinal began to crawl over the edge, and he reacted instantly, grabbing Wormer around the waist.

"Let me go!" Wormer cried. He had one leg on the wall, and he was holding on for all he was worth. It took all of Dagursson's and Ryan's strength to haul him off the stone ledge and force him back to the boulder, where they pinned him down.

Once he was freed from staring directly into the maelstrom, Wormer's strength dissipated, and he slumped to the ground.

"What . . . what *was* that?" he murmured, as though emerging from a drug-induced high.

"Just your run-of-the-mill natural phenomenon," said Ryan.

"But I felt . . . " Wormer stared from one of them to the other. "I felt . . . God," he said. "More intensely than ever before. I wanted to go to Him."

"Whatever this place is, it seems to have that effect," said Sam.

"It can't be," Wormer said. He seemed to be coming back from the brink of something. "This is false. A blasphemy. I . . . I must confront it."

He stood up, weaving slightly. Ryan let go of him, but he and Dagursson watched him closely.

"I think it's time to go see Amma," Sam said quietly. "If you want answers, Cardinal, that is where you may find them. Though I warn you, you may not like what you hear."

She led the way down the passage toward Amma. There was no question which way to go. She had merely to follow the wailing, and as they got closer, the crying slowly dissipated. When they finally came face to face with the ancient woman, she had her mouth open. Her face was stretched and elongated like some sort of parody of Edvard Munch's *The Scream*.

Wormer and the other cardinals stared at the horrifying sight, as though suddenly set upon by a thunderclap and revelation.

Then Amma's voice came out of that terrible face. She spoke in Norse, but they could understand her words. And there were only two, repeated over and over.

"Go awaaay," said Amma. "Go awaaay."

"This is the Norse woman you spoke of?" Wormer asked softly.

Sam nodded, unable to take her own eyes off the old woman.

"Can I speak to her?"

"You can try."

"Why are you here?" Wormer asked. His brethren gathered around, anxious to hear what the strange vision would say.

"I am everywhere," said Amma.

"What do you want?"

"Go awaaay," said Amma.

Sam looked perplexed. "If you are everywhere," she said, "How can we ever go away?"

"At least tell us who you are," said Wormer.

"I am God," Amma replied.

"Which God? Whose God?" Wormer asked.

"The first God," came the reply. "Before all others, I was here."

"What do you want from us?"

There was a long pause before Amma spoke again. "There is nothing you can do for me . . . or for yourselves."

"I don't believe you," said Wormer, his voice growing angry. "You are a false God."

Ryan moved to Wormer's side. "What are we seeing when we look into your center?" he asked Amma.

"My universe," came Laki's reply.

"The universe?" asked Ryan.

"Not your universe," said Laki. "*My* universe."

"Aren't they the same?"

Again, Amma seemed to hesitate. "I am not the God of your universe," she said finally. "I have moved on."

"But you created us?" asked Sam.

"Yes," replied the voice of Laki. "I have moved on."

"I do not believe you are my creator," said Wormer in an angry voice. "He would not abandon us."

"I am the only God you will ever know," said the voice.

"No. I reject you," said Wormer.

"As I have rejected you," said Laki. "Go away. Live out your useless lives."

"I . . . I will denounce you when I am Pope," Wormer said furiously.

The others all stared at him. He was losing it.

Ryan said, "Can't you help us? We have caused something we may not be able to undo. You know this. It's at least partly your fault. In the Southern Ocean, something is destroying our world."

"Your weapons, your *scientific* experiments have no significance," said the voice of Laki. "They have no meaning to my universe."

"They have to ours," said Ryan. "The laws of nature guide our investigations."

"The laws of nature are my own," said Laki.

"You mean you control them?"

"If you like," Laki replied.

Suddenly, Wormer leaped at Amma. He began to pull at her chrysalis, ripping it from the wall and throwing it to the ground, where the ancient woman lay, mouth still open.

"You are false!" he cried. "I will destroy you." He reached for a rock and raised it above his head to smash Amma. Dagursson grabbed his arm and stopped him.

"No," Wormer pleaded. "I must destroy this evil."

Amma's mouth moved. "Do not make him angry," she said. It was the first time she seemed to speak for herself alone. "Skari made Laki angry, long ago. That is why we are here. Skari could make anyone angry."

Amma spoke now in a different tone, as though being separated from the passage wall had liberated her somehow.

"I want to understand you," Wormer said.

"You want a god you can understand?" Ryan asked. "When have humans ever had that?"

"Skari became obsessed with Laki," said Amma. "Worshiped him, made amulets in his honor, lived beneath the Earth. It was not what Laki wanted."

Sam knelt beside Amma. Now moving freely, the old woman seemed more human, separate, no longer the voice of God. Sam put one hand behind Amma's withered back and lifted her into a sitting position.

"What does Laki want if not to be worshiped?" asked Wormer.

"Laki has no use for those who worship him," said Amma. "It is why he causes them to leap into the void. He prefers those who do not believe in him. That is what free will is all about. You humans . . . are on your own."

Sam could hardly believe what she was hearing. "Laki . . . God . . . *prefers* atheists?"

"It is the ultimate affirmation of free will," said Amma. "Laki does not wish to be worshiped by those who fear him. Those who worship Laki are only interested in their own salvation."

***

An hour passed, during which they rested, sitting in small groups on the passage floor. The cardinals seemed spiritually exhausted by what they'd seen. Wormer sat apart from them, lost in thought or perhaps prayer.

Dagursson, Sam, and Ryan sprawled next to the seemingly rejuvenated figure of Amma. Sam had tried to clean the sticky substance from the old woman and even attempted to run a small comb through the stringy, gray hair. Then Amma seemed to go to sleep.

Ryan spoke softly. "There's something I haven't been understanding for a while," he said.

"Are you kidding?" said Dagursson. "Who the hell understands any of this?"

"What is it?" asked Sam.

"Just this. Why is Laki expending so much energy trying to communicate with us?"

They stared at him blankly.

"Laki has gone out of his way to make Amma an avenue of communication. He even makes sure we understand the ancient Norse she's speaking. Why? If his only message is that we go away . . . why bother?

"He wants to make damn sure we get it," said Dagursson.

"Maybe, but he's put one obstacle after another in our path. If he only wants us to go away, why collapse tunnels, why get us lost? Why not just show us the way out? I mean, he's shown some of us the way out, eventually. It's as if there's some sort of selection process going on. Some are absorbed like Amma. Some just disappear like Akbari, and some are allowed to go away, as he keeps telling us. And anyway, if Laki is everywhere, as Amma said, what good does it do for us to go away? Where is 'away' to God?"

"So . . . what?" asked Sam. "You're saying Laki is lying to us?"

He shrugged. "I don't know. Playing with us, maybe. Amma said there was a kind of selection process. One that prefers atheists, if you can believe it. Or perhaps he has another agenda. What strikes me is that Laki seems at least as concerned with what we think as vice-versa. It's almost as if he gets some sort of perverse pleasure out of our presence. He tells us to go away but doesn't really mean it. He seems . . . I don't know quite how to say this so it doesn't sound ridiculous. He seems . . . interested in us. Conflicted, maybe."

"You think he's trying to test us?"

"No. It doesn't feel that way, somehow. It's more like he needs control, even if he says he doesn't. What was it he said? That we were nothing? If we are nothing, why is he spending so much time dealing with us? It would be like us trying to have a deep philosophical discussion with an amoeba. And why would he have preserved the Vikings and all those others as chrysalises if humans are nothing? It doesn't make any sense."

"So what's your answer?" asked Dagursson.

"He's sort of like the God of the Old Testament," said Ryan. "You know, the wrathful God who believes in punishment, fire and brimstone and the like. Who seems to exist only in regard to human failings, which, of course, he gave us. The God of the Old Testament always seemed schizophrenic to me. Angry at us for the failings *he* created. I think Laki may be a little like that . . . petty, self-important . . . a God who wants to control us even when he says he doesn't. Even though he says we have free will. Even though we are nothing. Laki needs us to . . . ratify . . . his own importance."

"Whoa," said Dagursson. "Do you have any idea how crazy that sounds? If God is that needy, how can he be God?"

"Good question. But maybe not one you should ask an atheist," said Ryan. "Up to now, I never believed in a higher being. I'm sure Wormer and his buddies could come up with some convoluted answer to your question.

"Besides, it seems to me that all the gods created by man have been incredibly needy. They want our attention. They demand it. They need it the way little children need the attention of their parents in order to thrive."

Sam considered him thoughtfully. "Sounds like you're saying Laki is throwing all this stuff at us, black holes, earthquakes, cosmic rays, holes in space . . . just out of petulance?"

"Amma said he didn't want us to worship him." Ryan shook his head in frustration. "The contradictions here are enormous. We're not supposed to worship him. He wants us to go away. We can't go away. Who knows where 'away' is? We are nothing. So why are we important enough for Laki to devote all this time to us? It's like the left hand doesn't know what the right hand is doing."

Dagursson looked utterly perplexed. "All I know is that after staring into that hole in space, at galaxies and expanding universes, it's hard to bring it all back to the petty, hurt feelings of some schizophrenic deity. He rules over entire universes, multiple universes, if we're to believe what Laki says, and yet here he is, negotiating with amoebas in a cave on a small planet that is one of billions in a billion galaxies and maybe a billion universes, for all we know."

"That could be what makes him God," said Sam. "That he can be involved with details down to that level."

"I think we need to ask him these questions directly," Ryan said. "Again." He looked at the sleeping form of Amma. "I don't think she's as connected as she once was, though."

"Maybe we should talk with one of the other chrysalises," suggested Sam.

"You think we could?"

"Amma said they were all there in the other room. Who was the one she talked about the most? A fellow named Skari? Maybe we should try to find him."

***

President Thurman listened with increasing agitation as Prescott Carlisle outlined their challenges.

"Sir," his science advisor said, "cosmic ray production has spiked in the last hour. Almost off the charts. It must have something to do with the expansion going on in the magma chamber. Something seems to be coming to a head. Have you any further information on activity in the Southern Ocean?"

"Last report," said Thurman, "was that fifty thousand square miles of ocean have disappeared—gone down the rabbit hole, if you will. Of course, that's just an estimate. The AWACS has to stay pretty far away to avoid being sucked in. The forces are powerful."

Carlisle thought hard. "Sir, this is the rankest speculation, but it may be that the disappearing ocean is being absorbed, somehow, by the hole beneath Laki. If there was some sort of portal that opened up allowing the bomb to pass through, it could have created a two-way street, a sort of feedback situation. The expansion we've documented in the magma chamber certainly suggests that something is being absorbed there. If so, we could eventually reach a point of critical mass."

"Meaning what?"

"I'm afraid your guess is as good as mine, Mr. President. All I can say with confidence is that there could be further disturbances in the fabric of space/time that can't bode well for any of us."

***

Wormer listened to the plan with growing skepticism. "You've already talked to this Amma," he said. "I don't see how she particularly enlightened us. By telling us that God prefers atheists? What rational thinker could believe that? Why should any of the other chrysalises be clearer?"

"For one thing," said Sam, "because Amma as much as told us so. She said Skari was the first to be *taken* by Laki. Perhaps Skari was the first to be actually punished for worshiping Laki. He'd become a sort of religious figure, a carver of amulets and tokens in honor of the volcano's god."

"Maybe Skari was the first human to whom Laki was ambivalent," said Ryan. "He spent virtually all of his time underground, the first of the Vikings to do so alone. If Laki really does need the attention of humans, it seems likely that Skari was giving it to him, even as he was being punished at the same time for revering their God. Maybe Skari figured out some way to give Laki the attention he craves while not actually worshipping him at the same time. A difficult tightrope to walk, it would appear. Seems to me if anyone can tell us something about Laki, it might be Skari."

Wormer looked completely frustrated. "Do you have any idea how crazy that all sounds? God isn't some schizophrenic nutcake. And this volcano isn't God. I guarantee it. My fellow cardinals and I will remain here and continue to pray."

Sam shrugged. She and Ryan moved away to where Dagursson was sitting. "Wormer won't have anything to do with the other chrysalises," she said.

"Doesn't surprise me," said Dagursson. "It's all about him and prayer. Nothing else matters."

"I say we just go see what we can find out," said Ryan.

"I think I should stay here," Dagursson said. "I don't trust Wormer. He may have something up his sleeve. I'm not willing to leave him alone."

So Sam and Ryan moved out together. They crossed the open cavern and approached the dark space that Amma had said held the rest of her clan. Sam felt a chill run through her entire body as they entered the forbidding chamber. The paranoia she'd felt several times before was nothing compared to the sense of being watched or controlled that overcame her now.

Chrysalises lined the walls, scores of the strange, gluey concoctions. They ranged from full adult size to much smaller versions that might have been those of children. Some appeared much older than others, their cocoons a darker, less transparent color. And they seemed to pulsate in a more regular fashion.

As they moved slowly past the strange figures, their handheld lights cast shadows that gave the entire place an ethereal feeling.

"My God," Ryan whispered. "What a chamber of horrors. How are we ever going to find Skari amongst this crowd?"

"I don't know. It seems almost impossible . . . yet . . . you see how much older these cocoons near the entrance look? Like they've been here forever? I'd bet Skari must be one of them." She took a deep breath. "Only way to tell is to pull the covering off of them."

"What good will that do? We don't know what Skari looks like."

"No, but we can ask. I was nearly comatose with fear when I first confronted Amma. About where I am right now, frankly. But she told me her name when I asked. It was almost as if she'd been waiting for someone to ask her. For centuries."

"Terrific." He stared at the most ancient looking of the chrysalises. "Okay, here goes nothing."

He stepped up beside the cocoon that was closest to the entrance, took a deep breath, and pulled the gluey covering down to reveal a frightening death mask of a face. He stepped back involuntarily as the ancient, wrinkled, and gray visage opened its eyes.

"You ask," he said to Sam. "You've had the most experience with this sort of thing."

She gave him a look. "Right," she said. "Thanks." She moved closer to the creature and asked, "Are you Skari?"

The horrible eyes were wide and fixed. They fluttered, then a hollow, echo of a voice, like someone who has had his larynx removed, came from the mouth.

"I am the first of us," the voice said. "I have not heard my name spoken in a thousand years. I am Skari."

"Wow. Right the first time," said Ryan. "What are the odds?"

"Not so bad. He was the closest to the entrance. Makes sense, in a weird sort of way, since he was the first to be placed here." She hesitated. "Were you brought here by Laki?"

"I am here of my own free will," said the voice.

"So this is what the exercise of free will gets you," Ryan said. "Hung on a wall in a gluey mass in a black cave for a thousand years."

Sam shushed him. "Why did you want to come here?" she asked.

"To be close to him," said the voice.

"You had a special relationship with Laki," Sam said. "You created religious offerings in his honor. Is that why he brought you here?"

The face moved slightly, the eyes fluttering back in their sunken sockets. "It was long ago," said Skari. "I discovered him beneath the Earth." The ghoulish figure spoke with a sense of pride. "The others of my clan did not know him then. I grew to understand Laki."

"Tell us, then," said Sam. "What does Laki want from us? Amma says he wants nothing."

There was a strange guttural sound, almost resembling a laugh. "Amma knows nothing!" the voice said forcefully. "The others always deferred to her age and to her wisdom. But she is nothing but an old woman. She *knows* nothing. Only I truly understand Laki."

"Jesus!" Ryan whispered. "He's a version of Wormer. Only *he* knows what God really wants."

Sam flashed her eyes at him, pleading with him to be quiet.

"I have been part of him for a thousand years," said the voice. "He brought me here when I asked him to. It was not a punishment. I did not belong in my clan. I was an outcast. Laki understood. He understands being alone. He does not want to be worshiped, but he is tired of being alone. He wants to be a part of us."

"A part of what?" Ryan asked.

"A part of our lives. He created us. It is his right."

"Can you ever leave this place?"

"Never."

"How does that give you free will?"

"I choose to be here," said the voice.

"Will you tell Laki," said Sam, "that we want to leave here? That we don't want to interfere, but he has made it impossible for us. The disruptions here in Iceland and around the world are causing problems for people everywhere. Can you tell him this? Will he understand? Will he help us?"

Again, the eyes rolled back in the figure's head. "I understand Laki. He is tired of the turmoil humans have brought to him through the ages."

"He's brought a fair amount to us as well," said Ryan. "If he is actually the creator, then we are the way he made us. He's as much responsible for what we do as we are."

"Perhaps he is more aware of that," said the voice, "than he once was. Laki is tired of being alone, but I sense an even greater desire to be done with you. You are not the only experiment he has crafted in the universe. Whether he will help you, I cannot say. The manifestations in the world are a sign of his anger. It is not good that Laki is angry."

"Amma said that too," said Sam. "That we didn't want to make Laki angry."

Skari's eyes closed and his head rolled back as though asleep. But then the strange voice spoke one last time.

"Go awaaay." The words echoed through the black chamber.

They stared at the figure on the wall. It was clear there would be no further communication.

"Do you suppose that means Laki will *let* us go away?" asked Ryan. "Free us to go on with our meaningless lives? Free the world from the disruptions he has caused? Let us go back to being nothing?"

Sam struggled with the enormity of it all. "What a mass of contradictions," she said. "He needs us but he's tired of us."

Ryan shrugged. "Tough job being a god. I'd probably be a little frustrated with humans as we are in the world too. If Wormer is an example of how we can best relate to God, that might be enough to disillusion any deity."

***

Dagursson sat on the passage floor and took Amma's still hand in his own. There was no pulse.

"Is she dead?" Wormer asked.

"I can't tell. No pulse that I can feel, but who knows if this thing even has a pulse. It may be that separation from her cocoon is depriving her of something she needs to survive." He looked up at the wall. "Help me lift her back in place," he said. "Maybe that will help."

Wormer recoiled. "I will not touch something that is evil," he said.

One of the other cardinals came over. "I'll help," he said simply.

"Don't be a fool!" said Wormer.

But the man knelt beside Dagursson and together they lifted Amma up and leaned her against the wall beside her chrysalis. At once, the strange tentacles emerged from the gluey mass and began to infiltrate Amma's body as if embracing her. In just a few moments, the old woman was once again part of Laki. Her eyes opened briefly and Dagursson thought he saw a smile cross her withered face. Then her head slid to one side and she seemed to go to sleep.

If he had once been skeptical that Laki represented some sort of life force, some vitalization, Dagursson no longer had any doubt. It was clear. Proximity to Laki provided at the very least, a boost to the human system. Senator Graham had been right about that, though it was clearly not a tradeoff he'd be willing to make any longer.

Wormer seemed stunned at the sight of Amma's rebirth, but also angry, as though his fellow cardinal's participation somehow threatened his authority.

"I tell you this thing is a false God," he said. "Look at what this woman has become. If this isn't a vision of hell, I don't know what is. We must go back to the hole in the Earth and pray to the real God for deliverance from this place. The true God will not forsake us. He will listen to us and bring Laki down as all false prophets are brought down in the end."

The cardinals stood, ready to do his bidding. They'd been placed under Wormer's leadership by the Pope and would do whatever the pontiff's emissary directed.

Dagursson considered them uncertainly. He couldn't stop all of them. Reluctantly, he trudged after them, fearing what would happen once they reached the hole. Would they try to throw themselves in as Wormer had attempted the first time? Was Wormer's desire to return the result of some irresistible call from the depths?

The wind grew stronger as they moved down the passageway and then, suddenly, it died away as they approached the opening in the Earth. For the first time they were able to stand beside the hole and stare in without the force of the gale in their faces.

Dagursson thought Wormer looked shaky. The cardinal leaned against the stone wall and raised his arms like some latter-day Elmer Gantry. "You are a false God," he cried. "I denounce you in the name of the Father and the Son and the Holy Ghost."

The other cardinals appeared to absorb some of Wormer's open anxiety. They began to chant and sway for all they were worth, raw fear etched on their faces.

"If you are God, send us a sign," said Wormer. "Or else, be gone, back to Satan's lair."

His fellow cardinals were looking around with wide eyes, expecting the wrath of . . . something . . . to descend upon them at any moment.

Dagursson edged closer to the stone wall in case he had to grab any of them should they feel compelled to climb in. He peered down and saw that the strange swirl of galaxies and stars was gone. In its place, far away, was what appeared to be water swirling and rising.

"Look," he said. "Something's happened. Maybe it's the sign you asked for."

But Wormer and the others were too far gone in their fear and mysticism to respond. Perhaps their denunciations had made Laki mad. Dagursson leaned over the wall and stared down, not believing what he was seeing. Where there had been stars there was now nothing but a tumult of water bubbling upward. He felt movement next to him, but he was drawn to the vision below and had trouble pulling himself back.

When he finally did, it was barely in time to see Wormer and the other cardinals all scramble over the wall with a newfound agility and tumble into the swirling maelstrom. Their bodies spun about and floated down, red robes billowing like falling autumn leaves, until they disappeared.

Dagursson pushed back from the hole, his heart pounding. Even he had felt the incredible pull of this place, and he was not a religious man. What he felt most of all was failure. That he'd failed to save the others. He didn't care for Wormer and had little feeling for the cardinals or religion in any sense for that matter. But he felt a personal failure as a police officer at being unable to save their lives.

He stumbled back to where the chrysalis of Amma hung from the wall. This was where Ryan and Sam would look for him. He collapsed on the ground, still shaking from the enormity of what had happened. In the distance, he could hear the sound of rushing water. Would whatever he'd seen soon boil out of the underground?

He turned his light onto Amma and stared in disbelief. Flanking the old woman on both sides were five new chrysalises. Beneath the glue-like and transparent exteriors, he could clearly see the movement of tentacles and what looked for all the world like red robes.

***

As Ryan and Sam emerged from the room where Skari and the other chrysalises hung, they heard the sound of rushing water.

"What's that?" asked Ryan.

Sam felt stone cold fear at the sound. "Whatever it is, it's massive. Maybe a glacial outburst. We need to get to higher ground."

They hurried across the open cavern and found Dagursson sprawled on the ground. "Something's coming," Sam said. "We need to get out of here." She looked around. "Where are Amma and the others?"

Dagursson pulled himself to his feet. His eyes looked dead in the shadows cast by the flashlights. "Amma . . . reconnected with Laki." He pointed to the ancient woman's cocoon.

Sam stared at Amma, then her eyes wandered to the new cocoons. Her heart nearly stopped.

"Where . . . where are Wormer and the other cardinals?" she asked.

"There," Dagursson indicated the other cocoons. "You're looking at them. They leaped into the hole. I couldn't stop them. When I came back here, I found them next to Amma."

Ryan went up to one of the cocoons and stared at it. He reached out a hand and pulled back the glue-like exterior. Staring at them was the clear image of Cardinal Wormer, his eyes wide open and filled with fear. There was no smile on his face as Amma had shown.

"Help me," he said, in a voice that was barely recognizable as his own.

"There's nothing we can do," said Dagursson. "When Amma became separated from Laki, she began to die. Once attached like that, they don't seem able to live on their own anymore. At least that's what I think."

The sound of water suddenly became much louder. They looked back into the cavern to see a rushing tumult entering the huge space.

"I don't know where that's coming from," said Sam, "but we've got to get out of here."

"I know where it's coming from," Dagursson said, speaking louder now, to be heard over the rushing water. "We looked into the hole and the stars and galaxies were no longer there. Instead, there was water far below, but it was rising. It must be coming out into the passageways now."

"It's got to be what Carlisle said was rising in the magma chamber," said Sam. "Not lava but water."

"It would appear that Laki is angry again," said Ryan.

They shined their collective lights into the cavern. The enormous space was absorbing the water quickly. The massive infusion would soon fill not only the cavern but the lower levels of passageways as well. Then it would continue to rise. They had very little time.

Almost as if connected at the neck, all three of them turned to stare at the cocoons. There was no way to save them. Truth be told, there was probably no way to save themselves. Maybe Laki would protect the cardinals. They'd been chosen after all—or was it punished?

"Help me," Cardinal Wormer pleaded again, his wide eyes staring at the water boiling into the cavern.

Ryan put one hand on the man's cocoon. He could feel it pulsating. Wormer's eyes looked bloodshot and filled with tiny tentacles spreading their fingers. "Now is the time, Cardinal," he said, "for you to trust in your maker. No one else can help you."

"I . . . I was going to be Pope," the distraught figure said in a heart-wrenching plea.

But it appeared that Wormer would rule only a very small part of the Catholic realm, that which encompassed his four fellow cardinals who hung from the cavern wall beside him.

They turned away and the three survivors began to race along the passage. At every turn, Sam led them higher. She knew the way out now. The only question was if they could beat the surging waters.

Chapter Twenty-Five

The scientists on the buses were subdued. All of their training, all of their computers and gadgets hadn't enabled them to determine what was happening on Laki. They were completely deflated. The fact that Carlisle, too, seemed drained only increased their sense of hopelessness.

Most of them had abandoned their stations and were sitting outside, staring with blank faces at the boiling clouds and ever-increasing lava flows. A few wrote letters to their families, though how they might ever be delivered or even found someday was difficult to imagine.

Two of the main streams of magma had finally connected, cutting the parking lot off from the main road. They were trapped, completely encircled by lava. Perhaps they had avoided the finality of a nuclear blast, but they now faced an even more terrifying end. The lava flows were increasing rapidly. New breaks in the landscape occurred every few minutes, as lava issued forth from a seemingly bottomless cauldron. Soon, the entire surface of Laki would be submerged in bubbling, two-thousand-degree liquid rock. There was no escape.

Carlisle and Senator Graham sat off to one side, apart from the others. Hauptmann, Kraus, and Gudnasson were nearby. Senator

Graham scanned the barren slopes of Laki constantly, searching for any sign of Samantha and the others. He knew it was hopeless. They had to be dead. No one could survive beneath a surface from which so much lava now flowed.

One of the scientists moved away from the rest and climbed a low rise. Suddenly, he turned back and began yelling something, waving a hand for them to come over.

Most paid no attention. They'd all seen enough weather and geologically created anomalies to last a lifetime. But Graham was still hopeful for some sign of Sam and Ryan. He and Hauptmann climbed to see what the fellow was making a fuss about. When they reached him, the man turned and pointed down the slope.

"Look," he said.

"Bloody hell!" said Hauptmann, barely able to comprehend what they were seeing.

Most of the ventholes had been issuing steady streams of lava flowing from the Earth. But now, instead of lava, water was bubbling up from below. The flow was substantial and growing by the second.

"What in the . . ." Graham stared at the strange sight in bewilderment. Where the water had come into contact with lava, enormous clouds of steam boiled forth, causing a loud sizzling sound, like bacon frying. Dozens of pockets of steam issued from splits in the Earth. The entire landscape was alive with heat and froth.

"I don't understand," said Hauptmann. "Where is the water coming from?"

Graham waved to Carlisle and the others. Slowly, one by one, they roused themselves and started up the hill. Carlisle was the first to reach them. He stopped abruptly and stared at the incredible sight.

As the rest of the small group of scientists gathered, all equally stunned by what they were seeing, the earth opened up less than twenty yards away and more water began to gush out.

One of Carlisle's men approached the gushing stream cautiously. He knelt down and reached out a hand, placing it gingerly into the water.

"It's hot," he shouted, drawing his hand back quickly. Then he put his finger in his mouth and exclaimed, "It's salt water!"

***

Sam led the way through a bewildering maze of tunnels. The entire subterranean complex was alive with the sounds of Laki. Lava bubbled, small quakes shook beneath their feet, ventholes collapsed even as new ones opened up. The passageways were filled with the sound of shrieking gas being vented. Over it all, they could hear rushing water coming ever closer.

"What a madhouse," Ryan shouted to Sam over the cacophony.

She nodded but continued to push hard through the tunnel maze. She was no longer certain where they were or even if they were moving closer to the surface. Too many vent openings had collapsed.

"Look!" Dagursson shouted, pointing behind them.

They turned to see water raging into the tunnel. It gushed in huge quantities, the sight alone enough to stop their hearts. It was coming toward them with the speed of a freight train. Steam poured off the water, giving little doubt that it was hot, possibly boiling from contact with the lava below.

"We're dead men," Dagursson said.

With the exception of his gender selection, Sam had to agree with him. No way could they outrun the pulsating water. It was barely fifty yards behind them. She looked around helplessly. For all her experience beneath Laki, this was something she could never have imagined.

The tunnel widened suddenly ahead of them, and Sam realized they'd entered into another cavern. This one was even larger than the last one but with much steeper sides. Far above, they could see daylight filtering down, lighting the enormous space.

There was no time to gape at their new surroundings. The hot water surged into the cavern, chasing them like a mad beast.

"Which way do we go?" Dagursson shouted.

Indeed, there seemed no sure answer. Another tunnel opening was visible far across the vast space, the only one they could see.

"That's our only hope," Sam said, sprinting ahead. "If we have time to reach it."

Behind them, water flowed into the cavern as though released from some mighty dam burst. It gushed into every nook and cranny. As it found each new subterranean fissure, its pace slowed until the deep venthole was engorged. Again and again, the water rushed at them only to dissipate as a new subsurface passageway had to be filled.

Gradually, the subterranean openings were permeated and water began to rise against the walls of the cavern. As they raced toward the tunnel opening, the ground began to slope upward. Sam stumbled and fell, and as the others stopped to help her to her feet, they looked back.

"My God," Dagursson said. "Where is it all bloody coming from?"

"I don't know," Ryan replied. "But it sure doesn't seem as though Laki has turned benevolent all of a sudden and decided to show us the way out. 'Go away,' Skari said. Well, if you ask me, Laki has loosed the demons of hell upon us."

"I don't understand it, either," said Sam. "If Laki wants to be rid of us and wants us to go away, why is he doing this?"

The cavern was filling rapidly. There was no time to discuss theology. They now looked out across a virtual sea of water. Steam filled the space as well, giving everything an eerie, mist-filled look, like a nineteenth-century industrial landscape, belching forth clouds of toxic waste.

"Keep moving," Sam said. "The water will follow us into the tunnel. "We don't have much time. We have to get to the surface somehow. This much water will completely fill the openings beneath Laki. If we don't find a way up and out, we'll drown."

"Or be parboiled like lobsters," said Ryan. "That water's hot."

They moved across and into the tunnel, which was widemouthed, unlike most of the others they'd encountered. As they started to climb the steep passageway, they heard something

CHRIS ANGUS

almost indescribable, which made them all stop and look back. Now what?

Across the vast sea of water, something was causing the surface to break into turmoil. There was the sound of screeching metal and a terrible, hollow, clanking noise unlike anything they'd ever heard.

"What in the Christ is that?" asked Dagursson.

And then as they stared in utter disbelief, the waters parted and something huge rolled over and uprighted itself in the frothing cascade.

"Oh, my god," said Sam. "What *is* that?"

No one answered, because it became immediately evident as an enormous metal behemoth rolled upright and began to float toward them, banging into rock outcrops and turning this way and that against whatever barriers presented themselves.

"It's a goddamned ship!" said Dagursson.

Indeed, it looked for all the world like an enormous battleship, its hull painted gray. The superstructure reached up toward the roof of the cavern, disappearing into the clouds of steam. They could even make out a few letters on the side of the hull: USS Thurman.

"I don't believe it," said Ryan. "I *know* that ship. It's a destroyer that was commissioned and named after President Thurman during his third year in office."

"Well, what the hell is it doing here?" asked Sam.

"Watch out!" Dagursson said. "It's turning this way."

They watched as the ship rocked back and forth, according to the vagaries of the current, but it did seem to be heading toward them, along with the water itself, which had now completely filled the floor of the cavern to a depth of at least a hundred feet.

"Up the tunnel, quick," Sam cried.

As they ran up the steep slope, the waters raced after them. Ryan looked back for a moment and saw something else.

"What are those things in the water?" he asked.

A number of white objects were lolling about in the foam at the base of the ship's hull.

Dagursson stared at them. "They're bodies," he said in a low voice. "Dead seamen."

But there was no time left. The water surged into their tunnel, right behind them, lapping at their feet.

"It's no use," Dagursson cried. "We can't outrun it." But then the huge destroyer rolled heavily in toward the tunnel opening. The cave was filled with the sounds of metal crunching against rock as the ship careened after them, then turned suddenly, bow first, and was thrown by the water directly into the tunnel opening. The superstructure broke off as it struck the roof of the cavern and fell back into the maelstrom, while the main body of the ship crunched and ground its way forward until it finally stopped, stuck fast in the tunnel opening, effectively, if temporarily, sealing the tunnel entrance.

The water at their feet abruptly stopped rising and settled calmly into a pool.

"That bloody thing, ghost ship, whatever you want to call it, has blocked the tunnel entrance," said Ryan. "The water can't get in."

"Maybe Laki's had a change of heart after all," said Sam. "There's no telling how long it will hold. We've got to keep going. It could break free any moment."

The bedraggled group moved forward into the steeply rising tunnel. The enormity of what was transpiring all around them was numbing. After several minutes of silent climbing, Dagursson was the first to speak.

"Where do you think the ship came from?" he asked, his voice small and hollow in the tunnel.

"No way a battleship floated down one of those small ventholes," Ryan said. "Only possibility is that it was transported here somehow, via the black hole or portal. That's got to be where all the water came from as well . . . that hole in the Southern Ocean the President told us about."

The others stared at him. It was the only rational explanation, if rational was the right word. But no one wanted to affirm what he'd said. It was just too bizarre.

CHRIS ANGUS

The tunnel leveled off and began to twist and turn. They followed it a long way. The sounds of grinding metal and surging water gradually fell away behind them. Then the venthole grew and quite suddenly opened into a larger space. Sam and Ryan stopped abruptly and stared at their surroundings. Dagursson literally ran into them.

"What's wrong? Why are you stopping?" he asked.

"It's the Nazi laboratory," said Ryan in an awed voice. "Somehow we've come full circle back to this place."

Far behind them they could hear the sound of water rushing again. Their temporary reprieve was evidently over. The destroyer must have worked its way free, and the tunnel was filling once more with water, like some implacable foe intent on chasing them down.

Sam gripped Ryan's arm tightly. "Come on," she said. "We know there's a way out of here."

He nodded and they began to push forward past the silent banks of files, vats, and ancient plumbing. Dagursson, for all his terror of the roaring water behind them, couldn't help but stare wide-eyed at the evidence of human construction all around them.

The rime-covered file cabinets, rows of vats and even the lavasicles and stalactites were no longer frost-covered and frozen. The heat of the volcano had begun to melt everything. They could see water pouring down from a thousand small rivulets, where the glacier itself had begun to melt.

Sam started to climb up the side of the great crevice that had been their path to safety once before. Only this time, it had melted to the extent that they no longer needed a rope, for the cascades of meltwater had flattened out the ice channel. The path ahead was now negotiable, an almost level, gentle slope upward.

Still, the meltwater made it slippery as an ice rink, and they often had to go down on all fours to keep from sliding backward. They quickly became soaked and frigid from the ice water. At one juncture, they paused to rest for a moment in an icy indentation. Looking below, they could see the relentless water rising behind them, climbing stolidly over file cabinets, tables, ancient Nazi plumbing, and vats now filled to overflowing with water. Slowly, Goering's insane dream was disappearing beneath the unstoppable tide.

Dagursson tore his eyes away from the deluge long enough to stare up at the path they still had to follow. He saw something moving above, coming at them out of the darkness.

"What's that?" he cried.

Sam and Ryan turned to look just in time to see the body of the strange, frozen, blonde-haired, and very unlucky young woman from long ago hurtle past them, just feet away, disappearing once again into the unknown, as she had seventy years before.

Dagursson lunged at the figure as it went by and stared after it in stunned disbelief. "I . . . I had a chance," he said. "I could almost reach her. I could have saved her."

Sam put one hand on his shoulder. "You couldn't save her," she said. "She's been dead longer than we've been alive. She was a frozen climber from long ago."

He stared at Sam incredulously. He'd only had a glimpse of the body as it went by and remembered only the sweep of blonde hair. She had seemed so real. "You've seen her before?" He couldn't get his mind around the incredible idea.

But they had no time. The water was rising rapidly. They crawled and slid and skidded higher, helping one another when they could, forming a human chain to get past occasional chunks of ice that jutted out of the side of the crevice.

Finally, they broke through to the surface. As they had before, they sprawled on top of the glacier, reveling in the sense of freedom and release. Far across the landscape, they could see Laki, still encased in boiling, black clouds, though it now seemed also to be covered with rising funnels of steam.

Then they heard the water beneath them again, like some awful living thing that wouldn't give them up.

"We've got to go higher on the glacier," said Ryan. "Or we'll be swept away once it breaks through to the surface."

They scrambled upward, even as the water gushed out of the crevice in a fountain that spurted fifty feet into the sky. When they had climbed a hundred yards higher, they stopped and looked back.

The water, pulled by gravity, flowed away from them, down the glacier and over the side in a mini-Niagara. Steam poured into the sky as the water bubbled over the frozen landscape.

"It's melting the glacier," said Sam, staring at the incredible sight. The subterranean waters were indeed carving a deep channel into the glacial wall.

"Come on," Ryan said. "We've got to find another way off this thing and get back to the others. They need to know what's happened."

But Dagursson seemed frozen in place. "Do . . . do you think Laki let us escape, after all?" he asked.

Ryan shrugged. "Who the hell knows? If this so-called escape was by design, it was about the most convoluted getaway of all time."

"Sort of like a test, wasn't it?" Sam said.

He stared at her. "I'm getting just a little tired of Laki's tests. If he's a god, He's a damned schizophrenic one. You think that's possible? A schizoid deity?"

"Be kind of hard to establish a norm in terms of behavior, wouldn't it? For God, I mean," said Sam. "You wouldn't have a very large sample to judge by."

***

Carlisle stood next to his communications chief, fretting over his inability to get a clear channel. Finally, the man smiled broadly.

"Got him," he said and handed a pair of headphones to Prescott.

"Prescott?" came the voice. It sounded distant and not very strong, but it was the President. "I can hardly hear you. What's going on?"

"Mr. President," Carlisle spoke loudly, as if the man were stone deaf. "We found your ocean, sir."

"What? Say again," said Thurman.

"The Southern Ocean, Mr. President. It's reappeared here, gushing out of the hole in the Earth. There's no doubt about it. No place else for so much water to come from . . . and it's salt water."

"Well . . . that's good," said Thurman. "Isn't it? Look, we've got news, too. Reports have been coming in from around the globe. Volcanic activity is dissipating. I don't know what you did over there, but it seems to be working. Maybe it was the power of prayer after all." A distant, bitter laugh came through the headphones. "Listen, His Holiness has been calling me every half hour. Wants to know where his delegation of cardinals is."

"Uh . . . no information on that, sir. Some of them are still here, but those who went underground, including Wormer, haven't been seen, along with our own people. To be honest, Mr. President, we don't hold out much hope for them. Things are pretty out of control beneath Laki. I don't think anyone could survive what's going on down there . . . cardinals and prayer be damned."

There was silence on the line. Then the President came back. "Sorry Prescott, I was just getting a report. Our AWACS says that the hole in the Southern Ocean appears to be closing. The waters are still swirling, but they're not disappearing. Hold on a minute . . ."

Carlisle waited, staring blankly at the computers above him.

"That's confirmed," the President's voice came back. "The hole has shut down. Our people report that the overall level of the oceans worldwide has declined nearly six inches. That's one hell of a lot of water gone down a rabbit hole."

"I don't expect it's disappeared for long, sir," said Carlisle, "the huge amounts coming out of Laki will eventually make it back to the sea."

"Yes . . . yes, I understand," said the President. "Listen, I've got to go. But it's good to have some positive news. Let me know if that idiot Wormer surfaces. Until he does, the bloody Pope won't give me a moment's rest."

Carlisle stared at the phone as the President clicked off.

Andy Pryne stuck his head in. "Good news, sir. The underground party has just reappeared, coming from the direction of the glacier. Should be here in a few minutes."

Carlisle threw the headphones down and pushed past Pryne in his haste to go see for himself.

Outside, sure enough, Sam, Ryan, and Dagursson were plodding across the flooded landscape. They looked like phantoms emerging from the clouds of steam. Senator Graham was already making his way toward Sam, and the rest of the scientists were close behind.

Carlisle puffed up beside the trio, shook hands all around, and said, "Whatever you did down there, it appears to be working. I just spoke to President Thurman. He says volcanic activity is subsiding worldwide, and the hole in the Southern Ocean has closed." He stared at the horizon. "Where are Wormer and the other cardinals?"

"They . . . didn't make it," Dagursson said. "A lot of people didn't make it out of that hell."

"What about Laki?" Carlisle asked. "Did you resolve anything with the volcano? Was it a god after all?"

"Laki was almost certainly someone's god," said Ryan. "The Vikings', maybe. I'm pretty sure he was never ours. He still seems unwilling to forsake Skari and Amma. The cardinals were turned into chrysalises too, though I don't think he had any love for them. It's kind of unclear if what Laki did by turning them into zombies like Amma was give them eternal life or punish them for worshipping him. What happens now is anyone's guess."

"Maybe Laki will go back to his own universe or dimension, or wherever he came from," said Sam. "I doubt we'll ever know for certain, but my guess is the dissipation of volcanic energy around the world suggests he's decided to leave us alone. Perhaps Skari had something to do with that. Who knows? Frankly, I'm tired of trying to figure it all out. Mostly, Laki seemed not to want much to do with us . . . except when he did."

"That sounds a lot like God to me," said Carlisle. "Utterly conflicted. We're probably a whole lot better off when he doesn't pay attention to us than when he does, if the past couple of weeks are any indication."

President Thurman's science advisor stared across the landscape. There were no longer any lava streams evident. They'd been replaced by flows of water gushing off the sides of the volcano, tumbling down like glacial streams of meltwater, making their way eventually to the sea. Through some miracle, they had thus far avoided the parking lot with its two big buses filled with hundreds of millions of dollars worth of equipment.

"Looks like we're out of immediate danger," said Carlisle, "but it will be a while before the water dissipates enough to allow us to get out of here." He turned to Ryan. "We need to report the loss of Wormer and the cardinals who were with him to the President. His Holiness is concerned."

"I doubt His Holiness will want to know precisely what happened to them," said Ryan. "That their prayer mission was ultimately a failure. If anything, it incited Laki. I think Wormer's holier-than-thou attitude angered Laki so much he wanted nothing more to do with humans. So he called the greatest offenders into the void. God knows, I can identify with that. Wormer made *me* want to get rid of him any way I could. If I'd had a hole to throw him into, I might have done the same thing."

Carlisle led the way to the bus. "I'm sure His Holiness will find a way to interpret things to his liking," he said. "It's one of the things religious leaders are particularly good at."

***

Dagursson emerged from the bus and went over to sit beside Sam and Ryan. Carlisle, Hauptmann, and Senator Graham were also there.

"My men finally grounded the helicopter that Rashid commandeered," he said. "But . . . ."

"What?" asked Sam.

"He wasn't aboard. According to the pilot, he was forced to put down near the coast where Rashid and his comrade were picked up by a fishing vessel. We have no idea where they are now."

"Can't you get the Coast Guard after him?" asked Ryan.

"They've been notified, but they're short-handed. The strange water phenomena, temperature, and weather changes and so forth have kept them busy rescuing small vessels. Besides, there are probably hundreds of fishing craft off the coast of Iceland. It would be like finding a needle in a haystack. Face it. Rashid has got away, scot-free."

"Maybe not," said Carlisle. "I'll tell the President to put out a worldwide Interpol alert for the man. Where can he go?"

"Back to Iran would be my guess," said Senator Graham. "International law has little influence there. Something I learned a long time ago."

They stared across the surface of Laki. It was slowly returning to something approaching normality. Though the water continued to gush, lava flows had dissipated or been cooled by the huge volumes of ice-cold salt water that could only have come from the Southern Ocean. Those waters had initially been turned to boiling cauldrons by the heat of Laki, but now the mass of icy liquid had overwhelmed the lava. There remained a loud hissing sound over all of Laki, as steam continued to rise in great, billowing clouds.

Even the skies had returned to normal. The boiling black clouds had reverted to the standard Icelandic overcast. There were no more mini-tornadoes and even the near-constant rumbling of subterranean earthquakes and collapses had subsided.

"What's happened to the cosmic ray output?" asked Ryan. "And to your other weird events, your strangelets and Kaluza-Klein particles, the Higgs boson and I don't know what all?"

"All our readings show things returning to normal," said Carlisle. "Which brings up an interesting question. Were they real in the first place? Were they examples of scientific phenomena or simply manifestations of Laki's anger?"

"My guess is the latter," said Sam. "I think Laki made up his own rules, including his own laws of nature. In a strange way, I think he was playing with us, enjoying our struggles, like a cat playing with a mouse."

Hauptmann turned a gimlet eye on her. "I know you're an atheist, my dear, but that's a pretty cynical view."

"I'm not an atheist any more, Ernst," said Sam. "I'm convinced Laki was real. I'm just not real sure . . . what. I guess you can put me down as agnostic from now on."

"I don't think your cat-and-mouse metaphor is cynical at all," said Carlisle. "There was a lot going on that we couldn't explain with all our instruments and computers and simulations. I think Laki pretty much did whatever he felt like, sort of like those ancient Greek or Viking gods, petulant, indifferent, and demanding all at the same time. So we had tentacles that seemed like some kind of fungus, but had no DNA. We had cosmic ray bombardment that had no outside cause or source we could detect. Same with the rents in space/time, black holes, strangelets, and so on.

"We were looking for scientific cause and effect. What we got instead were completely random events created by an ambivalent deity, acting on impulse. We had no more insight than the ancient Greeks who tried to explain events in their world according to the whims of spiteful gods."

"Well, one thing was real enough," said Graham. "Amma and the other Viking chrysalises were kept alive somehow for a thousand years. I'd still give my eyeteeth to know how Laki did that."

Carlisle shook his head. "Like everything else Laki had a hand in, I believe it was all for show, all an illusion. The proof is in how quickly things returned to normal once Laki tired of us. He simply lost interest and has probably turned to some other universe or some other creation for amusement. God help them. We were but a moment's diversion."

"Maybe Amma had it right," said Sam, "when she said the creation of humans *was nothing*. Perhaps Laki's goal all along was to show us how insignificant we really are."

Chapter Twenty-Six

Deep beneath the Vatican, Demetrio Ricci, the papal Secretariat, proceeded on his mission. His focus was not deterred by the many mysteries, some of them gruesome, that abided in the sub-basements of the Vatican.

The lower levels were dank and smelled of the age of centuries. Ricci carried a rack of large iron keys to locks that were rarely, if ever, used. Any normal mortal might be expected to feel the chill of the past run down his spine as he moved along these dark corridors. But Ricci was unaffected.

In one secluded room lay ancient Jewish relics, Torah scrolls, manuscripts and most precious of all, the Temple Menorah of pure gold. All had been stolen by the Romans from Jerusalem and taken to Rome in 79 CE. When the Roman Empire became Christian, the items were placed in the Vatican basement. Repeated calls by Israel for return of the sacred holy vessels were never commented upon by the Popes and had been met with denials by Vatican officials that such objects even existed.

Farther along was another chamber, this one filled with looted Nazi gold. Here were hundreds of millions of confiscated Swiss francs that had been sent to the Vatican for safekeeping by the Nazi puppet Ustasha government of Croatia in 1946. Keeping the gold company were piles of jewelry and other valuables taken from concentration camp victims.

Ricci paid no attention to any of these relics of the sometimes horrific past of the church. Soon he was striding past the pagan necropolis that had been uncovered beneath Vatican City in 2003 during construction of a parking garage for Vatican workers. Called the Necropoli dell'Autoparco (literally, the Necropolis of the Parking Garage), the tombs gave a glimpse of the ties between Christians and pagans during the Age of Augustus (23 BC – AD 14). Only recently, and against the wishes of the Pope, had part of the necropolis been opened to the public in honor of the Vatican Museum's 500th anniversary.

The display held two hundred and fifty excavated tombs, including forty elaborate mausoleums from a time when many pagans were on the verge of conversion to Christianity.

It was here, in a section of the necropolis still largely unexcavated and hidden from public view, that Ricci reached his goal. The Holy See had been aware of the pagan burials for hundreds of years prior to their unwitting discovery by construction workers. It was only one of many, many secrets of the Catholic Church. Ricci was here to assure His Holiness of the safety and security of another, one that related to issues much in the news of late.

The papal Secretariat selected one of the large iron keys and inserted it into an ancient, rusting lock. But though the lock was old, it had been well oiled and used frequently in recent years. It opened smoothly.

Inside was a single shelf carved of marble and resting on it a simple wooden box. Ricci took another key, unlocked the box, and grunted as he viewed the contents.

The box contained a single, oversized book or manuscript. It was the oldest known copy of the original Icelandic sagas. Older by far than the edition of the Heimskringla that Hauptmann had perused with such loving care at the university.

Ricci placed his hand on the book for the last time. It was an old friend. He'd spent much of his career deciphering the manuscript, comparing his translations with those of earlier papal Secretariats. The book's secrets had been known to the Holy See for many hundreds of years.

The aging manuscript was nothing less than proof that there was a living god. Yet it was a proof long denied by the church. For this was the saga of Skari, Viking carver of religious totems in honor of Laki.

The existence of Skari had long been known to Popes and papal Secretariats. The ancient sagas were clear. They spoke of a being who lived at the center of the Earth and who had bestowed eternal life on the Viking residents of southern Iceland in the tenth century.

The Pope had told Wormer only part of the truth when he said he knew of the cardinal's secret council of religions. In fact, the council's investigations and tenuous conclusions had been reported by the Vatican's spies to each Pope since the group's founding immediately after the war. What Wormer was not privy to was that the Vatican had its own copy of the sagas, one kept secret from all but the highest of the Catholic hierarchy.

According to Skari, Laki was both a pagan and a Catholic god. A bridge between two worlds. Such a confluence could never be openly accepted by the church.

Yet this was no legend to be dismissed. The sagas proved beyond any doubt that Laki was a power to be reckoned with. A living god who controlled the secret of eternal life. Skari provided authentication of Laki's power. Hard facts that could not be denied by even the most fervent members of the church.

And so the dilemma: How to deal with this perceived threat to the authority of the church, to its sole power to interpret the laws of God? For this was how the church viewed Laki. Not as proof of its belief, at long last, that there actually *was* a living god, one that revealed himself as no other ever had. Instead, the church rejected Laki. The hierarchy would never accept solid proof of God's existence. They were wedded to their concept of faith and beliefs unrooted in evidence or substance. This was the way forward for the church, as it had always been.

The Pope knew that Wormer and his fellow cardinals had been sent on a mission from which they would likely not return. What was Laki? God or devil? The church chose the latter, against all evidence to the contrary. In utter denial of Skari's proof.

Laki's anger at this rejection had festered for many centuries. For he was an ambivalent God. Willing to leave man to his own devices, yet fond of his creation in the way only a Creator could be. The conflict would send Laki into a rage that manifested itself finally in the real world.

The sudden appearance of that manifestation had chilled the hearts of the Pope and his papal Secretariat. For what if they were wrong and Laki was indeed God, as Skari insisted? Then the church had spat in the face of the Supreme Being and all was lost.

Ricci ran his hand over the ancient text, reassuring himself of its physical reality one last time. The subsidence of the Icelandic magma chamber and volcanic activity around the world was final proof, in his mind, that Laki had been the devil and that they had defeated him. After all, how could they have ever defeated God?

Maybe Wormer's prayer had done the trick. Saved the church from the wrath of Laki. Perhaps Ricci would suggest to His Holiness that Cardinal Wormer be canonized. It seemed the least they could do.

The papal Secretariat reached one hand into his robes and pulled out a small butane lighter. He held it to the pages of the manuscript until it caught and then watched contentedly as Skari's truths disintegrated into a pile of ash.

Chapter Twenty-Seven

It was a perfect baseball moment. Ryan stood at the plate and surveyed the infield. They were playing shallow. The game was tied with two out in the bottom of the ninth and the winning run on second.

The sky was that brilliant cobalt blue that comes only on rare, clear days in Iceland, where baseball was not a national pastime. He leaned over and picked up some dirt and rubbed it between his fingers. The smell of the newly mown grass was joined by the whiff of hot dogs and rosin. There was a satisfying roar from the crowd.

Sort of. The stands held a smattering of a dozen wives and girlfriends. Two young girls were making a weak attempt at the wave, standing up and down, raising their bare arms. He saw Sam, sitting halfway up the bleacher, her head in a magazine. *The Journal of Volcanology* or something. She didn't seem to know he was at bat.

He took a practice swing and stared out at the pitcher. The pitch came in low and probably inside. But he swung anyway. There was a satisfying crack and the ball headed for center field. The second baseman misjudged it and leaped, but the ball was already past him, rolling toward the fence, the center fielder in hot pursuit.

Gonzalez, the overweight smoker on second, took off on contact. He ran like greased lightning, jagged and erratic, puffing and grunting. As he rounded third, the outfielder threw the ball to the cutoff man, who turned and prepared to throw to home. The runner was going to be out by a country mile.

As Ryan prepared to slide uselessly into second, he watched the cutoff man's throw to the plate sail over the catcher's head and go all the way to the backstop. Gonzalez scored standing up and the game was over.

Sam had closed her magazine and was jumping up and down cheering. She had her hands in the air, thumbs up, as he trotted in to take the high fives of his teammates.

A perfect baseball moment.

A month had passed since volcanoes around the world had gone silent. The surface of Laki was peaceful once again. Prescott Carlisle and his scientists were gone, taking their incredible buses with them. It had required the importation of a crew of workers to construct a temporary bridge to allow the vehicles to cross the encircling lava trails, which still retained too much heat to risk driving over.

The government of Iceland sent a delegation to survey the extent of the damage to the southern Ring Road. Infrastructure had been severely compromised in the region, and the prime minister determined that it was too soon to decide if tourism could once again become a major part of the southern island's economy.

IranOil had begun to withdraw from Iceland. Oil prices worldwide were stuck in the doldrums and Iran's economy was in desperate shape. The contraction meant there was no longer money for foreign investments. The refinery on the outskirts of Reykjavik was shut down, and local businesses could no longer rely on the magnanimous, charitable contributions they'd become accustomed to.

Ryan kissed Sam and they began to walk off the field, when they saw Dagursson standing next to the backstop, holding a newspaper.

"Good game," he said. "I don't know anything about baseball, but I thought your runner on second was going to be dead on arrival."

"No sure thing in baseball," said Ryan.

"Thought you might like to see this." He had the paper open to a short news item.

Ryan read it with Sam leaning over his shoulder. In Tehran, one of Iran's most successful business owners, a man named Rashid, had been bankrupted. Without the protection of his influential friends, charges had been brought against him for compromising the nation's nuclear program. Details were thin, but after a quick, public trial, Rashid received twenty years in prison, along with sixty lashes.

"Couldn't have happened to a nicer guy," said Sam. "Any news on when they might reopen Laki?"

Dagursson shrugged. "There have been a handful of aftershocks still. Then they'll have to reconstruct the road. Why? You staying on to continue your research?"

"Well . . ." Sam hesitated, looked at Ryan.

"We're going to take a month off," he said. "Sam's father is insisting on a big wedding in D.C."

"It'll be a splash," Sam said, "knowing my father. Might even help his reelection bid. The President is opposing him."

Dagursson nodded. "Hadn't heard that," he said. "Congratulations on you two getting together. Don't ever ask me for marriage advice, okay?"

***

Deep beneath the volcano, the waters of the Southern Ocean retreated through cracks and fissures, down long passageways and cooling ventholes. Much had returned to the sea, but equal amounts flowed back into the hole at the center of the Earth.

As the waters dissipated, they left behind once more the vast, complex universe of stars and galaxies that had so stunned Ryan, Sam, and the others, though no one would ever know.

Once the last government experts, surveyors, and bridge builders had gone and Laki was again silent, seismographs in Reykjavik recorded a magnitude 8.3 earthquake, the epicenter of which was located at the volcano. A flyover by a government plane reported that the surface of the volcano had apparently pancaked in on itself, sealing forever the subterranean levels. The elevation of Laki had decreased by an estimated three hundred feet.

***

Laki observed the changes and saw that they were good. What frustrating, exasperating beings these humans were. He found them endlessly amusing. From this perspective, they were the best of his creations, even though they rejected his truths so routinely. He did not wish to be worshiped, and those few who rejected him completely, the ones who called themselves atheists, he found most interesting.

Perhaps, as Skari suggested, it was time to step back and leave them to their own devices. He would revisit them someday and see what new detours they had taken.

In a few million years, perhaps. There was no rush. They weren't going anywhere.